Selfish Is the Heart

MEGAN HART

BERKLEY SENSATION, NEW YORK

THE BERKLEY PUBLISHING GROUP
Published by the Penguin Group
Penguin Group (USA) Inc.
375 Hudson Street, New York, New York 10014, USA
Penguin Group (Canada), 90 Eglinton Avenue East, Suite 700, Toronto, Ontario M4P 2Y3, Canada
(a division of Pearson Penguin Canada Inc.)
Penguin Books Ltd., 80 Strand, London WC2R 0RL, England
Penguin Group Ireland, 25 St. Stephen's Green, Dublin 2, Ireland (a division of Penguin Books Ltd.)
Penguin Group (Australia), 250 Camberwell Road, Camberwell, Victoria 3124, Australia
(a division of Pearson Australia Group Pty. Ltd.)
Penguin Books India Pvt. Ltd., 11 Community Centre, Panchsheel Park, New Delhi—110 017, India
Penguin Group (NZ), 67 Apollo Drive, Rosedale, North Shore 0632, New Zealand
(a division of Pearson New Zealand Ltd.)
Penguin Books (South Africa) (Pty.) Ltd., 24 Sturdee Avenue, Rosebank, Johannesburg 2196,
South Africa

Penguin Books Ltd., Registered Offices: 80 Strand, London WC2R 0RL, England

This book is an original publication of The Berkley Publishing Group.

Cover illustration by Ilona Wellmann, Trevillion Images.
Cover design by Lesley Worrell.
Interior text design by Laura K. Corless.

PRINTING HISTORY
Berkley Sensation trade paperback edition / October 2010

Berkley Sensation trade paperback ISBN: 978-0-425-23456-3

Library of Congress Cataloging-in-Publication Data

Hart, Megan.
Selfish is the heart / Megan Hart.—Berkley Sensation trade pbk. ed.
p. cm.
ISBN 978-0-425-23456-3 (trade pbk.)
I. Title.
PS3608.A7865S45 2010
813'.6—dc22

2010027177

PRINTED IN THE UNITED STATES OF AMERICA

10 9 8 7 6 5 4 3 2 1

Praise for Megan Hart and her novels

"Ms. Hart is a master . . . I am absolutely in love with [her] writing and she remains on my auto-buy list. Take my advice and add her to yours!"

—*Ecataromance*

"Megan Hart is one of my favorite authors . . . The sex is hot and steamy, the emotions are real, and the characters easy to identify with. I highly recommend all of Megan Hart's books!"

—*The Best Reviews*

"Terrific erotic romance."

—*Midwest Book Review*

"Unique . . . Fantastic."

—*Sensual Romance*

"Megan Hart is easily one of the more mature, talented voices I've encountered in the recent erotica boom. Deep, thought provoking, and heart wrenching."

—*The Romance Reader*

"Probably the most realistic erotic romance I've ever read . . . I wasn't ready for the story to end."

—*A Romance Review*

"Sexy, romantic."

—*Road to Romance*

"Megan Hart completely wowed me! I never read an erotic book that, aside from the explicit sex, is [also] an emotionally powerful story."

—*Romance Reader at Heart*

"Uplifting . . . Fascinating worldbuilding."

—*Dear Author*

"Enjoyable erotic romances . . . Strong characters and intriguing . . . plots."

—*Genre Go Round Reviews*

Berkley Sensation titles by Megan Hart

PLEASURE AND PURPOSE

NO GREATER PLEASURE

SELFISH IS THE HEART

Once more for my family

Another time for friends

And of course to Superman,
who always tells me I can do it, no matter what it is

Acknowledgments

Special thanks must go to the artists who provided me with the music I listened to while writing this book. I could write without music, but I'm so glad I don't have to. Please support their work through legal means.

Little Fox—Heidi Berry

Look After You—The Fray

Come Here Boy—Imogen Heap

You've Been Loved—Joseph Arthur

Labor of Love—Michael Giacchino

Night Minds—Missy Higgins

And extra-special thanks must go out to Mick Lynch and Kevin May, The Guggenheim Grotto, whose song *Lost Forever* made me weep every single day for months in a row and was the one that most contributed to this novel. Thanks, guys—you're just as lovely in person as you are streaming from my iPod.

Chapter 1

"If I didn't care for you so greatly, cousin, I'd surely hate you." Caterina Marony turned from Annalise's bedroom window to stare at her cousin. "You'll be next."

Annalise, who'd not yet bothered to dress in the formal gown she'd be wearing to her sister's wedding, gave Caterina an uninterested grunt and bent back to the task of lacquering her fingernails. "After six weddings, my parents are hardly in any position to provide me with the sort of splendor in yonder garden. If Allorisa's betrothed was not wealthy enough, and besotted enough, to provide my sister with the finest party she could ever hope for, they'd be stuck having tea sandwiches and cordial, the same as I expect to suffer."

Caterina, Annalise's junior by but a year, frowned and let the lace curtain fall over the glass. She crossed her arms over her chest. "It's not the party that matters, Annalise. It's the marriage."

Annalise blew on her nails to dry them. "Surely you still cannot envy me my marriage if that's what you truly think. Not when you know as well as I that it's an arrangement, not a union of passion."

Caterina's gaze flickered. "But surely Jacquin will be a fine lover. He's so handsome, and . . ."

"A flirt? Yes, cousin, I'm well aware of my betrothed's charms." Yawning, Annalise got off the bed and went to the ewer and basin to bathe her face. The garden would be insufferably hot, worse even than this garret room, which was cooled only by an ingenious arrangement of vents and the windows that prevented direct sunlight from getting in to heat the room. The water was warm but better than nothing, and she dampened a cloth to press to the back of her neck while she made the rest of her toilette.

"He is most sincerely charming," Caterina said.

"Jacquin," Annalise replied without looking at her cousin, "has a fine cock and knows how to use it, which is not exactly the same as being a fine lover."

Caterina giggled and gasped, and Annalise threw her a sharp look. "What? The use of such frank language has scarcely teased you so, before."

Caterina fussed with Annalise's small jewel cask, mostly empty but for a few good costume pieces. "Oh, well. Perhaps I played at worldliness before."

"And now you play at modesty?"

Caterina looked up at that. "I can still envy you your future place, cousin. It's especially worth envy when I have no prospects for a ring of my own."

Hearing her cousin's wistful tone, Annalise couldn't find it within herself to tease. Instead, she hugged the other woman quickly. "You've had scads of suitors, Cat."

"And my parents don't approve of any of them!"

Annalise linked her arm around her cousin's waist and studied their reflections in the looking glass atop her dresser. Caterina was tiny and dark, with a slim waist and flat bosom, slim hips of a perfect span. Her figure was fashionable, just right for the current high-waisted gowns and straight skirts. In comparison, Annalise had high, full breasts, long legs, and ample hips less perfectly suited to the day's current style. Not that she'd ever had complaints. She'd had half a dozen lovers, and not a one had been anything but eager to sample her lushness in dress or out of it.

"Your father simply isn't ready to let you go, that's all," Annalise said. "Whereas mine is probably leaping in the air with joy to be rid of the last of his daughters."

Cat grimaced and turned her face from side to side, letting her dark curls tumble over her shoulders. "Even so, I'd far rather have someone waiting for my hand than look ahead to a future empty of a husband."

"Your future isn't empty. It can't be. Look at you, that beauty."

"If it were only beauty that brought me a husband, I'd have no worries!"

"Ah, well, it was scarcely my face that brought me the offer from Jacquin, as you well know. It was our fathers' doing more than ours." Annalise laughed. "Not, mind you, that I'm complaining. I've ever found Jacquin's company to be most merry, and if our fathers feel it will benefit the family businesses to join, well . . ."

Well, then at least she would be wed and need no longer worry about it.

Cat snorted lightly and looked away from Annalise. "You'd better get dressed. I hear the bells of the Temple priests' carriage, and you know your mother will wish you to be there to greet them."

Annalise sighed. "I suppose I should, else she work herself into a frenzy. Though why my presence is required for the blessing I don't know. And why, by the Void, did my sister believe velvet was a smart choice for a midsummer wedding? I shall expire of the heat before they've even said half their vows."

"At least she asked you to stand beside her."

Annalise rolled her eyes. "Dear, sweet, Cat. You know the only reason my sister has me as her maid is because my mother insisted, and our next closest sister is too fully with child to be expected to stand up with Allorisa. And the others must come from too far a distance for her to demand their service the way she can of me."

Cat laughed softly. "And you have such a natural inclination toward service, cousin . . ."

Annalise threw a damp cloth at the other woman, who ducked it, laughing. "I do it for the sake of my sister's betrothed, who will have to spend the rest of his years soothing her temper. There's no need for me to tease her into further fury when the wedding itself has sent her into a froth."

From outside in the garden, the toll of bells grew louder. The priests had arrived. Annalise could hear her mother's chatter even through the glass.

"Come, Cat. Help me into this Void-begotten gown and tidy my hair. I must go stand beside my sister and make certain she doesn't do something frivolous."

"Like faint?"

"Or run away," Annalise said with a lift of her brow. "Though what a merry scandal that would be!"

And another of the stairsteps has found her way to wedded bliss," Jacquin Kirkol whispered into Annalise's ear, knowing how it would tickle and make her squirm.

His fingers tightened on her hip. To anyone watching they would seem quite the happy pair, Annalise thought as his hot breath and the tip of his tongue on her lobe sent a shiver throughout her. Jacquin had been teasing her for the past hour or so as the endless wedding customs her sister had insisted on spun out the day.

"Just one more dance," he murmured. "And then you're free, yes?"

Annalise turned her face just barely to look at him. "You know I'm standing as her maid. I must attend her for the entire party."

"Ludicrous." Jacquin nipped at her neck so swiftly only someone staring at them would see it.

"Custom," Annalise sighed and poked him in the side. "Cease to pitch this woo with me, sirrah, I've no time for lovemaking today."

Jacquin pulled away with a pout that did nothing to sour his pretty face. "Bother. I might as well go home to Alyria and spend the days before our marriage tied tight in the chains of chastity."

Annalise, her eyes on her sister, who would require food and drink soon if she meant to keep dancing with every party guest without falling over, poked him again. Hard. "Hush, you. I know for a fact you came as your grandmother's escort and for the sake of trade, not for the mere pleasure of seeing me."

The music slowed, the dance close to ending. Annalise made to move toward Allorisa, who didn't look like she wanted to stop dancing, even though her face gleamed with heat and she'd made her way through every partner but for her newly bound husband. Jacquin arrested Annalise with a hand on her elbow, holding her tight. With the shield of her skirts and a turn of his body to keep most anyone from seeing, he pressed his groin to hers.

Her breath caught and she looked into his eyes. Jacquin had been a guest of her family's near to every summer since they were both children. He'd ever been fond of kissing and petting her, but as the months drew closer to their impending marriage, he'd grown more insistent about proving his affections to her. Annalise had no issue with this, as she'd long ago relinquished the prize of her virginity and had made no secret to him about it. What was consistently more frustrating was that Jacquin often made much of an effort at wooing her, but very little at actually fucking her.

"I must attend my sister," Annalise said through half-parted lips and laughed at his entirely too dramatic groan of frustration. "Surely you cannot expect me to slip away from all of this to service you?"

Jacquin laughed and kissed her cheek. "You, my darling, are a tauntress."

"I could say the same of you."

There were a bare few moments before the dance ended. Already Annalise felt the pull of expectation, of what was required. Of service anticipated. The weight of it slouched her shoulders and turned down the corners of her mouth. She could not wait for this day to end so she need no longer dance at anyone else's whim.

Allorisa looked as though she never wanted the day to end. Annalise could scarcely blame her sister, who'd not inherited their mother's winsome grace or their father's casual charm, nor any of their shared attractive features. Of all the sisters, Risa was the most like their grandfather in appearance, and though Grandda was a formidable, well-liked gentleman, his face sat rather better on his shoulders than on a young woman's. Even so, she had a lush figure and lively eyes and was as bright as a new-minted coin—but coupled with a determined disposition and no seeming ability to temper it, her intelligence had kept away suitors by the dozen. The fact that she was the sixth of seven daughters didn't help, for it meant her dowry was nothing to brag upon. Not that her own was anything to brag upon, Annalise thought as she waited for her sister to finish a last whirl around the slate patio laid especially for this day. But at least Annalise was ebon-haired and dusky cheeked, with a merry sense of humor. At least she had that.

"Annalise, I'm thirsty," Allorisa complained the moment her partner had bowed and left her. "By the Mother, the sun has fair roasted me!"

"Come, sister, and sit in the shade while I bring you something to drink." Annalise took Risa's arm and led her to the bride's bower, hung with expensive, out-of-season flowers and ivy that cast shadows, if not coolness. "Your husband has nearly finished his dancing, as well. He'll be along soon, I'm sure, and then we'll have the feast."

"I think I know the course of events at my own wedding party." Allorisa took the mug of chilled grape wine Annalise handed her. She quaffed it back and returned the mug. Her eyes flashed and softened. "Thank you."

"It's hot," Annalise said with a shrug, as though that made a difference in her sister's disposition, when they both knew quite well it did not. "I'm fair roasted myself in this velvet."

"But you look so lovely." Risa said this charitably and could afford to, for though the gown had been sewn of expensive fabrics and cut to current style, it did not suit Annalise half as much as Risa's did herself.

But then, that was the bride's privilege. Annalise gritted out a smile. "More wine?"

Allorisa was craning her neck for the sight of her husband, Denver, who was still locked in the final waltz with some distant cousin. "Yes, yes, before he's finished."

Custom dictated the bride's maid act the part of fetchencarry, so that was what Annalise would do. She refilled her sister's cup, dodging a few well-meaning relatives who wanted to congratulate her on her upcoming nuptials, and returned it just as Denver found his new wife. The couple made a show of kissing sweetly at the request of the guests gathered 'round, and the announcement of supper was made. Annalise hung back, though her stomach rumbled. Her corset had been laced too tightly for her to enjoy the meal, and as her sister had insisted on the most gourmet of every dish, Annalise knew there would be a great many exotic dishes with tiny, insufficient portions and long pauses between the courses. If she were going to make it through this as well as sit at her sister's elbow and serve her whatever her husband did not, she needed something to sustain her.

There was also the matter of the service her mother was now fluttering about. The Temple priests who'd performed the wedding ceremony even looked askance as Fluta Marony begged them with hands clasped to her bosom and fluttering eyelashes to lead a special afternoon service. Annalise's mother didn't notice the shifting sighs and looks the wedding guests gave, but even if she had, Annalise doubted it would matter. Her mother had long ago given herself fully to the Faith in every respect, though she'd left off forcing her children and husband to worship with her.

"It would be best to eat first," said the tallest priest, the one who'd been to the house before and who knew Fluta's eccentricities. "So that all might enjoy the service without distraction."

It said much, Annalise thought, when a priest found her mother too enthusiastic in her worship. She took the chance to slip from the crowd. Bread and honey in the kitchen would settle her stomach while she waited on the poached quail's eggs and copperfish roe. Annalise lifted her skirts, grateful at least for the flat-heeled slippers her sister had insisted she wear so as not to tower over her, and hopped across the kitchen threshold. Inside, the bustle and commotion did not dissuade her. Her mother preferred to cook most of their simple meals herself now that the family had so dwindled, but today all the cooking was being done by hired caterers. Annalise knew where to find the loaves of yesterday's bread and crocks of sweet honey gathered from her father's bees, and she ducked into the pantry without even speaking to any of the hired help.

Many manor homes had multiple pantries for wet and dry goods, chill and warm. At Marony House the kitchen had been expanded over time as money allowed and necessity dictated, so the main pantry had been carved from spare bits of space left when walls went up and others came down. Floor-to-ceiling shelves lined a narrow, short hall with a jog at the end that led to the stairs of the cold cellar. The cool shadows and quiet were welcome after the hours of heat and noise outside, and Annalise paused to acclimate.

The low sound of murmured voices around the corner alerted her that she was not alone, and though she was surprised when she turned the corner, she was not shocked.

The young man wore his golden hair pulled back into an intricate braid down his back. Annalise studied his clothes, the high-throated shirt, the brightly patterned cravat, the long-cut trousers and tight-fitted westcoat that gave him his figure, rather than his body providing the form on which the clothes hung. Dressed with fashion, but not taste. Jacquin could've found better.

"Blessed Balls!" cried the blond young man.

"Indeed," Annalise said with a quick sweep of her gaze over his dishevelment. She cast a longer look at his companion, who had the grace to look away. "I've just come for some honey. Please don't let me interrupt."

"But we weren't—"

"Hush," Jacquin said to the blond. "Mistress Marony is no fool. You should go."

The blond nodded and ducked his head before brushing past her. The click of his bootheels was very loud, as was the creak of the pantry door and the influx of noise from the kitchen, which cut off when the door shut behind him. Jacquin leaned back against the railing to the cellar stairs. Annalise gave him her back to look for the crock of honey.

"Anna . . ."

"Hush." She echoed him. "I am no fool."

"Truly, we were only talking."

One hand on the shelf to steady her, she turned with a throat afire from the effort of holding in a shout. "I believe your game involved the use of teeth and tongue, indeed, but you'll find me fair doubtful as to it being only conversation."

"And yet I swear to you that's all we had, love." Jacquin moved to touch her, and she pulled away.

They stared across the narrow space at each other. The sole

illumination came from the narrow, high windows set along the roofline. There was enough light for her to have seen everything, to see all of it now. Jacquin's frown and the flash of his eyes, the soft plumpness of his lips she recognized as the aftermath of passion.

"You dishonor me, Jacquin."

"I swear to you, that was not my intent."

"Then why do it? Here at my family's house? By the Arrow, Jacquin, we are to be married in a month's time. I know what you do in your own time before we are wed is of your own account, but . . ." Annalise swallowed hard.

"I plead your mercy. Truly, Annalise."

Jacquin came from Alyria, where it had long been known that men who preferred the company of their own sex were freer with their public affections than was the case in some other places. Here in Evadia such intimacies were rather less accepted, at least in public. Though anything a man and a woman could get up to seemed entirely allowed, no matter how decadent, Annalise thought with bare-boned scorn as she remembered a couple she'd seen standing by the fountain. The woman wore a golden choker that would have looked like nothing more than expensive jewelry if not for the slim leash of golden chain attaching it to the bracelet of the man beside her. It had been difficult to tell if the length allowed either of them sufficient room to move apart or if they always need stay at each others' elbows.

Annalise shuddered at the thought of it.

She sighed and leaned against the shelves, her appetite fled. She'd accepted Jacquin's troth a year ago, just a sevenday after Allorisa had taken Denver's. Annalise enjoyed the privileges of maidenhood and yet grew weary of being her father's chattel. Trading that in for the position of wife seemed a pleasant enough arrangement. And she'd known Jacquin for near her entire life, after all.

She knew him.

"Hush, love, don't cry." Jacquin pressed a thumb to her cheek and took it away glistening with her tear. "Please. I swear to you the lad approached me. In a moment of weakness I allowed him to pull me inside—I never meant to do more than speak with him about why I must needs refuse his offer."

Annalise captured Jacquin's hand between hers and kissed his knuckles gently before releasing it. "Sweetheart, I know that."

He startled and pulled his hand from hers. "Do you?"

"Think you I could know so well the color of your eyes, your favorite dessert, the way you cheat at cards, and yet not also know the other truths of you?"

"I think you don't know as much truth as you think."

"Jacquin, will you be happy?"

It was not the place to ask such a question, there amongst the bags of flour and crocks of jams and butters. Perhaps there was no good place to ask. Jacquin answered, anyway.

"I would do my best to try."

Annalise sighed and ran a fingertip along the shelf, which gave up only the finest hint of dust. She rubbed it between her thumb and forefinger. "As would I. But would it be enough?"

Jacquin tilted his head to look her up and down. He stepped back. "What exactly are you saying?"

She had to strain her ears to hear even a hint of the merriment outside and maybe even that was her imagination. Outside in the garden, her sister danced with her new husband. In nine months time or close to it, Annalise guessed, her sister's belly would swell with that man's child, giving him an heir and Allorisa a reason to occupy her time with somewhat other than herself. Outside in the garden, guests ate and drank her parents' hospitality, provided by their new son's coin.

And all of that would be hers in a few short weeks. The rest of her life would stretch out in front of her—marriage. Motherhood. A pleasant home of her own and a husband who would do his best to make her happy but would never love her the way she desired, no matter how he was able to force himself toward it. She'd been able to overlook all of this before, but today, now, seeing the joy on her sister's face and knowing it would never be hers struck something deep inside her.

"Jacquin," Annalise said. "I cannot marry you."

Chapter 2

Striking Serpent. Biting Dog. Leaping Monki.

Cassian Toquin moved through the forms of the Art with practiced discipline and ended with his feet together, hands tight-pressed palm to palm, fingers pointing to his chin. The sun had scarcely peeped over the horizon and yet sweat trickled down the line of his spine. He tasted salt when he licked his mouth. He opened his eyes.

Above him he heard the hushed titters of his audience, which he ignored. Instead, he bent to lift his shirt from the ground where he'd tossed it. With swift fingers he smoothed his hair back from his face, grateful he'd kept it shorter than fashion dictated. It fell over his eyes but not down the back of his neck.

The creak of a window caught his attention, and he looked upward. Once a novitiate had fallen from the third story as she leaned to get a better glimpse. Fortunately she'd fallen into the cart of straw and manure Felix the gardener had parked by the flowerbeds in preparation for their fertilization. The girl had been bruised and humiliated but she'd lived.

Though he glimpsed the forms and faces of several novitiates in the shadowed rooms of the Motherhouse, none of them were hanging from the ledge. Yet. Someone had cranked open the window either to allow in a breeze or to get a better look at him as he exercised, but now had retreated. It was better that way. Cassian found it easier to teach the young women in service when he didn't have to face them as admirers.

His other admirer was not so silent. "How long did it take you to learn the Art, Master Toquin? How long to become a master?"

"I'm not a Master of the Art, Kellen. I just practice it. I could practice it every day for the rest of my life and not master it."

Kellen, tousle-headed and blond, frowned. "I don't think I'd like to do something every day and know I'd never become good enough at it to be called a master."

Cassian smiled but stopped himself from ruffling the lad's hair. "There are many skills in life that can't be completely mastered. One can become proficient, and that should be enough."

Kellen followed Cassian to the pump in the yard where he ran the water, frigid from its source deep underground. Cassian splashed his face, blowing great breaths at the chill, and dripping, swiped at his face. Kellen already had Cassian's jacket ready, held out like an offering. Cassian took it.

"You needn't play the part of my fetchencarry, Kellen. I'm quite capable of gathering my own belongings."

"I know," Kellen answered cheerfully. "But I like watching you."

It would be a number of years until the lad discovered the joys of living in a house filled almost exclusively with women. Right now, all he saw were the pains. Cassian took the jacket, hung it over his arm. He meant to return to his quarters for a bath rather more private than he had opportunity for now.

"Do you?"

"Oh, yes. The Mothers say I'm to learn what I can from you, at any rate. Not the Art," Kellen added. "I don't think they care much for that."

"No, I don't suppose they do." The Art was a man's domain, though Cassian had heard tell of women who practiced it. He couldn't quite imagine what they'd ever need it for, but he'd heard stories. "Mothers don't always understand the importance of the same things men do."

Kellen laughed, eyes crinkling. "No!"

"I was a good deal older than you are now when I first took up the practice. I should think you'd be able to learn faster than I did."

Kellen's grin did its best to break Cassian's heart, but he'd grown accustomed to making it into stone. The Art was not the only thing he'd long practiced. The lad leaped into the air in a fair impression of Striking Serpent.

"Like this?"

"Very good. Not quite." Cassian hung his jacket on the pump handle and showed Kellen the form. "Like this."

Kellen did it again, better this time. He stumbled a little when he came down, but his hands were in the right place. In the bright morning sun, his hair shone like gold. His eyes, though filled with merriment at the moment, were dark. Cassian didn't like to look at Kellen's face overlong. It reminded him too much of what he'd prefer to forget.

From inside the Motherhouse, a chime rang.

"Come. It's time to go inside."

Kellen nodded obediently. "Maybe tomorrow you can show me more, Master Toquin? Please?"

"We'll see if you've made it out here so early, Kellen. But . . . yes. I see no reason why you couldn't join me." There was no reason, which was the only reason Cassian agreed. To forbid it would only hurt the lad with no excuse, and Cassian found himself unable to be so cruel to one who didn't deserve it.

"You'd best hurry, else you'll be late." Cassian waved a hand. "Go."

Watching the boy go, Cassian mouthed the first part of the morning prayer. The second part came as he crossed the yard toward the house. The third he muttered as he quickly stripped out of his dirty clothes in his room and bathed from the basin of cold water. In moments he was dressed again in the masculine version of the Handmaidens' high-necked, long-sleeved uniform, his a jacket instead of a gown of course, but with the same row of buttons down the front. He pulled the red of his shirt to show just below the black sleeves of his jacket.

None of the words had mattered. He said the prayers by rote and habit, and though he slid into his seat in the dining room with the final syllable still clinging to his tongue, not one part of the prayer had moved him. Nor did the words he spoke before he broke his bread, but he said them anyway, hoping to feel his maker's touch.

"Good morn to you, Master Toquin. I see you were hard at work already." Mother Harmony stopped by his table on the way to her own, a platter of biscuits and butter in her hands. "Such discipline is admirable, if not necessary."

"Not necessary," he agreed as the serving girl put a bowl of rice mush and simplebread in front of him. "But highly gratifying."

"It does keep you rather fit," Harmony said with a purse of her lips and a glance at her own well-rounded figure.

"I'd be happy to teach you, Mother. Any time you wish." It was easy to make an offer he knew would be refused.

Harmony laughed at this and gestured with her knife. "Oh, my dear, no thank you. I've long grown past the age when a bit of extra flesh discourages me. But you keep on with it, if it brings you pleasure."

There was more to it than that. Cassian didn't practice the Art for the sake of fitness, or even in anticipation of needing it for defense. There seemed little enough chance for that, seeing his position as

Master of the Faith here in the Order of Solace Motherhouse was fair guaranteed to never require him to fight anyone. No, Cassian kept up with the discipline because he'd already lost too many things that mattered. He couldn't bear to let go of another, even one that taxed his aging muscles and woke him earlier than he was naturally inclined, one that took much from him and gave him little. He would practice the Art as long as he could stand upright to do so because it reminded him of his brother. Of Calvis.

"You should eat more," Harmony continued, peering more closely at him. "You're too thin."

Cassian had little to say to that. To deny it would cause her to flutter and cluck; to agree was ridiculous. "I am as the Invisible Mother intends me to be."

Harmony sighed and wagged a finger at him. "Can't get around you, can I?"

Again, Cassian wasn't sure what to say and only nodded, relieved when Mother Harmony waddled away to her own seat. The Order of Solace had its roots in the Temple of the Book, but it was a purely feminine domain. Cassian was one of only three men in the room. One of less than a dozen men on the grounds. After close to ten years in service here, Cassian still had little to say to the women beside whom he'd worked for so long. The Mothers and Sisters-in-Service were no more familiar to him than his own mother and sisters had ever been, or any woman, for that matter. He enjoyed their company and knew they found his at least tolerable. He knew they respected his place within their Order, even as they all knew he'd never be a part of it. But he did not understand them, and doubted he ever would.

Breakfast finished, the novitiates dismissed, Cassian had little time before he was due to address his first class of the day. He meant to use the few precious moments in preparation, setting out the copies of the texts, making sure the room had not grown too stifling, lighting the scented candles. Girding his figurative loins. A hand on his sleeve stopped him in the hall, novitiates in their colored headscarves bustling all around him.

"Master Toquin, I would have you speak to my herb preparation class this morn, if you've time." The request came from Sincerity. In contrast to the novitiates in their bright headscarves, her long dark hair hung in an intricate braid to her hips. Her gown, though cut in the familiar fashion, was of lightweight and pale blue linen. "We are studying the trefoil today."

"Mistress, my knowledge of herbs is limited," Cassian told her, though he had a guess as to why she would request his presence. "I'm not sure what I could offer your students."

Serenity smiled. "The trefoil's properties are threefold, and many believe they're tied to the blessings of the Holy Family. If you would be so kind as to come and speak to my class—they're all first seasons, by the way, I've traded with Patience—about the comparisons between the story and the flower. I think they would find it most enlightening."

Cassian gave a quick look around the hall and found it empty, then allowed his gaze to slide over Serenity's familiar features. He liked her. Had known her for longer than he'd been here at the Order. An accident had left her right leg scarred and stiff; her limp had made it unlikely she'd ever be sent to serve a patron. Most patrons were men, after all, and no matter what any might say, men were all too often first concerned with appearance.

"And you would have me speak to your students on the lessons they'll eventually learn in my own class if they're unfamiliar with it already?"

Serenity ducked her head with a laugh. "I must confess my patience with these first-season novitiates is wearing thin, unlike that of my Sister."

"She is aptly named," Cassian said.

"She is, indeed. And perhaps they will attend to the lesson better should it come from your lips than mine. At least in this instance.

And I grow weary of them, I admit that as well. I could use a bit of a break from attempting to force knowledge into their heads."

Cassian tried not to laugh, but Serenity knew him too well to believe his frown. "Why did you trade?"

"Because after five years of teaching the same lessons without cease, my Sister and I have both grown . . . overaccustomed to our roles. We thought a trade of duties might enliven our circumstances."

It was the first time Cassian had ever heard Serenity even hint at dismay over her role as constant teacher instead of being sent out to serve patrons.

"And you've not found it to be so?"

"Indeed," Serenity said, "I have not. Please, Cassian. Come speak to my class and tell them the story, that I might have a rest from their constant prattling."

"And you believe they'll hold their tongues for my instruction?" Cassian shook his head. "Am I so formidable?"

"I have witnessed for myself your ability to strike women into dumbness." Serenity raised a brow. "And it is not always because of your temper."

Cassian's smile faded. He put a hand over his heart, made a formal half bow. "I regret I am unable to attend your class this morn, mistress."

"Cassian—"

But he was already stepping back, his back turned. His boots thudded on the wooden planks as he went down the hall toward the stairs. He did not look back.

Once in his own classroom, he closed the door and leaned against it, head bowed. Serenity, of all the Sisters-in-Service, might possibly be considered more than a colleague, but a friend. She, of all of them, knew the depth and breadth of his tale, for she'd been there for its entirety.

She wasn't wrong about his temper, which was both formidable and famous. That she could tease him about it said much of her fondness for him. He had behaved badly.

But he must. Respect, mutual kindness, even fear he could tolerate. Perhaps fear he would even encourage. But fondness and compassion he could not abide.

They were dangerous to him, and would remain ever so.

Jacquin. Enough." Annalise pushed him from her.

"I swear to you, I can make this work."

"I want you to stop."

Jacquin retreated, frowning, his mouth wet and swollen from kisses. Her own mouth felt swollen, too. Sore, in fact.

She sighed. Jacquin, who had spent the better part of the past two chimes attempting to convince her there should be no obstacle to their marriage, echoed the sigh. Over her head he drew in a breath of herb from the bowl she'd declined moments before. The fragrant smoke tickled her nostrils, and Annalise shifted on the settee to lean against its opposite arm. Watching him, she put her feet up and into his lap.

"They ache," she explained. "Pinch-toed slippers."

"Ah." Jacquin set the bowl onto the side table and worked her toes with his strong fingers.

She winced when he rubbed the soles. "My sister's doing. I told her my feet are too broad for pointed toes, but she insisted."

"Your sister is such a fancy slut."

Annalise barked laughter and nudged him with her foot. "Hush, Jacquin. My father would have you slaughtered if he knew you were here in my bedchamber sampling my sweets before the wedding."

"He would not, and you know it. You're far past the age anyone could expect an intact virtue."

Annalise nudged him again, though what he said was true and she'd certainly dispensed with her virtue a long time past. "Sirrah!"

"And far too beautiful," Jacquin added gallantly. He lifted her foot to his mouth and kissed the toes. "But I shall remain ever so silent if it causes you to rethink your answer."

"It's still no," she said.

With another sigh Jacquin put her feet from his lap, grabbed up the bowl, and got off the settee. With his hair unbound and falling in thick, golden sheaves over his shoulders, his body trim and lean, he cut a fine picture Annalise had no trouble admiring as he paced. She particularly enjoyed his long thighs and the sculpted mounds of his buttocks.

"Stop staring at my arse." He actually sounded irritable as he looked at her over his shoulder. "It's unseemly since you are so insistent upon denying me your hand in marriage."

"Jacquin, sweet, my love. My darling. You must admit I'm right. It would leave us both terribly unhappy."

"Don't coo at me as though I were some simpleton to be put off with a handshake."

He was truly upset. Annalise rose from the settee and slipped into a spidersilk robe, belting it at her waist before pursuing him. She put a hand on his shoulder and he turned, his mouth drawn into a frown.

He punched a fist into his palm. "I must marry. I must have an heir some day. I must have a wife to stand beside me."

"Why take a wife when a chatelaine and a good household staff could do the job as well and you'd not be beholden to her?"

"A wife lends ever so much grander an appearance than a slew of servants," Jacquin said dryly.

Annalise shrugged. "I adore you, Jacquin. You know that. You've long been my best companion. It seemed natural enough that we should marry. It seemed right when our parents proposed it."

Jacquin turned and took both her hands. "So, what has changed? Surely not the sight of me with that lad. I told you, he meant nothing. And as for the rest . . . I blame the worm and herb. I shouldn't have so indulged before making love to you . . . I swear to you, Annalise, I am capable."

"Capable, perhaps, but do you desire me?"

His gaze faltered a little at that. "I do desire to marry you."

Annalise looked at the settee, and the bed, the blankets rumpled from their efforts. "I would not be enough for you, Jacquin."

His mouth worked, but no words came for some long moments. Then he sighed and scraped back the hair from his forehead. The bowl had gone out and he put it aside. His eyes had grown red from the herb and his emotions.

"Nor," Annalise added gently, "would you be, for me. I think we've proven that."

"I told you, that lad meant naught to me. Less than naught."

Her fingers tightened, curling over something she no longer held and perhaps never truly had. "But someday, someone would. And what, then? Would you have me be the cuckold?"

"I would never ask you to keep your affections solely to me, Annalise."

"But I would wish to grant them so, to my husband. So, yes, seeing you with your lad is what swayed my mind from the idea that our marriage would be anything but a farce. And I refuse to live my life in such a manner. You would do well to have the same pride."

He stared at her, long and hard, then grabbed up his breeches. His shirt. He dressed quickly, without looking at her. "Do you know of the shame our families will feel if you dissolve this? Do you understand that I will still be expected to wed someone—a woman, yes, and that I will still intend to do so? And that you, for that matter, would indeed be expected to marry some other man?"

"I would be free to take a husband who—"

"And where will you find him?" Jacquin asked.

His cruelty was unexpected and unusual and set her back a step. "What do you mean?"

"I mean, sweeting, that you agreed to my troth in the first case because you despised all the other choices. You told me yourself a man who'd take a wife without a dowry must have other very good reasons—"

"Such as love," Annalise said.

"I love you!"

"And yet you cannot bring yourself to make love to me. Months of pitching your woo, of petting, of teasing," Annalise said, but gently, for she did care a great deal for her longtime friend. "And yet here we have it, the truth. You can't bring yourself to put your cock inside me, Jacquin. The very thought of it makes you shudder with distaste. I love you, too, as I ever have. But I cannot face a life of seeking my pleasure outside the marriage bed."

"I'd never have taken you for your mother's daughter."

Annalise frowned. "I make this choice not because I fear the Void or offending the Invisible Mother. I simply want to wed a man who . . . wants me. Really wants me. In all ways."

"I want the status of a bride. You wish to avoid the millstone weight of a husband who doesn't love you. We are both at a loss. And yet you refuse to marry me. What shall we do? Our families expect another ceremony. Your father has already agreed to take me into his trade, at no small relief to me as the youngest son of my own father, with no chance at gaining anything from his business. How shall we sever this bond without disgrace and without giving up our friendship? I will not allow that," Jacquin said sternly, raising a finger in lecture. "I adore you too fully to let that happen."

"And I you." She embraced him, then stepped back.

She tapped her teeth with her thumbnail as she paced. An idea was forming in her mind, amorphous and vague but taking shape as she walked. "I will think of a way to work this for us both."

She hushed him when he made to speak, and Jacquin gave in to silence. The scent of herb floated between them; she took some, though it was not her habit to partake. The weight of his gaze followed her around the room as she paced it, thinking. Thinking.

Her mother's daughter. Could she be that? Annalise held back a shiver of disdain. Her mother had given herself up to the Faith before Annalise was even born; she'd never known her mother to be anything but disturbingly devout. Yet something decent had come from her mother's devotion. Annalise had been well-schooled in the Faith. Better than well-schooled, she'd had the benefit of instruction most young women—indeed, most young men, lest they decide to become priests—could expect. She could not become a priest, of course.

But she could become something else.

"A vision," she said at last.

"Of what?"

"I don't yet know, but something that will lead me to . . . solace."

"What?" Jacquin, who'd been lounging, sat straight up on the settee. "Surely you don't mean—"

"It's perfect." Annalise clapped her hands and whirled to face him.

"Sweetheart, you could barely bring yourself to serve your sister on her wedding day. Surely you cannot expect to bind yourself in service to anyone else. By the Arrow, Annalise, at least with a husband you can say no. As a Handmaiden—"

"As a Handmaiden," Annalise said, "I shall never be required to wed. And you, love, as attached to me, a woman of faith, shall not be required to marry anyone either so long as our arrangement is not dissolved. Which, I might add, it need never be so long as I remain a novitiate and never a Sister-in-Service. Or so I understand it."

Annalise, in fact, understood very little of the Order of Solace and its workings. She did, however, know quite a lot about society, honor, and expectation. She'd watched six sisters walk ahead of her after all.

"And what of when you are no longer a novitiate and are expected to actually serve?"

She shrugged. "It could be years before I'm deemed ready. Longer, should I . . . linger."

"You wouldn't dare!"

She laughed. "I might. And by that time I'll be so old I'll never be expected to marry. And my father will have passed along the business to you. It will all be lovely and wonderful."

"I think you are either the most foolish or brilliant woman I have ever met. How will you do it?"

"Tomorrow. You will accompany me in a walk through the forest. You'll be a witness to my vision. Two days from now, you'll be betrothed to a religious woman and I'll be heading to the Motherhouse."

Laughing, they danced together, and his kiss fell upon her mouth with affection but no passion. And that was fine, Annalise thought, for physical pleasure could always be gained from one place or another, but true emotion was much more difficult to acquire.

Chapter 3

Inside the stone and brick walls of the Motherhouse, Cassian knew his place. It was not the one he'd been born to, nor the one he'd taken when he left boyhood behind, but it was the one he'd accepted when he'd first walked through the gates. Now, he admitted, he would scarcely know what to do with himself should he find himself put from it. He knew his place in the yard, as well, where he put himself through the paces of the Art. And in the town, where he sometimes frequented the tavern with his old friend Roget.

It was in the forest where he sometimes walked, seeking to follow the path of the Allcreator, that Cassian should have felt the most comfortable, and it was there he felt the least. In the forest, beneath the trees, he could strip away everything else he had become. He walked the woods anyway, knowing he would never find what he sought.

It was punishment, not reward.

Sometimes he was followed—not all the novitiates who came to serve were worthy of the Order. Just as they giggled at him from their view through the windows, so on occasion did one or two of them slip away from the Motherhouse to tread in his footsteps, to see what their teacher did when he was not instructing them. On those days he simply walked and walked until they grew tired of trying to discover his secrets, or weary of keeping pace with his much longer legs.

Today, however, Cassian had no audience. He'd not gone very far into the trees or strayed off the winding path that led away from the manicured grounds of the Motherhouse and toward the main road. This was nothing like the path Sinder had taken when He strode the world, bringing light into the Void and breathing the winds, but then Cassian had long ago ceased to expect he would ever feel what the Allcreator had.

He'd also long ago ceased to feel melancholy about it. Now he sat on a large rock to the side of the path, his face tipped toward the dapples of sunlight slanting through the tall trees. He had a hunk of bread, some dried fruit, and a flagon of sweet wine. Most importantly, he had time. His own time, under no obligations to anyone, and though he would never give up his place in the Order, Cassian relished these quiet moments here alone.

So when the sound of crunching heels came to him from beyond the bend in the path, Cassian didn't look up in pleasant expectation. There could be only one person coming this way. Merchants and tradesmen came to the Motherhouse from the other direction, by the main road. Visitors to the Order, of which there were few, also came by way of the road and not the path through the woods. Only potential novitiates came this way.

Judging by the sounds, the newcomer was far enough away that he could slip off into the woods and avoid her. Or he could simply turn back down the path and arrive at the Motherhouse before her. But the warmth of the sun and sweetness of the wine was too tempting. He didn't want to move.

Temple priests had no mantras, no five principles to repeat. Priests had the Word and the Law, and hours of study and interpretation.

A single sentence could take a year of dissection, a year after that of argument, and still not be accepted as fact. Some brothers devoted their lives to the eternal discussion of what determined the Word and the Law. Cassian had ever preferred the more mundane, the hands-on aspects of practicing his faith. Endless rounds of discussion and argument, the minutiae of interpretation, had never been his style. For Cassian, faith was black and white, not multiple shades of gray.

So he had nothing to muse upon now as he sat and waited, no thoughts inside which to lose himself. By the time the first sight of the woman appeared 'round the bend in the path, he'd finished a handful of fruit and broken a crust of the bread into small pieces that better fed the birds than his stomach. The soft *crunch-crunch* of her feet on the path's crushed rocks paused when she saw him, and he thought at first she would flee.

He'd not have blamed her had she turned heel. A woman alone, coming across a man in the woods, far away from any who might protect her—even though she wore the cloak of a Seeker, she'd be a fool not to have a moment's hesitation. There were men stupid enough to risk the Order's wrath to take their pleasure where it was unwanted.

Cassian took no pride in the fact that his gender made him suspect, but it was the truth, and any woman who relied on the protection of a garment was indeed a fool in Cassian's eyes. Yet he didn't move away. She would have to pass him, if she dared.

She moved forward, one foot in front of the other, her head high, her gaze direct. The closer she got, the more Cassian could see. It was not the cut of her cloak but the quality of the fabric that told him she came from wealth, and it was the force of her stride that told him she came from privilege. She might be a fool, at that. A privileged fool.

He broke apart the bread in his palms and scattered the crumbs on the ground. A blackbird came to snag a bite, then flew away before his hand could reach it, should he have been so foolish as to try. More crumbs. Another bird. By the time the woman had crossed half the distance between them, he'd fed half his loaf to the flock.

Again, she paused, perhaps taking his measure. And what, exactly, did she see? A man wearing the rough garb of a woodsman, no axe but a worn leather bag at his side. His hair worn too short for fashion. What might she make of his features, the length of his legs and breadth of his shoulders? Would she find him a threat now she could see him closer, or would she take the confidence of her privileged life and continue past him?

She answered his question in the next few moments when she again lifted her chin and strode forward with steps swift enough to flutter the edges of her cloak.

Ah. A bit of a fool, then.

She slowed as she approached, at least showing that bit of caution. Cassian paid her no mind, concentrating instead on uncorking his flask and sipping from it. He didn't need to see her to know when she came closer. The breeze brought the scent of her, and he muttered something like a curse at the foolishness of a woman who'd travel on her own and tart herself up before doing so. Did she wish to be raped on the roadside?

"Good day." Her voice, low and sweet, was tempting enough without the added seduction of her perfume.

Cassian set his jaw and looked at her. "Good day, mistress."

The woman kept her distance as she flicked her gaze over him. Now that she was closer he could see the sheen of sweat on her brow and upper lip, and no wonder, since her cloak, though fine, was sewn of heavy wool and not a fabric more suited for the weather. This interested him. Cassian knew from experience the fluctuation of wealth and how those whose pockets once hung heavy with coin could keep the appearance of all they'd gained even as their coffers gathered dust.

"It's warm," she said.

Her tongue slipped out to lick at her lips, a gesture a lesser man might've taken as invitation. Cassian was no lesser man. He knew the blatant attempts at seduction, and this miss meant none.

"I've been walking a fair distance. Longer than I'd been advised," the woman said.

She had pale eyes, the color startling against her dusky skin, beneath dark, shapely brows. He'd wager the hair beneath the hood was dark, too. It would be long and silken. It would be beautiful.

"The carriageman who left me off told me the Motherhouse was this way," the woman said when Cassian again made no answer. "A half day's walk, he said. Yet I've been walking since early this morn and seem to grow no closer."

"It would seem, then, the length of your stride was overestimated."

She seemed as though she meant to laugh but held it back at the last moment. "It would seem so."

He watched her gaze follow the path of his flask to his mouth, watched her lips part and her throat work as his did when he swallowed. She would be thirsty, trekking in that heavy cloak, even in the shadows. The distance from the main road to this point was indeed a half day's journey, made simple when provisioned appropriately. She didn't seem to have been so.

A gentleman would have offered her a sip from his flask, but Cassian had long ago been denied the opportunity to become one. He eyed her, wondering if she'd ask him for a taste. Wondering if he'd allow it.

"I hadn't expected the day to be so overwarm," she said.

"I would guess that, by your cloak. Perhaps you should take it off."

Her gaze flashed, but she didn't retreat. Her jaw tightened for a moment, only. "I can't."

Cassian drank again, slowly and on purpose. Yes, it was a dig, but what person of intellect ever set out on a path of unknown length without appropriate provisions, without the right clothes? The right footwear? She hadn't been limping, but he bet she wore a pair of pretty silken slippers beneath that gown, not sturdy walking boots. He'd seen enough young women staggering into the yard in half a delirium because the last leg of their journey to the Motherhouse had been so unexpectedly difficult.

To his surprise, however, the woman in front of him reached into her cloak and pulled out a small linen traveling bag. From within she drew a leather bottle closed tight with a cork. He watched her tip back her head. Watched her throat work as she swallowed. He had to turn his gaze, his mouth tight at the corners.

He didn't like that.

"I'm on my way to the Motherhouse," she said with lips still glistening.

Cassian said nothing. He tucked away his flask and stood to brush the now imaginary crumbs from his hands. He no longer felt like walking in the forest.

"The Order of Solace?" Her voice tipped up on the end of her sentence, quizzical.

She hadn't moved out of his way, and unless he pushed past her he'd have to go around the rock to get to the path. He glanced over his shoulder to the thick pad of needles on the ground, the spikes of shadow flowers pushing through. A few measures beyond were the trees growing close together, with just enough distance for a man to slip between.

"Do you know it?" she persisted.

He felt the tug of her hand upon his sleeve, and Cassian looked at her, finally. He stared hard at her fingers plucking at his elbow until she took away her hand. Then he looked at her face, her open eyes, her parted lips.

"I know it," he said.

The woman's expression tightened, her mouth pursing, brows furrowing. She crossed her arms and lifted her chin. Oh yes, this one was used to having her way.

"Could you tell me which direction I should choose?" She pointed ahead to the place where the path split.

"I could."

The forest would never be silent. Always, the wind would rustle branches, birds would sing, and animals would rattle in the undergrowth. The waterfall hidden in the trees behind him would rush and pound the stones below. But now, with this woman staring at him, a wave of silence swelled between them. It broke upon the hiss of her indrawn breath, and he imagined the sound of her lashes fluttering—surely he couldn't hear such a noise, though they be long and lush, seeming even to brush her cheeks as she looked down.

When she spoke, her voice was light but low. She looked him in the eyes, then, no shy cutting of the glance or false demureness. "Will you tell me the direction?"

It wasn't the first time he'd been asked such a question, and it was not the first time he'd given such an answer. "Certainly, mistress. The path you seek is just ahead, to the left. Follow, and it will take you where you need to go."

She narrowed her eyes and looked him over. Cassian had been observed, watched, spied upon, and giggled over. He'd never been so studied.

At last, she inclined her head. "I thank you."

He watched her set off down the path with a sure and steady step. She looked neither to the right nor left, but straight ahead. She didn't even look back at him, and Cassian, for the first time, found himself wishing he'd given a different answer.

For the first time in the many he'd been asked, he wished he'd told the truth.

"Damn him to the Void." Annalise muttered the invective as she plucked yet another piece of straw from her hair. "Damn him and all his spawn."

It was uncharitable, to say the least. Certainly not in keeping with the image she was set on portraying, that of the demure and spiritual Seeker. A Handmaiden.

Did Handmaidens curse?

He'd lied to her, the bastard. May the Invisible Mother turn her back on him. May the Holy Family bar him from the Land Above. May he rot in the Void for eternity—

"Mistress?"

Annalise, scowling, turned to face the small, round woman who'd lent her a place on the stable floor. That the stalls hadn't seen a horse for a long time hadn't made her night any more palatable. The wood had been hard, the straw musty and not thick enough to cushion her, yet invasive enough to penetrate her cloak, gown, and shift and fully infiltrate her hair. She'd spent too long a time trying to brush it out, and was certain bits still clung to her in places she couldn't see.

"Sun's up," the woman said carelessly, as though Annalise couldn't see for herself.

She had, in fact, been wakened after too-few hours of sleep by a sharp shaft of light stabbing directly into her eyeballs. Though her first retort was sharp, she tempered it. Not from the kindness of her nature, but from what her mother had always taught her of being gentle with those less fortunate. This woman would qualify, Annalise thought with a look around the stable and through the door to the bare earth yard beyond, where a few scraggly chickens pecked.

"You'd best be getting on," the woman continued, blithe, as though she had strange women stumble into her yard in the middle of the night all the time.

Perhaps she did. Annalise stretched, her neck and back creaking in protest at her hard night. Her stomach rumbled and she put her hands over it. "I don't suppose I could—"

The woman snorted lightly. "Impose upon me for something to break your fast?"

The accent she forced into her voice made it clear she was mocking. Annalise cut off her own snide reply to say instead, "Not if it would be an imposition. No."

"More than letting ya sleep in my stable with naught but your cheery smile as compensation?" The woman laughed and slapped her knee. "Ah, you're a fine one. Yes. Most of the girls who come this way make me laugh, but you . . . you're somewhat else, girl."

Annalise could deal with hunger for a few more hours. Surely they'd feed her at the Motherhouse, should she ever manage to find her way there. It couldn't be far.

"Tell me something, girly. What're you seeking at the Order?"

Annalise brushed at her skirts and sleeves and gave up detangling her hair. "I want to join it, of course. Why else would I go there?"

The woman's grin quirked. "Why else? There are as many reasons to seek the Motherhouse as there are women who go there. They all want to join, girly. But why? Why do you want to give your life?"

A dozen lies, the ones she'd told her family and friends, tripped over Annalise's tongue, but became trapped by her frown. She didn't owe this old woman any truth—not for the dubious pleasure of having been allowed a vile night's rest in a shoddy stable, at any rate.

"I had a vision."

Both of the woman's brows lifted so high they disappeared beneath the fringe of hair hanging down on her forehead. "So you say?"

Annalise frowned at the woman's tone. "I do, indeed!"

"Think ya visions are to be had by just anybody?" The woman laughed and tilted her head. "No, no, they are not, indeed. Think ya the Invisible Mother, blessed be Her name, has time to go 'round granting visions as though they's apples to fall from a tree?"

Annalise gathered her cloak at her throat and drew herself to her full height. "Madam. I thank you for your . . . hospitality . . . but I must get to the Motherhouse today. So, if you'll but point me in the right direction, I'll be on my way."

Her rumbling stomach refused to be silenced, no matter how she might wish it to remain so. The woman laughed and reached out to pat Annalise's belly, not noticing or unconcerned at the scowl she earned for her presumptuousness.

"Without breaking your fast?"

Before Annalise could say anything, the woman grabbed at her wrist. Her tone turned wheedling, her wrinkled face coy. She tugged, and Annalise stepped closer, unwilling even in her annoyance to be disrespectful to an elder.

"I have fresh eggs. Brown bread. I have cacao, girly. Steaming and steeped with milk."

It had been a day since Annalise had eaten a full meal, not a handful of nuts or dried fruit from her pack. Her stomach protested again, louder this time. She had ever been made irritable and clumsy with hunger and this morn was no exception. And with no telling how long the journey still might be, she would be foolish to step out upon it without eating.

"I would be fair grateful," she said while gently extricating her arm, "if you would grant me the honor of being allowed to eat at your table."

The woman shifted, the heavy layers of her gown brushing the bare, swept earth. She didn't reach again for Annalise's wrist, but instead gestured. "Come, then, girly. Come inside."

The small hut with its thatched roof and old-fashioned split door had looked to be as neglected as the stable from the outside, but inside proved to offer rather greater comfort with a cheerful fire and a well-scrubbed table set with two chipped but clean plates. A small bedstead filled the far corner and two chairs settled in front of the fire, while a rickety-looking ladder led to a small loft above.

"Sit, sit." The woman gestured. She moved faster inside than she had in the stable.

Annalise chose a seat at the table and watched the woman shrug out of several layers of clothes she hung carefully on hooks along the wall. Each layer diminished her until at last the woman who turned with a brisk clap of her hands seemed half the size of the figure that had greeted Annalise in last night's darkness. The woman, who'd kept the kerchief wrapped tight over her long braid, tied an apron around her waist and bustled at the small stove before turning with a platter of food that she set on the table.

"Eat, eat." The woman, who had yet to offer a name, flapped her hands at Annalise.

"Aren't you going to join me?"

"Ach, I broke my fast before the sun rose. You go ahead. Go on." She waited, expectant.

Annalise put a hand on her belly, aching with emptiness, and looked at the plate. Simple fare, but she'd never been above it. Scrambled eggs settled on a slice of brown bread oozing with butter. The smell of it set her mouth to watering.

"Thank you."

There'd never been a meal taken at Annalise's house that had not begun and ended with a prayer. Sometimes the prayers had lasted longer than the meals themselves. Annalise murmured some now, under her breath and without thought to the words.

"What say ya?" The woman cocked her head to peer. "What was that?"

Annalise paused with a fistful of bread and egg halfway to her mouth. Butter dripped onto her fingers. "Your mercy?"

"What say ya? The words you spoke. What were they?"

"Oh . . ." Annalise swallowed her hunger but held tight to the bread for the moment. "Naught but a prayer."

"Huh. Wouldn't-a thought you the sort to thank the Invisible Mother for Her bread before eating it."

"Old mother, I am on a vision-sent journey to the Order of Solace to become a Handmaiden. Why should it surprise you that I would honor Her before my meal?"

"Most do it silent-like, that's all. Not with open mouths."

"Silent grace so none might judge the sincerity," Annalise said. "I've no care if anyone doubts my sincerity or not."

Her hostess gave her a shrewd look. "You do know of what you speak. Huh. Well, don't let my yapping keep you from it. You've a meal to eat and a day's walk to make."

"A day's—" Annalise bit down hard on the words and the curse she wanted to lay on the head of the man who'd directed her so astray.

The woman laughed. "Your vision didn't tell you this part, eh?"

"No, indeed."

"You could turn back, girly. A swift few minutes' trek will take you to the main road. There's a village not far off from there. I'm sure you could send word to your people to come for you. You've been on the road what, a day?"

"A few more than that."

"They'll barely have noticed you're gone."

Annalise bit into the food with a sigh, then moaned softly with pleasure. She chewed carefully, aware of how closely the woman watched her eat. She swallowed. Bit again. She finished her breakfast swiftly and neatly, then wiped the corners of her mouth with a fingertip and stood.

"Thank you for the meal and the lodging. I'm sorry I have naught to offer you in recompense, but—"

"I know. The Invisible Mother told you to set off with naught but your clothes and a day's worth of provisions."

This was the description of any vision Annalise had been able to find reported, but she eyed the woman and licked the last slick of grease from her lips. She'd ever been one to stand apart from the crowd.

"Actually, no." Annalise had not shared the details of her "vision" with anyone—silent grace so that none might judge the sincerity. Or veracity. She'd done her research so she might know the details of what others had said, but she'd never claimed any of them as her own.

The woman smiled. “No? What did She tell you, then?”

Annalise rose with a lie’s thread upon her tongue, one more to add to the tapestry she’d already begun to weave. “She spoke in a voice that made my ears bleed. To be sure, there were words, but I couldn’t tell you what they were. She didn’t need words to convince me I should spend my life in the pursuit of Her return and that of Her husband and child.”

The words had begun as lie but tasted of truth.

The woman who’d given Annalise shelter and food but not her name, tilted her head to stare. Then she pointed out the hut’s small window to the yard behind the house and the forest beyond it.

“Take the path through the woods,” she said. “You’ll find what you seek there.”

Chapter 4

Cassian was not surprised to see the woman from the forest crossing the field beyond the Motherhouse. He'd known even when sending her in the wrong direction that she had the spirit necessary to find her way to the Motherhouse. The surprise came in how early she appeared. He'd not thought to see her any time before midday on the morrow, if not later, yet here she was, striding through the knee-high grass and flowers with the walk of a purpose-led woman.

This meant one thing of two—either she'd figured his ruse and made her way to the Motherhouse despite him sending her off in the wrong direction, or she'd so pleased the Sister-in-Service who waited for Seekers in the hut at the edge of the forest that she'd been granted approval rather than further misdirection.

Either way, Cassian knew enough to be impressed. Most Seekers were turned away as many times as it took to discourage them. Most never made it to the Motherhouse.

But this woman had, and as her gaze fell upon him, he waited for her to hesitate before passing. She did not, much as she hadn't paused upon their first meeting. By the time she reached him, he'd ceased the slow and careful motions of his hands and arms and had come to rest.

"You," she said.

"Me."

She looked beyond him, across the field and the low stone wall separating it from the yard, past the stables and to the Motherhouse itself. She looked tired, but not too tired. One night spent sleeping rough, perhaps two, but no more than that. He might've underestimated the length of her journey. Her boots and the hem of her gown bore the stains of dust and grass. When she pushed back the hood of her cloak, her hair proved itself in need of a thorough brushing but her face had been recently scrubbed. She lifted her chin. Here in the light of the morning Cassian could see what had been hidden from him in the forest shadows—this woman's eyes were more than pale, they were crystalline, the color of ice made faintly blue. Against the darkness of her skin and hair, her eyes were even more startling.

"Shall I bother to ask you if yonder mansion is the house I seek, or would you set my foot upon the wrong path again?" Soft anger tinged her voice.

Cassian couldn't help recalling the less formal tone she'd used with him upon their first meeting. It had suited her better, along with the tease of amusement in those spectacular eyes. He supposed he couldn't blame her for adopting a more formal stance today.

"Is it the wrong path if you end up where you wanted to be all along?"

She didn't answer right away, and when she did, her voice was pitched low. "Seek you to test me on philosophy?"

"A question only." He blew out a breath and scraped his hair back from his face, thinking it was time for another cut.

She looked him over, and again he was struck by her utter lack of self-consciousness in dealing with him. He, a stranger and a man, should have earned at least a slim margin of respect, if not fear. Of course, she had no idea who he was. He wondered if it would matter when she found out.

"Should I have called it the longer, then, instead of the wrong? It would be the same result, would it not?" Now her eyes narrowed, the dark, sleek brows furrowing. Her mouth thinned. "You deliberately misled me."

Cassian shrugged. "And yet you found your way."

She studied him. He waited for anger or accusation, but none came. Instead, incredibly, the woman dismissed him with a sniff and turned on her heel so suddenly she tore the grass from the earth. She gathered her skirts and flipped up her hood. Then she set off across the field toward the Motherhouse.

He watched her for a moment without following and deliberated if he should, but the morning sun had already moved in the sky and he would be late for classes if he lingered. He had yet to bathe and eat and was reluctant to relinquish either pleasure in the face of a long day in front of students who ranged from giddily distracted to purposefully inattentive. He caught up to her in the length of three strides and fell into step beside her.

She twitched a glance his way, the motion of her hooded head telling him of the look rather than any sight of her eyes. "What are you doing?"

"Walking beside you."

She stopped in front of the low stone wall that did nothing to keep anyone in or out. "Why?"

"Perhaps we have the same destination."

She turned to fully face him. "Perhaps? Or certainly?"

An uncommon smile tried to tug at Cassian's mouth, the feeling of it so rare he at first didn't recognize it. "Perhaps certainly. If your goal is to reach that large house ahead, then indeed, but I'm certain I wouldn't dare presume to speak for you."

The woman huffed before clamping her lips tight. She softened them with an obvious effort. "I believe you would presume a great many things, sirrah, not the least of which would be . . . obfuscation."

He blinked at the term, then shrugged. "Mistress, I assure you, I happen along the same path out of convenience, not malice."

"I should believe that? After what you did yesterday?"

"You may believe," Cassian said after the barest pause, "whatever you wish."

"Answer me this. Why lie to me? Why deliberately send me down the wrong path? The longer path," she amended when his mouth opened on the same answer he'd given her before. "To what purpose?"

"Perhaps I'm a trickster."

The hood shaded her eyes but he felt the weight of her gaze just the same. "No," she said after a moment. "I don't believe that's true."

"No?"

She shook her head. From within the depths of the hood he caught a glimpse of her mouth, curving now into a smile. Cassian stepped back at the sight of it.

"It was a test, was it not? To see if I'm worthy, or some such thing? Yes?"

In all the years he'd been with the Order, from the dozens of young women who came seeking service and whom he'd had a part in dissuading, Cassian had never been asked that question. They all figured it out, of course, or were informed of their passing upon their first meeting with the Mothers-in-Service. But not a one of them had ever asked him about his part in it.

"I'm right. I can see it on your face." She laughed.

Cassian scowled and turned away. "You see nothing on my face."

Incredibly, her hand reached to snag his sleeve, and this action so surprised him at first that Cassian didn't pull away. "Oh, but I do. Right there in the furrow between your eyes and the way you tried to keep from smiling just a few moments ago. I've surprised you, haven't I? I can see that, too."

"Mistress," Cassian said coldly, "I will thank you to unhand me at once. Your exuberance is . . . unseemly."

"Your mercy," the woman said without a speck of sincerity in the words. She let her fingers slide from his sleeve. "I suppose they'll expect a natural decorum, yes?"

"What you lack naturally will be trained into you." Cassian stepped back to give her a half bow. He had no more appetite, no need to follow her inside. She'd thoroughly unsettled him.

"Ooh, sounds delicious. I can scarce contain my excitement."

By the Arrow, the chit was flirting with him. Cassian's scowl deepened. "I'll leave you to find your own way inside."

"Are you certain? I might have need of an escort," came the retort, completely devoid of anything resembling respect, "lest I stumble and struggle upon my way. Would you care to remind me which direction I am not to follow, sir? I'd hate to think I'm depriving you of one last chance to send me astray."

"I'm fair certain you'll have no trouble finding the front door. Good day." Cassian turned on his heel and headed in the direction of the back kitchen with her bedamned laughter trailing him all the way.

It was amazing how a simple mug of tea and slice of fresh bread, a piece of fruit and a quiet room could make the world a brighter place. Hours before Annalise had woken in a dingy hovel in despair, and now she breathed in the soothing scents of gillyflower oil.

"More tea?" The woman sitting across the desk from Annalise had introduced herself as Deliberata, one of the Mothers-in-Service. "I've an entire pot."

"No, thank you . . . Mother." Annalise tripped a bit on the title. This woman, with her long, sleek braid and high-throated gown, was as far from Annalise's frilly, fluttery mother as any woman had ever been.

"Very well, then." Deliberata sat back in her chair and folded her hands on top of the highly polished desk. She watched Annalise without speaking.

Annalise had already shared the details of her "vision." There must be more for her to say, but she wasn't going to spout out a bunch of nonsense simply to fill the space between them. She'd already undergone a test of sorts, being sent down the wrong road. *Longer road*, she corrected herself once more. Apparently, she'd passed that one, but had no doubts there would be more. After all, if every person who wished it could enter the Order of Solace, Handmaidens would no longer be rare enough to hold value. On the other hand, she thought as she sipped from the delicate china cup and watched the Mother-in-Service watching her, perhaps there simply weren't that many women moved to join. The Invisible Mother knew she was only here to delay a marriage she didn't want, or to avoid it all together. While Annalise believed within her heart she was special, she knew she wasn't unique.

She set the cup in its saucer and placed it carefully on the desk, then looked around the room. Furnished with heavy, richly carved furniture and thick tapestries, the room was impressive. She'd expected it to be so, of course. While not many knew the details of a Handmaiden's purpose, most were well-informed of their cost.

"Annalise. A lovely name." The Mother tapped one finger atop the desk. "And you come from Evadia, yes? Along the border?"

"Yes. I do." Annalise settled into the creaking chair with a sigh.

"And how long did it take you to travel here?"

"Nearly six days, ma'am. Four by carriage to the town of Delvingdon—"

"I'm familiar with Delvingdon," Mother Deliberata said dryly. "It is where most of our novitiates from the southeastern provinces go first."

Delvingdon had a Sisterhouse. A small one, nothing like this grand Motherhouse with its walls of brick and stone and the dome of glass over the central observatory. The Sisterhouse in Delvingdon had only a high iron gate around it and a dour gatekeeper who'd refused Annalise entry and told her which direction to head. Perhaps that had been a test, too.

"I hired a carriage there upon the advice of the Sisterhouse's gatekeeper," Annalise said. "Though the carriage driver had little more idea of where to find the Motherhouse than the gatekeeper had given me."

Deliberata smiled. "We do not keep the location of the Motherhouse a secret. We simply don't advertise its whereabouts to those for whom the knowledge is unnecessary."

"Or for those who'd seek to harm it?"

Deliberata nodded slightly. "There would always be those for whom our Order is something to fear rather than revere. Thankfully few in these days, though in times past we've not been so fortunate. But nevertheless, those who need to find us, do. As you did."

"Not without effort." Annalise frowned, thinking of the man in the forest, the one she'd then met in the meadow. "But I suppose that proves my worthiness to seek a place here, yes?"

"Oh, no," Deliberata disagreed, but gently. "It only proves your determination, which is not the same as worth at all. Though we are very glad you've made it to us, Annalise, the worth of your presence here has yet to be determined."

Ah, she was being thoroughly put in her place. Annalise did not bristle. She knew when a bowed head was a better choice than lifted chin. "I'll do my best."

"Of course you will. They all do." Deliberata rapped the desk with her knuckles. "Well. I'm sure you're tired from your journey, such as it was. Let me ring for someone to show you to your quarters, and we'll get you situated."

Startled, Annalise looked up to meet the other woman's eyes. "That's it? I'm a Handmaiden?"

"A novitiate," the Mother corrected, again gently. Annalise

wondered if there was ever anything the woman did without quiet grace—and she wondered how long it would take her to learn such a consistent, measured response.

A very long time, she thought, if she were to ever master it at all.

"A novitiate, of course." Annalise stood when the Mother did. The chair snagged on the rug as she pushed it back and she struggled to shove it without looking like a graceless behemoth. When she looked up, Deliberata was staring with amusement tweaking the corners of her mouth.

"I thought there would be more," Annalise said in an effort to retain her dignity. "That's all."

"There will be plenty more, child, never fear. But not all at once. Nothing worth gaining is ever granted in one piece, you know."

Annalise could think of much of value that could be gained all at once, but she held her tongue. "I thought I'd be required to prove something of my knowledge, that's all."

Lots of people knew, or claimed to know, what Handmaidens did, but Annalise had never met a person who'd secured the services of one. There were stories. There always were. Of the landowner in the next province who'd taken on a Handmaiden to satisfy his every base need left unfulfilled by his lady wife, and how his absolute solace had ended with his death. A relief to his lady wife, to be certain, but not exactly speaking well of the Order of Solace. Other tales were less explicit, mostly whispered, many of the "wink and nudge" variety. Inevitably there seemed to be an element of sexuality involved, which made sense to Annalise. She herself couldn't imagine a life of sexual dissatisfaction, which was why she'd started this game.

Of how Handmaidens were trained there was far less information. Apparently, having a vision was not enough; or rather perhaps a true vision would have told her all she needed to know. Instead, she'd suffered the advice of well-meaning ignorants. "Go to the Sisterhouse," she'd been told, and once there had been directed to yet another location. That Handmaidens must be of strong faith and well-versed in religious practice seemed the common assumption, and Annalise had no difficulty providing that.

Now, truthfully, she felt a bit cheated that she'd spent so long in study all her life only to finally be unable to use what she'd been forced to learn to impress the woman in front of her. Deliberata didn't look like a woman who was easily impressed. Annalise admired that.

Deliberata crossed to the woven cord with the large tassel at the end and pulled it. From somewhere a bell presumably rang, though Annalise heard no sound of it, and the sharp rap on the door followed too quickly for the distance to have been long. A moment later the door cracked open and a blonde head peeked around it.

"Yes, Mother?"

"Tansy, we have a new little sister here with us today. I thought since you've not been assigned a roommate you'd welcome the opportunity."

Tansy had bright hair, full red lips, and blue eyes. She looked as though the top of her head would perhaps reach Annalise's shoulder, and she clapped her hands together in a glee Annalise would have assumed was feigned if Tansy's broad grin hadn't seemed to prove it true.

"Oh, lovely, Mother. Yes. I'd be delighted to share my room with . . . ?"

"Annalise," she said when the Mother didn't offer the introduction. "Marony."

"Tansy Kochendor." Tansy giggled as if even the sound of her own name amused her.

Annalise bit back a sigh.

"Tansy, please take Annalise to see Sister Precision, so that she may be dispensed a set of uniforms and other supplies, and then show her to the bathing chamber. I'm fair certain she'll wish to bathe after her journey."

Again, Tansy clapped her hands and bounced. Yes, bounced on

her toes as though she were watching a particularly amusing puppet performance. Laughter might not be prudent in this case, but Annalise couldn't help the short chuckle that escaped.

"Thank you, Mother. Come along, Annalise. If we hurry, I'll have time to show you around a bit before evening services!"

Annalise found her hand imprisoned in Tansy's and the pair of them heading through the office door before she had time to protest. "That's it?" she asked over her shoulder as Tansy tugged her through the doorway. "Mother Deliberata?"

"We find it best if your first day is spent in acclimation. Tomorrow will dawn early enough for us to determine what place you will hold here. Good day, Annalise. Welcome to the Order of Solace. May you find here what you seek, and may you seek what you find."

Chapter 5

The door closed behind them with a solid thud that left no room for argument. Annalise turned to Tansy, who was still bouncing. Annalise took her hand from Tansy's grip.

"Was this how it was for you, on your first day?"

Tansy's grin twitched, flattening. "Oh, no. After my parents left—"

"Your parents brought you?" Soft wall hangings muffled the sound of Annalise's voice, but she minded herself to keep it low and smooth, anyway. This hall had many doors, and she knew not what lay behind any but one of them.

"Oh, yes. When I became of age, my parents brought me. Right up to the doorstep."

Tansy didn't look much older than a girl now, and Annalise became conscious of what some might consider her "advanced" age. "How nice for you."

"Papa had a contribution, of course."

"Of course," Annalise said dryly. She understood, now. Tansy was one of those privileged young ladies who'd been sent to finishing school and changed their frocks every season.

"Don't make it sound that way." Tansy gestured as she led Annalise down the hall and up a set of narrow stairs that had been hidden behind one of the wall hangings. "I know you think that Papa's contribution is what gave me my place here, but I can tell you that's not true."

"I didn't assume your father's money is what gained you entry. The Order takes all who make it to the gates, isn't that true?"

Tansy faltered at the top of the stairs before moving toward the left-hand hall. "Well, yes. But you wouldn't be the first to believe that because my parents gave the Order a lot of money I've somehow been treated special."

"Have you?" Annalise was never fond of ignoring questions for the sake of politeness. She looked down the other hall, empty but for some dust motes dancing in the shaft of light from the window at the end.

"I—well—I—" Tansy stuttered and shrugged.

When Annalise caught up to her, the girl's cheeks had gone a painful shade of pink. "Tansy, if others have accused you of it unfairly, I won't be one to join them. But if it's true, it might be best to own the fact rather than pretend it's false. You needn't brag on a truth to admit it."

"I don't think so," Tansy whispered after a moment, her head bent before she looked up more fiercely than Annalise expected. "If it's so, it's not because I've wished for it. My papa granted the Order money toward my room and board, for the cost of keeping me. It could be years before I'm deemed suitable to serve a patron—"

"Or never," Annalise added in a murmur. "That's always a possibility."

Tansy nodded. "Yes. Or never. But I won't let it be never. My parents would be so saddened, and I couldn't bear to disappoint them so. But I know it could be a long time before my patron fees would begin to cover the cost of my time here. I don't think there's anything wrong with my papa giving the Order a contribution to its coffers."

That was interesting, that Tansy would be saddened to disappoint her parents should she never become a Handmaiden. "What of your own sadness should you never be determined ready to take a patron?"

Tansy blinked rapidly. "Of course I would be so saddened. It's just that my papa has made a great effort for my keeping here . . ."

"There are those who believe they can buy their way into the Land Above with boons to the Temple." Annalise shrugged, unconcerned. "Or upon the backs of others."

Tansy whirled, blue eyes wide, mouth open. "No! That is not my papa!"

Annalise held up her hands to counter the girl's alarm. "Your mercy, Tansy. I meant no disrespect to your father."

Tansy shook her head, her shoulders hunching. "The others . . . there are others here who do. They say I am treated especial because of Papa's gift, and I know they have reason to think so, but they never see what I've earned on my own merit."

"Perhaps you should be less concerned with what others think of your merit, then."

Tansy looked over her shoulder, red lips parted. "Mother Consolata said the very same thing to me!"

Consolata, Deliberata. Annalise knew Handmaidens were given new names upon taking their vows, but these were not names. They were characteristics. If chosen for their reference to the personality of the bearer, what name would she be given? She quirked her mouth at the corners.

"Do you mock me?" Tansy stopped in the hall, lined with more doors, these mostly half open with the murmur of voices coming from inside.

"Not at all," Annalise assured her. "I'm simply finding all of this rather . . . unexpected."

"There was a Seeker who came here last year. She claimed she had a Calling. She started the training. And yet all she ever did, day start to day end, was poke fun at what we do here." Tansy's bright expression dimmed. "She made a mockery of what we do. She was most particularly unpleasant."

"Did she become a Handmaiden?"

"She was not sent away," Tansy said with a sniff, but before she could continue, a door at the end of the hall flung open and a trio of young women spilled out.

"The color of this suits my eyes ever so much better," said the tallest, smoothing the skirt of her dress. "And that gray does bring out the pink of your cheeks, Helena."

The three paused when they spotted Tansy and Annalise. Helena, clad in gray, nudged the side of her partner wearing dark blue. The tall girl who'd spoken, her gown a deep plum and her hair a rich copper, lifted a brow.

"Tansy."

"Hello, Perdita. Helena. Wandalette."

Perdita gave Annalise an up-and-down appraisal. "And you are?"

"New," Annalise said. This girl was easily six years younger than she. Annalise could have consumed her for breakfast.

Perdita blinked rapidly, but if there was confrontation to be had, it was not going to happen then. Instead she gave Tansy a sly, sideways glance and smoothed her skirts. "I've a new gown, Tansy. One provided me by the Order."

Tansy looked at her own hem. "It's pretty on you."

Perdita shrugged as though the compliment, though deserved, was unnecessary. "We're off to our afternoon faith instruction."

Tansy snorted softly. "I'm fair certain you'll enjoy your class, Perdita."

Helena snickered while the still-silent Wandalette hid a grin behind her hand. Perdita's mouth twitched, but not kindly. She looked Annalise over again, then bowed her head in a gesture that might have been respectful had it at all smacked of sincerity.

Then the trio set off in a swirl of skirts and giggles.

"Allow me to hasten a guess. Those are the girls who give you difficulty over your father's generosity?"

Tansy sighed. "They share a room. Helena and Perdita can be . . ."

"Vile?"

"Irritating," Tansy said. "But Wandalette can be very kind."

Annalise looked back at them as the young women rounded the corner and disappeared. "I've grown beyond the age of posturing. But I suppose some never do."

Tansy giggled. "Perdita never will. If you ask me, I don't think she'll ever be assigned a patron. But I didn't say that aloud."

A halo of gray hair above a round, wrinkled face peered around the doorway through which Perdita and her companions had come moments before. "Tansy! Is that the new girl?"

"Yes'm. Come," she gestured to Annalise. "If we don't hurry, we won't have time to put away your things before the evening service."

"Good day, girl." The woman in the room put her hands on stout hips. She stood only as high as Annalise's chest and had to tip her head back to catch a glimpse at her face. "Step you up and let me take your measure."

Crates and racks all over the room teemed with bolts of fabric and gowns in all shades. Some hung haphazardly over the backs of chairs while others looped on hooks set into the wall. It was as though a dressmaker's cabinet had exploded. Other tables held jars of buttons, and pincushions bristled with needles adangle with thread.

"Sister Precision," Tansy said by way of introduction. "This is Annalise."

"No need for names, girl, just step up on the stool so I might figure your size."

Annalise did as she was told, but with a laugh. "I'm hardly a girl, Sister."

Precision snorted. "Anyone is a girl to me any longer. I passed my sixtieth year last month. I'll not be long denied the Land Above."

Tansy bit down on her lower lip as though to hold back words, while Annalise looked at the old woman. "My mother's mother lived until her ninetieth year. You could have a lifetime left on this plane, Sister."

Precision, who'd been reaching for a pincushion to strap to her wrist, now gave Annalise a lifted brow stare. "Bite your tongue!"

"Your mercy," Annalise said. "I meant no offense."

Precision wrinkled her mouth, which set the crevasses deeper against the sides of her nose and between her brows. "Sweet Invisible Mother, girl. Think you I wish to dawdle around forever here when I could be drinking the delights of the Land Above?"

The older woman snapped at Tansy to bring an armful of gowns from the rack behind her. Precision plucked the first and held it up to Annalise, then tossed it aside to take the next. This one made her cluck and tilt her head back and forth.

"Take off your dress."

"What?"

"Strip. There's no room for modesty here, girl. A Handmaiden must feel as comfortable in her own skin as in a gown of gold." Precision stared at Annalise. "Might as well get used to it now. Besides, it's not as though I've never seen a pair of plumpenpillows before."

Annalise couldn't hold back her laugh at the term for breasts she'd never heard before. She put her fingers to the buttons at the throat of her gown and swiftly undid them all the way to her waist. Beneath she wore a simple linen shift and stays.

"Those must go," Precision snapped again, and Tansy sprung to action to undo the laces at the back.

"Wait, what?" Annalise put her hands on her belly to hold the garment tight against her. "You'd have me believe I'm to go 'round without proper foundation beneath my gowns?"

"A Handmaiden's role is not for fashion, but for service. Too many a lady has fainted on her couch from the tightness of her laces. And no Handmaiden has time for frippery or can count on the help of a maidservant. Best you get used to making your own posture, not one made by fabric and bone. Off with it."

"No wonder you are sometimes accused of being slatterns," Annalise muttered.

Precision rapped Annalise on the knees with the edge of a measuring stick. "Bite your tongue! We may be called by many names outside these walls, but inside, none may impugn us!"

"Your mercy." Annalise winced.

"She's ignorant," Tansy offered helpfully. "As many are, when first arriving."

"And yet many have learned to sew shut their lips upon insult," Precision said. She grunted, flicking the hem of Annalise's shift. "Off with this, girl."

"You'll have me naked? This shift fits me well and is of fine cloth. Would you have me discard it?"

Precision sighed as though the weight of the world had come to rest upon her bony shoulders. "Sinder's sweet sin, girl. I'm not going to steal it from you. But one gown won't suit you for more than a day or so, perhaps three if you've no taste for sweetness upon your person, but if that's the case, I think you'd best find another Calling, for we don't admire lack of hygiene here."

"I'm not . . . I didn't mean . . ." Annalise clamped her mouth closed. It seemed best not to speak.

She stayed silent for the rest of the session while Precision measured and poked and pinned and tossed aside gown after gown. In the end she pressed three into a heap on the table next to Annalise and waved at her to step back into her original dress. The old woman fixed her with a sharp eye that belied her age, and when Annalise had finally dressed again in her shift, her belly unaccustomed to the room, Precision sighed.

"You've four for now. More might come, if deemed necessary. But that's what you get for now. Pick out your stockings and boots from the bins over there. You've your own cloak, so you can keep that, though by the time you're assigned to go anywhere it may no longer suit. Shifts are folded in the cupboard over there, Tansy can show you where. You'll have one for each day from those. Even if you bathe daily, you should change your shift every morning."

Annalise paused in front of a bin of mismatched stockings to look back at the woman. "With all due respect, Sister, my mother raised me properly."

Precision let out another snort. "You'd be surprised at some whose didn't. Now. Off with you, girl. G'wan. Get. I've more tasks to tend and no time for dawdling."

The woman shooed them both out and slammed the door behind them, leaving Annalise staring at the pile of clothes in her arms. Tansy laughed. Annalise wondered if there was aught that Tansy didn't find amusing.

"Come on, then. You'll be rooming with me. And won't it be merry?" Tansy shifted the pile of stockings and the pair of boots she was kindly helping to carry. "I haven't had a roommate yet. All the other novitiates do, and most have two. It can be very lonely at night."

Annalise forced her groan into silence and followed Tansy down another set of halls, down some stairs, and through a few sets of doors. She tried keeping track but knew she'd be unable.

"We have a good room," Tansy said. "It's at the end of the hall, away from the ones who stay up late making merry when they should be better served sleeping or studying."

Annalise had an idea of which novitiates that might be. She paused outside the door Tansy had opened. "Are there rules against making merry?"

"Not . . . exactly."

"But there are rules?"

"Of course. Every place needs rules."

Mother Deliberata hadn't mentioned them. "What are they?"

Tansy looked over her shoulder as she entered the room and Annalise followed. The other girl perched on the edge of a narrow bed made up with crisp, plain linens. Two others just like it, but bare of sheets and blankets, lined the other walls. Head to head or foot to foot, if all three were occupied. Annalise held back a grimace and sat on the bed across the room, against the opposite wall.

"Oh . . . simply that . . . well, we must at all times behave with decorum and represent ourselves as though we'd already taken our vows. It's not a rule, I suppose. More an expectation. And we must attend the studies we're assigned, of course, else we'll never learn enough to be ready for our vows. And we must not leave the grounds of the Motherhouse without permission from a Mother-in-Service. Some are granted leave to go into town, but I've never asked."

"What might one find in town that one doesn't find here?"

Tansy's cheeks pinked. "Oh . . . well, if one has coin to spend, one might find all manner of amusements. Or company."

"Male company? I suppose there must indeed be a fair lack of that around here." She thought of the dark-haired man, and her smile faded. Of everything she'd imagined about the Order of Solace, this description didn't fit. "It sounds like the worst years of boarding school. Worse than that, for school ends and service to the Order doesn't."

"One might leave the Order, if one chooses, Annalise. And of course once you're assigned a patron . . ." Tansy trailed off wistfully. "Well, all manner of things might happen then."

"Indeed." Annalise bit back further response. If she had her way, she'd never be assigned a patron. Then again, did she wish to spend the rest of her life face to toe with others?

She'd imagined a quiet life of learning and perhaps prayer—dull, to be certain, but bearable. A few years of it while she waited to be past the age where marriage was a necessity and not a luxury. What Tansy was describing was not at all appealing.

"I'd thought myself too old to need schooling," Annalise murmured with a sigh and looked 'round the room, noting that despite the bare block walls and stark furnishings, it wasn't entirely uncozy.

Tansy's father's money had made a difference. Subtle but not invisible. A carpet for the wooden floor, heavy drapes at the window. A rack of gowns, all of similar cut and color, but in fine fabric.

"One is never too old for schooling," Tansy said.

Annalise stopped cataloging the room's contents long enough to give Tansy a look. "It would seem I came unprepared for my term here."

Tansy's laughter was like the chirp of a bird in its nest. "Everyone does, I think! When I first arrived, my eyes were so wide I was fair certain I'd never close them."

"How long have you been here, Tansy?"

"Five years." She ticked them off on her fingers quickly, then closed them tight into her fist and gave Annalise a somewhat defensive look. "But I was very young when I arrived, you see. There was much to learn. Not everyone who arrives here requires the same training. You'll find out tomorrow when you're tested."

"Will I?" Annalise wasn't surprised, but it would have been nice if the Mother who greeted her had mentioned a test. "What sort of test?"

"Oh, all sorts."

"Reading? Figures?"

"Yes, of course." Tansy shifted on the bed, her chin lifting. She spoke by rote. "One who is not educated cannot properly serve."

"What else will I be tested on?"

"Oh . . . the canon of the Faith. Other skills. Have you any other skills, Annalise?"

"Ah, that depends upon whose opinion you solicit. Yes. I have skills. I can tat a doily, darn a sock. I can, if hard-pressed, compose a poem, though I make no boast of its merit. Is that the sort of thing you mean?" Annalise had heard stories of what tasks a Handmaiden might be expected to perform. Other, more intimate skills, she was not going to mention.

"Oh, you sound so accomplished." Tansy clapped with delight. "I'm sure you'll do wonderfully!"

"What happens if I don't?"

Tansy looked pensive. "Nothing harsh. Don't fear."

Annalise hadn't been afraid, only curious. "Do they turn you away?"

"Oh, no. Nothing like that. We're all placed in classes according to our skills. There's no term, such as there would be in school. We move from skill level to skill level, until we can take our place as teachers to those who need instruction, or we're assigned patrons. Handmaidens never stop learning."

"Lovely," Annalise said without enthusiasm. "I can only wonder that more poor families don't send their girlchildren here for their educations, especially since the Order doesn't indenture its novitiates."

Tansy tilted her head. "Oh, I suppose some might . . . but I can't imagine why anyone who didn't have a true Calling would come here."

"I can," Annalise said, but then turned the subject to other places.

Chapter 6

He knew her name, now. Annalise. It suited her, somehow regal but not royal. Cassian knew she would never be an Anna.

After a daylong session of testing to determine her path of training, she would no doubt be tired, hungry, even bristling with annoyance. He wasn't surprised that she'd sprung from the chair when he came in, or that her mouth had twisted and her brow furrowed. He'd have done the same, he thought, watching her.

"You!"

"Me," he said.

Annalise had woven her hair into a single braid in the style they all wore. If asked, he'd have said he preferred the tight ringlets falling down her back, but nobody questioned him, and Cassian worked hard to never let it be known he had a preference about which anyone might ask.

"Where are the Mothers? Deliberata, Consolata, Patience?" Sudden weary laughter erupted from her. "By the Arrow, I cannot tell you how difficult I find it to believe there are women who answer to such names."

Cassian had closed the door behind him and now he moved forward into the room. "It would behoove you to believe it."

She watched him warily. "And you? Your name. Let me guess. Arrogance? Liar?"

"Men don't enter the Order of Solace."

"But men can become Temple priests."

"Priests keep the name of their birth unless they choose otherwise. They're not given other names."

"You mean the men get to keep their identities." She gave a small sneer. "They're not required to take on a new persona to perform their service."

"Priests must take on many things. A name, at least, changes only what others call you. It can't change who you are."

She sniffed and crossed her arms over her stomach. "So, what is your name? Who are you? You must have some place here, not in the stable or the yard. You said yourself they don't allow men in the Order."

He waited without giving himself away while she circled 'round him, looking him over. Cassian had been so scrutinized before, many times, and even her hottest gaze could not move him. Or so he told himself as she moved closer to look at the high collar of his jacket, the length of his sleeves and hem, the cut of his trousers. She studied his hair and then focused on his face.

"Temple priests," she said thoughtfully, "shave their heads. So you are not a priest."

Even now, so many years later, this struck a small pain just below his breastbone and deep within his gut. "No."

"So. What are you here to test me on?"

At least she hadn't burst into tears. "What might you think I'm here to test you on?"

"Ha!"

She stepped back, twirling so the hem of her gown swirled around her boots. They were not Order-given, he saw that, but a fine travel pair she must've worn here. So she had been better prepared for her journey than he'd thought. The gown, though, was different. It didn't suit her as well as her own had.

"Is that my test? To figure your purpose?"

Cassian sat in the empty chair and put his hands on his knees. He didn't turn to look at her, even though she stood in his line of vision. He said nothing.

The sound of their breathing grew very loud.

"You won't tell me? The others all told me. It was tedious but not shocking, any of it," Annalise murmured finally. "I knew my letters and numbers. I knew the story of the Holy Family, more than one, in fact. I knew how to serve tea without spilling. But now . . . now, sir, what could you be here to test?"

Her voice had dipped low, Sinder help him, deep and thick and rich as puddled honey. Women of all ages came to seek service in the Order, and they all went through the testing—but Cassian was not always called in to assist. Most often he dealt with the girls, the simpering gigglers with youth and exuberance propelling them swifter than wisdom.

Annalise was no girl.

"I know. You're a man. I am a woman. I know what you're here to learn of me."

"If you know," Cassian said, "you'd be one of the first to guess without prompting."

She had a lovely laugh, sweet but edged with wickedness. It was designed to turn men's heads and draw women in close. Cassian didn't look. He did not move.

Annalise moved around him in a slow circle as she spoke. "They tested me on many skills, but have said naught so far of what a Handmaiden is expected to do for her patrons beyond making tea and reading aloud. We all know there's more to it than that, yes?"

"Sometimes. I would not presume to speak for every patron or every Handmaiden."

"And I should not, either," she murmured. "You need not say so aloud to chastise me. I understand when I've overstepped."

At this, finally, he looked at her. "Do you? I find that difficult to believe, given our previous conversations."

"You mean the ones in which you insulted me and led me astray?"

"And yet here you are."

She stopped in front of him. With him seated and her standing, his gaze leveled at her breasts. He looked at her face, instead.

For the first time since their meeting in the forest, he saw hesitation in her gaze. Her tongue slipped out, soft and pink, to trace the fullness of her bottom lip. She stiffened her shoulders.

"Here we both are."

He looked, and looked again. Annalise didn't turn her gaze from his. He admired her for that.

"You are not here to see how rapidly I can divide a column of numbers."

"No. Not that."

She swallowed, and the motion of her throat working drew his gaze despite his best intentions to keep his eyes on hers. Her breasts lifted and fell with her breath. Her hands clenched at her sides.

Then, slowly but with grace, Annalise sank to her knees.

The sight of a woman in such a pose ought to no longer move him, but Cassian was still a man. Something tightened inside him when she tilted her face to look up at him from her place a scant measure from his feet, placed so firmly on the floor. Her skirt had tangled about her legs, and he reminded himself she was new to this—perhaps not to being on her knees, but to serving.

She'd not yet learned to Wait, and that, too, would come in time. Yet Annalise sank naturally back onto her heels with her hands in her lap. The pose wasn't quite perfect, but the ease at which she set the posture sent another tight, sharp thrill through him until he forced it away.

"I suppose there are all sorts of service," she whispered. "Are you here to judge my willingness, sir, or my skill?"

Neither, in fact. He was sent inside the room to judge a novitiate's comfort level with a strange man and her ability to sense what might set him at ease, since service to men was far different than that to women. Only some assumed from the start, as Annalise now did, that he expected sexual service, and none of them had ever been right.

Until now.

The thought froze him in place. Her gaze flickered over him. Cassian strained to show no reaction.

"This would be ever so much easier if you were not so lovely," the woman on her knees breathed, and Cassian was at once on his feet.

"I am here to test your capacity for empathy," he said harshly, voice rough but not with anger.

She got to her feet. "My what?"

He gestured at the fireplace, the teakettle, the scattered pillows on the floor. "To judge your ability to put others at ease. To sense what might make another comfortable."

Annalise blinked rapidly, lips parting. Then she put her hands on her hips, eyes narrowed. "Are you saying I've failed?"

"My purpose here was to see how easily you figured out what another person might need," Cassian said sternly, without looking at her.

"Have I failed? Tell me, sir, if you find that to be true."

"I'm saying you should seek further training. Much further training!"

Incredibly, she laughed again. "You accuse me of overstepping again."

"This is not an accusation. This is a fact. A Handmaiden is not a kitchen slut, sent to flip up her skirts at the first crook of her patron's finger!"

"Tell me no Handmaiden is ever asked to get on her knees and suck a patron's cock, and I will call you a liar. Which I already know you to be," Annalise told him.

"I did not," Cassian said tightly, through gritted teeth, "desire you to perform such an act upon me."

Annalise looked, as he had, at the teakettle and pillows, the props and tools that had gone unused. She looked back at him, her gaze hard as iron. Ungiving. And, Sinder help him, knowing.

"Liar," she told him. "If a test was failed, I do not think 'twas me who failed it."

He could say nothing, found no words. Cassian hissed in a breath and shook his head. Annalise shrugged and turned away.

"Shall I be sent away before I've begun? Was this what determines my place in the Order, or not?"

"No."

She slanted a sly smile at him along with a glance. "No?"

"You'll begin your training tomorrow," Cassian said, his voice so tight it hurt his throat.

"Lovely," Annalise said.

He thought he heard her laughing as the door closed behind him.

I don't believe the Holy Family will return any earlier based on the time I awake." Annalise said this from the safety of her blankets, which had twisted around her ankles during the night.

"You don't wish to miss morning services!" Tansy, already up and about, had washed her face at the basin and turned dripping cheeks toward Annalise.

"And if I do?"

"They're the shortest ones." Tansy tugged on Annalise's toes through the blankets.

At this, Annalise peeked out from beneath the covers to see if the younger woman was teasing. It wasn't quite possible to tell with

Tansy. Two days in her presence hadn't been long enough to learn her sense of humor.

"And the sooner we finish, the sooner we can get to the dining hall to break our fast. And," Tansy paused dramatically, "there are cinnamon cakes."

"Ah, well, if there are cinnamon cakes," Annalise replied without moving.

Tansy giggled. The sound might have worked Annalise to irritation from another source, but there was simply no hating Tansy. Perhaps those spoiled girls they'd met in the hall could do it, but Annalise, whose patience for trivialities was notably thin, couldn't. It was the girl's overwhelming aura of joy, undeniable.

"You do wish to attend morning services, don't you?" Now Tansy sounded concerned. "Annalise?"

Annalise cracked open an eye and yawned. "Not particularly."

"Not . . . !" Tansy swallowed her shock and shook her head, sending the bright blonde braid swinging. "Oh, you are teasing me. You must be."

"I assure you, I'm not." At last Annalise threw back the covers and stretched, then put her feet on the floor beside the bed. "I can list ten fingers' worth of tasks I'd rather set myself to this early, and attending Temple services isn't on it."

Tansy covered her mouth with her hand, her eyes wide. "Oh, Annalise. How can you say such a thing?"

"Because it's true. Ah, you've filled the pitcher for me. Thank you."

Annalise hadn't thought to do it before climbing into bed the night before. At home, the housemaid would have made certain to make it ready for the morn. Annalise supposed she'd best become accustomed to remembering, for what better way to learn to serve others than by serving herself?

Annalise was aware of Tansy's gaze upon her as she washed quickly and dressed in one of the gowns the Order had provided.

It still felt strange to go without her stays, but somehow liberating, as well. She fumbled with her braid and felt Tansy's hands helping her a moment later with the headscarf Annalise had not yet grown accustomed to wearing.

Annalise looked over her shoulder. "Thank you, Tansy. You're very kind."

Tansy still looked worried. She gnawed her lower lip before speaking. "Annalise, I have to ask you something. Are you . . . do you not have . . . faith?"

The truth of that answer was no, but though Annalise liked Tansy, she didn't fully trust her. Not with the truth of her reasons for becoming a novitiate, anyway. Annalise had passed all their tests, all of which seemed bound to determine her ability to become a Handmaiden. Her faith hadn't been called into question.

"Must one attend services to prove one's faith, Tansy? It's been my understanding that prayers make their way to the Land Above no matter where they're said."

"Yes, but . . . in the Temple the priests lead the service."

"In the Temple," Annalise said, "the priests say aloud what the rest of us speak within our hearts. Tell me, which prayers do you think the Invisible Mother hears better?"

"The priests speak for those who can't."

"Ah, but I am not unable to speak, Tansy."

Tansy bit at her lower lip again, her expression troubled. "Attendance at services is mandatory, I think."

"But you don't know?"

"Nobody has ever said otherwise. We only miss services if we're ill, or not here. Everyone goes to services. All the Sisters and the Mothers. All the staff." Tansy worried her fingers together into a knot, then loosened them only to start all over again.

"Then I shall attend as well." Annalise patted her headscarf over her hair and smoothed the front of her dress.

"But not with joy in your heart!"

Annalise paused to look at her. "No, I can't say that is true."

Tansy shook her head, fretting. "I don't understand."

Annalise patted her shoulder. "You needn't."

At this, Tansy nodded, the storm clouds on her expression breaking apart to reveal the sunshine of her smile. "Well. I shall pray for you, Annalise. Extra hard. How is that?"

"If you must." Annalise laughed. "Far be it from me to turn away such an offer."

"I still don't understand," Tansy murmured as they left their small room and followed the long corridors and stairways toward the chapel. "Why enter the Order if you're not of the Faith? If you don't believe?"

"Believe in what? Allowing others to speak for me?"

They'd joined a group of other young women, all dressed in the same style gowns, identical braids under matching headscarves. We are a flock, Annalise thought with a pang of dismay-tinged amusement. All of us with the same feathers.

"In the return of the Holy Family. That's why we become Handmaidens. To fill Sinder's Quiver."

"Ah yes, of course I believe in that." Surely the Invisible Mother would forgive the lie.

Tansy, whose legs were shorter, had to do a double-skip in order to keep up with Annalise. "And you do believe we can do that, don't you? Handmaidens? Provide our patrons with absolute solace?"

"Certainly. Of course." It seemed the right answer, but Annalise didn't believe one person could provide another with even a moment's happiness, much less one of absolute solace. Anyone who depended upon another for such a thing would never find it, she thought. "Do you believe we can be taught how to do that?"

Tansy blinked. From not far away came the sound of the chime calling them to the chapel. "We'd better go. We'll be late."

It had been ages since Annalise had been inside a chapel, much less attended a Temple service. The last she could remember had been for the Fast of Sinder, not the most pleasant of holidays and certainly not the one she'd recommend to anyone attempting to convert the unconsecrated to the Faith. She could still recall the sting of incense in her nose and the buzz in her ears as she fought not to faint from hunger and lack of sleep. Her sister Adorette had in fact passed out, twitching and jerking on the floor in front of the priests who'd stepped over her and moved on as though she weren't there. It was the last service Annalise had attended, no matter how many times her mother had pleaded. Or threatened.

Now here she was again, in the largest chapel room she'd ever seen. Long benches with carved backs made four rows each on either side of the center aisle. The beemah in the front, raised a step off the floor, was circular. Three priests, their heads shaved and oiled, sat there. Their bare chests gleamed with oil as well, the crimson silk of their folded robes lying over one shoulder and pleated at their waists to hang to the floor.

Contrary to what she'd been forced to in childhood, nobody was silent. The women of the Order chatted and laughed as they filled in the rows. The priests were silent, intent on lighting their casks of incense and making mystical symbols over everything with their hands, but unlike the priests Annalise could remember, none made stern faces toward the noise their audience made.

The service began without fanfare, just the simple chiming of a bell rung by the tallest priest. The three turned their faces toward the draped alcove at the back of the chapel then bowed from the waist, then once to each side. Upright, they began to sway and mutter.

Annalise, who'd followed Tansy into one of the last rows of benches, looked to either side of her. On her right, Tansy mimicked the priests, her eyes closed and smile rapturous. She clutched a prayer book to her chest, but didn't read from it, apparently having memorized the service. At Annalise's left, a broad-shouldered woman in a dark green gown squinted at the words in her prayer book. Her mouth moved as she read, her words a whisper. All around, the women chanted and muttered, each at her own pace.

And in the middle of it, Annalise stood still and silent. She didn't open the prayer book. She didn't whisper along with the prayers—though she could have. She knew them all, even if she'd done her best to forget. They came back to her not in pieces but all at once, chunks of pleas and supplications, poems of praise to the Invisible Mother that she hadn't written and, therefore, could not feel were her own.

She'd never known how to pray in this manner. Someone else's words but her own pace. Always before she'd sat and listened to the priests speak them for her, which made all the prayers theirs and never hers. Faced with wildness, this twisting and turning of the body to portray the joy of the supplicant, Annalise froze. It was too much even to feign.

Suddenly, it was all too much.

"Your mercy," she said in a low voice as she pushed past Tansy. "Please let me by."

Tansy paused in her litany to move aside, but didn't try to stop Annalise. Looking 'round, Annalise saw others who'd finished the service preparing to leave. Her exit would scarce be noticed as strange.

"I'll see you in the dining hall," she told Tansy, who nodded and bent back to her worship.

Annalise didn't go to the dining hall. When she ducked out of the chapel, it was with an exhale of breath she'd not realized she'd been keeping held tight within her lungs. It whooshed from her and left her light-headed. She ducked into an alcove just beyond the chapel doors and put her hand to the cool brick wall, her head bent. She could hear the voices from inside the chapel more clearly here, and looked up to see that the alcove opened to the chapel but with a high, curved railing and curtain to shield it from the main chapel.

She was not alone. A figure stood in the shadows of the far corner. She didn't need to see his face to know him. She still hadn't learned his name.

He stayed as still and silent as she had in the chapel, not a sway or mutter to betray him. Perhaps he wasn't praying, she thought, but as her eyes adjusted to the dim light the stiff set of his shoulders told her she might be wrong in that assumption. He was certainly concentrating fiercely enough not to have noticed her, she was fair certain of that, for not a hair twitched her way. And his eyes were closed, she could see that now by the deeper pools of darkness in his face. If he'd been looking at her, surely his eyes would have caught the light.

The common rise and fall of voices inside the chapel changed as she watched the man from the forest do nothing. The service was over. Annalise backed out of the alcove, her sleeve scraping the bricks as she did. She caught a flash of motion from his corner just as she joined the crowd spilling from the main chapel doors.

In less than a breath she was caught up in the throng, again one among many. When the man appeared in the doorway, his dark eyes searching the crowd, Annalise knew there was no way he could know she'd been the one spying on him. Yet when his gaze caught hers from across the hall, just as she was jostled and tugged along toward the dining hall by an exuberantly chatting Tansy, Annalise could tell he knew she'd been the one.

He had looked into the crowd and plucked her face from all the others as easily as he might have tugged an apple from a tree.

Chapter 7

Silence was Sinder's Blessing and for the moment, Cassian had it in abundance. He needed it. After the incident at morning services he'd found himself sorely incapable of suffering giggles and frothy questions designed to prick at him. He'd assigned his class a lesson too difficult for them, apurpose to keep them from plaguing him, and watching the ten or so sleek heads bent over their texts, Cassian had no regrets he'd set such a hard task.

Classes in the Motherhouse didn't run on a yearly cycle the way traditional schools did, just as he wasn't a teacher in the traditional sense. None of the instructors here were—they were all members of the Order, or in Cassian's case, a member of the priesthood, whose skills and temperaments had provided them capacity to instruct others. As novitiates entered and were tested, they were placed in groups according to their skill levels. As they became more proficient, they moved to different groups where they could be further challenged, or if they were not yet assigned a patron, they became instructors themselves.

Cassian had been teaching the Faith for near ten years. In a school he'd likely have been given a brass pocket watch by now in recognition of his service, but here in the Order where service itself was considered the reward, he'd merely gained a reputation.

Not undeserved, he knew, as a particularly timid novitiate looked up from her text with a yawn and closed her mouth on a squeak when she saw him watching. Yet Cassian would have challenged even one of the women he'd tutored to show proof of his temper. He knew what they whispered about him. What was said of his fury, and what had happened to novitiates in the past who'd overstepped him. But not a one of them had ever witnessed him so much as raising his voice, much less destroying furniture in a rage, or striking a wall so fiercely he put a hole through the plaster. He knew what they said about him, but he never denied it.

He liked being able to quiet a room with no more than a lifted brow or downturned corner of lip. Obedience and submission pleased him greatly. There was a reason he'd found a place here amongst the Sisters-in-Service . . . and there was a reason they allowed him to stay.

"Please, sir, if I might ask . . . ?" The timid girl, Wandalette, cleared her throat.

Cassian, leaning back in his chair with his feet propped upon the desk, flicked a fingertip at her by way of answer.

"I would like to know why the stories diverged? Why is there more than one version of the Book? Do the priests not know which is the true word of Sinder?" Again, she cleared her throat. "I mean, sir, why is the story the same until the end?"

"Yes, sir, I'd like to know that as well," piped up another of the newer novitiates. Perdita, he thought her name was. "My grandmother always told me the tale of how Kedalya was set upon in the forest by wolves in the form of men. They took Her virtue, and left Her for dead."

"And when Sinder found Her so sullied," Wandalette said, "He blamed Her for the attack and took their son away."

"But this text here," Perdita pointed out, "says that Kedalya betrayed Sinder of Her own accord, and the commentary states that it was the Invisible Mother's fault the Holy Family split up. Which is the truth, sir?"

Perhaps the lesson had not been too difficult for them to understand, after all. Cassian let his boots thump to the floor and leaned over the desk. "The version I gave you is the correct text."

Wandalette and Perdita exchanged glances. Perdita shrugged and bent back to her book. Her fingers smudged with ink, she carefully copied a passage into her small parchment booklet, the one that would attend her during her entire time of service to the Order. Wandalette did not copy the passage, but sat back at her desk and thoughtfully flipped through the pages of the text.

Cassian waited for another challenge from her, but she seemed sated by his answer, and he allowed the silence and heat of the room to lull him into a near doze. He'd slept unwell the night before, dreams of old plaguing him for reasons he wished not to explore. Now with the soft scratch of pens on paper and the occasional low sigh, he let his eyes drift shut.

"Your mercy," said a voice he hadn't known long enough to be so familiar. "I was told to report here for . . . instruction."

Again his boots thumped to the floor, this time hard enough to rattle the inkpot upon his desk.

Annalise tilted her head, a smile in her eyes but not yet upon her lips. "Your mercy, sir. Perhaps my greeting was . . . unseemly?"

Ten pairs of eyes flickered back and forth between their instructor and this stranger. Annalise was easily six years older than the oldest of them—a woman grown, and well aware of it, too. She was out of place in this group, who'd been placed together mostly because of their youth and inexperience.

Unless, of course, it had been determined she knew too little of the Book to be placed with any other group.

"We meet only until the next chime," Cassian said. "There's scarce enough time for you to attend today's lesson."

"I don't mind." She smoothed her skirts as she took an empty seat at the back of the room. She folded her hands atop it and fixed him with a steady gaze. "It's been a good long time since I was in class. I think I should seek to gain as much from the experience as possible. Don't you?"

Ten mouths gaped. Cassian shifted in his chair and linked his fingers together as he stared at her. She'd been in the alcove this morn, he was fair certain of that. Watching him. But to what purpose? More importantly, to what impression?

"You'll need a text to read. And something to write in and write with."

"Such as this?" She reached into her pocket and pulled forth a leather-bound book the size of her palm, along with a pen carrier of folded felt. "They gave me this already."

Their eyes locked. Her smile had faded even from her eyes, and she met his gaze with naught but seriousness. Her look did its best to unmake him, and Cassian did not like this. Not at all.

None of the novitiates were required to share texts, as they might have done in a school. The Order used its funds wisely for provisions. Cassian had a stack of books ready for dispersal in the storage closet.

"Wait," he said and returned in a few moments with a text for her. "Today we're studying the final four chapters."

Before he even had the chance to sit back at his desk, Annalise had flipped through the pages and looked up at him, her brow furrowed. "This book is unacceptable."

Nobody said a word, but the sound of their shock nevertheless echoed throughout the room. Cassian himself swallowed a grunt of surprise at Annalise's calm tone. He turned.

"Is it?"

She held it out to him. "The binding has cracked, the pages are bent. Should not a copy of the Book, even one meant for regular study and not holy translation, be kept in better condition? I thought texts in condition such as this were burned."

He took the text from her. She was right, though not a single other woman in the room would've known it. He set the book aside and looked 'round the room at the other novitiates, none of whom were daring to look back. When his gaze settled upon Annalise, she smiled.

"Or so I recall being taught by the priests at home."

In silence, Cassian went to the storage closet and brought forth another text. He set it in front of her and, this time, didn't turn away. He watched her look through it. When she looked up at him, those pale-ice eyes jabbed him someplace deep inside.

"Your mercy, sir," she said quietly. "But this text is in no good condition, either."

"Perhaps," he said tightly, "it would benefit you to choose the text for yourself."

She rose smoothly. "Perhaps it would."

He could not feel her breath against his back as she followed him, but he imagined he did. He imagined, too, the weight of ten gazes following them. He did not imagine the low hum of conversation that began the moment he and Annalise entered the closet.

Lined on both sides with shelves stacked high with texts, translations, and commentaries, the only light coming from a narrow window at the far end of the room. A low desk had been pushed against the wall there, with a single, straight-backed chair. Nobody ever sat there in study, but it had been that way when he'd inherited the room and he'd never changed it.

There was plenty of room between them, so much not even the hem of her skirt needed to brush his boots as she turned to look at the shelves. They weren't touching, but he felt her. More so when he looked away and knew she'd cast her gaze upon him.

"You choose," he said hoarsely.

"Many of these texts look unkempt," she said. "I'm sure their wear is from their use in study—"

"Of course it is," he bit out. "Think you I'd have them ruined for sport?"

"Your mercy," Annalise said, though he doubted she meant the words as sincerely as they sounded. "I meant only that constant use would make it difficult for anyone to have attempted their upkeep."

Though he ought to have done, was the unspoken but understood end of her sentence. And again, she was right. The books they used here weren't sacred by any means, but they were copies of the sacred texts, of the Book itself, and though they'd not been anointed, they were due respect nonetheless.

Moreover, it was his duty to do so, and he'd ignored it for a long time. Not because he hadn't been aware of the task, but because nobody else had ever seemed to know, and because he simply hadn't cared. Now he looked at her. She didn't shrink from him.

"You might choose your own copy," he told her. "And set those aside you deem . . . unacceptable."

Her mouth looked soft, especially when she smiled. "You would trust my judgment?"

"It would seem you know enough for that to be sensible."

She shifted, titled her head, cast a look up at him from lash-shaded eyes. She was flirting with him. The sight of it set him back a step, against the shelf where the sharp edge of a book dug between his shoulder blades.

"By calling me 'sensible,' sir, you prove you don't know me overwell."

"I don't know you at all."

One sleek brow lifted. "Yet of all the people I've met here at the Order, you seem to be the one with whom I've had the most interaction."

"That will change."

"Will it?" She studied the stacks of texts and ran a finger down their spines, then met his gaze again. "Now that I find myself compelled to attend your tutelage, sir, I believe we will but spend all the more time with one another."

"You will have other instruction," Cassian said. "And I, many other students."

At this, her eyes narrowed. "Indeed."

She gave him her back and made as though to choose a text. Cassian, released from the snare of her pale eyes, relaxed. He knew, now, how to keep her at a distance from him.

She would not ever be the same as all the others, but he must make her believe he thought her so.

For a fortnight, Annalise did as she was told. Go here, sit there, eat now, and sleep then. It was easier than she'd expected, to bend to the instruction of others. To obey.

Not that the Mothers or Sisters-in-Service ruled the Order with fists of rock. Not at all. Unlike many of the other religious orders or guilds, the Order of Solace didn't indenture its novitiates. Though a few, such as Tansy, had families who contributed to their keep, the Order ran solely on the proceeds of the fees it charged patrons for the service of its Handmaidens. Sisters who wished to leave were free to do so at any time, and return if it so suited them. Novitiates not yet entered into the Order were required to attend appropriate instruction and work toward the time when the Mothers above them determined them ready to Serve—but Annalise could discover no time limit as to how long this could take.

"How do the Mothers-in-Service decide when a novitiate is ready to become a Sister? And how long past that time does she take a patron?" Annalise asked the question into darkness from her narrow bed, with Tansy across the room and the third bed yet empty between them.

"The Mothers know best." Tansy didn't sound sleepy, though

the tenchime had just sounded and the fivechime would wake them even before the sun. "They always do."

"But how do they know?"

Tansy shuffled in her blankets before answering. "I don't know how, Annalise. They just do. It's their purpose to know, as it will be ours to serve when they decide we are ready."

"Purpose and place." Annalise mouthed the words she'd heard so often since her arrival. "And pleasure. But what of the pleasure, Tansy? I've yet heard little of that part of it."

"Do you not gain pleasure from the learning? Each new skill I master brings me great pleasure!"

That wasn't what Annalise had meant. She shifted, too, down deep into her covers. "I speak of a different sort of pleasure. The sort that nobody has yet spoken of to me, yet I know must exist within service to a patron."

"Oh." Tansy cleared her throat, then giggled. "You mean the pleasure between a man and a woman?"

"Between two people, yes." Annalise thought of Jacquin and his penchant for the company of his own gender. "Handmaidens are always female, but they're not always assigned to men."

Tansy drew in a sharp breath. "We are assigned to patrons to whom we would be best suited."

Amused, Annalise turned her head on the pillow to look at the dim shape across the room. "And for you that would always be a male?"

"Well, yes," Tansy replied hesitantly. "I do believe so. I'm fair certain the Mothers wouldn't give me to a woman who expected . . . that."

"Lovemaking?" Annalise asked, just to make her roommate blush, even if she couldn't see the pinking cheeks.

"Oh, Annalise!"

"What? Surely you know there are those who do so prefer the

company of their own sex. And though nobody's said as much to me since my arrival, I also know it's a Handmaiden's duty to provide solace to her patron in any way necessary, and I know that often includes . . . intimacies. Everyone knows that."

"And many believe that's all a Handmaiden does," Tansy retorted.

Annalise herself had heard the tales and was therefore much astonished at how long she'd been in the Order without anyone instructing her on the etiquette of orgies. She laughed at the sound of Tansy's outrage. "And yet I daresay to those who matter, those who have actually sought the company of a Handmaiden, such stories are of no import. Anyone who is granted the service of a Handmaiden has been well-instructed in her function, yes?"

It had been one of the first things they'd discussed, the lengthy process by which patrons were assigned their Handmaidens. Mother Complacence had spent the better part of two chimes with the group of young women gathered in her classroom, Annalise the newest among them, but the others there no more than a week ahead of her. Mother Complacence had shown them the files every patron was required to complete, including full medical, financial, and personal histories. Thick binders of information that would take hours, if not days, to complete.

And yet nothing comparable was kept for the Sisters-in-Service, nothing concrete that could be used to match them to a patron.

"How do they do it?" Annalise asked again, more for her own musings than from hope of getting an answer from Tansy. "How do they know how best to match them?"

"Perhaps when I am a Mother-in-Service, I might tell you." Tansy sounded a little breathless, though still not sleepy.

Annalise yawned. "Seek you that honor?"

"The Mothers are well-loved and well-respected. Why wouldn't anyone wish to become one?"

"Mothers-in-Service no longer serve patrons, that's all. I'd imagine you'd wish to perform the function for which you so long trained.

Especially when it does seem to take such a long time. Longer than I'd expected." Not that she minded. The longer it took for her to be considered patron-ready, the better, in Annalise's opinion, as she had never intended to actually enter service.

"I hadn't thought of that. Why are you so wise, Annalise, when I am not half so bright and yet have been here for so much longer?" Tansy sounded sad.

"You said yourself, they know best. I'm sure your time is coming, Tansy. You've accomplished much, have you not?"

"Oh, yes. Of course. But I've not yet been taken for my final testing before being granted the title of Sister. I fear . . . I sometimes think . . ."

Annalise waited, but Tansy had shut up tight, and sometimes it was better not to pry. If Annalise pressed her, Tansy might confide her deepest griefs, and then Annalise would be expected to do the same. Or at the least, comfort the other girl, and Annalise felt in no position to offer such a service.

Yet she wasn't utterly without heart, so she said quietly, "All things in their time, Tansy."

Tansy said naught in reply, and after some time Annalise fell to sleep.

Kellen. What is this?" Cassian spoke more severely than he'd intended, but the boy had near run him over as he rounded the corner.

The boy held something behind his back, face a guilty mask, mouth smeared with what looked, suspiciously, like tumbleberry jam. "I don't have tarts in my trousers!"

Cassian crossed his arms and pressed his lips together so as not to laugh. "Indeed?"

Kellen shook his head but couldn't look Cassian in the eye. Cassian, however, had been a boy, and even though it felt like a hundred score years ago, he could still recall how grand an idea stealing a tart might be until the thief were caught.

"Show me your hands."

They were dirtier than the lad's face. Cassian sighed, shaking his head. Kellen hung his, scuffing a foot along the bare wooden floor of the hall.

"Kellen, you know I'll have to ask you to turn out your pockets."

Kellen looked up, eyes wide. Raised in a house of women, he'd had no shortage of coddling, this Cassian knew. He'd been disciplined as well, never harshly and always with love . . . but never by Cassian.

"Sir?"

"Turn them out."

Kellen did, reluctantly. The left held naught but a few stones and bits of paper folded into boats. The other, several tumbleberry tarts wrapped in a napkin. Falling apart, oozing jam, they smelled delicious and probably tasted so, but they'd made quite a mess.

"Not only did you take what wasn't yours without permission, Kellen, but you made a mess of your trousers, and they'll have to be washed. I know you don't launder them. You've created work for someone else with your foolishness. But worse than that," Cassian said sternly, "you lied to me. And that, lad, is what I find most deserving of punishment."

Kellen swallowed hard. His eyes glinted with tears, but he didn't cry. He looked into Cassian's face bravely, then nodded. "Your mercy, Master Toquin. I . . . I shall prepare for my beating."

"What?" Cassian stepped back, appalled. "Mother Above, Kellen. I don't intend to beat you!"

"You don't?"

"Lad, have I ever raised a hand to you? Has anyone in this house ever?"

"Mother Harmony once washed my mouth out with soap," Kellen confided.

"For what reason?"

Kellen sighed and looked shamefaced. "For cursing."

Cassian's own mother had done the same to him when he was about Kellen's age, and more than once to Calvis. He sighed. "Walk with me."

They fell into step. Cassian looked down at the lad, who'd clasped his hands behind him in an identical fashion, whether in direct mimicry or by natural inclination, Cassian didn't know. He took the boy into the kitchen, where Cook was dozing by the fire. She startled to consciousness when Cassian cleared his throat.

"Ah, Master Toquin. And you," she said with a jabbing finger at Kellen. "Didna I chase you and yon companion out of here already once tonight?"

"Kellen. Return the tarts."

"But sir!" Kellen looked distraught, small face turned up, eyes wide.

Cook snorted. "What? Stole some tarts, did he? Well, think you I'd want them back after them grubby hands has been all over them?"

She narrowed her eyes and heaved herself up from the chair to put fat fists on her hips. "It was the other one put you up to it, eh? Don't tell me it wasn't, I heard him whispering to you, when I'd have given you summat to fill your bellies, eh? But he wanted the tarts, not my day-old biscuits."

Cassian looked at the boy. "Is this true? Was it Leonder who put you up to it?"

Leonder, a year or so older than Kellen and another of the Order's Blessings. Kellen shook his head. Cook tutted.

"Kellen, remember what I said. It wasn't the theft but the lying I've issue with."

Kellen looked up at him again. Cassian could see the struggle in the lad's eyes. He waited for the boy to speak.

"It was me," Kellen said with the barest wobble in his voice that led Cassian to believe he wasn't being utterly truthful. "I am the one who stole the tarts."

"This fact isn't in question. But tell me, lad, if it was Leonder . . ."

"It was me."

Cook snorted and waved her apron at them. "Never no mind, Master Toquin. It's not the first time someone's snitched a tart or two from the rack, and it won't be the last. The lad'll suffer enough the next time he's denied his dessert, which I think should be the punishment."

"For the stealing of the tarts, yes. I'd say a full three days of no dessert should suffice." Cassian did his best to look stern. "But for the lying, I'm afraid there will have to be somewhat else."

Cook snorted again. "That I'll leave to you, and you'll get yourselves gone from my kitchen before you do it!"

Cassian took the boy out the back door and into the yard, though not beyond the light spilling from the windows. Darkness cloaked the rest of the yard, a light from the stables in the distance. Here they were mostly in shadow.

"Sit," he said.

Kellen sat on the wooden bench outside the kitchen door. Cassian sat beside him. He said nothing, remembering full well how the anticipation of the punishment was oft more difficult to bear than the punishment itself.

At last, he looked at the boy. "When I was your age, my brother discovered a desire for a certain kind of apple grown in a neighbor's orchard. We had apples of our own, and peaches, and ferlas, but Calvis decided that the golden apples of our neighbor were sweeter. The neighbor, unfortunately, was no friend to our family and had refused to allow us permission even to gather the fallen apples, the ones he couldn't sell."

"So what did your brother do?"

"He decided the sweetness was worth the risk, even though it was wrong, and he snuck into the orchard to gather as many as he could.

The problem was, Calvis wasn't content simply to take the fruit from the ground. Since he'd been denied what he really wanted, he thought to pluck fresher apples from the trees themselves. Only he couldn't do this alone. He needed someone's shoulders to stand on so that he might reach."

"You?"

"Yes."

Kellen looked at his hands, still sticky and dirty from the tarts. "Did you want to go with your brother, or did he talk you into it?"

"My brother was ever able to talk me into trouble, but I was the one who decided whether or not to follow him. In the end, I was the master of my conscience."

"What happened?"

"We were caught. Calvis fled. I was not so swift. Our neighbor, Lord Veldant, was well-deserved in his reputation for fury, and our father was not inclined to defend sons who'd done so blatant a crime. I'd been caught with the apples in my hands, you see. Foolish. Lord Veldant took it upon himself to beat me with his own belt."

Cassian could still remember the sting of leather on his bare flesh, the crack of the belt. The pain. The shame. And below it all, the anger that he'd been left to take the punishment for both when it had been his brother's idea.

He looked at the lad next to him. Kellen's face, shadowed but still lit enough by the kitchen lamps to see, had gone still. His mouth worked. Cassian put a hand on the boy's shoulder, feeling the small muscles twitch and strain.

"I took the punishment for my brother because I had no other choice."

"Leonder said he would fight me if I told it was his idea. And . . . sir . . ." Kellen coughed with a shrug. "I wanted the tarts, too. It was Leonder's idea, but I did it. I took them. I should take the punishment."

Cassian could take no pride in this lad, nor shame either. But as he squeezed the boy's shoulder again and stood, he felt a little of both. "You'll suffer the next few days after meals. But no more than that."

Kellen stood, too. "You're not going to beat me?"

"I told you I wouldn't. But never lie to me again."

Kellen nodded, then held out his hand. "I won't."

Surprised, Cassian took it, and they shook. A moment later the lad hugged him hard around the waist, surprising him further. Cassian's hand went naturally to the boy's soft hair. Kellen's cheek pressed Cassian's belly, his arms tight 'round him, and then he let go and stepped back.

"Thank you, sir!"

"Go on," Cassian said quietly. He could still feel the softness of Kellen's hair. He watched the boy dart through the doorway, but it was some long moments before he followed.

Chapter 8

Annalise had thought to find her time in the Motherhouse, if not torture, at least somewhat unpleasant. Yet she discovered much of what she was required to learn she'd already been taught. The art of brewing tea, of tatting lace, of how to properly fold a napkin—these paled next to the skill of unobtrusiveness, of comfort. Of grace. Annalise had no doubts she could learn to arrange flowers or play the pianoforte, if required. She could be taught to *do* anything.

What challenged her was learning how to *be*.

She looked at the other novitiates, the Sisters and Mothers. Some more accomplished than others, to be certain, but most of them with the same common serenity Annalise had not yet discovered. She chafed, frankly, not at the tasks she was set but at the notion she should perform the dullest or most odious of them not only without hesitation, but with cheerful, consistent pleasure.

Even so, there was pleasure to be found in domesticities, in simplicity. In combining the perfect measures of herbs to provide just the right brew or setting a table, making a bed with clean, sweet sheets. No matter her previous skill, Annalise learned there would always be new ways to perform.

Annalise had only been put in one place she knew to be incorrect. With other classes, once she'd proven she either already had the ability or learned it quickly enough, she was allowed to sit with other students of her level. In herb-mixing and elementary baking and pantomime she was advanced several levels within the span of a sevenday, and even in the discussion of art and history, for those two subjects she'd studied for her own pleasure and upon which could converse competently with even a scholar. Yet in the one group with whom she absolutely did not fit, Annalise was not moved.

Master Toquin's Faith instruction.

Annalise had spent her childhood so fully immersed within the practice of the Faith she could pray in circles 'round the other women in her class. She could read with more proficiency, dissect the simple passages with greater clarity, and in addition she knew by heart dozens of other texts and commentaries Toquin never once mentioned.

He didn't like being challenged, she'd learned that early on when she brought up an alternative argument about one of the stories. She'd thought at first perhaps it was because she was a woman, but then decided a man who'd decided to live and teach in a house solely composed of women would have to be stupid to also refuse to believe a woman could be literate, educated, and understand the Faith. No, it wasn't her sex that kept him from admitting she could hold her own in a discourse.

It was her.

She'd asked to be removed from his class and been denied. No explanation. Just a simple refusal. It was the only time since she'd arrived Annalise felt the silent admonition that she could do as the Mothers had decided, or she could leave. She wasn't ready to leave. She stayed in Master Toquin's class.

This is what Annalise had thought she knew about the Order of Solace—that it was a society of women bound to practice their faith through service. That they believed each moment of absolute solace they provided their patrons sent one more arrow to fill Sinder's Quiver, and that when it was full, the Vacant Father and the Invisible Mother would be reunited with their son and the time of peace would be at hand.

Annalise was no blush-cheeked virgin, but the idea of taking a stranger to bed—of being in charge of a patron's satisfaction, or of being required to service a patron's whim, had heated her. Annalise had no desire to pretend even to herself that she wasn't curious about this part of a Handmaiden's duty, even if she never intended to actually take her vows. Yet of all the classes to which she'd been assigned, of all the instruction she overheard other novitiates discussing, there seemed to be nothing to prepare them for the more intimate side of taking a patron.

"How do you know if you're ready?" Annalise asked Tansy one evening in the quiet of their room.

"For a patron? We don't have to know when we're ready," Tansy answered. She turned from her place at the basin where she was washing her face.

Clad in the cream-colored shift, her hair tied atop her head with a bit of green ribbon, she looked younger even than she was. Earlier she'd been wearing a layer of cosmetic, applied by a too-heavy hand, and the remains of it clung to her eyes, lips, and cheeks.

Annalise got up from her bed and crossed to take the cloth from Tansy's hand. "Because the Mothers-in-Service know for us, is that it? Here. Let me. Who did this to you?"

"I did it to myself," Tansy said with a sigh and tipped her face up as would a child. "Some patrons would require such."

"Some might require you to dress as a brothel whore?"

Tansy frowned. "I meant some would require the use of cosmetic! Did I—was it too much?"

"I suppose that depends upon the eye that views it." Annalise scrubbed gently. "And I'm fair certain you need no such heavy touch to bring out your own beauty, Tansy. Good cosmetic enhances one's features, not obscures them."

Tansy sighed again. "No wonder Perdita was making sport of me."

"Perdita," Annalise said darkly, "makes too much sport."

"And yet she's so far advanced. She's already accomplished so much, and I heard that she'll be granted a patron before the year's end. She's been here only a sixmonth, Annalise, and I've—"

"The Mothers know their business." Annalise swiped the last bits of cosmetic from Tansy's mouth. "There. If you like, I can show you how to apply it so none would even know you're wearing it at all."

"Would you? Oh, thank you!" Tansy went with skipping steps to her armoire and pulled out a casket of pots and brushes. As with everything she had, all were of the finest quality.

Annalise studied the wealth before her. "Would you take this with you to a patron?"

Tansy caught her bottom lip with her teeth. "I . . . suppose not. We're to take only the clothes we travel in and a few other small items. The patrons provide us with what we need."

"Do you think most men would think to provide a Handmaiden with tools such as these?" Annalise plucked a pot of lip rouge. "This is lovely, Tansy, but very costly. Patrons must be able to afford us, true, but most of them are men. And men, in my experience, think naught of such feminine fripperies as cosmetic."

"I *could* take it with me, I suppose, even if it's not usually done." Tansy sounded doubtful.

Annalise smoothed Tansy's damp hair from her forehead. The girl had skin like milk. Against it, Annalise's fingers looked ever the darker. "It would better serve you to learn to use what you've access to in any household."

"But Seducta said—"

Annalise laughed aloud, unable to help herself. Handmaidens were granted their names based upon the quality the Mothers-in-Service determined their most prominent, not necessarily the best. "Seducta? She's the one who favors crimson lip rouge and lightens her hair, yes? The one with the overlush figure?"

Tansy, Sinder bless her, wasn't likely to say a negative word against any of the Sisters, but her blush meant Annalise was right. Annalise laughed again and hugged Tansy quickly. The girl was sweet beyond belief.

"There are some men, true, who prefer such a woman. But you, dear one, are not that sort of woman, and I daresay will never be. Perdita might be, if she doesn't watch the number of creambuns she stuffs into her sly mouth, and if she relies on the charm that lies between her legs rather than any other skill. And I suppose she will be granted a patron before the year's end for that reason, as what I know of men leads me to believe there are many who require such simple solace as that. But Tansy"—Annalise made sure the girl was looking at her face before she continued—"you are different and special. You know better than I that a Handmaiden's pleasure and purpose is never the same from patron to patron, nor from Sister to Sister. When you are granted your patron, it will be because only you can satisfy him. I know it."

Tansy's blue eyes welled with tears, and she clung to Annalise with a small sob. "I fear I shall never be granted a patron! Never! I stumble so, I cannot learn grace! I know the five principles, I know all the positions of Waiting, I am mired fully in my faith . . . and yet . . . I stumble, Annalise! Over and over, when it comes time for me to shine, I do not!"

"Hush." Annalise pushed the clinging girl from her, but gently. "If there is a Handmaiden in this room, it's surely you, not I."

Tansy wiped at her eyes. "Oh, no. You . . . you are so bold and certain. You'll be granted a patron soon enough. You already know so much more than most of the women who come here."

Annalise thought of the hours spent in Master Toquin's class and felt her mouth thin. Just two days before he'd ignored her when she tried to interject into his discussion. She hated to be ignored. "Just because I can quote the Book from back to front makes me no more ready for a patron than you, and perhaps less so, for I've not yet mastered the other skills necessary."

"But you shall, easily enough. Is there aught you've ever set your mind to you've not managed?" Tansy laughed. "I would not believe it of you."

"There are many tasks to which I've set myself I've left unfinished." Annalise forced away her frown. "But come, let's to the kitchen, where I swear I will show you tricks that will charm any patron, no matter how stingy he might be with frippery."

She was not there to become a Handmaiden, she reminded herself. She was there to wait out her time until the engagement contract between her and Jacquin could be safely annulled without harm to either of them. All the rest of this was simply to pass the time.

She would not admit how she longed to set Toquin in his place. No. Nor how the way his gaze slid over her without reaction had so maddened her she'd considered launching herself into his arms to see what he'd do. How every time he turned his face she wanted to step in front of him to force him to look at her. How each time he passed she wished to move so that he might be forced to rub against her.

How much she wanted him to . . . want her.

"Annalise?"

"Put a gown on," Annalise said absently, trying to shake off the sensual image her mind insisted on painting. "It won't do for you to be running the halls in your shift."

No man for whom she'd set her cap had ever resisted her. Not since she'd first grown breasts and discovered the way a turn of the face, a flip of the hair, could draw a man's eyes the way a lamb is tracked by wolves in the meadow. Annalise knew she wasn't commonly pretty, but that had never mattered. If she wanted a man, she'd had him, always.

And why did she want him? she thought as Tansy, chattering incessantly, shrugged into her gown and bid Annalise help her with the buttons at her throat. Why did Toquin so capture her attention? It was more than his face and form, which were a delight to any woman of discerning taste. And it was not his attitude, that arrogant coldness, the superiority. It was somewhat else, perhaps that sense of being unattainable. Of being so aloof.

She wanted to crack him open and climb inside. She wanted to see him want. She wanted, Annalise thought as she led the still tittering Tansy toward the kitchens, to see what it was like when Cassian Toquin broke.

In the kitchen, she simpered and wooed Cook, a fat biddy with a mustache and chin hairs who was just finishing the dough for the morning's rolls when Annalise and Tansy entered. The cook, who was likely used to young women plundering her stores at strange times, waved them toward the pantry where she warned them to keep their fingers out of the crocks of honey and butter, and to clean up any messes they made. Tansy, wide-eyed, let out a deep breath when the door closed behind them.

"How did you get her to agree?"

Annalise, eyes seeking the ingredients she'd use instead of Tansy's expensive cosmetic, shrugged. "Think you she's never had anyone in her kitchen past hours?"

"The evening snack is the last mealtime! I never thought . . ."

"Which do you think the Order prefers, Tansy. Girls whose bellies empty in the night nibbling something in the kitchen, or being forbade such privilege and therefore sneaking food into their rooms where the bugs and rodents might congregate?"

Tansy looked so suddenly guilty Annalise knew she'd been one such girl. "Nobody ever said we were allowed to come for food . . ."

Annalise sighed and put her hands on Tansy's shoulders to square them. "We are not children here. This is not a school. There is no punishment, for there aren't any rules. We're required to study and learn and grow toward the day we're determined capable and ready to take our vows, yes?"

"Yes," Tansy said doubtfully.

"So, if you are hungry, then why not eat?"

"But . . . I'm not hungry now."

Annalise gave an inner sigh. "Fine. Come here to the table and let me show you how to make up your face using what any household will have."

It took little time and effort to paint Tansy's lips and highlight her eyes with pastes made from spices common enough Annalise could near guarantee no kitchen would lack them. The end result was lovely, as Tansy proclaimed when taken to the cloudy-looking glass hung by the kitchen's back door.

"I'm pretty!"

"You're always pretty, Tansy."

Tansy touched her face in awe, then turned to Annalise. "It's so much prettier than using all those pots of color, and so fast!"

"And so easy, so simple, that none but the most inquisitive patron need ever even know you've used anything at all."

"How ever did you learn such tricks?" Tansy looked again at her smiling reflection.

Annalise wiped her hands free of the remnant of spices. "You learn to make do with what you have. Or have not."

Tansy hugged her again, and Annalise suffered the embrace because to put Tansy off was much like trying to keep an overeager kitten from climbing one's skirts. Tansy even went so far as to kiss her cheek. Annalise laughed.

"I'm well-pleased to have made you so happy, Tansy."

Tansy took Annalise's hands. "I thank the Invisible Mother every day you were assigned to share a room with me."

"I wouldn't go that far, Tansy, my goodness."

"Life brings what the Invisible Mother provides."

Annalise didn't believe that for an instant, but she smiled and patted Tansy's cheek. Before she could say anything, the back door flew open and two laughing figures stumbled through on a cloud of distinctive-smelling smoke.

Annalise didn't know their names, but their clothes showed them as stable hands. Both tall, both fair-haired, both ruddy cheeked, they might have been brothers but seemed too intimate a pair for that. Perhaps not lovers . . . at least, not yet, she mused, watching as the hand of the slightly taller one grazed the other's back low enough to almost touch his buttocks. Neither of them saw the women in the kitchen.

"Herb," she murmured, and a sudden longing rose within her. She could taste it on the back of her tongue, and not merely from the scent the young men had brought in the door with them.

Tansy let out a startled squeak, and Annalise wondered at an Order that most often served men but had so few about to inure its novitiates to their presence. At the sound, the shorter man turned, eyes wide, and his companion a moment after.

"Ah, your mercy, mistresses. We'd no idea you were here," said the shorter with a swipe to get his hair off his brow.

"Let's go," Tansy said with a tug on Annalise's hand.

"Hello, lads." Annalise looked them up and down.

Both straightened, flushing. The taller glanced at his friend. Both had red eyes and spots of color on their cheeks. Definitely herb.

"You go," she told Tansy quietly. "I've somewhat to which I must attend here."

"What? But you . . ." Tansy sputtered, then quieted. "Oh, my!"

Annalise shot her an amused glance. "Go on, little kitten. I'll be fine."

Tansy ducked her head and backed up, turning only at the last second but still looking behind her at Annalise before she left the kitchen through the hall door. The young men simply stared. A stomach rumbled loudly.

Annalise smiled. "Well, lads. Let me guess. You're here for a snack?"

"Aye." The taller seemed bolder now, by the way he eyed her. "Will you tell Mirinda?"

"If you mean the cook, no, I won't. What concern is it of mine who raids the stores at night?" She looked from one to the other. "I could be additionally persuaded to hold my tongue, lads, at little cost to you."

"Oh?" The shorter grinned. "What might that be?"

"A bowl of your herb. I'm fair to aching for lack of entertainment here." She grinned in return.

"Huh, and here I thought they kept the ladies occupied," said the shorter.

"Oh, indeed, in all manner of pursuits. And yet I find myself in sore need of something a bit more . . ."

"More exciting?" The shorter man inched forward. "You'd not be the first, I wager."

"Indeed," Annalise murmured. "I would also so wager."

Chastity was not a requirement of the Order, and yet like so much else, none spoke of what erotic pursuits its members might seek on their own accord. With so few men on the grounds, Annalise suspected a goodly number of the novitiates took to self-satisfaction, if not mutual intimacies, just as she supposed the sisters who'd returned to the Motherhouse between patrons might be fair grateful for the time to be alone.

It had been, she realized, a full few months since she'd last taken her pleasure—any pleasure. At the thought of it, her nipples peaked against the fabric of her shift. Heat collected between her thighs. The question, she thought, watching her new companions, would be if the men who so freely enjoyed each other's company would welcome hers, as well.

She found out soon enough, in front of the small fire built in a circle of stones in the earth behind the stable. Terran and Eagen, their names were, and they were indeed not brothers but boon companions, friends since childhood. And not yet lovers, it became clear to her, though what held them from it she could not be sure. They both wanted it, Eagen more so, based on the heated looks he gave his shorter friend. But Terran as well, for though his focus might be upon her, his attention was easily enough distracted by the other man.

This was going to be most merry, Annalise decided as she took the bowl from Terran and drew in the smoke, deep. She held it. She closed her eyes. It was not the quality Jacquin had oft provided—dear Jacquin! How long it had been since she'd even thought of him, and had penned only the briefest, bare letter to him and not had one in reply.

Terran sucked a few breaths of smoke and passed the bowl to Eagen, then sidled a bit closer to her. "We've not had any of the ladies out to smoke with us."

"No?" Annalise slid her tongue over her teeth, tasting herb. "I imagine a pair such as yourselves are rather popular with the ladies, yes? Surely you've done somewhat to . . . earn . . . your positions here."

"Aye, but they most often just have us flip up their skirts in a spare stall," Eagen told her.

"You're intoxicated." Terran laughed. "Watch your tongue."

"I'm not offended. Tell me more, sweetheart," Annalise prompted with another draw on the bowl.

Eagen shifted on the bench. His thigh pressed hers. On her other side, Terran leaned close.

"None of them care to share more than that, is what he's saying." Terran poked at the fire, sending up some sparks, then leaned back against the stable wall. "We're studs, like. Stallions."

"Who's the one intoxicated?" Eagen muttered.

Annalise only laughed, relaxing as the herb sent its tendrils all throughout her. The attentions of not one, but two handsome men, the calming effects of the drug, the star-sprinkled night sky and orange-red glow of the fire. Lovely.

She shifted so that she might give Eagen the full benefit of her gaze. "Show me."

"What?"

At her other side, Terran snorted soft laughter. Annalise leaned closer to Eagen. Her lips parted, as did his, but she didn't kiss him.

"Show me," she repeated slowly, so that her breath caressed his face. "Show me, you and Terran both, how stallions behave."

Terran was on his feet before Eagen was. He pawed the ground with a "hoof," his fingers curled as he pretended to rear. He whinnied, then shot her a grin and danced around the fire. Eagen was up a moment after that, imitating his friend. They faced off, playacting two stallions battling but laughing too hard to make it anything but a jest.

"Yes," Annalise murmured as Eagan fell into Terran's arms and nuzzled at his neck. "Just so, boys."

They held each other a moment too long, hands drifting a little too gently over the other's limbs. Terran caught her gaze over Eagen's shoulder. Annalise sat back on the bench and toyed with the end of her braid.

"Eagen," Terran breathed. "We're ignoring our new friend."

She gestured. "Yes, come here, the pair of you, else I smoke all the herb and leave you bereft."

"Not that!" cried Eagen and, laughing, leaped the fire to slide into place at her side.

This time, she held the bowl between them so they both might draw from it at the same time. She let the sweet smoke seep from her mouth and into his . . . but she did not kiss him. When Eagen drew away, Terran sat down behind him and reached around him for the bowl.

"Together," Annalise suggested. "Let me see you two do it together."

She thought they would refuse, but after only a moment's hesitation, Terran lifted the bowl and he and Eagen shared the smoke the way she'd done with Eagen. Their mouths hovered, the smoke slipping between their lips, and Annalise held her breath, waiting to see if they'd give in to the pleasure it was clear they both craved.

Eagen did it first. He cupped the back of his friend's head and pulled him closer. The kiss lasted no more than a heartbeat, only to start up again when Terran moaned into Eagen's mouth.

She'd known it upon first glance at them, but took little pleasure in being right. It reminded her too much of Jacquin and her reasons for being here in the Motherhouse when she could've been at home preparing for a wedding. She must've made a sound, for the men broke apart and both looked at her as though she'd caught them out at something shameful.

"Very pretty," Annalise said, and reached for the bowl.

Terran was the first to move for her, and she let him kiss her, their tongues tangling and tasting of herb. When he pulled away, his fingers loose on the back of her neck, Annalise glanced over his shoulder at Eagen. She smiled.

"And of the other ladies, those whose skirts you've flipped. Have you put on such a pretty show for them, as well?"

"No," Eagen said hoarsely.

Terran tried to kiss her again, but Annalise held him off with a hand pressed to his chest. The bowl had nearly gone out. "I rather liked it."

Terran, his hands still upon her, looked over his shoulder at his friend before looking back at her. "How much more would you like?"

"How much more do you have?"

Terran shifted so as to lean against the stable wall, his legs in front of him, with Annalise on one side and Eagen on the other. He reached for his friend's hand and brought it to his mouth, licked the tips of Eagen's fingers. Eagen swallowed a groan. Terran looked at Annalise.

"Let it never be said I dint do my best to please a lady what's asked it of me."

There was much more she'd want, but these were not the men to grant it and this not the place to take it. Yet there was no denying the swell of heat inside her at the flash of Terran's gaze, the swipe of his tongue over soft, full lips.

"Unless the lady's changed her mind?" Terran whispered.

Annalise shook her head. "No."

She'd come out here with them with the intent of indulgence, of distraction. Of forgetting what she'd come here to do, what to escape, of what she'd found instead. To put aside the thoughts of what she could not have and what she did not want—to focus on, however briefly, that which she could have. Did want.

"Kiss him," she whispered to Terran with a glance at Eagen. "And then I would see him on his knees for you. I think he'd like that, yes?"

Terran's gaze flashed again. "I know I'd like it."

Eagen shifted on the bench. "Terran—"

"Hush," Annalise said and slid her hand over Terran's thigh to cup his cock, already hard. "In the morn you can blame it on the herb, and none will be the wiser. But I guarantee you, sweetheart, you'll love it better than flipping up my skirts."

"And you?" Terran breathed as Eagen slid closer on the bench to nuzzle at his neck. His eyes got heavy lidded, his mouth parting as his head fell back against the wall. "We'd hate to see you neglected."

Eagen looked up at her, his mouth wet, eyes glazed. "Aye, lady. What of you?"

"What of me, indeed?" Annalise murmured, stroking gently. "I'm certain you'll think of something to occupy me. Now, Eagen. Let me watch you take him in your mouth, and I believe we'll all be fair pleased with the results."

With another groan, Eagen did as she said, Terran's fingers already fumbling to release his prick from the confines of his trousers. And it was lovely, watching one pretty mouth devour that equally beauteous cock. It was sensual and breathtaking and it ought to have moved her to her own pleasure, but all it did was leave her cold inside.

She could blame an overindulgence of herb or sentiment, but Annalise knew the real reason she found herself unable to respond to the erotic scene she'd deliberately instigated.

His name was Cassian Toquin.

Chapter 9

Roget only came to the Motherhouse once or twice a year, but he always dragged Cassian off to town for a pint or four when he did. This visit had been no different but for the number of pints consumed. Six or eight for Roget compared to Cassian's single mug. The man could drink and did so with gusto, and would walk with barely a stagger.

"Come, old friend," Roget demanded with a thump on the table. In his civilian clothes, his shaved head gave away his profession even if his behavior didn't. "Tell me you're still satisfied with your work. Convince me, and I'll not ask you again."

"You ask me every time I see you," Cassian replied mildly, sipping at his mug of bitter ale.

Roget tipped a finger at him. "'Ware, else I slip your mug full of worm and see what answer you give."

"Would worm make me a liar? For I tell the truth now."

Roget snorted and eyed a serving wench swaying past them with her hands full of mugs and pitchers. "Does she not even turn your head? Not even a little?"

Cassian laughed a little. "No."

"Again, I fear you misspeak to me." Roget shook his head in sorrow. "Come back to us. You were ever well-skilled at your vocation. We miss you."

"You know I can't do that."

"I know you won't do it. *Can't* is something else entirely." Roget drank deeply.

"Can't. Won't. The difference is not so great as you'd have me think." The noise in the pub was giving Cassian a headache. Such places always had. He came here because Roget refused to be entertained in Cassian's quarters with a jug of kitchen spirits and a bowl of stew.

"Ten years, Cassian. Ten long years. Is that not a long enough penance?"

Cassian shook his head. Roget sighed. Cassian poured his friend another pint from the pitcher between them.

"You could come back at any time and be welcomed. You know that."

"I know it. I don't wish to return to the priesthood."

Roget let out a truly astonishing belch, even by the standards of those whose company they currently kept. "And yet you stay on with the Order. Tell me again why this is so, as I know it's not for the abundance of opportunities to partake in sensual exploits. Presuming you've kept to that vow as well, which I've no doubt is true based upon what I know of your stubborn nature."

Cassian shrugged.

"It truly is a penance," Roget said when it became apparent Cassian meant not to answer. "By the Arrow, Cassian. Truly? I meant it in jest before, but I'm right?"

"You're drunk. We should go back so you can sleep it off. Have you not a service to lead in the morning?" Cassian stood.

Roget didn't. He shook his head and pushed away his mug. "Oh, brother. Still, now? Think you she'll come back? And what then? What do you hope to gain if she does?"

"I don't stay—"

"You have ever been the poorest of liars," Roget said.

Cassian sat. He poured himself another mug of ale, meaning just to sip at it, since drunkenness did naught for him but bring about an aching head and regret. "I made a promise to my brother."

"Your brother," Roget said as though the words tasted bad, "is dead, ten long years hence. He's unlikely to hold you to such a promise from his place in the—"

"Don't you say it," Cassian warned. "I know what you thought of him. He was my brother, my true brother of the blood, not merely of the heart."

"Your mercy."

The men both drank while around them the merriment went on. Roget leaned back in his chair and ran a hand over his bald head. He looked younger without the thick lines of ceremonial cosmetic around his eyes. Cassian blinked, remembering suddenly the sting of it.

"He's gone, Cassian."

"I know it."

"Yet you still punish yourself for what was not your fault?"

"I played as much a part in it as anyone."

"If anything, the blame rests upon her and him. Not you."

"This story," Cassian said, "will never have another ending no matter how many times the tale is told. Say no more, Roget. I know full well what you think of it. Of me, and my choices. I tell you now as I've told you before, I can't return to the priesthood. Nor do I wish to. I'm . . ."

"Say that you're happy in your place and I'll reach across this table and punch you in the teeth."

Cassian raised a brow. "Not very peaceful of you."

"I'd be acting as your friend, not a priest."

"You are still and will always be a priest first, Roget, it's your nature and your life. Aside from that, you know that I could whip you easily, even if you were not eight mugs ahead of me."

He'd meant to make Roget laugh, but his old friend only shook his head. "Even if she comes back . . ."

"You would do well to bite your tongue," Cassian said coldly, "brother."

Roget sighed, shoulders lifting. "Ah, you wound me, but then you have ever done as you pleased and none could stop you. I think that's why I miss you so."

"You needn't miss me. You see me every time you make your rounds to the Motherhouse."

"Once you'd have been there with me during every service. Now you don't even attend."

"You know I can't."

"I know you won't," Roget said.

Cassian drained his mug and pushed it aside. "The hour grows late. I'm for home. Are you joining me?"

"I supposed I'd best, else I'll never make it back." Roget cast a grin toward the pretty barmaid he'd ogled earlier. "And as much as I'd like to discuss the finer aspects of philosophy with that lovely maiden, the morn will come too early and I'm older than I was yesterday."

Cassian laughed despite himself. "We are ever older than we were the day before."

Roget sighed and stretched, rubbing a hand over his pate. "Ah, lad, but not all of us live the good, clean life you do. All that exercise. You still rise with the sun and practice the Art?"

"I do."

Roget grimaced, but made no comment. "Come, then, brother. Lead me home by the hand as though I were the bumbling, drunken fool you'd have me be."

Again, Cassian laughed. "I'll lead you, but not by the hand."

"Sinder's Balls!" Roget exclaimed. "You'll not suffer me even such affection as that! I'm mortally offended."

"You're mortally intoxicated."

"Mayhap a bit of that is truth," Roget admitted. "But know you this is the only time I ever become so. With you."

Outside in the night's crisp air, Cassian breathed deep. "And why is that?"

"Because I know you'll not indulge. And because"—Roget spit into the dirt by their boots—"I know it gives you pleasure to look at me in such a state, that you might feel superior. And as your everlong friend, I like to make you happy. If such a thing were possible for you to be and which, my friend, I fear is not so."

"You are drunk," Cassian said and slung one of Roget's arms around his shoulders. The words, barely slurred, stung. "You'll remember none of this on the morrow."

"But you might."

"I'll do my best to forget it."

"You would do your best to forget other things," Roget said, but thankfully kept his line of conversation from continuing, instead bursting into a song that kept him occupied during the walk from town to the grounds of the Order.

"Quiet!" Cassian laughed, knowing it would do no good.

"What? So that all who reside here, all those lovely ladies, the simpering twits, the giggly gadflies, might maintain their view of you as the imposing and cold-as-stone Master Toquin?"

"Yes." There was no point in denying it.

Roget snorted laughter and made pause to loose himself from his breeches to piss in a long, hard stream into the bushes at the edge of the drive. "You might be better served if they knew you as I do, Cassian. As a man who can make the best of jokes."

It had been overlong since Cassian had been that man. He watched as Roget tucked himself away. The moon had gone behind some clouds. The Motherhouse loomed in the distance, but he heard the faintest sound of laughter and voices from behind the stable and caught the scent of woodsmoke.

"Someone's having a party," Roget remarked.

"Not of our concern."

"Tell me something, brother."

Cassian sighed as they trudged up the gravel drive toward the back of the manse. He'd regret this late night in the morn, but not as much as Roget would with his swollen head. "What?"

"Do you really think you're so strong?"

"I do."

Roget straightened, his voice steady and no longer slurring. "Because you hide yourself away from everything in the world and avoid all that would tempt you to life? You think that's strength?"

Now angry for the first time this night but not the first time with Roget, Cassian threw off his friend's hand. "You shouldn't drink so much. It makes you stupid."

"What makes you stupid, Cassian? Ah, that's right. Naught. Not a bedamned thing, is that so? Not drink, not drug."

"Why would I seek to be stupid?"

Roget laughed, low. "Ah, and there I hear the glimmer of anger in your voice. Careful, brother. You'll have me thinking I've had a rise out of you."

Cassian swallowed hard before answering. "I'm going to bed."

"Alone."

"Of course alone," he snapped.

"Of course," said Roget. "As ever. You know something, Cassian? This vow you took. The promise you made. Were they truly for your brother? Or were they mayhap instead for your own sake?"

"Please don't make me—" Cassian broke off.

"What? Hit me?" Roget laughed, tipping his chin up to offer a better target. "If I thought I could make you, I would keep taunting."

Sickness nudged at Cassian's gut and he breathed through it. "I think you'd better find your own way to bed."

"Resisting temptation is only admirable when you put yourself in front of it, Cassian."

He stopped a few steps away from Roget but didn't turn. "As a glutton in front of a banquet?"

"Just so."

"I live in a house full of women," Cassian said wearily. "Think you that's not enough to tempt me?"

"No. It's not what they have between their legs but what they have in their brains that's bound to tempt the likes of you, and I'll wager you refuse to allow yourself to engage in more than the barest conversation with any of them. You keep them at bay with that glower. You make them fear you, brother, so they might not love you."

Cassian had no answer for this. He walked, instead, as fast as he could without running. Roget didn't catch up to him.

By the time Cassian crossed the yard in front of the stables, the low murmur of voices had grown louder. Not quite the sound of argument, but definitely not a friendly sound. He'd have ignored it as none of his concern, if not for the sudden and familiar feminine lilt.

He stopped, listening.

"No!" It was Annalise.

Cassian ran. He skidded on the gravel and rounded the corner of the stable. On the far side and around the other corner he saw the flash and flicker of a fire. Shadows. He heard the scuffle of feet in the grass.

In his early-morning practices the names of the positions never failed to accompany the movements themselves, but here and now he found he had no time for even silent words. He moved. He rounded the corner and had the lad by the back of the collar before any of the three people there knew Cassian had arrived.

The lad hit the dirt with a thud and a cry and his partner, the one standing too close to Annalise, didn't even have time to turn before Cassian had grabbed him as well. He stopped himself from jabbing the young man's throat with the points of his fingers—that would've rendered him unable to speak, and Cassian meant to demand answers.

He hadn't counted on Annalise leaping at him. She clung to his arm with her full weight. She didn't quite break Cassian's grip, but she almost broke his arm.

"What are you doing?" She yanked again.

The young man in Cassian's grip struggled weakly, gasping and choking at the pressure of his collar bound tight to his throat. Cassian let him fall. He put his now free hand over Annalise's and pulled her off him. He didn't let her go.

"What, by the Void, are *you* doing?" He was breathing too hard, sweating too much. The ale he'd drunk sloshed uncomfortably in his gut, and Cassian realized too late he was quite a bit drunker than he'd thought.

The lad on the ground groaned. The one in front of him backed up. Annalise, hands on her hips, glared. Cassian looked from her to the two lads. They were disheveled, Annalise less so, but perhaps her fierce glare was distracting him from noticing if her mouth looked kiss-swollen. Cassian took another step back, swallowing against a rush of saliva.

"Annalise—" This came from the lad on the ground, who shut up when Cassian turned his stare upon him.

"Hush," she said.

Terran, Cassian thought his name was from seeing him 'round the estate. The other was Eagen. Neither of them looked ready to go against him. Cassian realized he'd maintained a threatening stance. He relaxed even as his head swam and heart pounded. He spat to the side.

"You should go inside," Cassian told her. "This is not the place for you."

"I was unaware I was beholden to you for my every move," Annalise said tightly, "or that I was required to ask your permission for anything I do."

The scent of herb was thick around all of them, even her. Cassian jerked his chin toward Terran and Eagen. "You two. Get gone. I think you've other places to be than here."

Eagen drew himself up, foolishly brave. "Annalise, are you all right?"

Cassian had no more patience. His head had gone from swimming to pounding. He changed his stance, subtly this time, but no less threateningly. "Sirrah, your desire to protect yonder woman is admirable, but think you I mean to harm her? Me?"

"You . . . ah, no, sir. No." Eagen gave Annalise an apologetic look. "Mistress, you'll be all right?"

"Yes," she said with another glare at Cassian. "I'm certain Master Toquin will do me no harm."

Terran and Eagen gathered themselves and left with bowed heads. Only when they'd gone did Annalise turn on him, and then she was in his face at once. True, she had to tip hers to look at him, but with her angry eyes and frowning mouth, she showed not a lick of fear.

"You are insufferable! How dare you? Who do you think you are?" She pushed him. Actually pushed him.

Cassian reacted without thought, capturing her wrist with one hand and yanking her arm at the same time to turn her. She ended up with her back pressed to his front, his arm imprisoning her against him. His mouth found a natural place at her ear even as she struggled. When he spoke, though, she quieted at once.

"Your behavior, mistress, is unseemly."

They were breathing in time, shoulders rising and falling. Bodies moving together. Her hair hadn't come entirely loose from the long braid but she wasn't wearing a headscarf, and loose tendrils, sweet-smelling and silky, tantalized his cheek. Her body, pressed against his, was warm and solid. Curving. Lush. Entirely woman.

Cassian let her go.

Annalise stumbled a step or two from him and turned. Her red-rimmed eyes would've given her away even had he not smelled the herb clinging to her like perfume. She licked her mouth.

"Did you come 'round the corner like a daemon unleashed so that you might . . . protect me?"

"You sounded as though you were in distress," he said without meaning to. It pained him to admit he'd been mistaken, and so foolishly. Clearly the chit hadn't been fending off unwelcome advances.

"Did you know it was me?" she asked, tilting her head to look at him. "Not some random woman in need of assistance, but me?"

Her eyes flashed, looking him over. She might as well have stripped him bare. Cassian turned. He walked away. From behind him, he heard the sound of feet on the grass and he stopped cold, eyes closed, world spinning around him and not solely from the alcohol. Maybe not from the ale at all.

"Cassian."

He wanted to ask how she'd learned his name, demand of her what right she had to use it with so familiar a tongue. He said nothing, hands clenched tight at his sides, eyes still closed. He didn't see her move closer, but he felt her.

"You thought I was in trouble, and you came to help me. Where is the shame in that?"

"It is your shame for behaving so boldly," he said hoarsely, still without looking at her. "Cavorting with stable hands?"

"I wasn't cavorting."

He looked at her then. "No?"

"I . . ." she hesitated. He could see the swipe of her tongue along her lips again. "No. I was not. But if I were, why would it be of your concern? If there are rules against it, I'm unaware of them."

He drew himself up, shoulders stiff, making himself a rock. "You are required to act as a Handmaiden, Mistress Marony, whether you've taken your vows or not."

Void take her, she laughed at that. Low and sweet, the sound set the hairs on the back of his neck upright. She shook her head.

"Ah, Master Toquin. I've seen you practicing the Art in the mornings. How do you figure any of us learn to please a patron in the most basic manner if we don't practice our own . . . art?"

He didn't want to think of her with those men, and didn't want to think of why the thought so set him back. He wasn't blind. He knew the women sought their pleasure from the few men here upon the estate—he'd been approached more than once himself, after all. Roget was wrong in that Cassian never faced temptation.

"Then go back to them," he said in a voice thick with disdain. "Finish what I interrupted."

He walked again, putting her behind him. Her voice followed, if she did not. He didn't want to let it slow him, but it did, so that he might fully hear what she had to say.

"Thank you for rescuing me," Annalise called softly.

"You didn't need rescue."

"But you were there anyway."

He wanted to denounce this as coincidence, of no consequence, but his mouth knew it as a lie and wouldn't form the words. He kept his silence, then. From behind him he heard another laugh, then the soft swish of her slippers in the grass.

When he turned at last, she wasn't there, and where she'd gone Cassian could not tell.

Chapter 10

At last, a letter came. Annalise recognized Jacquin's hand on the envelope before she flipped it to reveal the wax pressed with his family's seal. Her betrothed had sent her a missive and her own parents had not. She couldn't say why this so amused and touched her, only that it did.

She found the letter slipped beneath her door upon rising in the morning, but as the chime for morning service had already sounded and she was going to be late no matter how she might run, Annalise had folded the soft paper into a double square so the thickness of it became unwieldy and slipped it into her sleeve. It scratched her arm, gouged her deep, left her distracted. What had he written? What had happened since she'd been gone?

Services had become no more bearable, the only point of light was the fact she never had to explain her reason for silence. If she could not, or would not speak for herself, the priests did it for her. Even so, she could scarcely pull out the letter and read it right there in the temple, nor at the morning meal after. Not if she wanted to read it in privacy without someone seeking to tug it away from her, either the letter itself or the contents.

No, she wanted to read it, but alone, and there was very little time or space to be alone as a novitiate. So Annalise kept the letter in her sleeve where it might remind her without cease of news from home.

By the afternoon, anticipation had worn a hole in her patience. She took her customary place in Master Toquin's classroom and slipped the letter from her sleeve onto the desk in front of her. The man would begin his lessons, talking on and on, and the other girls would spend the time with vapid questions, grasping at the most basic philosophies and yet never catching them. He'd never called on her because she always had an answer or another question for him, and since three nights ago when he found her behind the stables, he'd ignored her even further. She'd have plenty of time to read her letter.

In her school days, Annalise had perfected the art of reading notes slipped to her by her classmates and hidden in the text or beneath the slateboard. She made no such effort now. She was no longer a girl and these classes earned no grades.

So when the shadow sifted over the letters, words, sentences, Annalise looked up expecting to see one of the other girls, curious about what she was doing. Toquin stood over her desk. He did not look happy.

"This is not the place for personal correspondences."

Annalise did not often find herself without words, and this occasion was no different. "I've read the text you assigned already."

"There are others to be studied."

Annalise took the time to look around the room at the other novitiates, all of whom had left off their studies to watch. Her stomach had clenched and dropped at the sound of his voice, but she drew a deep breath before she replied. She was not a child.

"I know those as well, sir, which I believe you might well have guessed."

"Are you saying you so well understand the Word of the Book you need study no further?" He had thick, dark lashes that closed over eyes the deep, bitter brown of cacao.

"I've studied the words in this text, yes."

"Scholars tend their lessons for lifetimes without fully comprehending the entire Word, and you'd have me believe you've accomplished what they give their lives to do?" Toquin looked over the letter Annalise hadn't tried to cover up. "And for what? This?"

He snatched up the letter and read the first line, his eyes shifting over the words. "A love letter?"

"Is it a love letter? It would appear you've more knowledge of it than I, since I've barely had the chance to read it." She held out her hand, but he didn't return it.

"This is not the place," he said again, "for your personal correspondences."

Annalise pushed away from the desk and stood, her fingers stiff not from fear but anger. "Then I shall tuck it away to be read another time."

She held out her hand, but Toquin backed away, letter kept tight, reading it as he went. He backed up against his desk and stopped, eyes roaming over the words as Annalise could only stare in sick and silent outrage. She looked 'round the room once more, but nobody dared stare this time.

Annalise clenched her fists at her sides but didn't stride to him or yank the paper from his grasp. "Give me back my letter."

He looked up at her then, the letter folding into squares in his long, strong fingers. "Tell me the name of the forest in which Sinder came upon Kedalya."

"What?" Annalise opened her hand. Her nails had left small marks in the palms.

"The name of the forest. A scholar would know it."

Murmurs and shuffles smoothed over her, but if anyone were looking at her, she ignored them. Annalise swiped her tongue over her lips and swallowed against sudden dryness. He watched her as she did, not with the quick, sharp eyes of a cat with its prey but a flat, dead gaze.

"I've made no claims to be a scholar—"

"Your mercy," he cut in smoothly. Snide. "You're greater than a scholar, for you've studied all these texts and know them well enough to need no further instruction. So tell me the name of the forest."

"You hold my missive prisoner for the sake of a name?" She gaped at him but only briefly before she thought of how such an expression might give him pleasure. She sealed her lips, tight and straight, bit her tongue to keep from saying more.

"I would."

As the youngest of seven daughters, Annalise had been long accustomed to taunts and teases. Favorite dollies stolen and held above her head while she wailed, treats promised but never given. Handed-down finery she'd spent hours in refitting only to lose when the sister who'd given it up found new desire for the fabric or ribbons she added to make it her own.

"The forest in which Sinder first came upon his bride is not referred to by name in the texts you've assigned us." Simple texts, not detailed. Not deep. Perfect as a base for study, but she'd absorbed more than what lay between the pages in her first six years.

His palm closed around the paper of her letter. It would be so well-creased by now, so dampened by being kept next to her skin for so many hours and now held tight in his palm, the ink surely would have run. She'd only read the first few lines. Now perhaps she might not be able to read any of it.

"But it has a name."

The forest could be said to have more than one name. She didn't know all of them. "If I tell you the name of the forest, you'll return my letter to me? That is your price?"

"Indeed, mistress. I shall."

Her jaw went so tight the clicking of her teeth sounded too loud in her ears, blocking even the sudden harsh thump of her heart. Without the assistance of her stays, Annalise had found her posture much less stiff than had been her wont, but now a rod of iron could not have made her back any straighter.

She had options. She could run and snatch at the letter, perhaps struggle for it. She could leave the room and seek a Mother to whom she could complain. Or she could give him what he wanted.

Instead, she sat back at her desk. She settled her journal to one side of the text and her pens in their flannel atop the journal. She folded her hands together, fingers linked tight to keep him from seeing any sight of them trembling.

"No."

Someone, Wandalette, perhaps, gasped. Toquin held the letter tighter in his fist for one breath, then two, before reaching behind him to place it gently on the top of his desk. He straightened. The high band of his collar bulged with the motion of his throat as he swallowed.

"No," he murmured.

The chime sounded for the session's end, but not a person in the room moved. Annalise focused on his face, on the ache in her fingers from clutching them so tight together, on the hard bench beneath her rear and the faintest whiff of breeze come from some unknown source.

"You," he told the room, "are all dismissed."

It was as though he'd set them loose, hounds from a gate, the way they all sprung up from their desks and fled the room. Only Annalise lingered, rising slowly from her seat and gathering her belongings while his gaze did its best to weight her shoulders or trip her step.

His voice caught her at the door. "You would leave behind that which you desire to prevent me from gaining?"

She stopped, but didn't look at him. "The others may be giddy, silly bints. I am not."

"This show of temper may describe you as otherwise."

Annalise gave a half turn on the toe of her slipper so that it squeaked on the wood floor. "I've not raised my voice. This is no show of temper."

"Of disobedience, then."

Again her hands clenched and ached. "I was not aware I'm required to obey you."

He hadn't moved even a hair since she'd stood from her seat and made to leave without approaching him. Now he passed a hand along the edge of the desk, over the letter. "You act as no Handmaiden."

Now she turned fully, so fast her skirts swirled. "I am not *your* Handmaiden, sir. Good day."

Without a further word or look, Annalise left the room and slammed the door behind her. He would not come after her. Would he?

"Annalise." Mother Deliberata, who'd been the one to first welcome Annalise to the Order, had just rounded the corner. "Is all well?"

Sister Merriment, who'd been walking arm in arm with the Mother, gave a curious glance to the door behind Annalise. "You fair to shook the door from its hinges."

"Your mercy. In my haste I was overexuberant in its closure." Annalise, upon the second curious glance of Sister Merriment at her fists, relaxed her fingers. "If you'll excuse me?"

"And how are you finding your first days here at the Order?" Deliberata asked calmly, ignoring Annalise's request. "Have you settled comfortably?"

"Ah, yes, Mother. I have." It was no lie—aside from the abominable, irascible man inside the room behind her, Annalise had been fully welcomed, or at the least ignored, by everyone else she'd encountered.

"It's no small thing," Deliberata continued, "to leave one's home and family behind, to seek a life of service. If there is aught I can provide for you, Annalise, you must let me or one of the other Mothers know. We seek only to encourage our future sisters, you know."

Which was a far cry from what she could have expected from other apprenticeships, Annalise well knew. "I understand, Mother. Thank you."

"It can be difficult to adjust," Deliberata said with a tilt of her head. "Should you ever feel you cannot mold yourself to our expectations . . ."

Before Annalise could protest against such an event, the door opened behind her. Cassian stepped through it, his mind clearly on other pursuits, as he nearly collided with her. Only his swift reaction, grabbing at her elbow to move her slightly out of the path of his feet, kept her toes from being trod upon. Annalise shivered, remembering how gracefully he'd moved three nights ago.

"Master Toquin," Deliberata murmured. "I see that you are making haste, as well."

He would denounce her now. She could be cast from the Order, Annalise knew it, though nobody would dare speak of those who'd been thrown out. There were rules and as Deliberata had said, expectations. Now he would reveal her to be unsuitable or worse, unwilling.

"Your letter," he said, and her throat closed tight on the breath she'd been sipping. "You left it behind."

He'd not yet left off his grip of her elbow and now his fingers twitched. The heat of his touch could not possibly have penetrated the weight of her sleeve, and that wasn't where Annalise felt it. Her belly took the spark and kindled it to flame, fanned higher when she looked directly into his eyes.

He let go of her as if she'd burned him.

"Your letter," Cassian said again.

Annalise took the proffered paper, folded neatly. She didn't thank him, not trusting her voice. He was still looking into her eyes, and now he cut his gaze toward Deliberata and Merriment.

"Your mercy, ladies, for the interruption." With that, he disappeared back into his room.

The door shut behind him with a small, soft click.

With both women staring at her, Annalise slipped the letter discreetly into her sleeve and cleared her throat. "It would seem I have much to learn from Master Toquin in how to properly close a door."

Merriment laughed and tucked her arm through Deliberata's again. "Ah, I've known Cassian to slam a few doors in his time."

"Sister," Deliberata chastised gently, never taking her gaze from Annalise's face, "one must not speak ill of Master Toquin, for without him, we'd be left to tend much for which we have not the skill or patience."

"Perhaps not the skill," Merriment replied with another small laugh, "but certainly we might be considered as having more patience."

Deliberata did not laugh. "Tell me, Annalise, how are you finding Master Toquin's instruction? Do you still feel you were placed incorrectly?"

Annalise looked at the other woman and wondered what she'd seen, what she thought she knew. "I find him most thoroughly knowledgeable in the Word of the Book."

Deliberata inclined her head. "Most well. Come, Annalise. Merriment and I were about to take a turn around the gardens before afternoon services. We should love to have you join us. The fresh air will do wonders for your constitution."

The command, worded as a request, might have been denied if Annalise knew how lightly Deliberata would take such refusal. Since she didn't, she nodded and smiled. "I'd love to join you. Thank you."

"I find a brisk walk in the fresh air wipes away all the cobwebs and brings a new outlook upon any situation." Deliberata offered Annalise her other arm.

Annalise took it. "I suppose a new outlook is not something to be disparaged."

Now, finally, Deliberata chuckled. "No, indeed, it is not."

No matter how many days had passed since he'd been the one on the beemah, facing the Book and speaking for those who could not, Cassian ever remembered how it had felt to be there. Now he made it his practice to watch not from the chapel but from the small side room that had long ago been built to accommodate visiting luminaries. Not that he equated himself with persons of such importance they required a special room, but because he knew for a fact the room itself had not been blessed for such a purpose in so long a time he felt no hypocrisy in its use.

None questioned his use of the room instead of his presence in the chapel, because none knew. Or none had, at least not until the Marony woman had discovered him there.

She was a burr, ever-snagging.

He could not stop thinking of her.

She challenged him, and though he didn't want to enjoy being so challenged, he did. Most of the women who sought the Order of Solace were intelligent—they had to be, to pursue their craft. Many were beautiful, if not classically at least with some feature or presence or attitude that made them lovely. Scores of women had passed through the Order in his years and more than one had turned his head.

Not a one of them had ever struck at him some other place.

She did not, could not know, not unless she could look inside his mind and divot out the truth. He'd seen the look in her eyes when he'd snatched the letter—a foolish, childish gesture forced by some emotion he wished not to name. She thought him arrogant, mayhap cruel. It would be better if she did.

But even now he could recall the tone of her voice and her lifted chin. How her eyes had flashed with fury she'd been strong enough to keep from spilling over. She had tight rein on herself, a restraint he admired but that had only moved him to taunt her into an outburst.

And for what? So that he might bring her before the Mothers and demand punishment? It would take more than a disagreement for them to turn her out, particularly when he'd been the one to urge it forward. He'd had no good reason for taking her letter and naught to defend himself with should Annalise decide to level a counter-accusation.

She thought him cruel, at the least. Cassian watched his once-brothers move about their tasks, their words falling over and around him. Across his lips, silent. He listened to them speak for him, who would not.

He'd not always been known as fire-headed. In boyhood, Cassian had fended off his share of jeers and attacks from bullies who'd assumed his quiet demeanor meant he was vulnerable. Since he'd never fought in return, his reputation as soft grew.

Calvis, on the other hand, had never stood still long enough for a blow to hit him. Those who believed he shared his brother's temper as well as his features discovered swiftly enough the sting of Calvis's biting wit and the harsher bite of his fists. Woe to any who harmed those he loved, for Calvis was protectively, fiercely loyal.

He was quick to fury and amusement both, easily led to laughter and passion. Cassian could only ever watch his brother in every pursuit—a fight, a kiss, joke. Calvis loved and was loved. Cassian, on the other hand, was most often forgotten.

If they'd not shared a womb, they'd never have been friends. Cassian knew it deep within his soul, though Calvis would ever deny it. Calvis's arm 'round his shoulders, his knuckles rasping along his scalp, the slap of his brother's palm on his back while Calvis's laughter rang all 'round them—these were things Cassian knew he'd have been denied if they weren't brothers.

"Shite and bollocks," Calvis had said the first and sole time

Cassian made mention of it. "Shut your mouth, brother, else I shut it for you."

It had been late, the room dark, Calvis's breathing heavy from indulgence in worm and herb. The stink of a brothel wafted from him so that even in the darkness Cassian could tell without hesitation his brother's position. He could hear the thump of Calvis's boots being flung to the floor.

"You think because I didn't ask you along that I don't like you?" More thumping. A stifled belch. The tang of herb drifted across Cassian's wrinkled nose. "I know you overwell, brother, that's all. I know you'd take no pleasure from the company of whores and the sorts of men who join with them."

Cassian, in his bed, had turned his face to the wall and drawn the covers up high. "Go away, Cal, you're drunk."

"Oh, oh, oh." The sound of bare feet slapped the floor, coming closer. "Oh, brother dear, such condemnation in your tone."

"I condemn you not, but go away." Cassian dug deeper into the bedclothes.

"Have you, little brother, ever been drunk? Methinks the answer is no, but you've ever been one to surprise."

Cassian had, in fact, overindulged on sweet tumbleberry wine once the summer before. It had made him sick enough to pray for unconsciousness, and he'd not repeated the act since. "It's late, and I—"

"You," breathed Calvis as the bed settled and he crept close, "have to be up early for those bedamned devotions. Yes, little brother. I know your bent."

"Don't call me little."

Calvis laughed and a fresh waft of herb-scent drifted across to tickle Cassian's nose. His brother's weight, the heat of his body, pressed him. Cassian, bound tight by the blankets he'd pulled up so high, couldn't move. With Cal at his back and the wall at his front, he could only twist a little.

"As the elder brother, I can call you whatever I like."

"By no more than a moment or two."

"By the span of four or five good convulsions, according to our dear mother, from whose womb we were ejected. And I should think that dear woman would know the length of time between my first greeting to the world and thine, brother mine." Cal snuggled close, his chin biting into Cassian's shoulder. His arm slipped tight 'round his brother's waist. "Be not angry with me. Next time I shall ask you to join us, I swear."

Cassian wriggled in the blankets and yet could not break his brother's grip. Not without much struggle, anyway, and past experience had taught him such an effort would be useless. They were matched in strength and size, but Calvis would ever be the stronger in his desire to win.

"Go to sleep, Cal. In your own bed."

"But why? When I've found myself in yours?"

"Because it's late and you snore when you've been drinking." Cassian wriggled again, harder, to get past the blankets at least, if not his brother's arm.

"So do you. Snore when I've been drinking." Laughter and hot breath caressed the space between them, until Calvis said seriously, "Let me stay. The hour, as you said, is late and I'm fair busted. Would you have me walk to my room in such a state? Waking the house? Subjecting our blessed mother to her beloved son in such a shameful state?"

"Mayhap you shouldn't have gotten yourself into such a state, if you're so ashamed of it." Argument was futile, Cassian knew, as was denying his brother what he wanted.

Cal's chin bit deeper as his nose pressed Cassian's neck. "I am ever shamed over what I do."

This was the first time Cassian had heard such an admission, and he made no comment. Cal's breath grew softer, deeper, slower. His arm relaxed, though it didn't release him.

"Next time," Calvis said quietly, "I will ask you, brother. If you so wish. But I know you. You'd gain no pleasure from such jaunts."

That Calvis was likely correct in his assumption served naught but to twist Cassian's determination to be included the next time. "You think me less a man than you?"

Cal's arm tightened. His mouth sought the flesh of Cassian's throat, where he bit once, just lightly. "No, little brother. I know you to be much greater. Much, much, greater."

And with that, the bastard had fallen asleep, immovable and stinking, and had snored the night through while Cassian lay awake and trapped.

Chapter 11

There had been times when Cassian took great joy from discussion of the Word and the Law. The Book had been everpresent in him. It had led him to every path. It still did, he thought, catching sight of the leather-bound text on his desk. He didn't need to open its pages to quote it word for word. He wished he could forget, sometimes, but never could.

"I fail to understand," he said now, "how you could have grown to such an age and have found such faith as to seek a position in the Order of Solace, yet be so unknowledgeable about the contents of a very basic passage."

Wandalette cleared her throat and blinked rapidly. The sheen of tears gave her away, and Cassian kept his sigh locked tight in his throat. He didn't want to make her cry, but the bedamned chit would insist on allowing emotion to overcome her. He told himself it was a lesson she needed to learn and best taught by him rather than a patron, but it nevertheless left him with a churning in his belly that had naught to do with hunger.

"Well?"

"Sir, I . . . my parents weren't of the Faith."

He studied her. All around, the other young women had paused in their scribblings to watch him test their novitiate sister. Annalise, the only one sitting in the back of the room, glanced up at the pause in his reply but looked away again, her pen moving smoothly over her parchment. She wasn't studying, and he could only guess at what she was writing.

Since the day he'd taken her letter, neither had made any pretense that he had anything to teach her, or she anything to learn.

"Not of the Faith. They didn't practice? Or they didn't believe?" Cassian focused on Wandalette again.

She swallowed hard and spoke in a voice thick with tears. "Not of . . . nor did they believe . . . I mean, sir, they didn't practice it nor allow its practice in our house."

Cassian had heard of such folk, though few. Even those who didn't have a heart-deep belief in the Faith most often at least celebrated the holidays. "And yet here you are."

"I wanted to make a difference, sir."

"Tell me, Wandalette, why you'd seek to make such a difference in the Order of Solace? Why not take up nursemaiding, instead? Why not raise a family yourself? Surely the birth and raising of children would make a difference."

Void take her, now she was weeping. He hadn't meant to force her to tears, only an answer. He scrubbed at his face in resignation, palm over his eyes so he could gain a breath or two without having to look at her distress.

"I had a vision."

From the back of the room, Cassian heard the sound of a chair scrape. He looked from behind his hand. Annalise was staring, too.

"Of the Invisible Mother?"

"No." Wandalette shook her head. "Of her sons."

"In your vision she had more than one?"

Cassian had heard many tales of visions. He believed those who'd seen them believed in their veracity as firmly as he understood not a one of them to be genuine. The Holy Family had gone away, never to return for any amount of solace provided the world they'd left behind. He'd never heard of a vision that was not of the Mother.

"I know the text says there's only one." Wandalette gestured at the book in front of her. "I've read it front to back, sir. I promise you. But why does it not say she had two sons? Twins."

His gut twisted on the word. "No text states Kedalya had more than one son with Sinder."

Annalise spoke. "There are commentaries that say she had more children. After the first."

Wandalette looked back and shook her head. "The boys were twins. I'm sure of it. And Sinder's sons."

There *was* a little-known commentary that stated much the same—that after Kedalya had left the forest and her god of a husband, taking their son with her, she discovered she was again with child. That the sons she bore after leaving were twins, identical in every way but for the fact that one was a murderer and the other a victim of his brother's anger.

But how could one such as she, not even raised in the Faith, know such a story?

"Nonsense," Cassian said in a voice that brooked no dispute. "Read the text in front of you for the answers. When you've mastered this level, you might move on. But know you it takes years if not a lifetime to fully understand everything and not a man yet who's been able."

"Perhaps it's not a man's place to be able," Annalise said from her seat at the back, "but there's naught to say a woman is incapable."

"I don't want to know everything!" Wandalette cried, alarmed. "Must I know everything to serve? Must I be a scholar of the Faith to be a Handmaiden?"

"If your patron requires it, you shall be." Cassian flicked a hand at her. "That, among everything else."

"Not every patron shall wish his Handmaiden to decipher dusty texts, surely." This again from Annalise, whose tone might be sweet but whose gaze was most definitely meant to prick.

"The best Handmaiden is not the one who knows everything, but understands what she does not know and how to best learn it," Cassian said. "Besides, the patron who requires a scholar of the Faith will be assigned one who can so serve. No, Wandalette. You need not know everything. But you must know at least something."

She drew in a hitching breath but looked him full-on without more tears seeping. "Thank you, sir."

He'd done naught. It had been Annalise who'd forced him to reassure the girl. "Study the texts as I require and the Mothers request, Wandalette. You can do no more than that."

"It was a true vision," she said. "The Mothers-in-Service said so. They believed it was so."

"The Mothers-in-Service believe all visions are true," Cassian said with a glance toward Annalise.

Annalise cocked her head to look at him but said nothing. The chime sounded for the class's release, and he watched them file out of the room, their chatter instant and exuberant and exhausting even in the few moments to which he was subjected.

He ran his palm over his eyes again and gave a sigh, and when he looked, expecting the room to be empty, he found instead Annalise, still at her desk. She'd gathered her belongings but not yet stood. She was half smiling.

"They . . . weary me."

"They would weary anyone, but I should imagine you'd be well accustomed to girls like that by now."

"I'm too old," he said without thinking.

Annalise looked faintly surprised. "Surely you're not. You're not old at all."

She didn't sound combative, but he took no flattery from it. "I *feel* too old."

At this she laughed, and the light bell-tinkle of it made him want to join her. He held back. He waited for her to go, and when she didn't, he pointed at the door.

"You're dismissed."

"I know it. I'm going." She gathered her things and gave him another look before she went to the door. "I've read commentary that said Kedalya bore other children when she left Sinder, and that's why the Holy Family will never be rejoined no matter what any of us do. Sinder accused her of infidelity and she proved him right when she came up pregnant."

The depth of her knowledge impressed him. "If you so believe, why are you here? There can be no use to your future as a Handmaiden if naught you do brings about the return."

"I didn't say I believed it, I said there's a commentary. There are many, as you well know. One can't believe them all."

"What do you believe?" he asked, curious.

Annalise gave her head the barest shake. "I believe whatever I shall be taught by you, Master Toquin, so that I might be released from this class to the immense relief of us both."

"Some do say Kedalya bore twin sons with Sinder as their father." He'd not meant to share this, but his tongue tripped out with it and once spoken, the words couldn't be called back.

Annalise lifted a brow, her hands closing her pen flannel. "I've heard no such commentary, yet it makes sense."

"Does it?"

"It makes . . . connection," she compromised. "It fits with the others I have heard. Stories of what happened after Sinder's accusation of her betrayal. For who, if Sinder created the land and the sea and the air, did Kedalya cuckold him with?"

"Who created his lady wife, if not himself?" Cassian asked.

"What happened to the twin sons?"

"They went brother against brother," Cassian said after a moment. "Spilled the first blood. The commentary says that's where we come from. Us of the Faith. That we sprung from the drops of blood one brother drew from the other."

"Do you believe that?"

"Does it make any more sense than that Sinder grew the first of us like flowers, plucked us from our beds, and thrust us out of the Land Above so that we might make merry for his amusement?"

She laughed, and again he wanted to join her. "As I said, sir, I believe what you deem it fit for me to know."

"You already know much I've not taught. Or ever would."

"And why is that?" She chewed the softness of her lower lip for a moment. "What use is knowledge if you never share it?"

"Sometimes it's the having of a thing that gives it the most value."

"So instead of gold you're a miser of your knowledge? Why become a teacher, then?"

"I'm not a teacher. I'm—" Cassian stopped himself. He didn't want to tell her he'd been a priest. Some knew it, but none who'd spread the truth. He shouldn't be ashamed, and yet he always was.

Annalise looked him over thoroughly but only nodded, didn't speak. When she left, the door swung closed slowly behind her, and Cassian waited for some long moments before he went to it, so that he might be sure she didn't wait on the other side.

The days continued passing quickly. Annalise was grateful for the sunup-to-sundown schedule that kept her too busy for ennui. The skill she'd thought would be the easiest turned out to be the worst to endure. Annalise had ever chafed at bending to the command of another, and so when she first learned of what was called Waiting, the series of kneeling positions Handmaidens employed to center themselves, her gut had clenched along with her jaws.

Waiting, Readiness. On her knees, buttocks resting on her heels, the back of one hand resting against the other's palm.

Waiting, Remorse. On her knees, buttocks resting on her heels, her hands this time placed palm down on the floor in front of her, presumably with downcast gaze as well, for a Handmaiden in this position was in an act of contrition.

Waiting, Submission. The position that curled Annalise's lip. On her knees, back straight, hands clasped behind her neck. There were women who craved such a place, but that would never be her, she thought as her skin crawled the entire time she was required to keep the stance.

And finally, *Waiting, Abasement.* On her knees, stretched so her forehead rested on the floor, arms stretched out, palms down, on the floor in front of her.

"Why would anyone require such a stance?" she asked upon its demonstration, appalled.

The other novitiates had taken it at once, following the Sister-in-Service's command. Annalise, whose knees and back ached, thought it would at least stretch her muscles and provide some relief, but the concept of the position's necessity lifted her gorge into her throat.

Sister Merriment looked at her. "One hopes one must never need to use such a position. This is the position for a Handmaiden who's failed so grievously in her function that she has disgraced herself and the Order."

Annalise couldn't hold back the curling of her lip this time. Remorse she could understand. Submission, tolerate if necessary—she was, as one of the five principles stated, a woman at the start and the end, and femininity had well trained her for submission no matter how she might despise it.

But abasement? Failure? Dishonor and disgrace?

Watching the others bent forward, their faces pressing the floor, Annalise shook her head and didn't move. "What could possibly be so horrible that a Handmaiden would feel it necessary to proclaim herself so disgraced?"

Sister Merriment neither laughed nor frowned. "Would that you will never know, Annalise."

"But I would like to know, now." Annalise Waited in Readiness.

Merriment faltered, her mouth pursing. "I honestly can't tell you, I'm afraid. If any of my Sisters has so failed in her function, I'd not be privy to it."

"Surely there are stories. There always are."

Around them, some of the other novitiates shifted but didn't remove themselves from their Abasement. They'd not been told to get up, and so they did not. Annalise looked at Merriment and waited for an answer.

"We don't speak of such things."

"Of failure? When learning from another's folly we might gain knowledge of how to prevent our own?"

Merriment frowned, now, and shook her head so the end of her pale braid swung against her hips, one to the other. "A Handmaiden who's been so shamed would be unlikely to return to the Order."

This raised both Annalise's brows, even if it didn't bring her off her knees. She'd discovered in the hours required of her that Waiting, Readiness, was an infinitely comfortable position to hold. "Even more reason to have heard tales. Women talk, Sister. Women we begin and women we shall end, yes?"

Though nobody else had dared raise a head, there was no doubt all were listening. Annalise watched Merriment carefully, her intention not of rudeness or rebellion, but curiosity. Merriment paced a few steps and set the hem of her gown swinging.

"I . . . I don't know of any, personally," she said finally before halting her steps to look back at Annalise. "I would venture I hope to never know of any."

"Yet by teaching us this, you put the notion of its possible requirement in our heads."

Merriment blinked rapidly. "I can do no less than to prepare you for whatever you may encounter, Annalise. Perhaps if this is too much of a burden for you, you might reconsider your desire to serve."

Annalise sighed and drew back her questions. She shifted herself, hands and forehead on the floor, and closed her eyes.

"I will never," she murmured so softly none but she should have heard, "perform this for a patron."

Cassian made his way through dim, quiet halls and out a back door into the courtyard, past stone benches and flowerbeds being tended by a pair of lads dressed alike. Like brothers, but not brothers. These boys were Blessings, children born to Handmaidens in the service of a patron. Fathered by kings or thieves, rare in their existence, but well-loved for it.

"Good day, Master Toquin!" Kellen, the smaller. Blond hair fell over one dark brown eye and his merry smile tilted on its side. He waved.

His partner, Leonder, nudged him. Taller, with dark hair the color of harvest leaves, he'd outgrown his last pair of trousers and exposed a full finger's length of limb between the hem and his clog. "Don't bother him. He's on his way somewhere, can't you tell?"

"Where are you going?" Kellen dusted his hands on the seat of his trousers and hopped along the crushed stone path to make it to Cassian's side. "For a walk? Out to the pond? Or to the forest where the waterfall is?"

"I haven't yet decided." Cassian resisted the urge to ruffle the boy's hair. It was already a tangled mess, with bits of grass caught up in it.

"The pond's got an eel in it," Kellen said. "I've seen it. Just a wee one, about this long."

Cassian studied the boy's measurement. "That long? 'Ware, else you'll find yourself the eel's supper."

"They don't eat people!" Kellen's small mouth rounded and he turned to his companion. "Do they, Leonder?"

Leonder shrugged. "If Master Toquin says . . ."

Kellen took a leap back. Leonder laughed. Cassian smiled. The boys began an argument over which was better, steamed or roasted eel, and the best way to catch one, and what to use for bait.

Cassian left them to their rough and tumbling, the sound of their boyish shouts following him. He'd wrestled with his brother much the same way. He'd sometimes even won, if his brother felt magnanimous enough to refrain from dirty fighting.

Now, he walked. And thought. He often sought the forest, but today he went through the grass and fields toward the pond. It had been hand-dug when the Order's first manse was built. The original founders had thought to breed fish in it and eels, for which the depth and brackishness of the water was better suited. He didn't think they'd ever thought of boating or ice-skating, though sometimes the sisters came out here to take part in such pastimes. But not today.

He couldn't imagine the hours of labor that had carved the pond. Boulders lay piled around its edge, proof of how hard the ground had been, how difficult the effort. Cassian had never swam in it—nobody did except the sorts of foolish boys who might tempt an eel to nibble. But he had gone out to the center in a small skiff on a day so bright the sun had cut through the dark water like a flame. He'd seen the pond's depth as well over a tall man's head. It wasn't overlarge, but it was deep enough to drown.

Of course, it didn't need to be deep for that. He knew of an upstairs maid in the home of a childhood friend who'd drowned herself in a bucket. Nobody had said why. As a man, Cassian could guess at any number of reasons she'd done so, especially since she'd taken her life in the bedchamber of the house's master with a bucket dragged all the way from the stable. But as a boy, he'd only heard the tale of how she'd been found, facedown, her skirts not even wet. How she hadn't struggled or fought but simply put her face into the few inches of water at the bucket's bottom . . . and breathed.

Calvis had seen her himself, he claimed, and been the one to tell the tale. How he'd managed to get inside the bedroom and view the maid he never quite explained, but he'd told the story often and with few embellishments. The lack of frills convinced Cassian his brother had indeed seen the dead girl. He'd been envious at the time, thinking it some treat to witness the subject of the story that had the county buzzing.

"You don't want to see it." Calvis had said this with clouded eyes and a shake of his head. "Not really. It's not a sight for the likes of you."

Later, when they outgrew short pants and slateboard lessons and had moved on to the pursuits that would shape them as men, Calvis had told him a different version of the worn-thin story. Not frilled or furbelowed.

"She put a bar of soap between her teeth," he said.

"Why that? Why a bar of soap?"

Calvis had shuddered, his mouth working. "To keep from screaming? I don't know, little brother."

"Don't call me that."

Standing at the pond, the dirt soft beneath his boots and water squelching around his toes, Cassian could still hear Calvis's voice. He could smell the acrid scent of the soap his brother'd been using to clean his fingernails before eating the dinner their mother had called them to. And in the rippling water at his feet, he saw the reflection of his brother's face.

An image from the looking glass. Reversed. They'd only ever been identical to any who didn't look overclose or didn't know them overwell. Now he looked, and then again, trying to put his own features in their place. The lines at the corners of his eyes helped. So did his hair, blown a bit by the wind around his face. Threads of silver had woven in the darkness. Calvis had ever been, would ever be . . . young.

"I miss you, brother." The mouth in the rippling reflection moved, echoing the sentiment. "Ever and always."

It wasn't enough. A memory and a few words would never bring him back.

Life will bring what the Invisible Mother provides. Cassian had long ago ceased believing that. It hadn't escaped him that in a faith based on the story of a man and woman split apart by betrayal, real or imagined, it might have been the male who created the world, but it was the woman who oversaw it. People might invoke Sinder's name, but it was to Kedalya the prayers were sent.

There was no use in praying for his brother's return. Death was a chasm not even the Invisible Mother could bridge. His brother was gone, whether to the Void or to the Land Above, both places in which Cassian had also ceased believing. He'd never see his brother again.

Whatever life brought, it wasn't at the bequest of the Invisible Mother. And what did life bring him now, as he made his way around the pond to the gazebo on the pond's far side. Annalise, her hair covered with a headscarf and her face scrubbed clean of cosmetic, her gown hitched at the sides and tucked into a belt tightened at her waist. She had a basket covered with a towel settled in front of her, and a loaf of bread peeked from it. A jug sat next to it.

She didn't see him. She was Waiting, her eyes closed, her mouth moving but no sound issuing forth. Was she praying? That didn't seem right. Handmaidens knelt in Waiting, not in prayer.

It felt illicit, this watching her when she couldn't see him, but Cassian made no move to step away. The crunch of his boots on the gravel hadn't yet alerted her, but if he moved now, would she hear and open her eyes? Would she think he'd been spying on her apurpose?

Did he care?

". . . no greater pleasure . . ."

Ah, she was reciting the five principles. It wasn't enough to learn them by heart, a novitiate must believe in them. Live them. Be consumed by them. Annalise did not impress him as a woman to be consumed by anything, but what did he know?

And still he stood, boots grounded to the earth as though he'd grown roots. His breathing soft, held tight in his chest, so as not to alert her. His hands curled into fists he noticed only when his fingers ached.

Move. He didn't obey his own silent command. He drew breath after breath, ears straining for the sound of her voice.

Cassian had been with the Order for ten years, with another three before that in service to the priesthood and assigned to the Motherhouse. He'd been surrounded for years by women, inundated, immersed. He knew beauty.

Annalise wasn't beautiful. Her features were too bold, her smile crooked, her eyes too shrewd. If she'd been perfect, would he have been able to ignore her the way he did the others, the many others? Cassian thought so, and cursed himself for being so swayed by what he'd long ago decided to forgo.

"Oh," she said when she opened her eyes and saw him there. Nothing more, no accusation, no smirking smile to show him she'd known all along he was there. No alarm, either. Only curiosity. She gave him that tilt-headed glance that Cassian was equally as disturbed to discover he found as familiar as her voice.

"I plead your mercy," he said.

"For what?"

For what, indeed. For staring? For not alerting her that he'd come upon her? Cassian cleared his throat.

Her mouth tightened. "Is this your special place? Have I encroached?"

"No, no. I often walk here, but no, it's not . . . mine."

She chewed the inside of her cheek and looked at the basket and jug in front of her. "I'm required to learn the five principles, front to back. I'm having difficulty."

"Surely not in the learning. A child could memorize them." He meant no insult and so of course that was how the words sounded.

She got to her feet, not with swift grace but a heave and a sigh. "A child can learn many things, sir. I'm not a child."

"No. I daresay you're not." He stepped away from the gazebo's wooden railing.

"My difficulty is not in the rote memorization, but in the acceptance," she told him bluntly.

If nothing else, her honesty was what made her so much the lovelier. "Many find it so."

"Well, Master Toquin," Annalise said dryly, "I am not many. I am myself. And I struggle with this, knowing particularly that I'm not unique in it and yet unable to convince myself to go toward the other spectrum, of those who find no quarrel in such statements as 'true patience is its own reward.' "

"Do you not find that to be the truth?" He watched her as she shifted her weight from foot to foot.

"What? True patience being its own reward? For what? How?" She shook her head and dusted her hands, then bent to tear a hunk of bread from the loaf and offered it to him.

Surprised, he took it. She tore another for herself and chewed it thoughtfully. He kept his in his hand but didn't eat.

"Obviously you've not gained the skills yet to become a Sister-in-Service."

The look she shot him was full of disdain he could not begrudge her, as his statement, bald as it had been, had also been stupid. "Surely you make merry with me, sir, for I thought I'd take my vow upon the morrow, so that I should be the first to attend the Order and join its service in so swift a time."

Knowing his own words had brought forth such a response didn't keep Cassian from bristling. He'd been too long revered, even feared, to accept such a reply with a different reaction. He made a half bow, hand upon his stomach. "Your mercy at the interruption. Clearly, you'll need hours more of meditation before you come even close to understanding the most basic tenants of the duties you claim to so long for."

Her gaze flickered at that and her chin lifted. "Everyone needs hours of meditation."

"Not everyone. I've known novitiates to earn their vows within a sixmonth." Not quite a lie, mayhap a slight exaggeration, and yet he could still not be certain why he told her such a thing beyond that something about this woman set him on edge and he found himself incapable of doing otherwise.

"You think it's a matter of strength of will," Annalise said flatly.

"I would call that an apt description, yes."

"And how long," she asked with narrowed eyes, "would you estimate it will take me to fully embrace these principles?"

Tension coiled in his gut at the way her voice dipped low. It scratched at him in places he hadn't known itched. Cassian swallowed, throat tight, and kept his voice steady, without emotion. His face carefully blank, as had served him so well, so often.

"You ask me to make judgment on when you'll be ready to take your vows of service?"

She nodded. "You seem the man to ask."

"Have you spoken to any of the Mothers? The other Sisters? Surely they'd be better judges than I—"

She laughed, tipping her head back, nary a trace of irony in her chuckle. When she looked at him, her eyes gleamed and her mouth twisted into a smile that had too little humor to be pretty yet had him wishing to take another step back. "Ah, ah, ah. False modesty, sir, is as unattractive as boastfulness, if not more so, for arrogance can never play at being anything other than what it is."

By the Arrow, she forced his blood to boiling. He felt the heat of it rush to his cheeks, and only by serious strength of the will she so claimed would lead her to her service was he able to keep his voice from shaking when he replied, "You think me arrogant?"

"I ask your judgment on how long it shall take me to be worthy of being called to service."

She'd taken not a single step in his direction, yet touched him all over. Cassian had no five principles, no mantras to repeat in times of duress to bring his thinking back to the Faith, and even if such practice had been a habit during his time in the priesthood, he'd have long forgone it now. So he reacted as he'd taught himself—by snipping the threads of his emotion, one by one, the way a weaver would clip the extra strings from a garment to keep it from unraveling.

"Do you ask to hear the answer I'll give, or the one that will spare your feelings?"

She laughed again without humor. "Oh, please, worry not of sparing my feelings. I've known you too short a time for you to grant me favors, sir, and long enough to know you've never worried of sparing me anything."

Cassian drew another breath and let it out. Neither peace nor calm filled him, but rather a welcome blankness. This was how he acted best, devoid of emotion that would lead him to rashness. "I think, Annalise Marony, that you could study for the rest of your life and never become a Handmaiden."

She blinked rapidly and took a single, staggering step back. One hand went flat to her chest, over her heart. Her fingers clutched just once before her hand fell to her side. Her back straightened. She looked him in the eye.

"I'll prove you wrong."

"Prove nothing to me," Cassian said, "as I care little for the outcome. Take your vows of service or not. You'll not be the first to leave before you have, nor would you be the first to remain here until you die without ever being granted a patron."

Her mouth parted, but in the next moment her teeth clicked together as her jaw clamped. It didn't make her ugly, this fierceness. If anything, it gave her the beauty she normally lacked.

He watched her throat as she swallowed hard, and her mouth

closed over whatever words she'd meant to speak. She would cry now, he thought dispassionately. They almost always did, and even though he hated it, he hoped she would weep so that he might be justified in his disdain.

Annalise didn't cry. She blinked again and drew a breath. Then another. She turned her face so as to look at the ground and not him. She gave her head the smallest shake.

She was, incredibly, dismissing him.

"You don't know me," she said in a tight, hard voice, sharp.

It would've been easier had she cried, for tears he could despise. If she'd railed, or sought to insult him, that, too, he could've swept off with ease, for nothing anyone ever said could hurt him when it was all most likely true. Her disdain he could've also borne as well-deserved, even if not for the reasons she thought.

Instead, she unmanned him with pity.

"You could never know me," Annalise told him. "Do you know anyone? Have you ever?"

He had, too well and more than one. Cassian stepped away from the gazebo. Away from her. He gave her another half bow he knew she'd see as mockery.

"I plead your mercy for the intrusion."

"Have you?"

Void take her, she moved toward him, following. She put a hand on the gazebo railing and a slipper to the gravel. It crunched beneath her foot, as loud as anything he'd ever heard.

"Is this another test?" Annalise asked in a voice too gentle to be borne. "Have I passed it?"

Cassian shook his head and let her gaze catch his. It tried to burn him and he refused to let it. "No test. Not this time."

She made as though to move toward him again and stopped herself, a hand on the railing. Her gaze swept him up and down, but Cassian had found the place inside that allowed him to remain cold.

Unmoved. It hurt, this place, but it was an old and familiar pain and one he welcomed. One he would always welcome.

"Another time?" she asked as though she'd never been denied an answer in her life. "You will test me another time, yes?"

"If the Mothers call me to do so."

"And will I know when you are testing me, or must I guess?"

"I daresay you will know."

Her pale eyes flashed then. "Mayhap by then you will have sought to know me, so that you might better judge my performance."

Cassian slowly, slowly shook his head. "But as you said, I could never know you."

At that, at last, he turned on his heel and left her behind him. She didn't call after him, for which he would later be grateful, though at the moment he could feel nothing like gratitude.

At that moment, Cassian made certain he could feel nothing at all.

Chapter 12

Every day they met after the noon meal in Cassian's dim-lit room, scented with incense, the texts of fine paper and tang of ink adding to the weight of the air. Bellies overfull, eyelids drooping from rising early, no matter how the students struggled, coherence was difficult and yet apprehension kept them on their toes.

Well, all of them but for Annalise. She understood the other girls' fear. Cassian was not only a man, which had become to seem a strange enough creature in a house full of women, but he was also a discontented man. Eager to scowl rather than smile, of a mysterious past about which she could unearth no amount of gossip. He was a brooding puzzle.

He was, Annalise thought, watching him through the fringe of her lashes, delicious.

Every encounter made him more so. Annalise had ever been one to crook her finger and gain the attention of men she desired—she'd learned early on how to provide those sorts of pleasures. It was one of the reasons she'd believed herself capable of at least pretending she wanted to become a Handmaiden. But not this man. He balked her, always. He insulted her. He ignored and chastised her, infuriated her.

He quite possibly despised her.

She watched him now as he stared out the window, lost in his own thoughts. What fantasy would a man like that use to occupy his time? Did he dream of carnal pleasures, or did he set his mind to loftier pursuits? Annalise craved knowing.

Not a one of the young ladies in her group could handle him. His gruff voice sent them into knock-kneed twitters, and his slightest glance set them writhing. The worst part of it, she thought as her pen scratched out nonsense syllables in the parchment booklet, was that he knew it, and encouraged it. He set fear into them like a diamond in a ring, something to be admired and cooed over. Something to be coveted.

And this the man to whom they assigned the newest, who were not always the youngest, but the ones who definitely needed the most nurturing. Annalise shook her head at the reasons of the Mothers-in-Service and kept bent over her booklet. She was supposed to be writing passages that particularly spoke to her so that she might keep them close for the future.

Bollocks.

None of it spoke to her. She knew the text word for word, front to back and in reverse, and not a bit of it had ever made sense. Annalise suspected it never would.

She stifled a yawn behind her fist, grateful that unlike her school days, the master wouldn't be traveling the rows with his ruler, ready to smack her knuckles for not completing the lesson . . . though on second thought, she might prefer that to his current alternating habit of ignoring and scorning her. She drew a small pattern of stars and bars. Underneath it, the scroll of her initials, just as she had so often as a schoolgirl.

Finally, at long last the chime sounded. An hour of leisure, then the afternoon service and evening meal, then more leisure pursuits until it was time to sleep. Annalise had already wiped her pen and replaced it in its flannel and capped the inkbottle, her booklet in her pocket, by the time the chime finished reverberating through the halls. She'd have been first out the door, too, if not for the silly bint Perdita, who spilled her text and booklet on the floor and her friends who bent to help her clean the mess but blocked the way.

"Mistress Marony, if you please."

Annalise looked over her shoulder. "Yes?"

"Would you stay a moment after the rest of the group?"

Ah, now the silly gits were staring at her, eyes wide, mouths propped open in identical expressions of dismay. Had she ever been so wind-headed? Annalise sighed. Yes, in all likelihood, she had.

"If it pleases you." She'd picked up the phrase without knowing it, but when it slipped from her tongue, she was glad she'd found it for no other reason than the way it widened his eyes.

"You needn't address me in such a manner," he told her when the others had gone and left them alone, the door left wide open so they could hear the voices and shuffle of feet in the hall that had replaced the soft chiming of the bell.

"With respect? I thought you insisted upon such a manner."

Master Toquin—she knew his given name was Cassian, but here in this room he was more a master than a man—narrowed his eyes. "Yet something in your tone never lends itself to such an honor."

Her lips thinned and tightened, and Annalise bit the tip of her tongue to keep from speaking with haste. This man held a place of importance within the Order. Power.

"It was the phrase," he added before she could speak.

She bit her tongue again so as not to leap to words she couldn't retrieve. He studied her, noting her silence. He rested his fingertips, protruding from the red hem of his shirt below the black sleeve, on the desktop close to where she'd left her pot of ink.

"You've not yet taken your vows," he said.

"Everything I do here is meant to lead me to that place when

I do all in the name of service. When it becomes second nature." She'd seen most if not all the other novitiates living as if they'd already taken their vows, and had seen it encouraged by the Sisters and Mothers-in-Service. "The best way to become a Handmaiden is to live as one, yes?"

"But you are not one. You are not mine," he told her with an edge to his voice she neither understood nor cared to decipher.

"Your mercy." Annalise bit the words so they had an edge of their own. Ragged. "You kept me for a reason?"

He looked toward the closet. "The texts. Your eye was keen in determining which were of quality too poor for use. I've noted your hand is steady, as well. And your attention to the work is . . . less than attentive."

"I'm in the wrong group," she told him flatly. "Perhaps you should petition the Mothers to move me from it, as I've done several times and been refused. Surely that would ease the burden of having me as your student."

His fingers drifted in a slow pattern of circles over the desktop. Her gaze fell to the circling, the tender way his fingertips stroked the polished wood. How precise his touch—and how long it had been since she'd had any such caress upon herself.

"I should think the burden is upon you," Toquin told her. "Since you so clearly need no instruction from me as to the text. I can see how dull you find it. But I can do naught to change the course to which you've been assigned. Only the Mothers can do that, and never in my experience do they do so from a plea, no matter who brings it."

His hand stopped the slow, steady pattern. Annalise swallowed the breath threatening to slip out of her on a sigh. When she looked up at him, he did not meet her gaze. He, too, stared at his fingers on the smooth wood.

"It has long been our habit to have those with greater understanding instruct those with less," he said in a low voice. "It would seem beneficial to us both, since the Mothers have determined that you should remain in study with this group, if you would become my . . . assistant."

"Your . . . but you don't even like me!" The cry shot from her lips before she could stop it, and Annalise stepped back from him.

Cassian looked at her then, eyes faintly wide. "I've never made such a claim!"

"You don't have to say it aloud, it's evident in your every word to me. Although"—she paused, thinking—"I suppose one could say the same of the words you say to everyone. It's generally understood you don't like anyone. But I thought, particularly, you disliked me."

He took a step back, his hand knocking the inkpot and rattling it. "Land Above, Mistress Marony, why would you believe I had any especial dislike of you over any other?"

Because she was different, she knew it by the way he looked or did not look at her. By the way his voice snagged on her name the rare occasion he chose to use it, and because he so rarely did. She knew she set his teeth on edge with her questions, her forthrightness, her simple unwillingness to be a single bird in a simple flock.

"Because I can assure you," he continued, "I harbor no such preference."

She lifted her chin to study his face. Color tinged his cheeks, not a blush but perhaps a flush of temper. His eyes glittered. A stray hair clung to his forehead. As if he noted her perusal he pushed it away with impatient fingers.

"If you choose not to accept the position—"

"I'll do it."

This stopped him, as her words seemed to do so often. Annalise shrugged, keeping her expression neutral so as not to reveal how much his dismissal of her had stung. Toquin's gaze traveled over her face before settling so briefly on her eyes she wasn't sure he'd even looked into them before he nodded and stepped back again.

"Very well. In addition to the classes, you'll be expected to assist me in preparation of the lessons, lend your hand in sorting the texts. Correct lessons, if necessary."

"I'm to become a teacher? How merry. I'd never thought myself patient enough for the task, else I'd have become a governess." Her lips quirked despite her all-to-recent distress at his tone and words.

Toquin didn't give her a smile in return. Did the man ever? "A good Handmaiden is oft asked to play the part of tutor in any manner of subjects, Mistress Marony. Or so I hear tell. There are many patrons for whom solace can only come at the instruction of another."

"Or so you hear. I thought nobody shared such stories here. At least, such was the tale I was told."

His gaze slid over her, and she thought she might have seen a twitch of lip, but too late, it passed and his mouth, full and lush though it was, stayed as firm and tight as it always did. "Talebearing is certainly not encouraged."

"I will be your assistant, sir, if only to relieve myself of the interminable dullness of the role of student."

Toquin lifted his chin. Changed his stance. If she didn't know better, Annalise might have said she'd challenged him and he rose to it, but the timbre of his voice didn't change. Nor did his expression.

"I am aware how less than challenging you've found my instruction. I can't speak for the Mothers who've placed you with me, but they have their reasons for all they do."

"Is there a person alive who has no reason for their action?" she asked, partly to poke him but mostly because she believed it to be so.

"I've never known one."

She laughed, knowing he wouldn't join her and yet hoping he might, just this once, slip a little. Not a hint of it. But something eased between them, some small bit of tension no longer jerking them back and forth like a dog on the end of a too-short leash.

"Tell me when you want me," she told him, "and I shall do my best to accommodate you."

His lips parted and sealed a moment later, and exasperated, she sighed. But since he'd not made comment, Annalise kept herself to silence as well.

The first time Cassian Toquin set his gaze upon Bertricia Miltrelli the sun had just come out from behind a cloud and covered her in fire. Golden hair, golden gown, even her skin had been cast with a sheen of gold. In the span of two heartbeats, mayhap three, she'd turned in conversation with her companion, and Cassian had stumbled so clumsily he went to a knee upon the stones and tore his trousers.

Calvis had helped him up.

"Leave off the ale if you're going to be a fumblefoot. Must I carry you?"

"No." Cassian shook his head.

Calvis was already following his brother's gaze. "Ah, the lady? Really, Cass? Her?"

"She is . . ." Cassian was unable to find the words to describe her.

"She's the bosom companion of yonder lemon-mouthed lass, Raeletta Demanns."

Cassian knew Raeletta, the daughter of their father's old school friend, and her sister Sarenissa, too. "She grew up."

"We all do." Calvis slung an arm around his brother's shoulders. "Don't tell me you're going to let a new-sprung set of breasts distract you from the fact that Raeletta Demanns is a pain in the arse."

"I'm not looking at Raeletta."

Calvis scoffed and knuckled Cassian's hair until he pulled away. "Her bosom companion is no less the she-hound. Home with her for the holiday. They're both here because our mothers have determined a brannigan is the best way to matchmake."

Cassian started, tearing his gaze at last from the three young women now examining his mother's bush of captain's buttons. "With us?"

"By the Arrow, I should think not. Think you our mothers find either of the pair of us ready for wedding? And I daresay neither would like to imagine us ready for bedding, either."

"Raeletta is a year younger than us. Sarenissa a year younger even than that."

Calvis shrugged. "Girls are settled quicker than us. Besides, no matter the affection Madame Demanns has cultivated for our mother, she thinks we two are Void-spawned."

Cassian shrugged away from Calvis's insistent grip. "She thinks that of you."

"Oh, ho, ho." Calvis grinned, not at all insulted. "What's the difference between us aside from an inch or two of prick I gained somehow when you didn't?"

Calvis's taunts wouldn't work today. Not in front of their guests. Bertricia, Cassian thought, his heart already lost. Only when his brother poked his ribs did he look again.

"Give it up, Cass. She'll never look at you the way you're already staring at her. She's not born for the likes of us."

"What's that supposed to mean?" The breeze carried the sound of her voice to him, and Cassian flushed with deep-seated heat even though the day wasn't overwarm.

"It means she's meant for courting by someone established. Wealthy. Probably for Grayson Delenard. He has a commission in the king's guard."

Cassian looked at his brother. The man in question was, indeed, a guest of their parents. "He's too old for her."

"Ah, but still fit. The man practices the Art every day and could fight off a room of men bent on killing him. Or the king."

Cassian stared at Bertricia. Was she looking across the yard at him? She wasn't looking at Raeletta, who could talk for hours just to hear the sound of her own voice. She was, he thought. She was looking at him.

Or at them.

Calvis was standing on his hands, showing off, until Cassian knocked him over. Cal, laughing, tumbled to the grass and bounced up at once, showing off the green stains on his hands.

Raeletta put her nose in the air and gave them her back. Sarenissa watched them both solemnly, but Bertricia laughed, one gloved hand over her mouth. At least until her companion saw her looking and tugged at Bertricia's sleeve to turn her gaze as well.

"Pay her no mind, brother. She's naught but heartbreak, that one."

Much might have changed had Cassian listened to his brother.

"Cassian?"

He looked up from the text at which he'd been staring without reading. Serenity beamed at him from in front of the desk. She held out a small basket of simplebread and a crock of butter.

"The remains of today's lesson," she told him. "I had them seed it with rosemary. I think it turned out rather well."

The fragrant bread sent a rumble through his stomach, and Cassian tore a bite from the loaf. "Thank you."

"You looked pensive," she said.

Cassian raised a brow. "Now more than any other time?"

"Yes, actually. You have for the past few days." She settled herself on the edge of the desk, one leg swinging. "You always do after Roget's been and gone, but this time it's lasted longer. You didn't come to the morning meal, nor the noontime. It's not like you to miss meals."

He broke off another piece of simplebread and buttered this one thickly before biting. "I've been busy. No more than that."

Her wordless murmur didn't sound convinced. Cassian forced himself to meet her gaze so she couldn't accuse him of looking away. Serenity looked back.

"Roget has ever been my friend," Cassian said at last.

"Friends are those who feel comfortable in telling us what they think we need to hear, not always what pleases us."

Cassian scowled. "At what point are you pressing?"

Serenity smiled at his irritation. "I believe you've spent so long in the company of women whose duty is to not pluck that you've grown too accustomed to never being so poked."

"I assure you, I've plenty of thorns pricking me on a daily basis."

She laughed. "Ah, but a flower is made more beautiful by its thorns."

A sharp crack against the glass turned both their heads. He was at the window before she could get there. The glass hadn't chipped but rattled a little more loosely in the wooden frame than it might have moments before. He saw naught but the kick of small feet and dust as whatever creature had lobbed the ball ran away, leaving it behind. Serenity peered over his shoulder and stayed at the window some moments longer as Cassian returned to his desk.

"Was that Kellen?"

"I would guess so. Him or his conspirator."

She laughed gently. "They're hardly that. Lads only, and young at that. They've little enough time to play, much less conspire. You should talk with them about the consequences of carelessness."

He sat back in his chair with a lifted brow. "I wasn't aware they were my responsibility."

"Cassian," Serenity chided and returned to her spot on his desk's corner. "I love to dance as much as any, but the steps of this gavotte are tiresome."

He pushed the basket of simplebread back toward her. "Did you come to bribe me into giggling over my secrets with you? Because it won't work."

"Because you can't be bribed?"

"Because," he said, "I have no secrets."

Serenity shook her head. "How long have I known you?"

"I don't keep count of such things." He crossed his arms and put his feet up on the desk, already knowing her reply.

"A long time. Since before you were a priest and I a Handmaiden. Do you forget we have also been longtime friends?"

"As I said. No secrets."

"Not from me. Not from Roget. But . . . there are others from whom you've kept much."

He looked toward the window without meaning to and bit down on the inside of his cheek at Serenity's triumphant look. "You speak of the boy."

"I do."

He shook his head, silent.

She sighed and pulled a hunk of simplebread from the loaf. Forgoing butter, she bit, then winced and swallowed. "Invisible Mother, that's dry. No solace to be gained from that, to be sure."

"Butter helps."

She put the bread down and hitched closer to him. "Would it be so difficult for you to acknowledge him?"

"To what end?"

"A boy needs a—"

"Hush," Cassian ordered. "If you would seek to truly be my friend, hold your tongue."

"The influence of a man," Serenity said. "Kellen is a bright lad, with much promise. A true Blessing, Cassian."

She knew as well as he the boy might not be a Blessing, really, for any reason other than fortuitous timing. Cassian closed the text he'd been pretending to study when she came in. Serenity stared at it, then him.

"Have you no desire at all to know him?"

"I know him as well as I need to know him."

Serenity sighed again. "She's not coming back, you know."

At this he stood so suddenly the chair flew back and hit the wall behind him. "You and Roget! Are you in league with him?"

Startled, Serenity hopped off the desk and landed on her twisted leg. She almost fell but righted herself with a grip on the desk. Frowning, she focused on him.

"If he said the same, it's because we both speak the truth. Bertricia isn't coming back to the Motherhouse. Kellen needs a parent. You're the one he has!"

There it was between them. Cassian sewed his mouth closed on a retort and jerked away when Serenity came 'round the desk to touch his sleeve. He refused to look at her, as well, no matter what she might accuse.

He moved from her to stalk toward the closet at the back of the room and return the text. "You can't know it."

"*She* believes it."

This stopped him, and he turned. "She's been in contact with you?"

Serenity nodded after half a breath. "She writes to me upon occasion."

"What does she say?"

"What do women say when they write to each other?"

He kept his mouth from a sneer only by forcing himself to blankness. "I'm not a woman beginning or end, Sarenissa. I don't know."

If the use of her name from before her life in the Order startled her, she didn't show it. "She writes of daily charms. Of the weather, of conversation. Of her life, Cassian. Her happy life."

He swallowed a rush of bitterness. "Not of . . ."

Me, he'd almost said and choked it back.

"Not of the boy? No. She knows he is in good care, here. And she has . . ." Serenity hesitated for longer this time.

He turned to face her. "What? Don't call yourself my friend and then not finish. Tell me."

"She has someone, Cassian."

"Yes. A patron. I know."

It was Serenity's turn to shake her head. "Not only a patron."

He could no longer keep his neutral mask. The sneer twisted his mouth, and Cassian covered it with one hand, but only for a moment. The taste of simplebread crumbs turned his stomach.

"She's not coming back, and even if she did, what would you do?"

"I would . . ." He cleared his throat and then again. The chime had sounded for the afternoon lesson. They wouldn't be alone for much longer.

Serenity gazed at him overlong before she sighed again. "You would what?"

"I would ask her to forgive me."

She showed no surprise at his words. She nodded as the door opened and young women, led by their chatter, began to enter. She moved closer to touch his sleeve only, knowing him well enough not to try for a more intimate embrace than that.

"How could she, when you won't forgive yourself?"

Then with another tug on his sleeve, Serenity moved through the gaggle of novitiates and out of the room. Cassian watched her go. He folded the towel over the remains of the simplebread. He smoothed the front of his jacket, though nary a wrinkle dared mar it.

He faced the room.

"Good afternoon, Master Toquin," Wandalette said cheerfully.

"Good afternoon, Wandalette." His voice, steady, betrayed nothing, yet she looked at him with some astonishment. "Yes?"

"You . . ." she hesitated.

Cassian, having no more patience today than any other, and in fact in possession of rather less, raised a brow. "Yes?"

"You never say good afternoon, or call us by our names!"

"Pull out your texts," came his reply. And then, spying her at the back of the room, "Ah, Mistress Marony. I believe I've a chore for you today, after class."

She nodded. Neither of them gave any indication they noticed the low buzz his words had produced among the other novitiates. Annalise looked at him from across the room, her pale eyes heavy lidded and thoughtful, and then she turned her attention to the book in front of her as though she might study the words he knew full well she'd long ago memorized.

Roget's accusation that he never faced temptation had shamed Cassian into asking Annalise to assist him, and now Serenity had forced him to thinking of much he didn't wish to know. He was in no mood to parry with Annalise, but it had been done and there was no going back now. Roget would be back again in a sixmonth or so, on his rounds to serve at all the Sisterhouses. By then the woman would be gone, one way or another.

Cassian had meant what he said when he told Annalise he didn't believe she'd ever be granted a patron. She was not the sort to bend. The question, therefore, was would she break, instead?

Chapter 13

Their time with him ended, the other novitiates left for the afternoon service with backward glances and hushed speculation Annalise ignored. Only when the door had closed behind them did she move to the front of the room, where he sat behind his desk. He'd been staring out the window the entire time.

"You needed me?"

"I need your assistance." Toquin gestured toward the closet at the back of the room. "We have texts to sort, I believe."

Annalise looked toward the closet, then at him. "Why now?"

His brow furrowed. "Plead your mercy?"

"Why do you want to sort them now, when you did not before?"

"Why do you question what I want and what I don't?"

She smiled at the rise in his inflection. He was not so cold as he'd like to feign. The question would be whether prodding him to anger would be better than enduring his disdain.

"Because I am insufferable," she suggested.

Toquin stared a long moment before answering. "You take pride in being so?"

"Should one take pride for what one cannot take credit?" Annalise asked coyly, testing him further with a drop of her lashes, the slightest jut of her hip.

Ah. He noticed that, sure enough, for his eyes narrowed and his mouth thinned just the barest bit. He noticed, and did not like it. It was different, his reaction, not the bored irritation the others wrung from him.

"You claim no credit is yours, yet you could change that quality."

"Oh, I've tried, with little luck. It's going to be the most difficult task I've faced here," she told him honestly, yet with the intention of teasing. "Perhaps that and . . . humility. Perhaps that, too."

"So much for proving me wrong."

Ah, that slap stung, and was well-deserved. "I spoke out of turn that day."

"Only that one?" He got to his feet, big boots thumping the boards.

He smoothed the front of his jacket, toying briefly with the flash of red at his throat and then at the sleeves, pulling them to fully cover his wrists. He was meticulous in his grooming, but Annalise thought it was meant to distract her more than tidy himself.

Distract her from what?

"Why do you wear that?" She pointed at his jacket.

Toquin looked at himself, then at her. "Why do you wear that?"

"It's what I've been assigned to wear. It's a uniform."

"So is my choice of garment."

She laughed. "Really? A uniform for what? Is that what men would wear if they allowed them to join the Order instead of merely working for it?"

Incredibly, he laughed. So briefly it might have been a sneeze, but nevertheless, a chuckle. Toquin looked as surprised as Annalise felt.

"It could be. I find it . . . comfortable."

"It's not fashionable, that's for sure. Though I'm fair certain you might set such a fashion should you ever present yourself in finer company than what you find here." She looked him up and down. "It suits you."

"I find the company in the Motherhouse as nice as any."

"Ah, you'd have me think you've had other company then, sir, and I know for a fact this is untrue." Annalise leaned against his desk, her fingers gripping the polished wood and the edge of it firm against the backs of her thighs.

"I have company enough. The closet, Mistress Marony."

She sighed. "It excuses me from afternoon services, yes?"

"Do you wish to be so excused?"

"I do indeed." She lowered her voice as though to tell a secret, when in fact she meant only to encourage him to lean. "I find myself fair weary of them, altogether."

He made a noncommittal noise and did not lean as she'd hoped. "Your presence is not required at services."

"But everyone stares if you don't attend."

One corner of his mouth twitched. "How can they stare if you're not in attendance?"

"They stare later, and drop remarks about how much you were missed. Women have a way of cutting to the quick of things with even a dull blade."

"Indeed." He looked over her shoulder. "The closet? Must I remind you of your task?"

"You might show me to refresh my memory," she said, though she needed no such thing.

Toquin sighed, broad shoulders rising and falling. "You'd have me believe you need instruction now? I am to believe such a charade? Tell me, think you I'm a fool?"

"I think you'd like to tell me how you wish the books sorted, and I fully believe you'd leap at the chance to chastise me for doing it in any way but yours."

Ah, she had him, now. He bristled for a moment before smoothing his features. He moved a little closer and she kept her smile from giving away the fact of her small victory.

"You cannot argue with me," she murmured and this time, he did lean. Just a bit. "You know it's true."

His fingers twitched, not quite fisting. Annalise bit her lower lip and kept her eyes innocent. He narrowed his. He knew her game, she thought with a small tingle of expectation. But would he play it?

"Come into the closet with me, and I will show you how I wish the task to be completed."

She nodded and waited until he'd brushed past her before she followed. Inside the closet, he turned to face her. He put a hand on the shelf at the level of her hip. His fingertips brushed the stack of texts. Annalise moved a little closer.

"Are you ready?" he asked.

"For every lesson you mean to teach."

She watched the bob of his throat as he swallowed. The air in the closet was thick and warm. She could smell him—and Annalise swallowed hard, herself.

"The texts, as you pointed out, have fallen into disrepair. I want you to sort the ones that might be salvaged from those that are unusable. The ones with no damage put aside on a separate pile." He slid a fingertip along the shelf, gathering dust. "You might clean in here, while you're at it."

She blinked prettily. "Oh, the honor."

He blinked, too, and turned his head. To hide a smile? Land Above, the man was worse than difficult.

"And am I to use *my* judgment as to the condition of the texts, or yours?"

"Mistress Marony," Toquin said in a low voice, "you plague me apurpose."

She fought a smile and kept her eyes wide. "Oh, never."

He pulled a book from the pile and took it to the table beneath the window. "Come here."

Annalise had hidden her grin by the time he looked at her. She took her place beside him, standing close though he shifted almost at once. Almost.

"You tell me if you think this text is to be saved, destroyed, or repaired." He touched it with one fingertip, sliding it in front of her.

She flipped open the cover then riffled the pages. "You know I must do more than peek at it. I must actually pay attention to each page to be sure they're unblemished. This is not a task for one afternoon."

"I didn't intend it to be."

"I do need your opinion," she told him seriously. "Not because I don't know enough, but because it's necessarily a task for two."

He said nothing, and she drew in a breath. He'd known it when he gave it to her. She'd thought herself the mistress of this game, but was she, truly?

"Don't tell me a cat's stolen your breath," he said.

"No. Not a cat."

She'd spoken in honesty, not to tease. His gaze flashed, mouth thinning, and though many times she'd meant to poke him into anger, she regretted it now. She moved when he did, blocking his way.

"Move," he told her.

"I meant no insult!"

"Get out of my way or I'll move you myself."

Annalise stood her ground, chin lifted, eyes boring into his face though he wouldn't meet her gaze. "No."

He looked at her then, his eyes flat and glittering with fury, his mouth set so grim the near smile he'd given before seemed like some sad dream. "I said—"

"I know what you said," she interrupted. "Stop. Would you listen? Why do you take such offense to such . . . levity? Such meaningless jest? You're not a man to be moved by worthless flirtation. I know this about you."

"You don't know me."

The words she'd thrown at him now bounced back, and Annalise discovered how much they could hurt. She flinched, but stayed in place. He was so close now she could feel his breath on her face, the heat of their bodies even through layers of cotton and wool.

She was not the sort to stammer and was mortified to find herself doing so now. "I spoke what leaped from my tongue without thought."

"It was not a cat that stole your breath."

"No," she said in a murmur that was the loudest she could speak, without additional intention. "It was you."

"Tell me the first principle." His voice had pitched low, too.

The tiny room had grown sweltering. Annalise tasted sweat when she swiped her tongue over her lips. She could see it beading on the top of his and couldn't stop herself from wondering what he would do if she licked it and how it would taste.

"What?"

"The first principle. Tell me." He'd not yet gripped her, but neither of them was moving.

"There is no greater pleasure than providing absolute solace."

She breathed out. He breathed in.

"And the mantra?"

She couldn't think of it at once, and he grew impatient, scowling. It should've frightened her. He meant it to, she was fair certain of that. It would have scared others in her position. It only made her want to kiss the expression away.

"You've studied it. But do you believe it?"

"I'm told I must," Annalise whispered without looking from his eyes. Those deep, dark eyes in which she was going to drown.

"No. Not must. It's not a question of must, or need. It is a simple question of belief. There is no greater pleasure than providing absolute solace. Do you believe it?"

She paused for a breath and nodded, surprised by her answer. "Yes. I do."

"Then how," he said with grit in his voice, a snarl on his mouth, "do you ever expect to grant it to someone when all you can ever find it within yourself to do is taunt?"

"I wasn't taunting you!"

Toquin stepped back at the cry. Annalise moved with him, so no distance grew between them. He turned his face again, but she took his chin in her hands and forced him to look at her.

Fast as anything, Toquin grasped her wrists and yanked her hands from his face. It didn't hurt, his hands if anything were big enough to encircle and bind her without actually touching her flesh. But the swiftness of the motion, the fierceness of it, startled a gasp from her.

Her heart thudded, marking time with thunder in her ears as she waited for him to speak. Or to strike. The violence in his eyes hinted it could be either.

"What I said was the truth," she told him at last. "All else, yes, I'll admit I did it to tease. To make you do . . . something. Anything. Even to rouse to anger, since that would be better than having you look at me like . . ."

His fingers tightened. His thumbs pressed the pulsing point on the insides of her wrists. He felt it, she could see it in the glance he cast there before his gaze returned to hers.

"Like what?" Deep and low, rough as gravel, smooth as river-tumbled rocks. That was his voice. Hard as his gaze that pinned her hard enough to make her wonder what by the Void she'd been thinking in ever seeking to tempt this man.

"Like I don't matter," Annalise whispered. "As though I mean naught to you."

How did they shift so that their bodies aligned? That his hands still bound her wrists between them, but his face was so close to hers she could have counted his lashes had they not been so thick? And how had she lost control of this situation?

"But you do. Mean naught to me."

Annalise twisted her wrists in his grasp, not seeking release but proving she knew him to speak a lie. "Then let me go."

For a bare second she thought he would. That in fact he might not only release her but thrust her from him so that she stumbled. It was there, that possibility, in the heat of his eyes and set of his mouth.

He did not let her go.

Her lips had already parted when he kissed her and his tongue slid inside without warning. Without resistance. He kissed her like he meant to eat her up, and Annalise leaned into it, open, eager, and gave him everything he seemed so determined to take.

Only then did his grip bruise her, but by then she didn't care. His hands found her hips; hers linked at the back of his neck, beneath the softness of his hair. He bent her, turning, one hand sliding between her shoulders to support her even as he pushed her onto the table.

He used his chin to nudge hers up so he could get at the small sliver of her throat exposed above her high collar. His teeth nipped. Annalise bit down on her gasp, willing to risk nothing that would stop him from his task. She arched, her fingers threading through his hair, holding him closer.

His hands moved over her body, breasts, hips, thighs, belly. The table cut into the backs of her thighs, but she didn't care. He pushed between her legs as she settled atop the table, thighs wide to receive him. The heavy folds of her gown got in the way, as did the length of his jacket.

He captured her mouth again and they kissed for a long time as he held her close. So Annalise said naught even when she wanted to speak. To say somewhat that would draw him to her. Instead she let her hands and lips and tongue, her eyes, meeting his, urge him to continue.

He groaned, his forehead dropping to hers. His hands ceased their roaming. His breath, sweet with mint, caressed her face. He'd closed his eyes, his lips parted.

Annalise froze with the thunder of her heartbeat making her deaf. They were tangled, limbs and clothes, yet she dared not move even to pull him closer, for fear he'd pull away entirely.

She'd never been with a man who seemed so desperate for her, yet so determined to deny himself. Moments ago she'd been certain he would take her there on the table and now . . . now she could feel the twitch and strain of the muscles in his back and shoulders as he kept himself from doing so.

It was her gown, she realized, and his jacket. There was no flipping up of skirts here. Too much material bunched between them, and even if he were to get her skirts past her thighs, what was he to do about his own clothes?

With other lovers, she'd have laughed at this predicament, but such an act would send him from her. She knew it. Her body strained, too, singing with the pleasure his touch had already brought.

"I—" she began, uncertain what she meant to say, and then he moved.

Swift and steady, graceful, he pushed away from her to slide her skirt to her hips, where he grasped her to shift her rear to the table's edge. Annalise gasped, fingers clutching at his shoulders to keep her balance. She needn't have worried. Cassian—her pleasure-sodden brain refused to call him Master—had her firm in his grip. He would not let her fall.

And then, sweet Sinder's Arrow, he was on his knees in front of her. No more hesitation. He drew his mouth over her knee and the inside of her thigh as she twitched at the sensation of wet heat against her flesh.

He was going to—oh, sweet Arrow. His mouth found her center, that dark sweetness so long unfulfilled. He kissed her there the way he'd kissed her mouth, with skilled hunger and delicately probing tongue.

She cried out then, unable to keep herself from it even if it should send him from her. Annalise dug her fingers into the thickness of his dark hair. Her hips tilted. His tongue found her clitoris and stroked it; his lips in the next breath tugged gently while his hands held her still despite the squirming.

This, she'd not imagined. That he would so pleasure her, take the place on his knees. No, she'd not thought it of him, and very quickly, Annalise could think of naught else. His mouth, tongue, lips, the heat and wetness against her own heat. It had been too long without such ecstasy, and her body responded quickly. She tipped herself against his mouth.

Now the words came, a slew of them tripping off her tongue in slow whispers of encouragement. *Yes*, she said. *Like that. Just that way.* He did what she said, and more, until she could no longer keep gathered the many glittering stars of her pleasure.

She let them go.

She sank into desire, consumed by it for the span of heartbeats and gasps she couldn't count. Her fingers tightened, pulling. She thought she heard him gasp but could do naught but ride the waves of ecstasy until, shuddering, she could at last see and hear again.

Blinking, she looked down at him. Men had smiled at her from this place between her legs. Most had crawled up her body to slide inside her. Smiling, she reached to cup his cheek.

None had jerked away from her touch as though her hand were made of fire.

Toquin got to his feet. His hair fell over his face. He didn't push it away. He paused for a moment, his hands on the table to either side of her hips.

"Your mercy. I should not have—" Voice like gravel, he cut himself off. Then, incredibly, gave Annalise a half bow and turned on his heel.

She was faster than she'd thought she could be after pleasure had so weakened her knees, but she got to him before he'd even opened the closet door. Her hand pushed it closed as he tugged it, and he turned, back to the door, eyes wide for but a moment before they narrowed.

"I'm warning you—"

"What?" she snapped, fair grateful though surprised to discover she had a voice with which to challenge. Her hand pressed the door, palm flat.

Her arm wasn't long enough to reach around him without also pressing her body against his. He could have pushed her away. He was big enough, strong enough. She'd felt that strength in his grasp already, knew what he was capable of doing.

He didn't move.

"Your mercy," he began again, and she cut him off with a shake of her head.

"I do not grant you mercy. What are you thinking? That you can so . . ." *Ravish* was not the right word, for she'd been a more-than-willing participant in the lovemaking, such as it was. "That you could perform such an intimacy without a word, without . . ."

Annalise sputtered to a stop. Both were breathing near as fiercely as they'd been just before when he was kissing her. The heat hadn't faded. If anything, it was greater, as she could feel the bulge of his cock against her belly. She pressed her hand harder on the door to keep him from opening it even a crack. She pressed her body to his, too.

His eyelids fluttered. She saw it, though he forced his gaze steady so fast she'd have missed it had she not been staring so keenly into his gaze. He licked his mouth. Drew a breath.

"How can you leave with the taste of me still on your lips?" she whispered. "How can you walk away from me without even a word?"

"I assure you, it can be done." His voice cracked on the words, making them a sweet lie that brought her no pleasure for knowing they were so.

"No." She shook her head. Leaned against him. Her own gaze grew heavy lidded, her mouth parting, inviting his kiss. Between them, the thickness of his cock grew.

She stood on her toes to kiss him, and at the last moment he turned his face so her lips found the corner of his mouth. Without taking her hand from the door, Annalise used a fingertip of the other to press his chin. To turn his face toward hers.

This time, he didn't push her away.

Chapter 14

The knock on the door behind his back saved him. The sound of it pushed them apart, Annalise taking two stumbling steps back as Cassian turned to face the door, gripping the door handle to keep it from opening. She muttered an invective that should have offended him, but didn't.

"Annalise? It's Tansy! Are you in there?"

Desire had blurred his vision, and Cassian blinked to clear it. Annalise had backed up another few steps, almost to the table where he'd . . . where he had . . . Cassian swallowed.

He could still taste her.

She turned her back on him, her hands seeking the pile of books. He opened the door. Tansy, on the other side, let out a squeak of surprise. Her gaze hit him midchest, then rose to his face.

"Oh, Master Toquin, I was looking for Annalise!"

He stepped aside to allow Tansy to pass. His back straight, shoulders squared, his groin aching. He didn't look toward either of the women in the room too small for three.

"Good day," he said.

"Master Toquin," Annalise began, but he couldn't stand there and listen to the sweet syrup of her voice.

He couldn't look at her face, even as his tongue swept lips still flavored with her. He left. She didn't, thank the Arrow, follow.

The hall was crowded, novitiates, Sisters, and Mothers-in-Service all leaving the afternoon service and moving toward the dining hall for supper. He'd taken the wrong route, but kept his steps steady and swift. None stood in front of him. All moved out of the way. And if they whispered about him as he passed, Cassian made certain not to listen to what they said.

In the peace of the yard he pumped a bucket full of icy water and plunged his hands into it, wrist deep, soaking his sleeves. He splashed his face, the water so cold it shocked a gasp from him. He spluttered, then dunked his face in the bucket.

When he came up, he had an audience. One solemn young lad, eyes wide. Kellen. The boy held an armful of paper-wrapped packages, a delivery of some sort.

"Sir?"

Cassian wiped his face with his sleeve, but as it was as wet as his skin, it did little good. "Aye, lad."

"Are you ill?"

"No." Cassian's breath blew out from between teeth that would have chattered had he not gritted them shut.

Kellen looked dubious. "You don't look good."

"Run along, lad. I'm fine."

Kellen shifted the packages. "Want I should fetch someone?"

"I told you already, I'm well!" Would the boy not leave him alone?

Kellen smiled then. "One of these packages is for me!"

There seemed to be no way to move him along without reply. "Is it?"

"It's candy. I sent away for it from the shop."

"And where did you find coin enough to pay for such a treat?"

Blessings, raised in the Motherhouse, were given all they needed. Clothes, food, shelter. Affection and discipline as required. But coin?

"Sometimes, I run errands for the ladies. Or if I help out extra in the kitchen, sometimes Cook will slip me a penny or two. Leonder is saving his for a saddle, but he hasn't a horse." Kellen rolled his eyes to show what he thought of that. "I bought some candy with mine."

"You'd be wise to save yours for the future, if not for a saddle. What good will candy do you?"

"It tastes sweet. That's all. Sometimes it's all right to have a little bit of something that does nothing but taste sweet, that's what Serenity told me." Kellen gave Cassian a shrewd glance. "Don't you like candy?"

"I cannot say I am overfond of it, no."

"That's too bad. I'd have shared a piece with you."

The boy looked too much like his mother to be borne. The same fair hair, the same spatter of freckles over the bridge of his nose. Yet there was something else to him in the manner of his walk. The tilt of his smile. Somewhat of his father in the low burble of his laughter.

Cassian looked away. He was ever looking away from what he could not bear to face. "You'd best deliver the rest of those packages, else you find yourself due for a scolding."

"I suppose I should. I promised Leonder I'd share some of it with him, if he will let me ride someday on the horse he doesn't have for his saddle." Kellen burst into giggles. "Good even, sir!"

"Good even, Kellen."

The heat in his belly had burned to a coal. His cock ached, his balls like two stones beneath it. Cassian put a hand on the pump, eyes closed, willing away the remnants of foolish desire and unable to fully rid himself of it.

Void take him, he'd been a fool. He'd meant only to push her from him, but the moment he'd bound her wrists with his hands all he could think about was holding them above her head while she writhed to the torment of his mouth and prick.

And tasting her . . . by the Arrow, he'd been a man possessed. Too eager to fuck, too blocked by their layers of clothes to get inside her, he'd gone to his knees like the greenest of lads. He could still feel her slick heat against his mouth, the tremble and quiver of her muscles as he sent her over the edge.

He'd made her do that.

Head bent, Cassian swallowed a groan so that any of his regular, curious spies upon him wouldn't overhear. He splashed more water that only chilled him and brought little relief. She had opened for him. She had moved under him. She'd given herself to him without hesitation, and he'd taken her.

And then, when he tried to walk away, she'd refused to let him.

There was nothing to make this go away. He could blame Roget for forcing the idea or Serenity for her part, but in the end the only person who could take responsibility for this was himself. He'd been weak. He couldn't take it back. The best he could hope for was to avoid her, and even that seemed unlikely, as she was not the sort to be ignored.

In the years he'd spent in service to the Order, countless young women had made themselves available to him. Some boldly, others more subtle. None had turned his head, none had forced him to lose control. He'd give her credit for that, at least.

He was by no means an expert at the Art, though he practiced every day, but he'd practice it now to keep his mind from the ache in his balls and the slowly fading flavor of female. He stripped out of his jacket—so easy when he wasn't fumble-fingered with lust! And hung the sopping garment on the pump handle. Bare-chested, trousers still uncomfortably tight, Cassian set about losing himself in the patterns he'd learned to honor his brother.

Heron in Flight became Striking Serpent and Slinking Tiger, but even though his body moved, his mind stayed in its place. Whirling. He couldn't stop thinking of her face.

"Sinder's Aching Balls," he muttered. This was useless. He gathered his jacket, slipped it still-damp and now cold over skin humped with deadman's knots.

He'd missed the evening meal, but his stomach didn't care. The low throb of ache from his unsatisfied cock kept hunger at bay. Chastity had never meant a lack of satisfaction—though he'd avoided lovemaking, he'd never denied himself the comfort of his fist.

He took a longer route to his chambers than normally necessary, seeking to avoid anyone in the halls. In his room he stripped out of his clothes and rang for the maid to take them away. Naked, he paced, thinking to distract himself, but there was no use for it.

And no shame, he told himself as he lay back on the bed, prick already in his hand. Better to do this than give in to desire, to break his vow. Better to grant himself this ease than lose himself again in that woman.

"Annalise." He couldn't say her name without her taste flooding his tongue. Cassian groaned, cock already hard, slick fluid gathered at the tip.

He painted himself with it down the shaft and cupped his sac. Then up again, palming the head while his balls tightened at a pleasure that was near pain. He hissed out a breath, eyes closed, her face in his mind. Her eyes, pale as ice, those lips the color of crushed berries. Her maiden lips had been the same dark hue, as sweet as berries, slick with her own honey. Her clit a tight knot under his tongue.

Ah, Land Above, he wanted to feel her beneath him. She would scald him when he sank inside her. His hand was a poor substitute for her heated depths, but he gave himself up to the images of her his mind provided while he used both hands to work at his cock.

Her breasts would be a bounty. Her nipples tight and begging for his tongue. The same color as her cunt and mouth, mayhap, or a paler shade against the dusky cream-lightened cacao of her skin. She would writhe when he sucked. Writhe and jut her hips up to take him all the way in to the root.

His fist was too dry, even with the help of the fluid leaking from the tip of his cock. He licked his palm and fingers, thinking of how he should have used them inside her while he lapped at her clit, and how if he had he'd be able to taste her on his skin, now.

Wet, his fist closed around his cock and he pumped into it. Feet on the floor, knees bent, eyes closed, sheets wrinkling with every stroke. If he fucked her in his bed, they would tear it apart and leave naught but tangled blankets in their wake. He would take her with the softness of the pillows beneath her buttocks to lift and tilt her tunnel so he could plunge balls-deep.

He said her name again, a low growl that embarrassed him though nobody was there to hear. His hand was her body. His mouth parted to taste a memory. He imagined her low, snagged-silk voice whispering his name, then crying it out loud.

Begging him. Begging for his mouth, hands, tongue . . . teeth. Ah, by the Arrow, he wanted to fill her with every part of himself. He wanted to ruin her. Own her.

He came at the thought of that, at last, pleasure boiling up from his balls and out his cock. Sticky heat on his fingers and his belly, the sea-smell of his desire making him gasp. And once more her name forced itself up his throat and over his tongue to hang in the air, a shameful reminder of his utter and complete loss of control.

Breathing hard, Cassian let his hand rest on the stickiness coating his belly. He couldn't remember the last time he'd brought himself off in such a fashion, hard and fast and needy. Greedy.

A thought came to him, so startling his eyes shot open and he sat so fast his head spun. He'd not thought of Bertricia once. Annalise had so filled his mind there'd not been room for memories.

With the ache in his cock and balls eased, Cassian nonetheless felt no weight had been lifted. He would still have to face her on the morrow, and now she knew how to urge a reaction from him. Or thought she knew. He had no hopes she'd not press the advantage.

At the basin, he washed himself and pulled a cotton night rail from the armoire. He didn't know if he should wish for sleep so that he might escape into dreams, or if he should hope they eluded him. It could go either way.

At least, he thought with a glance at the bed, he might not make an adolescent of himself, spending himself in his sleep.

The knock came at the door and he strode to it, intending to send the maid who'd come for the clothes off to bring him some bread and ale from the kitchen. Of course he flung the door wide, a command already on his lips. Of course it was not the maid outside.

"Annalise."

He sounded lost even to his own ears. There was no doubt she heard it, too. He wanted her to give him that smirking smile so that he might push her aside with anger, but all she did was tilt her head in that maddeningly charming fashion.

"Will you let me in?" Annalise asked.

And he did.

His room was luxurious more by its size and obvious touches of his long-term residence than by any of the furniture or decorations. It suited him, spare and functional, with hidden touches of beauty in unexpected places. A tapestry hanging on one far wall, the carved wood of the armoire. The bedding.

The rumpled bedding.

Annalise looked at it, then him, taking in the tangle of his hair and wetness around the neckline of his night rail. He would be naked beneath it. The thought dried her mouth and throat so as to fair choke her when she swallowed.

He was looking behind her, to the hall beyond.

"There's no one," she told him. "If you're worried someone might see."

He closed the door but didn't turn right away to look at her. This was familiar to her now, the way he avoided her gaze. Even after bringing her to climax with his mouth, he couldn't look at her face.

"It is of nobody's concern who I entertain in my quarters," he said.

"Even so, I'm assuring you of my discretion."

He locked the door and put his back to it, not leaning but straight and stiff as brick. "It's not necessary."

Annalise frowned. "I'm fair certain it is, else you'd not be so insistent that it's not. Tell me, Master Toquin, can you not simply accept my consideration? Must you fight at everything I offer?"

She wasn't prodding him to anger, like the other times. She was tired of that at the moment. The game had gone too far, the prize won and she uncertain of its value.

He nodded. "Thank you. Yes. I appreciate your consideration."

They faced each other, and though his gaze would not settle upon hers, he wasn't turning aside his face. He went to the armoire and pulled out a handful of clothes, then disappeared into the privy chamber without a word. Annalise, never one to allow herself to not be made comfortable, spent the time he was gone to acquaint herself further with his room.

A spare few books on the shelves, not a one of them religious. No portraits, no sheaves of letters tied with ribbon. Nothing to indicate he had, or ever had, a lover. Nothing to show, in fact, he had anything but the Order.

The armoire door gaped and she peeked inside, expecting to see a row of somber dark outfits. The puddle of crimson silk draped over a hook at the back gave her pause. She ran the material through her fingers, jerking her hand back at the last moment when Toquin appeared and shut the door without waiting overlong for her to remove it.

"You were a priest?"

He nodded. He'd put on a pale shirt, open at the throat and loose-sleeved. Dark trousers. Nothing close to fashionable and yet suiting him as much as the severity of his normal wear but in a different way.

"That explains much."

"Does it?" He scowled, brows knitting. He made certain the armoire shut with a click before he backed off. "Do you always invite yourself to peruse the belongings of strangers?"

"Are we strangers?" She glanced from the corner of her eye. Maybe such a sideways look would keep him from spooking.

"I—"

"You do not impress me as the sort of man who oft finds himself without words, and yet with me you would insist upon cutting them in half. Why is that?"

He moved away from her to a table by the window, where he fiddled with the cork on a glass bottle. "It has been my experience with you from the start, Mistress Marony, that you have words aplenty so that I need none."

She laughed. "Is that so?"

"It is."

"I would not presume to speak for you, sir."

His fingers stroked the bottle but didn't open it. He looked out the window, avoiding her. She crossed to it to make a show of looking out, too, and caught his glance when they both turned.

"I didn't come here to spar with you. You might find that difficult to believe, but it's true," Annalise said.

He sighed, not the reaction she'd expected or hoped for. "Tell me, then, your reason? For I suspect you'll not leave until you've had your way, no matter how gained."

She didn't want his words to sting, but they did. She straightened her shoulders. "I think we need to talk about what happened."

He did look at her then, straight on. "That was a mistake."

Again his words pricked her. She swallowed to keep her voice from cracking in her reply. “I don’t agree.”

“If I declared that the sun rises in the morn and sets at even, you wouldn’t agree.”

So untrue and yet she could find no blame for his statement, not based on anything that had gone between them thus far. Hateful tears pricked her eyes. This was not why she’d come. This wasn’t what she wanted.

Vision blurred, Annalise stumbled at the doorway only to discover his hand upon it the way hers had kept him from escape earlier in the closet. He wasn’t touching her, but she felt the heat from his body against her back. She waited until he retreated before she turned.

“I plead your mercy,” he said. “That was cruel.”

She blinked rapidly, but the tears would not be held back. She swiped at them, angry and mortified that she should so break down, now of all times, when he was actually being kind. His thumb touched her cheek, capturing a silver droplet he lifted and rubbed away with his forefinger.

“Please don’t cry.”

So of course she did, bursting into ungainly, unattractive, and wholly inappropriate sobs. Annalise covered her face, but strong hands guided her to a seat upon a chair made of strong thighs and backed by a broad chest. And oh, that it should be him who so comforted her only set her to further weeping as she pressed her face to his soon-sodden shirt.

Maybe her tears softened him, or like her, he was tired of the battle. All she knew was that his arms rocked her gently until she ceased her sobbing and curled into his warmth.

“Have you finished?”

She pressed her cheek to the damp fabric and smiled. “Will you let go of me if I say yes?”

“So swiftly you may find yourself upon the floor.”

"Then no. I think I shall cry the rest of the night."

He sighed, this time not so wearily and tugged at her braid until she looked at him. "Annalise . . ."

Again, he sighed, and shifted, but she held fast to her place on his lap and he didn't seem intent upon tumbling her to the floor, no matter his threat. "Cassian."

He frowned but didn't correct her.

"It's a lovely name."

He raised a brow. "I take no credit for it, my mother named me."

"Your mother had good taste."

"So my father always said."

"I like you when your tone is light," she told him softly and put her hands on his shoulders, just lightly so as not to ruin whatever this was between them.

Cassian. The name suited him. He traced the line of her brows with one fingertip before letting his hand drop back to the small of her back to keep her in place. Her weight might've begun to press upon his legs, but he showed no sign of it.

"A smile would suit your mouth, as well," she teased.

"My face aches when I smile."

"For a man whose curmudgeonly reputation is outranked only by the rumor he likes to make women cry, you have a merry sense of humor. Subtle, but merry nonetheless."

His mouth didn't even twitch. "It's not true."

"It is, I heard your jest not half a moment ago."

He shook his head. "No. The rumor isn't true. I don't like making women cry. I despise it. It is, in fact, a weakness, Annalise, and one I strive desperately to keep secret, so that none might take advantage of me with it. And yet now you know. Why do you suppose that is?"

"I don't know. Why do you suppose you told me?"

"Because," he said gently and pushed away a tendril of her hair clinging to her damp cheek, "if I did not tell you of my own accord,

I have no doubt you would pull it from me in your own good time the way a medicus hunts for a splinter in a festered wound."

She wrinkled her nose. "What a disgusting and unflattering comparison, and yet, sir, how much better does the wound feel when the splinter's been removed?"

"I've been fortunate enough to never have earned a wound such as that."

"You wouldn't want one," she told him and slid her fingertips along his throat to the back of his neck. She didn't link them. She didn't want him bolting away as though she'd bound him.

"No, I daresay I would not."

"Cassian." She rolled the name on her tongue. "Are you telling me you are not the man everyone believes you to be?"

It was the wrong question. He got up, not tumbling her from his lap but setting her neatly on her feet so she had to grab the front of his shirt. He put his hands over hers to loose her grip, and she didn't force it upon him.

"Is anyone ever the person everyone else thinks they are?"

"You think I am brash, persuasive, and slightly wanton," she said.

It had been a guess, based on what she'd been told by others in the past. Cassian's gaze flickered. She'd hoped to see another glimmer of a smile, even the tiniest hint, but nothing. He shook his head.

"You have no idea what I think of you, Annalise."

"So tell me, then." She watched him go back to the table, this time to take the cork from the bottle and pour. "Worm? I'd no idea you so indulged."

"I haven't in a long time. But as this seems the night for indulgence, I might as well. I have but the one glass, I'm afraid."

"I could drink from yours."

His gaze flashed again, and then he nodded. "As you said, we are no longer strangers."

They both drank, one after the other, and he corked the bottle tight. He handed her the glass, half full, after only a few sips. He shook his head when she offered him more.

"No. I shouldn't."

"You think you might lose control of yourself." *Again*, she didn't add.

He nodded. "I know myself."

She put the glass down without drinking. "Cassian. We do need to talk about what happened. What this is, between us."

"This is—"

"If you say nothing," she warned, "I shall weep again. And this time I shall be forced to wail, as well."

"You would use my weakness against me?"

She grinned. "Certainly."

"Fine. Let us discuss what happened." He gestured at the chair on the opposite side of the room as he took a seat in his.

Annalise was having none of that. She hadn't ridden his face to climax, been turned aside, wept in his arms, only to sit across the room from him like two dowagers at a garden party discussing the fertilization of roses. She hitched her skirts to her thighs and straddled him.

He froze when she did, and tried to turn his face, but she moved hers so he must look into her eyes. "You find me very wanton."

"I find you . . . very much a woman." He closed his eyes a moment too long, then settled his hands upon her hips.

She wasn't certain he didn't mean to toss her off his lap again, and waited, but it appeared he only meant to shift her to a more comfortable position for them both.

"I have been a plague to you from our first meeting. I know it. But you," she said, "you have been infuriating, and apurpose, too. Don't deny it."

"I cannot."

"And yet there is something here. I feel it. You must feel it. Unless you take many women into your closet and—"

He cut his gaze from hers, and recognizing that sign of his discomfort, she stopped. “You are unlike any man I’ve ever known.”

“Because I don’t take what’s tossed my way every time it’s offered, you mean.”

“Why don’t you?”

She got the laugh she’d been after, but wasn’t satisfied by it.

“I took a vow a long time ago.”

She glanced at the armoire. “Priests aren’t required to be celibate.”

Cassian shifted her weight a little, his hands twitching. “I’m not a priest.”

“The vow came . . . after?”

“Yes.”

“I’ve never known anyone to leave the priesthood.”

“Annalise,” he said, sounding annoyed, “how many priests have you ever known?”

She thought of her childhood. “I’ve made the acquaintance of more than you could ever guess, but I suppose I’ve known not a one. Not really.”

“There are priests who leave their faith just as there are merchants who cease to sell.” He frowned. “Few speak of it, but that doesn’t mean it doesn’t happen.”

“Ah, much like the Handmaidens who fall in love with their patrons.”

“What?” He startled.

“I’ve asked about it,” she explained. “What happens to the Handmaidens who grow overfond of their patrons. Or those who bear children . . .”

“They’re called Blessings, and I assure you, they happen.”

“But nobody speaks of them.”

“Nobody denies them, if that’s what you mean.”

“It’s not.” They stared at each other. “I like you when you look at me.”

Cassian made a disgruntled noise. "I wish you didn't."

"I also wish that were so. It would save me a great deal of emotional distress if I could continue to heartily dislike you."

And then, at last, he smiled. Both sides of his mouth quirked up. Even his eyes crinkled at the corners. "I could make it so you still do."

Solemnly, Annalise shook her head. "I fear it's too late for that."

He sighed, his smile fading. She thought then he would put her from his lap again and she moved forward, this time to lock her hands behind his neck and grip his sides with her thighs, that she might imprison him. Cassian, for his part, gripped her all the tighter, and she felt again the strain of his muscles.

"There is naught to forbid us from this, Cassian."

"There is."

"Nothing formal," Annalise whispered into his ear.

He smelled so good, so delicious. The heat of his skin warmed her cheek. Layers of fabric once more separated them, but she imagined the press of him growing between them.

"I can't," he said so simply and yet in so tortured a tone she stopped herself from nipping his ear.

She pulled away to look into his eyes, and Cassian didn't look away. "Why? What happened to make you deny yourself something I know you desire?"

"I can't."

She thought on this a moment. She could've been mistaken about the press of his cock earlier. "Are you . . . have you been unmanned?"

"What?" His brow furrowed, he frowned, ever the man she'd come to know over the past few weeks. "By the Arrow, no!"

"Then why can't you?"

"I simply cannot." His expression told her he'd reveal no more.

The past few months had treated Annalise to far more denial than she liked. "I think you can. You simply don't want to."

"I would not disagree with you."

"Ah, another first for us?" She laughed curtly and shifted on his lap to press her body close to his. "Parts of you want me."

"Parts of me are not the whole."

It was her turn to sigh. "Tell me you don't want me, and I shall leave right now. This minute."

"Annalise," Cassian said, "I do not want you."

This stung worse than anything ever had. At least Jacquin had claimed he *did* want her if only he could stomach the fact she had a cunt and not a cock. Annalise got off Cassian's lap, eluding him as he grasped for her and stepping away even as he stood and tried again to hold her wrist.

"You were right. What happened was a mistake. You may plead my mercy again, if you like, and mayhap I shall grant it this time." Her voice came out jagged, but she fought the tears.

"I don't want your mercy. I want . . ."

"What? Finish a sentence and look me in the eyes, Cassian, I dare you." She stood on tiptoe to make it easier for him. "You brought me off with your mouth, have you forgotten that? Regret it if you must, but don't act as though you can't stand the sight of me! I can't bear it!"

He caught her wrist, finally, and held her from moving away. "I don't regret it."

"Well," she snapped, refusing to yank at her wrist and give him the satisfaction of the struggle, "I do!"

He let her go. "So are we to head back to discord? Will strife make it easier for you to face me?"

"Will it make it easier for you?" she retorted.

"It will indeed, as it ever has. With everyone."

"Then no. I don't wish to go back to it," Annalise told him. "I shall insist upon us being the best of friends, boon companions."

Both of his brows lifted. And again, he smiled, Void take him. Insufferable!

"It would please me," he said in a low voice, "to merit your friendship."

"Why? So we can discuss the finer aspects of the Faith? Dissect the stories? So I can take over your teaching duties and leave you to . . . stare out the window and twiddle your thumbs while I endeavor to bludgeon the simplest tenets into the heads of the novitiates?"

"It would be better than when I make them cry," he said.

"You," Annalise told him archly, "are just like every other man I've never known."

"I thought you said I was like no other."

She sniffed, though her irritation was fading. "I misspoke."

He spoke gently. "I am not an easy man to know. I have ever made it so on purpose. But Annalise, I cannot keep myself from you. I've tried from the moment I laid eyes upon you in the forest—"

"When you sought to send me astray."

"Aye, then. And still you have turned up, over and over. Until you leave the Motherhouse to serve a patron, it would seem we are bound to keep each other's company."

"You think . . . you think I shall indeed gain a patron, after all?" She didn't mean to make her voice so small, but as the tears had come earlier so now did this softness.

"I think there are few who come here who don't manage to ever be assigned, and you are determined enough, and smart enough, and lovely enough, that you shall have no trouble being exactly what someone needs."

"Someone other than you."

Cassian spread his fingers slightly. "You've heard the tale about the seamstress's children going without clothes."

If ever there was a man in need of solace, here he was before her, but Annalise didn't say so. "If we are to be friends, you might tell me about your vow."

She'd pushed him too far again. His gaze shuttered. He withdrew without taking a step.

"I would rather be your friend than your enemy," Cassian told her, "but it would seem we have equal experience being both. I shall leave it to you to decide, Annalise."

She'd wanted him near from the first moment she saw him because of his face and form. Now, seeing this small part of him she knew he revealed to so few, she wanted him for something more.

"Friendship," she said in a voice made steady so he'd not suspect her of other motives.

He smiled again, brilliantly this time, and this time, she was the one who had to look away.

Chapter 15

Three years is not such a long time to be in love, unless that love is not returned. Cassian knew the full length of that time, every measure the sun traced in the sky, every breeze that blew, every season's cycle. All of it became as nothing but a way to track how long he'd loved her. For three years, Cassian loved Bertricia, until at last, one day, she loved him back.

He knew the moment she did. It was a change in her laugh and the tilt of her smile, a shift of her gaze. She'd tolerated him before that, accepted the small gifts he gave, partnered with him during the games of snap me and quoites that characterized the annual brannigan his mother held in concord with Raeletta and Sarenissa's mother, and to which Bertricia was invariably invited. Once or twice she'd even allowed him to kiss her chastely when they walked in the garden, only ever on the cheek or the hand, and she never offered but only allowed.

And then one day, she loved him.

He could never know why. He'd never asked. He'd taken the gift of her affection without question, fearing to ask for too much explanation lest she change her mind. Decide she loved someone else.

His brother, perhaps.

Cassian would've worried less if Calvis had shown any inclination toward "she-hound the second," as he liked to call Bertricia. Calvis had an eye and taste for feminine flesh that Cassian both understood and reviled. Women, to his mind, were meant to be adored and cherished, mayhap pursued but with respect. The way he'd courted Bertricia.

Calvis, on the other hand, made his way through the women of their acquaintance like a farmer in the fields, plucking, tasting, tossing aside. Only unlike a farmer, Calvis never kept what he harvested. It had made him near irresistible.

If his brother had set his gaze on Bertricia, Cassian would've known not to fear. No woman kept his attention for longer than it took for him to bed her a few times. But as it was, Calvis never looked at her twice without curling his lip. If the two were in the same room, Calvis left it, no matter how prettily Bertricia might flutter her lashes or attempt to draw him into conversation.

"I don't understand how you can fawn and mewl over her, brother."

"I love her. It's not fawning or mewling, Calvis, it's . . . courtship."

Calvis snorted into Cassian's ear, his arms bound tight 'round his brother from behind. He'd caught Cassian in Snapping Turtle. Cassian didn't struggle to get away. It would only lead Calvis into further demonstration of his growing prowess with the Art, a pastime rapidly becoming more than a hobby.

"And do you think she'll concede to wed you, little brother?"

Cassian turned his face so he and Calvis were cheek to cheek. It was a surer way to get his brother to release him. "I hope she will. That's all I can do."

Calvis let him go. "You have nothing to offer her."

It was not the first time his brother had tried to taunt him into an argument, and Cassian's patience was wearing thin. How was it he could love his brother so much, more than any other, more than their parents, and yet grow to loathe the very sight of him?

"I have myself. I have everything to offer her."

"You're going to be a priest, Cassian. What woman wants a priest for a husband?"

"A woman of the Faith might find a priest a very fine husband."

Again, Calvis snorted. He took a few steps away, his fingers curled into loose fists he slowly raised to waist-height before putting one foot forward into one of the positions of the Art. Cassian didn't know which one. Cassian didn't care.

"Priests have no wage. What will you use to buy her those pretty gowns she so adores? The cosmetic for her face? The cream pies to stuff her gullet?"

Cassian crossed his arms, watching his brother and wondering at how they looked the same and yet were nothing alike. "Priests have their living granted them—"

"Priests do. It's not enough to support a family."

At the thought of it, a family with Bertricia—children—Cassian smiled. Calvis saw it, and scowled. He moved forward, jabbing and ducking while Cassian did little more than shift out of the way.

"Fight me, little brother."

"No."

"Fight me," Calvis wheedled. "You know you wish to."

"I don't wish to!"

"Fight me!" Another jab. Calvis circled.

Cassian stood his ground, jaw set, gaze steady. "Why? So you might take comfort from knowing you can beat me?"

"So I can take comfort from knowing you are yet a man, not a smooth-groined eunuch." Calvis danced closer, then away, forming his body into the bends and dips of the Art with greater skill than he'd had even the week prior.

"You are good at what you do," Cassian said.

This stopped his brother in place. "Are you too afraid?"

Cassian shook his head. "Why can't you accept that I'm good at what I want to do, too?"

"Being a priest?" Calvis spat the word to one side. "Is that what will please you? Shaving your head, dressing in robes, smelling of oil and incense? Spending your days in the temple or in study, dissecting ancient words written so long ago none might know their meaning but only guess at it, and your nights in the arms of a woman who will never be satisfied with what you might offer?"

"I want to speak for those who are unable!" Cassian cried, pushed at last to anger. "What is so wrong with that?"

"She will make a cuckold of you!" Calvis shouted, and was upon his brother in the time it took to exhale.

Toe to toe, eye to eye. A matched pair. Calvis began it.

Cassian was the one who ended it.

Thinking of it now, the past long gone, he remembered the pride he'd felt at beating his brother. It had been good at the time, bitter later. It was a lesson well-learned.

Things would not change, Cassian told himself and knew it to be a lie no matter how many times his mind formed the thought. Everything would change. He'd opened himself to Annalise, just the least small bit, and there was no taking it back.

All had changed already, based on the smile she gave him from her seat in the pew during morning services. She'd sought his gaze deliberately, though he stayed in the shadow of the alcove, and she found it with unerring ease. She lifted a brow, pursed her mouth, waggled her brows in a mockery of the priest on the beemah that even Cassian could not deny was perfection.

She sat down with him at breakfast, too, settling her bowl of porridge on the table and sliding into the chair across from his while he looked in shock. Then she lifted a brow and dug her spoon into the porridge as though daring him to say anything against her presence. Which of course, Cassian did not.

Not that the meal was silent. He guessed no man could remain quiet in Annalise's presence, for she would insist upon discussion. Call and answer, he thought, when she drew out of him a reply to a question he never thought he'd give.

"But which do you believe?" She spread a hot buttered scone with a thick layer of tumbleberry jam. "Of all the commentaries you've studied, which do you hold most dear?"

Cassian had chosen a plate of fried eggs and thick sausage to break his fast, but had eaten little since Annalise first sat. Now he sliced the sausage into even slices and listened carefully to the click of his knife up on the plate. "Must I choose one?"

"Yes. If you were led to the edge of a cliff and forced to decide or be pushed off, which would you pick?"

Around the room, the rows of benches were alive with wriggling, chatting women. Most of them were looking at the table he shared with Annalise. It wasn't the first time he'd been the subject of such scrutiny, but he'd always found it easy to ignore before. Now, with her there, he felt as though they sat beneath a crimson banner designed to draw every eye. Annalise didn't seem to notice. More likely, she simply did not care.

"What are my choices?"

She pointed at him with her spoon. "You tell me."

He bit, chewed, swallowed. She watched him. Cassian drank some bitter tea. "I've studied a full score and twenty different versions of the discovery story. Some differ by so bare a margin as a word or two in their interpretation. Yet you ask me to pluck one from the air as a street performer might pull scarves from a sleeve?"

"Pretty analogy." She tilted her head and gave him a smile he didn't deserve. "But not a pretty answer."

"Why is this so suddenly a topic of such import you must accost me with it over our breakfast?"

Again the smile, this time with a sly look 'round the room. "I thought mayhap it would set you more at ease to feign we are discussing topics of import rather than simply sharing a table. If you like, I can merely gaze upon you with fluttering lashes and a few winsome sighs, so that all who are watching us so indiscreetly might have something over which to gossip."

Cassian tightened his jaw and stared at his plate. "I'm well aware of how we're being observed. Would you insist upon drawing attention?"

"Cassian," Annalise said in a dropped-low voice meant for him and none to overhear, "I would not. Which is why if any should decide to listen they'd hear only a subject of what is unlikely to be of any interest."

He looked at her, the knot in his stomach easing. "Should I fear your deviousness, or admire it?"

She reached with her knife to spear a chunk of his sausage and tuck it into her mouth. She chewed it solemnly but didn't swallow before saying, "I'd prefer admiration."

The chime sounded for the end of the meal and the beginning of the day's study. They both stood at the same time. Annalise ate the last bit of her scone and licked her fingers, one by one.

He pretended not to notice.

"You didn't eat," she said.

"I found my appetite much diminished."

"By the company?" She laughed. "I should take umbrage, sir, to such a statement!"

"The company was fine," he said, surprising himself.

The room emptied quickly while they stayed in place at the table. "The conversation, then."

It had been that, but not for reasons she might think. "I'm unused to such talk first thing in the morning, that's all."

Annalise gave a soft snort he found utterly endearing. "I daresay you're unused to a good many things, Cassian."

He stared in reply. "I should go. I have groups of study to lead."

"And I," Annalise said dryly, "have napkins to fold and tea to pour. My goodness, however shall I fend off the palpitations of my excitement, I do not know."

She made it so easy to laugh, and if the laughter itself sounded like a creaking door and stuck like a cushion full of pins in his throat, it wasn't because of her. "Do your best."

She waved a hand at him. "I shall see you later this afternoon, for our study group, yes?"

"Yes."

She stood then, on tiptoe, and he thought for one wild moment she meant to kiss him right there. After all they'd said, all he'd done, she'd done, she would be so bold. But, with a bedamned grin quirking her lips, all Annalise did was pluck a few crumbs from the front of his jacket.

"There. We can't have you entertaining the scores of novitiates looking as though you had nobody to care for you."

"But I—" He began and fell to silence at the slow, small shake of her head.

"You do. Now."

The mask of blankness fought at his features; he felt it struggling to turn him into a puppet. "We agreed . . ."

"To be friends, yes?"

He was helpless against that tilted head, that quirk of her mouth. "Yes."

"Friends take care of one another, Cassian. I would expect as much from you, should I cover the front of my gown with my meal or should my smile reveal a mouthful of green. Surely you've had friends before."

Serenity was perhaps his longest acquaintance, and she'd never have dared brush his crumbs. Roget wouldn't have cared. "None like you."

Annalise laughed, bright and merry. The sound of it rang through the empty dining room. "Never a one like me. I am the only me."

"I need to go."

"You do. We both do."

Cassian watched the light fall from the window and across her hair. "I shall see you this afternoon, Annalise."

"And I," she told him, spinning on her toe and moving toward the door so he might watch her go, "shall look forward to it."

He saw her before that, at the noon meal when she again took her place at his table.

"In all the years I've been here, nobody has ever dared sit in that chair when I am in this one," he told her when she put down her plate.

Annalise arched a brow. "I wonder why? Could it have been your disposition?"

"There is a reason for my disposition." And it wasn't helped by his rumbling stomach, empty since he'd been unable to finish the morning meal. Looking at his plate of cold sliced meat, a biscuit, a side of greens, he wondered if her presence at the table would cause him to forgo this meal as well.

It hadn't dampened her appetite. Annalise tucked in with the efficiency of a sailor, managing conversation and chewing with nary a pause between bites—and yet with the most impeccable of table manners. And she talked, oh, how she talked. Of all she'd done that morn in her various studies. Of her friend Tansy, who even now was staring at them from across the room, and who'd begged an explanation from her after the morn meal and whose answer had been waved aside by Annalise, who explained around a bite of biscuit that it was nobody's business but theirs.

"I am in awe of your ability to run your mouth," Cassian said at last when she'd paused long enough and with such an expectant look he understood he was expected to reply.

"If you don't cease your pretty flatteries, I fear I shall become overenamored of my own worth."

She'd made him laugh again. "And your plate is nearly clean amongst all the chatter."

"I speak because you will not. Mayhap I eat because you do not."

He looked again at his plate and carefully folded a slice of beef inside a biscuit. "I'm eating."

She watched him silently while he chewed, then gave a soft shrug. "Do I so unsettle your stomach that you find it difficult to eat? I don't mean to."

"You could eat at a different place, as you used to." Cassian wiped the corner of his mouth, his appetite flaring to life so that he gobbled the rest of his beef and biscuit.

"And be deprived of your company? No. Besides, I like you when you talk to me."

He paused with his mug halfway to his mouth, then drank so as not to answer. This didn't mean they passed the rest of the meal in silence, only that she kept the conversation light for the rest of it. At the end of it, unlike in the morn, Annalise didn't linger overlong.

She smiled at him over her shoulder as she caught up to a few of the other novitiates, women Cassian knew by sight but not name. They bent their heads together the way women did, and he wondered if the soft rise of their laughter was directed at him.

And he wondered if being the cause of laughter was better than being the reason for tears.

Chapter 16

Tansy was giving her longways glances, never meeting Annalise's gaze but looking away every time Annalise lifted her head from the square of linen upon which she was stitching. It was fair irritating the way she did it, as though Annalise wouldn't notice. Annalise, for her part, had aching fingers, sore eyes, and a headache from squinting at the intricate design she thought would never bring a person a second's solace, no matter how pretty she made it.

"What?" she asked finally, when Tansy had looked up from her own piecework again. "I know my flower knots are uneven, but truthfully, Tansy, I need no judgment from you upon my handiwork."

"Oh, no, your work is lovely!"

Annalise watched the deep flush creep from Tansy's collar up her throat and over her cheeks. Even her forehead pinked. "What, then? You've been goggling at me since we began."

Tansy pricked at her linen square, embroidered 'round the edges with a pattern of leaves and flowers. She looked at every other woman in the room rather than meet Annalise's eyes. "It's just . . . you didn't eat with us today."

"Oh. That." Annalise looked at the work in her hands and pressed her lips together. "I'm sure I'll be at your table again. I wasn't aware you were so regretting the loss of my company."

Perdita shifted in her chair. Annalise had been wondering how long it would take her to speak. "What Tansy means to say is, why on earth were you eating with Master Toquin?"

"I like him."

There was nobody in the room who even pretended to work, now. Annalise looked at them all in turn and set aside her own piece. She rubbed at the aching tips of her fingers.

"Is it so difficult to believe I might enjoy his company?"

"Because he made you his assistant," Tansy put in helpfully with a look 'round at the other women. "Annalise is so well-acquainted with the verses—"

"Yes, yes, we know all about how wonderful Annalise is," snapped Perdita impatiently. She leaned forward to pin Annalise with a beady glare. "But really, Annalise, what we want to know is how, by the Land Above, did you get him to allow it?"

"What? Sitting with him at his table? I didn't ask his permission, first of all. I wasn't aware we had assigned seats." It was the sort of non-answer that would pinch madness into Perdita, and sure enough, the other woman's eyes flashed.

"It's not your proficiency in the Faith, is it?"

"I'm certain I don't know what you mean." Annalise spoke calmly, though she felt anything but. She felt like reaching across the space between them and slapping the smile from Perdita's fat face. "Master Toquin and I are . . . friends."

Not by her choice, and despite what he'd said, mayhap not by his. She'd tried, by the Arrow, but he'd done his best to stop her. Not with coldness or anger as had been his previous habit, but his implacable resistance to even the most mild of her overtures was disheartening, to say the least. And worse, actually, than his annoyance, for at least then he'd been reacting.

"There's naught against an instructor and a student sharing a meal," Tansy said boldly.

Annalise looked at her. "Tansy, you needn't defend me. If Perdita wishes to make much of my acquaintance with Master Toquin, she might do as she pleases. I've no issue with her queries."

"It seems so sudden, that's all." Perdita lifted the gentlemen's shirt upon which she was sewing. The work was beautiful. Even, tight stitches, soft fabric, a masculine yet fashionable design. Annalise had no difficulty imagining how a shirt such as that might bring a measure of solace to the man who wore it.

"Friendships are never sudden. They grow like flowers," Annalise said. "Which you seem to have a lovely skill for embroidering, Perdita, but not such a great skill for cultivating."

Perdita frowned. "I am quite proficient in the garden, Annalise Marony. The roses I grew at home outlasted any others in the garden, and my captain's buttons were coveted for centerpieces by all my mother's friends."

"I'm sure your skill with plants is as impressive as your every other," Annalise said serenely, focusing on her own work, "but I wasn't speaking of flowers."

Perdita looked 'round the room, first to Tansy, then at Helena and even Wandalette. "I have friends."

Annalise shrugged. "So do I."

"And you count Master Toquin among them?"

"I do."

Perdita sniffed. "Master Toquin has never fraternized with the novitiates. It doesn't seem appropriate, actually."

Annalise could no longer maintain her placid demeanor. "Speak plainly, or speak not at all."

"I speak very plainly. What I mean is, that such a friendship between the two of you seems sudden and unexpected, considering the way the pair of you were previously at such odds."

"How would you know what we were?"

Perdita smiled. "Everyone knows. We all heard about the words you exchanged in his classroom."

"It was my understanding that Master Toquin was no favorite of any. Whatever words we exchanged were naught but the usual for him, yes?"

"No," Perdita said. "Nobody ever stood up to him before the way you did."

At this, Annalise scoffed. "Oh, really? You think in all the years of service he's provided the Order that nobody, no novitiate, ever spoke back to him? Not a one? The man's insufferable and arrogant, and not all of us were bred to be meek little lambs led willingly to slaughter."

"I haven't been here as long as some." Perdita gave Tansy a significant stare. "But it's my understanding that he has ever been as he is now, and that none dared cross him."

"If he were such an evil figure, causing so much grief, why would the Mothers-in-Service allow him to stay? In an Order full of young women, most of them impressionable, bound for service to the Faith? Why on earth would they keep him on if he were so . . . so. . . ." Annalise sputtered on her lack of words. Her linen lay scrunched in a ball on her lap. It was made of ugliness and lack of skill, unfit even to wipe a nose. She wanted to toss it aside but kept it close, so as not to give Perdita the satisfaction of comparison to her own exquisite work.

"Mayhap because we should get used to such a man." Wandalette, who'd ever seemed as uncertain and awkward as a mouse, now spoke with conviction. "Because we do need to know this, us. Because it's what we'll have to face when we go out among them. To them. The patrons. Because they'll all be like him, or worse."

Silence. Every woman in the room turned to stare at Wandalette, who shrugged and bent back to threading her needle. She licked the thread and poked it through the eye, then drew the strings together with the tips of her fingers and twirled them at the bottom to make a knot. She held it up, the needle glinting, then noticed all the stares.

"How else would we learn?"

Perdita, for once, had no comment. The other girls bent back to their work, and in a few minutes the soft murmurs began again, the worthless chatter Annalise despised and had no interest in repeating. In her lap, the square of linen had not been ruined. She could save it. She could thread her needle the way Wandalette had done, and prick it through the cloth. She could imprint colored flowers on the creamy linen and make a pattern where there had been none.

She could, she thought, make beauty from something that had near been ruined, make something pretty that had seemed just moments before impossible to fix.

"I believe I'm finished," she said aloud to nobody and stood. She gathered her sewing basket and materials and put them all away. She handed them to Tansy. "I'm going for a walk."

"Do you want me to go with you?" Tansy was already on her feet, but Annalise shook her head.

"No, thank you."

Tansy looked disappointed, but Annalise didn't care. She needed to be alone for a while, to contemplate this, making something pretty that didn't seem possible.

Even a dual-headed calf ceases to gain a second glance from the people who've grown accustomed to it, and so it was with the friendship between Cassian and Annalise. She knew he didn't think so. She could tell by the way he still looked from side to side when she took her place at his table.

"Loosen yourself," she told him. "We are no longer the current fashion in gossip."

At least he was no longer holding himself from his food while she was with him. He broke off a piece of bread from the small loaf between them and slid it across to her. She looked at it for half a moment but made certain not to react in any way that might alert him to her knowing how charming she found his offer.

"I never assumed we were . . . fashionable."

Annalise sipped sharp cider from her mug, grimaced, and put it aside. She didn't care overmuch for cider and had poured it from the pitcher without thinking why. "You worry about it. I can tell."

When he got up from the table, her first thought was that she'd driven him from his seat. It wasn't an outrageous assumption to make, considering their past confrontations, and yet she hadn't meant to poke him. She stared at her plate, stomach knotted, wondering if this would ever be easy, if the effort had reward.

He returned before she had time to even look 'round. He'd brought a pitcher of water, and a new mug. He filled it for her and pushed the cider aside.

"What?" he asked, startled at the way her mouth gaped. "By the Land Above, Annalise, are you going to . . . cry?"

"No, absolutely not." She shook her head. "Tell me, sir, of today's lesson, so that I might come prepared to plague you with all the questions those other women won't think to ask."

He spoke for quite some time before noticing she'd made no reply.

". . . the passage regarding descriptions of the Land Above and the Void, both . . ." Cassian trailed away. "Annalise, are you unwell?"

She was very well. That simple act of consideration he'd shown her—something with so little meaning on the surface as to be unremarkable, yet so significant at the same time.

"I like you when you're talking about the text," she managed to say in a voice only slightly scratched.

"I am well pleased to discuss such matters with you. You know that." He looked up as the chime sounded. "And the mealtime has ended. It feels so sudden."

Mayhap she needn't try so hard, she thought as they both got up and merged with the crowd leaving the dining room. Mayhap this might happen on its own, should she cease to push so hard for it. In the hallway they both paused, Cassian's destination in one direction and hers in another.

"I shall see you this after, yes?"

She heard the inflection of her own voice in his and found it so charming she wanted to weep again. "Yes."

"Annalise." Cassian said her name slowly without looking even once at anyone passing by them to see if they might be listening. "Are you sure you're well?"

"I'm most well, thank you. I'll see you later. Go, now, else your students rebel and begin reading ahead in the texts."

"I find there little to suggest that is at all likely," Cassian said.

Annalise laughed. "You never know. I'm not the only novitiate who knows obscure bits and pieces of the Faith."

Cassian made a face. "Have I heard you aright? You are admitting to being the same as any other?"

This could not go without response; Annalise poked his chest. Hard. "I take affront at your tone."

He captured her hand before she could poke again, but whatever retort he meant to give was swallowed when a cool feminine voice interrupted them.

"Your mercy, Master Toquin, Mistress Marony. Annalise," said Deliberata with a small smile that revealed naught, "I've some letters for you."

In an instant, the warmth of his fingers vanished as he pulled away. Cassian gave the Mother-in-Service a formal half bow and one to Annalise. When he straightened, the teasing light in his eyes had vanished.

"And I must be away, as Mistress Marony so aptly pointed out to me."

"May the Invisible Mother keep you," Deliberata said.

"Today and all your others," Cassian replied after a hesitation. "Anon."

Both women watched him walk away. Deliberata spoke first. "Do you still feel you are too advanced for Master Toquin's instruction?"

"I . . . no, Mother. Actually, I've found Master Toquin a fine instructor."

Deliberata smiled. "Finer than you'd suspected?"

"Yes." Annalise paused, not eager for the older woman to question further. Not from shame on her part, certainly, but out of respect for Cassian. "He's a man of impressive intellect."

"And a fine-featured face never hurts."

Annalise laughed. "Yes, Mother, I suppose a handsome man is always more a pleasure to be around than an ugly one."

"Oh, I don't know. Ugly men seem to have their own charm. Mayhap it's because they're more used to pleasing than expecting pleasure. It makes it ever so much more satisfying to provide it."

"You speak of patrons?"

Deliberata's laugh belonged to a much younger woman. "Oh goodness, child. Not necessarily. It's been a good long time since I've had a patron, as I've made it my service to attend here at the Motherhouse. It's been far less time since I've taken a lover. Walk with me. I've your letters in my office and would give them to you at once."

"Yes, Mother." Annalise fell into step beside her. She wanted to giggle at the older woman's frank admission, but held back. When she was old and wrinkled and gray she hoped the idea of taking a lover would seem no sillier than it did to her now, even though it might to someone else.

They chatted of inconsequential things on their path to the same tidy office to which Annalise had been first admitted upon entering the Motherhouse. Inside, Deliberata pulled open a drawer and removed a packet of letters bound with a rough cord. She handed them across the desk.

"They were delayed in their delivery, it appears. The man brought them this morning from town."

"Thank you, Mother." Annalise tucked the letters into her palms and placed them against her belly.

Deliberata smiled. "Do you know how much you've improved since your arrival here, Annalise?"

This was not what she'd expected to hear. "I . . . have?"

"The young woman who arrived upon my doorstep several months ago would have fallen upon those letters like a dog tossed a bone with meat still on it."

Annalise looked at the letters. "I thought it would be unseemly for me to tear them open to read in front of you and dismiss our conversation."

"It's been quite some time since you've heard from anyone at home, and I'm fair certain you're eager to read what they've sent. I'd have understood if you preferred the company of their words to mine." Deliberata sat with her hands folded on top of the desk and gave Annalise another smile.

"I was being polite."

"It's more than being polite. I've known you to be spirited since your arrival, but never rude."

The cord scratched at her palms while the corners of the letters poked her, too. Letters, three of them, and from who? One from her parents, perhaps a sister or two? Was there a letter there from Jacquin?

She'd not written him in more than a week and should not have felt guilty for it. After all, beyond the first letter he'd sent, he'd not bothered to send another.

"It is more than being polite," Deliberata said again. "It's about finding a certain level of calm, Annalise. A certain way of being, so that no matter your eagerness to accomplish a task, you maintain the ability to assess all aspects of the situation and decide your course."

"It makes me no less eager to get to the letters, Mother, pleading your mercy."

Deliberata laughed. "Child, there is little to be done for such excitement as comes from something as special as a letter from loved ones far away. I would never prefer you to lose that joy. But I am well pleased to see how you handle yourself, and it. It shows me somewhat about you."

"Which is what?"

"That you are becoming a Handmaiden."

Fire and ice both split her at the same moment. Annalise swallowed past a sudden lump. "Mother?"

"Few arrive here with it instilled inside them. And, unlike some of my Sisters-in-Service, I'm unconvinced it can be taught to those who have no skill for it. There is somewhat special about being a Handmaiden, as you well know, Annalise. Somewhat beyond a manner of speech or deportment. Many leave the Order before taking their vows. I thought, I truly thought, you'd be one of them."

Guilt still plagued her, that Deliberata should have so seen the truth Annalise had tried to hide and yet now was no longer certain applied. "Your mercy, Mother."

"No need to apologize to me, child. Some have it. Some do not. Some want it. Some think they desire a life of Service and yet discover they cannot stomach it." Deliberata waved a hand. "We are all called to serve the Invisible Mother in ways we are never granted the ability to imagine. It's not up to us to discover them. We must rely on Her guidance to lead us to Her, and it may not be in ways we anticipate or even like.

Annalise held the letters closer to her stomach. "Mother, I think I should tell you something."

"Your vision. The one you had in the forest. The one that sent you to us."

Annalise swallowed again at the memory of the lie. "My vision."

"Your description of it was quite compelling, as I recall. I'd never heard one quite so detailed, or vivid. You must have put a lot of thought into it."

Fortunately, the Mother-in-Service had a chair on the other side of her desk, because when Annalise's knees gave out, she sat so suddenly she'd have hit the floor had it not been there to catch her.

"You know? You know I . . ." She still could not quite bear to admit a lie. "Embellished?"

"My dear, do you think you're the first young woman ever to seek sanctuary among us who's not been a true seeker of service? My goodness, I myself came to the Motherhouse to escape a particularly domineering mother and passive father, neither of whom had my best interests at heart, or so I believed in my youth. Still believe, actually." Deliberata shook her head, mouth pursing for a moment. "Many come to us with reasons that are less than pure."

"I plead your mercy. I've done what's requested of me. Most of the time."

"Ah, you've chafed at much we've asked of you. Take no shame in it. Some who come to us have no quarrel with time spent on their knees, and yet are never granted a patron."

"I should not have come on false pretense."

"Was it?" Deliberata looked at her.

Annalise opened her mouth to say yes, but stopped herself. "Was it not?"

"Did you truly go into the forest and fall to your knees in front of an image of the Invisible Mother created in the bark of a tree, which then spoke to you in a voice so terrible it caused your ears to bleed? Did She truly tell you to seek the Motherhouse and devote your life to service? Did She blind you for a day and a half, from the rise of one sun to the set of one moon, and cause Her name to be raised on your flesh in wheals of crimson?"

"No, Mother." Listening to it now, Annalise wished she'd not spent so much time on the craft of the tale. Compared to what Wandalette had said in class, Annalise's story was overblown and ridiculous.

"Ah. But does that mean that your vision was a lie?"

"None of that happened, Mother."

Deliberata raised a finger. "Sometime you might feel the need to confess your reasons, but I am not to play the part of your confessor. Tell me where you came up with the idea for that story."

"I made it up."

"All of it?"

"Yes. From the commentaries and texts I knew."

"You took bits and pieces and put them together to make your own?"

"Yes, Mother."

Deliberata's girlish laugh rang out again. She clapped. "Delightful. But ask yourself, Annalise. How did you know which bits to choose? Which to put together? How did you know how to weave that particular tapestry?"

Annalise thought about it. "I don't know."

Deliberata raised a finger. "Do you not think She had a hand in it?"

"The Invisible Mother? Kedalya?"

"Yes. Do you not think perhaps She led you to decide this path, no matter what reasons you thought you had? Do you think it possible She led you here, Annalise, to devote yourself to service so that you might do your part in bringing about the Return?"

Annalise had not, in fact, thought any such thing, but there in the Mother-in-Service's office, anything seemed possible. "Do you think that's what happened?"

"Perhaps it's not so important what I believe, as what you do."

Ah, there was the rub. Annalise's belief had gone away long ago. Stolen or lost, mayhap just forgotten.

"Think about it," Deliberata urged. "You might be surprised to learn that even a made-up story of bits and pieces is a true vision, after all. Go on, now. Read your letters. Go to your studies."

And Annalise, unexpectedly obedient, went.

One letter was indeed from her parents. All was well at home. Several of her sisters were with child. They were proud of her, of

Annalise, for taking this path and hoped that when she took her vows they would have a chance see her before she left the Motherhouse. One from Allorisa, filled with bragging of her new life.

And the third, the final and thickest letter, the one that made her fingers tremble to open . . . was from Jacquin.

Chapter 17

Annalise?" She wasn't looking at him, and Cassian realized how quickly he'd become accustomed to her attention now they'd declared the truce. "Have you something to add?"

She'd had her head bent over her desk, still at the back of the room, and now didn't look up even at the sound of her name. As one, the other novitiates turned. Concerned, Cassian made his way down the aisle to stand before her. Was she truly unwell, the way he'd thought earlier?

"Annalise?"

She looked up then, her eyes tinged with pink in a too-pale face. She wet her lips before speaking. "Your mercy, sir. I was distracted."

He looked to the desk, to the text, closed. To her journal, also closed. She had a letter spread on the polished wood, her hands flat over it. She'd smudged the ink onto her fingertips and must have touched her forehead with them, for a smear of darkness marred her dusky skin.

"Are you unwell? Ought I send one of the girls to fetch a

medicus?" He touched her shoulder, wishing instead to put the back of his hand to feel for fever but too mindful of the eyes of so many.

"I'm fine." She cleared her throat.

Her eyes said otherwise.

"You are all dismissed," Cassian said.

Annalise's eyes widened. Her mouth thinned, clamped tight on some protest he would refuse to hear. The class murmured, texts closing, papers shuffling, chairs squeaking.

"Now," Cassian said in the voice of thunder that had never let him down.

"Sir, should I fetch a medicus?" Wandalette asked from his elbow.

"No," Annalise said.

"No?"

She looked at Wandalette, then Cassian, then at the letter on her desk. "No. I'm well, truly. I think perhaps I ate somewhat that disagreed with me. That's all. Truly, Wandalette, you need not fret."

Wandalette made a doubtful noise, then looked at him. "Well, you're with the master, and I suppose we know he'll make sure you're taken care of. So if you're sure."

Her simple acceptance—that he would take care of Annalise—set him back a step. "Go, please."

Wandalette nodded. "Yes, sir. Annalise, I hope you feel better."

Cassian stood straight and tall without bending until the last novitiate had filed from the room. Then he pulled a chair toward her, so fast the legs scraped curls of wax from the floor. He sat, knee-to-knee. He took her hands in his and chafed their chill.

"Tell me what has you so distraught?"

"Not distraught," she told him. "I am quite undone with joy."

She looked as far from joy as the Void was from the Land Above. He squeezed her hands again and settled them onto her lap. She blinked at him, her eyes bright, but no tears sliding down her cheeks. For that he supposed he ought to offer gratitude.

"It's a letter from Jacquin. My betrothed. My former betrothed, I suppose I should say, though he has now said he wishes me to reconsider our engagement."

"And . . . do you wish to?" He tried to think what she'd said of him, this other man, and could not. He wished he'd more thoroughly read the letter he'd so childishly stolen from her before, so that he might know better how to judge what she was telling him now.

"Of course! Why would I not?"

"I thought you were finding your place here," Cassian said.

He pushed away. Had to move away from her, lest he open and everything inside him tumble out onto the floor where she might see. He made a show of tidying the texts on his desk but neither saw them nor felt the leather covers in his hands.

"You're going to undo all the work we made." She said this from just behind him.

He didn't turn. He didn't want to think about that day in the closet. How she'd tasted, and her heat and how she'd writhed. He didn't want to remember how tightly her fingers had tangled in his hair.

"What are his reasons for seeking to renew your agreement? Can you be certain they're honorable?"

"Jacquin was ever honorable," Annalise said, a bit of bite in her tone. "It was not he who ended our agreement. I did it."

Cassian turned. "You must've had good reason."

Emotions slid across her face as they always did, but this time he could not read them. He couldn't tell what she thought or felt. He bit his tongue to keep from saying more and hoped for the taste of blood to distract him, but even that eluded him.

"I have ever had good reason for all I do."

"I'm sure that's so."

She tilted her head to look at him, but he didn't find it as endearing now. "He says he wants to come here. Speak to me in person.

He feels we might be able to work out our difficulties. He wants to try, at least."

"Now? And not before?"

"Before," Annalise said, "we tried and were unable to accomplish an agreement."

"And you think now it might be different? What's changed?"

The slow, small, and secret smile she gave was not for him. It churned his stomach. This was the smile she had for another man.

Cassian hated that smile.

"I suppose I won't know until he comes, and we see if we are able to . . . improve upon the situation."

This had the tone of intimacy and it set his teeth on edge. He turned from her. "My best wishes for you both."

"Cassian," she said as though just now realizing she might have been being self-involved. "He says he loves me."

The words hurt worse than the smile had, for he might combat *her* feelings but he could never compete with those from another.

"But I—" he began, and as so often with her, stopped himself from saying more.

And Annalise, unlike so often with him, did not ask him what he meant to say. With another slow and secret smile that was not for him, would never be for him, she tucked her letter against her chest and sighed. Then she turned and left the room.

Cassian stayed behind.

Once as a child Annalise had been taken ill with a fever so fierce her parents later told her they'd feared she would die. All she recalled of that time was being in her bed, too weak even to wail for her mother's cool touch, and the underwater burbling of adult voices that sounded far away but came from beside her bed.

And then, one day, she'd opened her eyes and sat up in her bed. She could see again. She could hear. She could move her limbs, unweighted.

That was how she felt now.

Unweighted.

Where had the vision she'd created come from? Had the mix of bits and pieces from commentary and text been random, as she'd intended, or had the Invisible Mother truly had a hand in its creation? The more Annalise contemplated it, the more convincing such a possibility became.

She didn't want to discuss such a matter with Tansy, nor Perdita or Helena. Not even Wandalette, who might understand the best of all the other novitiates.

The letter from Jacquin had been delayed, which meant the visit he'd proposed to make in a sevenday's time would, in fact, happen sooner than that. Annalise spent the day in the sanctuary, forgoing her studies and even meals, though her stomach gnawed itself and her head began to spin.

Cassian found her there after even the priests had gone. She'd left the pews to Wait in front of the beemah. For the first time, the position didn't feel forced. The back of hand resting inside the palm of the other in her lap, her buttocks comfortably settled on her heels, her back straight, Annalise had finally discovered the peacefulness of Waiting.

"What are you doing?"

She opened her eyes. "Waiting."

"I see that. Why here? We don't kneel to pray."

"I'm not praying. I'm Waiting."

Cassian grunted, looking down at her and shifting from foot to foot. "What are you waiting for?"

"A vision."

Another grunt. "Wouldn't you be better served to seek that in the forest?"

"I think if the Invisible Mother wants to visit me, She'll do it wherever I might be," Annalise told him.

He didn't look good, she noticed. His shirtsleeves hung unevenly from his jacket sleeves, and his hair had been rumpled. A fine shadow of beard dusted his face. It was the first time she'd seen him anything other than utterly clean-shaven.

"So then why do it in here?" He looked around the sanctuary with thinly veiled distaste.

She'd never realized before that he actively disliked the sanctuary. It seemed an odd distaste from a man who'd once made his life's work in places such as this. She frowned.

"I wish you'd get up," Cassian said. "I don't like you when you're on your knees that way."

Her brows went up. "This is Waiting. It's what Handmaidens do. It's what I'll be expected to do when I have a patron."

Cassian's grunt sounded a little more strangled this time. "Get up."

"I shall," she said, annoyed, "as there's no point in meditation with you jabbering in my ear."

She got to her feet. He watched her. He looked angry, and she sighed.

"Cassian, speak the complaint I see so clearly in that furrowed brow and angry mouth. I've no patience for pretense."

She knew him so well, now. Could tell when she'd struck a nerve. His jaw tightened, relaxed.

"You didn't come to the dining hall today."

"I was here. I've much to think upon."

"I waited for you," Cassian said stiffly.

This stopped her. A spiral of warmth coiled inside her. "Your mercy, but I was otherwise engaged."

"Ah, yes. That." He curled his lip.

He wouldn't allow her to know him overwell, but this response made little sense to her. "You know of my struggle?"

Did he know her so well, beyond providing her with water instead of cider, that he could guess at her state of mind, too?

"You did tell me somewhat of it as was in regards to your letter."

More surprise. "Oh, that. Think you I stayed here upon my knees the day through in order to clear that matter?"

"Why else?"

Annalise had been raised in the Faith. She'd seen how the strength of it could pull families together or tear them apart, how it could elevate as well as destroy. That she'd ever felt broken by it had mattered little to her before. But now . . .

"Something has changed," she told him.

If there was anyone who might understand it was he, for had he not taken his own vows, made a life based on the Faith? Even now, no longer a priest, Cassian's every act was bent toward understanding and teaching the Faith. And beyond that, he was her friend, or supposed to be. Annalise wasn't quite sure how shallow or deep their acquaintance ran.

"I believe the Invisible Mother spoke to me."

He looked around the room as though expecting the Invisible Mother to spring from beneath the beemah. "In the forest. Before."

"No, not then. I lied about that."

He had a lovely smile, when he cared to use it. He wasn't using it now. "Did you?"

"I thought I did. I intended to. But now . . ." Annalise sighed, unable to shake the sensation she'd woken with today of being bright-eyed and clear-headed for the first time in . . . well, for as long as she could recall. "Now I feel as though perhaps Her message to me was too subtle to understand the first time. That She has more for me to learn."

Cassian squared his shoulders almost imperceptibly. "Maybe the lie you're telling is to yourself, this time."

She blinked, then accepted the chastisement with a bowed head. "You have every right to be disappointed in me."

"Disappointed? Disa—" Cassian coughed into his fist. "By the Arrow, Annalise. Is that what you think?"

"Is that not what you meant?" Confused now, her mind on her revelations, she moved toward him.

"I waited for you, and when you did not come to the meals, when you didn't come even to our session, I worried somewhat had happened to you," Cassian said suddenly and sternly. "None had seen you since the morn. I looked everywhere for you. I didn't expect to find you here, waiting for a vision that will never come."

"Why do you think it will never come?" she cried. "Why would you say such a thing? I should think you, of all people, would be happy to hear I've felt a connection to the Invisible Mother that's strong enough for me to wish to pursue it!"

"Me, of all people? What does that mean?"

"You," Annalise said, "believe. You are learned. You, your knowledge, the depth of your faith, are to be admired."

He made that strange noise deep again in his throat. His hands made fists at his sides. "You find me admirable, do you?"

"Yes, yes of course, I do. No matter what else has ever come between us." She thought of his mouth between her thighs, and a small shudder ran through her. "But especially now that I believe I understand, even more."

"You understand nothing," Cassian told her. "You aren't even listening to me."

"I'm right here."

"I waited for you," Cassian said in a low voice, "and when you didn't come, I looked for you. Everywhere. I looked for you, Annalise."

"And you found me!" She tossed out her hands, unable to comprehend why he was so chastising her. "Right here. Here I am in front of you, Cassian, trying to tell you what's happened to me, and how it makes me feel. What is your issue with this?"

"I thought you were worried about your betrothed!" he shouted, sudden and loud in the hushed silence of the sanctuary that never bore such an insult. "I came to be certain you were not . . . that you were not . . ."

"What?" Frustrated by his continued inability to ever finish a thought with her, she advanced upon him. "Just speak to me, Cassian. What do you think I will ever do or say in reply to you that you cannot bear?"

"Many things."

She softened. "I like you when you're honest with me."

He looked away from her; she hated it. "I thought perhaps you were reconsidering allowing him to reconcile with you. That perhaps you'd become distraught. That you might . . . bring harm to yourself."

Such an idea had never occurred to her, but that he'd worried about it so moved her she touched his sleeve. "Never. I loved Jacquin and I may still . . ."

He took his sleeve from her grasp in order to pace away from her. "I was worried about you."

She caught up to him and captured his wrist. She turned him, gently, until he faced her. "I've not yet even seen Jacquin. And when I do, I know not what shall happen. I came to the Order for the wrong reasons. I'm fair certain Jacquin seeks reconciliation for the wrong reasons as well, but I won't know until I hear his argument."

"And of the rest?"

"That, too, is somewhat I must think upon, Cassian. I don't know what to say, or what you wish of me. But I thank you for your concern." Her hand slid from his wrist into his palm, and she squeezed his fingers. She smiled, teasing. "I like you when you're concerned."

"You've missed every meal today. You must be hungry," Cassian told her. "Let's go to the kitchen for something to eat, yes?"

It wasn't until some time later, with her belly and her mind still full, that Annalise realized he'd taken his hand from hers so gently and without fanfare, she hadn't noticed, and nor had he touched her again.

Chapter 18

Leaping Tiger. Striking Serpent. Cassian knew all the forms so well his body could create them without benefit of his mind's assistance, which was quite well, since he was unable to concentrate upon them today.

He practiced the Art in memory of his brother, but today there were too many memories crowding his brain for him to focus. He kept on, anyway, forcing himself to stretch and bend. It would've been easier against an opponent, one who'd strike back. Make him think. But as it was, he'd never had one, never fought using the skills he'd bent himself to learn.

Not like Calvis, who'd ever been a Master of the Art and who'd died at the hands of another less skilled than he.

The sun was too new in the sky to provide heat, but Cassian sweated anyway. His body ached. His soul ached, too. He heard his brother's voice and saw his face, too. If ceasing this practice would've put the memories from Cassian's mind, he'd have gladly abandoned it, but there was no forgetting today.

"I plan to ask her to marry me." Cassian knew his brother would mock. He wasn't prepared for the look of disgust twisting Calvis's face. "What? You think she won't?"

"I think she will," Calvis told him. "And moreover, I think she's been angling for you to ask her for the past three months. You've only been waiting because you're a great bloody prat who can't see what's right in front of his face."

"I see what's in front of my face. I see you, brother, drunk again. Unshaven, unwashed. Your clothes dirty. Who were you fighting?"

"Whoever someone paid me enough coin to fight, as usual. What do you think? I head myself toward the local pub and hurl random insults until someone takes up the challenge?"

"I think you might," Cassian said. "In between the others."

Calvis snorted laughter and went to the drawer where he pulled out a bowl and a jug of worm. His bedchamber already reeked of both, as did his breath and clothes. He gestured for Cassian to sit on the low, sprung-cushioned couch. "Make yourself at home, brother. What's mine is yours and all that nonsense."

The house was more a hovel than anything, two tiny rooms with an arch between them and outdoor plumbing in the yard behind. No wonder Calvis looked so rough. Cassian sat, careful not to snag the hem of his tunic on the wood sticking out from the seat.

"Look at you." Calvis lit the bowl and waved the fragrant smoke forth before breathing deep. "Land Above, I can't get used to it."

Cassian ran a hand over his newly bald head, still smooth. "It does feel strange."

"Cold?"

"Yes. That." More than that. Watching the dark strands pile up at his feet while the priest ran the razor over his skull, Cassian had felt distanced. Aloof. Only after, staring in the looking glass at his strange reflection, had he understood for the first time how it felt to be different than his brother.

"Nobody could mistake us for each other now," Calvis told him. He quaffed from the jug of worm and handed Cassian the bowl.

Cassian held it in his palms and breathed, knowing his brother would expect him to put it aside. Smoke coated his throat, his lungs, and he held it in until his head buzzed. Calvis stared.

"Nobody," Calvis said again. "By the Arrow, Cassian, you've done that before."

Cassian had, in fact, partaken of both herb and worm many times, just never with his brother, who couldn't be trusted to keep himself together when he was indulging. It had always seemed more important to be sure one of them remained sober than for Cassian to participate in his brother's vices.

He returned the bowl. "Yes."

Calvis snorted low laughter and pulled up a chair across from his brother. "You have unplumbed depths and secrets from me?"

"No secrets."

Calvis shook his head, watching his brother with grave eyes. "Would you tell me of the rituals of the priesthood?"

"You know I can't."

"Then, my brother, you have secrets."

"Would you tell me who's hired you to kill for them?"

Calvis lifted a finger. "If I tell you the names of those who pay for my skills, you might be called to testify against me. I can't have that."

"So you have secrets, too."

"A thousand of them, brother, and more. Which I've never denied. Drink up."

They both drank, then smoked. Calvis brought out a platter of stale bread and hard cheese, but flavored with intoxication, the food was delicious. They laughed and joked, much like they'd done as boys. It was the closest Cassian had felt to his brother for a very long time.

Later, both of them so tired as to have thrown themselves across Calvis's bed, Calvis ran a hand over Cassian's head. The sensation of his fingers rasping over stubble still invisible sent a chill down Cassian's spine, and he drew away. Calvis rolled onto his back.

"No mistaking one for the other," he said again.

"No. But those who know us wouldn't confuse us, anyway." Cassian yawned, thinking of how he should return home, how Bertricia would be waiting for him to visit her upon the morrow, and how he had duties to fulfill at the temple. He tried rolling onto his side to get up, but fell back with a laugh.

"Stay here," Calvis said with a glance. "You can't possibly walk the distance tonight."

"No." Cassian yawned again, eyes closing. "Though I fear the journey might be even worse in the morning, with daylight splitting my head."

Calvis laughed. The bed shifted. Cassian felt the weight of his brother's gaze and turned onto his side to face him. Head to head, foot to foot, with a handspan between them. This, too, they hadn't done since they'd been boys.

"I've missed you," Calvis said.

"You went away, brother."

"I came back," Calvis pointed out. "I was never gone for long. I could never be gone for long."

Cassian didn't say that Calvis had gone away and come back, true, but it hadn't ever been the same once he'd left. "Nothing stays the same, you know."

"Ah, but once we shared everything. A womb, a room. Clothes. Once we ate from the same plate, drank from the same cup. Wore the same face." Calvis's palm passed over Cassian's head again, then pulled away. "I thought we'd always have that, at least."

Cassian yawned again, jaw-cracking. "You'll ever be my brother. You know that."

"Ever and always?" Calvis asked.

"Of course."

The bed shifted as Calvis turned once more onto his back. "Cassian, would you love me no matter what I did?"

It was too late and Cassian too drunk for this sort of conversation, but he struggled up onto one elbow anyway. "I do love you. Of course. And I suspect you've done much."

Calvis looked at him. "Becoming a priest doesn't mean you condemn me for what a brother would forgive?"

"No. Of course not. Well"—Cassian paused, struggling to think around the fog of herb and worm—"I suppose I should say no, that now I'm a priest I should urge you toward redemption. That I should send up supplication for the saving of your soul."

"You don't think my soul worth saving?" Calvis sounded amused but looked sad.

"I don't think you've done anything that would endanger your immortal soul."

"Ah. The taking of coin in exchange for taking of life isn't enough?"

That was a tricky question, one Cassian should've known the answer to and would have, had the asker been any other but Calvis. "Were the men you killed villains?"

Calvis shrugged. "To those who wanted them dead, yes. I'd imagine so."

Cassian chewed on his answer in an attempt at speaking coherently. "Murder is wrong."

"I know that," Calvis said, annoyed. "Sinder's Balls, Cassian. I do know that."

"I can't condone it, but I can't condemn you for it. Because you are my brother, and yes. I love you, no matter what you do."

Calvis rolled onto his side again to stare. "You'd not say such a thing if you knew all that I'd done."

"Worse than murder?" Cassian looked dubious.

"Yes."

"What's worse than killing?"

Calvis shook his head, and the sheets beneath his head rumpled. He yawned, eyes closing, and Cassian thought perhaps his brother was feigning sleep to avoid the question. Which might not be a bad idea, his weary mind thought as his eyes closed, too. Whatever could be worse than killing was naught he wished to learn of his brother.

When the knock came at the door, Cassian didn't get out of his brother's bed to open it, but when the soft scent of perfume wafted over him, and a low, throaty feminine laugh tickled his ear, he sat straight up. Too late. The woman in the bed had her hand on his crotch, her mouth on his ear. Her tongue traced a delicious pattern on his skin, down his throat, which she nipped. She laughed when he pushed her away.

She looked at Calvis. "He doesn't look so much like you."

"Believe me, he's not very much like me at all." Calvis stripped off his shirt and joined them on the bed. "But you won't care about that, sweetheart. Will you?"

"I daresay I shall not," she purred, and reached again for Cassian.

Head heavy and drunk, Cassian was slow moving but managed to hold off her grasping hands. "What's this?"

"Consider it a gift, little brother." Calvis had stripped out of his trousers, too, and lay back against the shabby wooden headboard, idly stroking his cock.

It was far from the first time Cassian had seen his brother naked, and not the first he'd seen him with a woman. If he hadn't been so intoxicated, he might've tried harder to push her away again when she slipped into the space between him and Calvis and nudged at Cassian's jaw with her chin so that she might again press her lips to his flesh. Her hand found his thigh, moved higher.

He was a man, after all.

"You didn't lie, love. You and him are not a thing alike." The woman said this afterwards, from across the room as she pulled on her shift and slipped into her shoes.

Cassian could still taste and smell her. Had been the last to have her, while his brother watched. It was not his finest moment. Calvis didn't seem to care, and he padded across the room on bare feet to put a clinking bag into the woman's palm. He even kissed her, murmuring in her ear until she giggled.

When she'd gone and Calvis had closed the door behind her, he came back to the bed where Cassian had pulled on his clothes but couldn't move beyond that. Calvis pulled on a pair of trousers and climbed into the bed. Cassian turned his face to the wall and waited for his brother to explain, to brag, to apologize, but Calvis did none of those things.

In the morning, Calvis woke him with a bucket of cold water to the face and laughed at him when Cassian stumbled to the yard to heave and choke. He could well remember why he'd so rarely indulged in worm, and with aching head and roiling stomach he waved aside his brother's offer of a stroll into town to break their fast.

"I have to get home, Cal."

Calvis snorted, looking as fresh as a flower, wet hair slicked back from his face and showing no signs at all of how intoxicated he'd been the night before. "To your lady love."

"She'll be expecting me."

"You might wish to bathe first. Wash your mouth. You'd not wish to kiss her tasting of vomit. Or another woman."

Cassian shuddered, holding back another round of heaves. He wiped his mouth with the back of his hand. "Why?"

"It's been my experience women don't care for that sort of thing, that's all." Calvis feigned surprise, brows arching, mouth quirked.

"No. Why the woman?" A long drink of cool water settled his stomach. Barely. Cassian took another, willing his guts to cease their churning.

"I thought it might be good for you. Before."

"Before what?" Cassian scowled. "Before I wed the woman I love?"

Calvis shrugged. "Yes."

Cassian ran his hand over his wet head, still missing the touch and tickle of his hair. "If you loved me, as you say, you'd not have encouraged such a thing."

Calvis looked up, then. "I didn't tie you down and force you to fuck her."

This was the truth, but didn't make Cassian feel any better. "You brought her there apurpose to—"

"To what?"

"To test me," Cassian said.

Calvis shook his head. "No, Cassian. Not to test you. I told you. To give you a taste of somewhat different before you go off and shackle yourself—"

"I have to go." Cassian shrugged away his brother's half-hearted grasp. "You needn't think you'll be invited to the wedding, since it's clear you've no love for the bride or me."

He stalked out of the hovel and through the yard, only to be stopped by Calvis's voice before he hit the street.

"It's not that I don't love enough," Calvis told him, "but that I love overwell. Don't walk away from me, Cassian."

But Cassian, head still swimming and stomach sick, had walked away. Things might've been different if he hadn't. He'd never know.

Today, remembering, his stomach was sick again, though not from overindulgence. He finished the final position, his feet unsteady enough they scuffed the dirt instead of planting firmly. He almost fell, but didn't.

"I say," came an unfamiliar voice, male, which caused it to stand out all the more. "I'm here to visit someone. Perhaps you might direct me?"

Cassian knew without having to ask that the man in front of him was Annalise's betrothed. For one wild moment it occurred to him he'd sent enough travelers on their way in the wrong direction, and how simple it would be to do the same for this man. It would do him no good, though. He'd find his way, eventually.

"She's in the house, most likely."

The man who had to be Jacquin turned toward the Motherhouse, then glanced back at Cassian. He had an open, friendly, and overhandsome face Cassian longed to punch square in the nose.

"That's a broad description, sir. That house looks to have any number of rooms."

"Go to the front door and you'll be let in to see the Mother-in-Service who decides to see you. She'll tell you where to find Annalise, if they determine you're fit to step inside the doors." This was an overexaggeration—unless they had reason to believe Jacquin would harm Annalise, as some men who'd come seeking the women who'd left them behind had done, none of the Mothers or Sisters-in-Service would keep Jacquin from her.

Jacquin held out his hand. "Many thanks."

Cassian could've broken that hand. In reality, he knew he could've done more than that. He understood his brother better than he ever had in that moment. He didn't take Jacquin's hand.

Jacquin blinked, frowning.

"In there," Cassian told him. "Go."

Chapter 19

It's been overlong," Jacquin told Annalise as he took both her hands. "You look . . . well."

He moved to kiss her mouth, and she turned so his lips grazed her cheek instead. The action surprised her as much as it did him, but Annalise hid hers rather better. Training had done that, she thought as she looked at her former and possibly soon-again, betrothed. Made her calm.

"Is there a place where we can go?" Jacquin kept hold of her hands a moment longer, squeezing her fingers gently before letting go. "To talk?"

"Of course."

"You're left unrestricted?" Jacquin looked over his shoulder as Annalise led him from Deliberata's office, where he'd been waiting, and into the hall beyond.

"I'm not a prisoner, Jacquin."

"Even so . . ." He had to take a double step to catch up to her, his hand snagging her sleeve at the elbow. "You needn't explain yourself to anyone? Be granted permission?"

"To entertain a guest? Certainly not!" Annalise plucked his hand from her elbow and settled it into the crook of her arm, her other hand atop it.

They earned a few curious looks from some of the novitiates, but Jacquin was the one straining his eyes to stare at everything. He went so far as to stop for a look in the open door of one of the classrooms, so that Annalise had to tug him firmly to move him. Even then he dragged his feet like a child, goggle-gazed at all they passed.

"Jacquin, you act the part of a copperfish trying for a crumb. Close your mouth and mind your manners," Annalise chastised.

He focused on her. "It's nothing like I expected."

She took him through a glass door and to a small courtyard, then along a stone path and through the scrolled metal gate toward the pond. "Allow me to guess what you expected. Near-naked women servicing the pleasures of men all over the place? Collared and bound, perhaps, or at the very least on their knees?"

Jacquin's boots crunched on the gravel as he again caught up to her swift and unhesitating step. "Well . . . yes."

Halfway up the hill, Annalise stopped and turned to tease him. "We only do that four days of the seven. You arrived on one of the wrong four days."

Jacquin had ever known her humor and shared it, but this time his jaw gaped again and his eyes bulged. Annalise sighed and patted his arm.

"Love, I jest. You'll find none of that in the Motherhouse. It's our haven, after all, not the place for our patrons."

He followed her again when she moved toward the pond and the gazebo beyond. "But . . . surely you must . . . I mean, everyone knows . . ."

"Everyone knows what? Rumors and stories, Jacquin." Annalise glanced over her shoulder, watching his unsteady progress. Perhaps the shock had unsettled him, or more likely it was the heels of his fashionable boots unsuited for heavy trekking.

"Fair enough. But you can't blame me for the thought. Tell me you believed differently when you arrived. Tell me how relieved you were to find it not so."

"I was, of course. Ah, here. Sit with me." She took a place on the stone bench in the gazebo and spread her skirts. She patted the spot next to her. "But it's always possible I shall have to learn such skills."

Jacquin drew forth a fine-woven handkerchief from his pocket to mop his brow and upper lip. When had he grown so foppish, so ill-equipped at the physical? Annalise thought she should've brought a jug of cider.

"Why?" He put away the hanky and turned toward her on the bench. "By the Void, Annalise, sure you can't be serious about this. Your time here was never meant for permanence!"

They might have been any courting couple, though the fashion of her gown didn't match the elaborate outfit Jacquin had chosen. Sky blue jacket with a matching waistcoat, shirt of pale blue gray linen, dark gray trousers, dusty now but of fine material. He looked every inch the dandy gentleman, complete with lace at his throat and cuffs.

Had it been only a few short months ago she'd found him so lovely to look upon? And now everything about him seemed overblown. Priggish.

"Things change, Jacquin."

She'd spoken calmly. She might well have shouted, for the reaction he gave her, one hand on his heart and the other briefly at his brow. When he looked at her again, he'd gone a little pale.

"You can't mean you intend to go through with this. Become a Handmaiden?" Jacquin slid closer to take her hands, and Annalise, taken aback, allowed him.

"That *is* the reason I'm here." She said it more gently than she would have before her time here, and that, too, she recognized.

He thrust her hands back in her lap and stood to pace the gazebo's wooden planks. "No. No, you're not truly here to take your vows and enter the Order of Solace. That was only a ploy. A distraction. It was never meant to be real!"

"Much like our betrothal, you mean?" The words came out more cruelly than she'd thought. So much for training. She still had a long, long way to go.

He whirled to face her, the hem of his jacket swinging. "It was never meant to be such."

She softened, reaching a hand he didn't take. "It would have been. And you know it."

"No. I told you then, as I tell you now, I would be a good husband to you. Better even than many who claim to wed for love alone and no other reason. At least with me, you'd know my intentions were ever to you and our family first, before all else."

Annalise put her hand back in her lap and shook her head slowly. "A husband who cannot make love to his wife? You said you wished heirs, Jacquin. How would you expect to get them upon me, when the . . ." She swallowed at the memory, which still stung after all this time. "When the very act of touching me intimately caused you such distress?"

He paced afresh, boots clacking on the wood. "I was a fool. I allowed myself to depend too much upon the aid of worm and herb, thinking I needed—"

She stood, then, to pace herself. Heart pounding. Stomach just a little sick at the memory even now. "I don't want a husband who has to drug himself to make love to me!"

"It would be different now," Jacquin said in a low voice. "If you would only allow me to prove it."

Somehow, Annalise found herself in his arms, her hands cupping his face. It seemed strange to look into his eyes without having to tip back her head or stand on her toes. Stranger to smell a whiff of pomade and sharp-spiced cologne.

"It's true I came here for the wrong reasons. But I think now I've discovered the right ones."

Jacquin shook his head, took her palms and kissed each one. His gaze bore into her. "I know you don't believe me, but I do love you."

"I do believe it. In your way."

He let her go and stalked to the railing to look out across the pond. "I shouldn't have let you go."

"You had no choice."

He shook his head without looking at her. "I had a choice. I could've kept you close to me. Brought the priests, had a wedding . . ."

She laughed. "You think you might have forced me to be your bride? Oh, Jacquin, I thought you knew me better than that."

She frowned a moment later when she saw he was serious. "You mean it."

"We'd have been wed a month already. My babe already planted in your belly, perhaps." He turned to her, jaw set and eyes icy. "None of this nonsense with you running away, me having to face your parents—"

"My parents! You were happy to have me come here so that we might delay the wedding without dissolving it! So that you might still have the benefit of working at my father's side without the mess of either of us being expected to find another partner! This was what we agreed together, Jacquin, yet now you make it out that somehow this was all my decision? All my fault?"

She stomped her foot, not calm or composed, unable to keep her voice from rising. "You blame me?"

"The only person who finds your service here worthy is your lady mother! And her only because she's so far gone into her religious madness she believes you'll be the one to do it, to provide your patron with that moment of solace that will at last fill Sinder's Quiver."

Jacquin had ever been respectful of her mother, no matter the woman's fantasies. To hear him speak of her with such derision sent a wave of unease through Annalise. She swallowed the bitter taste of bile on the back of her tongue.

"Why did you come here?"

"When you didn't answer my first letter, and weeks had passed without hearing from you, I realized how much I missed you, Annalise."

She gave a soft snort at that. "Surely you had enough to occupy you, what with working for my father and your other pursuits."

"None of it was as merry as my time spent with you, this I swear. I missed you. I understood why you left, and I wished to make amends. Where's the harm in that?"

"No harm. But this changes naught." Annalise leaned against the gazebo's other railing. "Much has changed for me, in ways I'd never thought possible."

"We have a contract," he reminded her. "If you dissolve it, your father will have to pay the price. And it's a steep one. The business has flourished since I joined him."

Her brow furrowed. "Are you threatening me?"

"No, no. Land Above, no," Jacquin protested. "I swear to you, not that. I'm merely telling you I've come all this way, at no great ease—"

"I know the hardship of the journey, Jacquin. I made it without benefit of your luxurious transportation, as a matter of fact."

Solemnly, he nodded. "I know it. And I can see your time here's been good for you. Made you . . . amenable. It's most pleasing."

This raised a brow. "Surely I've not changed so much."

He laughed a little. "Sweetheart, you've ever been unhesitantly spoken and forward with your thinking. Why else have you found it so difficult to find a suitor?"

Anger, thin and cold, burned in her chest. "My difficulties with courtship cannot be traced to my personality, for I know full well my face and figure more than made up for it. Men—most men," she amended with a slightly derisive look at him she didn't bother to hide, "seem to put up with a lot in order to wet their wicks. If I had difficulty finding suitors, it was because of my father's lack of business sense and the six sisters who came before me, eating up all the dowry."

"All the more reason for you to renew our betrothal."

"Why? Because I might never have another offer?"

"That's not what I said."

Annalise sniffed. "It's what you implied, Jacquin, and you know it. I must be honest. If this is how you've come to plight your troth, you're fair disappointing in the execution of it!"

"Please, please, sweetheart, can't we talk about this? Will you not allow me to show I've changed? Not my heart," he said quietly, "for that ever was yours. But my body."

She allowed him to take her in his arms and kiss her. His mouth, so familiar, no longer urged her to sighs, but she parted her lips for him anyway to let him stroke his tongue inside. His groan startled her enough to pull away, but his hands gripped her hips and held her close.

"See?" He whispered against her mouth. "Or rather, feel."

True, the heat and hardness of his groin between them seemed to indicate arousal. Annalise sighed into Jacquin's kiss this time, closing her eyes and letting his tongue and hands urge a reaction from her. It wasn't working, not when her mind filled with an image of dark eyes, dark hair, broad shoulders, and that stern, unforgiving mouth . . .

"See? Yes, sweetheart, you see, we could be good together." Jacquin's voice had gone hoarse. He pushed her to the bench to slide a hand between her thighs, her gown a barrier to his touch. "Just allow me to prove it, and I swear you'll have no more qualms."

They'd kissed many times before, much this way, and Jacquin was correct. It did feel different. It felt . . . wrong.

"No." She pushed at his chest until he left off.

Breath hitching, pink on his cheeks, eyes a little glazed, Jacquin blinked. "What?"

"This isn't right."

"Of course it's right. It's as right as anything ever was. We're betrothed, sweetheart. You agreed to be my bride and I your husband, and I'm here to show you it can work. It will work."

He kissed her again, for even longer this time, but though his hands roamed over her body Annalise felt nothing but resignation. Was this what it would be like to serve a patron, she thought, her mouth taking his kiss but naught else.

"Where is your head?" Jacquin snapped, and got up from the bench to run a hand over his hair. "Not with me, I'm fair certain of that."

"Your mercy," Annalise said.

He turned. "You'll not even give me a chance?"

"I . . . Jacquin . . . I . . ." Annalise sought words she couldn't find.

He got on his knees in front of her, clasping her hands tight. "Sweetheart, I do swear to you I will be ever the most faithful of husbands to you, if only you'll come back to me."

Annalise kissed his fingers and put aside his hands, then stood. The wooden floor might well have worn through, the pair of them had done so much pacing. She ran a hand along the railing, skipping fingertips over the possibility of splinters.

"I believe you would be miserable," she said at last and turned to find him slumped upon the bench, a cut-stringed marionette. "Look at you, you're miserable now."

He drew a heavy sigh, shoulders lifting. He gave her a naked gaze she couldn't bear and yet refused to ignore. "Annalise, just come home. There are circumstances."

"What circumstances?"

He held out his hands, fingers spread. "Your father and I don't see eye to eye on the business. I've made your father more money since you've been gone than he's made in your entire lifetime, yet he balks me at every turn. He refuses to grant me the partnership he promised would be mine upon our wedding. Instead he holds me off with promises he cannot possibly produce. That would change if you came back. Became my wife, the way we'd planned. It would be a good life for you, Annalise, I can promise you that."

Emotion, twisted and tangled, tightened her throat, hoarsened her voice. "But will it be a good life for you, love?"

Jacquin blinked, mouth pressing tight closed on whatever he meant to say. His shoulders sagged. And there it was, the truth of it all.

She went to him because she could, now, in a way that had been impossible for her even a few weeks ago. She went to her knees in front of him on the hard boards, her gown doing little to cushion but not caring. She took his hands in hers, this time, reversing the roles. She squeezed gently.

"I could never," she said, "ask you to give up who you are to make a life with me. Not ever, Jacquin. I care for you too fully to expect such a sacrifice."

He took his hand from hers to touch her cheek, then slide it to the back of her neck and anchor there. To pull her close and kiss her, softly this time, and without forced passion. He rested his forehead to hers, eyes closed, for a full long moment before he let her go.

"Care too fully," he echoed with a hollow laugh. "But not love."

So much had changed, as she'd said, and Annalise felt wrung out from it. Torn up. What she'd thought was love had turned to somewhat else; what she'd believed was loathing had become somewhat new, as well.

"I will always care for you. And love you as my dearest friend. The way we have ever been, Jacquin."

His brow lowered. Another grim look. He stood, leaving her behind to once again look out over the pond. His fine clothes hung off him as though somehow he'd shrunk in the past few moments. He put his hands on the railing, shoulders hunched, and when he spoke, he sounded nothing like the merry Jacquin Annalise had always known.

"Tell me something."

"Anything."

"Is it because you've truly found a calling?"

Annalise hesitated in her answer to be certain she didn't lie. Jacquin didn't turn to look at her. She sighed. "I wish I could tell you yes, or no, but the truth is I have no answer for that. If you asked me that yestermorn, I'd have easily said yes. But now, here with you, I can only be certain I know what I do not want rather than being sure of what I do."

He kept his back to her. "So you would continue on this path?"

"That of training in the Order? I don't seek to leave it now, no."

"That's not what I meant. This path, this refusal not to break our betrothal."

At this, she hesitated again. "If I dissolve it, will you require of my father the full price of the contract?"

"Yes."

She flinched at that, thinking he'd never been so stern before, but knowing he was in the right to demand her father pay.

He turned. "I could earn a pretty sum for the expense of losing you, Annalise. I could live quite well upon it, should your father have it to give, which I know for a fact he does not. He'd have to tithe himself to me for a goodly long time, not to mention that I'm fair certain such a break would urge him to put me from the trade altogether and leave me with naught but the pittance he could provide each year."

"It does so often come to money," she said. "I told you."

Jacquin didn't laugh. His gaze darkened. "You know I'm the youngest son, not the heir, not even eligible to inherit a bedamned thing from my father, should he ever even die. You know my chance of making any success for myself came from aligning myself with your father, taking over his business, for he's made a good reputation even if he's had no success with keeping hold of his coin. It was to be the perfect arrangement. You the last daughter, I the final son. And now . . . there is nothing. If we don't wed, your father will put me from the trade and I will have naught but the taste of success to sustain me. Even if I were so bold as to attempt to simply take his business, I'd have no capital for it. How much longer do you think your father will accept this arrangement, Annalise? Or the Order? At some point you must decide, become a Handmaiden. Or come home."

"I can't decide now."

"How long can you stay here without it?"

She shrugged. "They don't judge by how long the journey, only the destination. Forever, I suppose, so long as I'm still working toward my goal."

"Could you be happy here? Really, sweetheart, in that drab gown, in the company of women, no outlet for your passion?"

"In years, perhaps my father would have enough to pay you off appropriately," she said, "should I break from you then. Or you could have earned enough, built enough of your own contacts, to be a success out from beneath his wing."

"Do you really want to stay here for years? Do you really expect me to wait that long, putting off the questions, convincing your father to keep me on as the son-in-law his daughter refuses to take? Your father's a sorely poor businessman with a tendency toward indulgences, but he's far from stupid. He's already begun questioning your progress. My intentions. And he knows . . . he suspects, sweetheart."

"What? That this was a plot?"

"Your reasons for making it," Jacquin said. "I've been discreet, but people do talk."

"Allow me to ask you this. If not for my father's business, would you wish to marry me?"

"I care for you fully," Jacquin said from twisted lips. "We have ever been the best of friends."

What she'd meant as compliment, he'd turned to insult. "Answer my question."

He said nothing.

She wanted none of this. Not his anger or disdain, not knowing everything for which she'd wished for the past two years had become as naught. She didn't touch him. They stared at each other, a distance between them that had never been there and she feared now ever would.

"I will not break with you, Jacquin. Go and tell my father I have doubts about my calling, but I need a bit more time to discern if what I feel is true. Go and . . . do whatever it is you wish."

He gave her a stiff half bow. She couldn't recall if he'd ever been so formal with her. She curtsied, knowing she'd never done such a thing for him.

"This can't go on forever, Annalise."

"I might be asked to take my vows. If I discover this is a true calling, and I become a Handmaiden, what then?"

"Then you'll have no choice but to break with me."

"Then I suppose you'd be well served to do your best in filling my father's coffers, so that when the time comes you might profit." Cold words said with too much heat.

The kiss surprised her, harsh and fierce as it was, and she froze in his embrace. When he moved his mouth to her ear, the wet heat of his words made her shiver. His hands gripped her tight, too tight, and for the first time since ever she'd known him, Annalise feared the man holding her so close.

"Everything I have I would hold as close as this. And yet you are forcing me to let it go."

He let her go as he said it. She pushed away from him. "Has it come to such a thing, that we should be enemies?"

"Such a decision, I would say, is yours to make. As you've made it clear I can do naught to otherwise sway you."

Her jaw tightened, briefly. "Did you really think all it would take was a few kisses to convince me?"

"It could've been more than that."

"Here? In the gazebo? Where any might see? Surely you don't think I'm such a doxy as that, Jacquin!"

He stared hard and made no reply.

She gasped at the affront and turned on her heel. She was already halfway down the hill before he caught up to her, fingertips snagging her sleeve and turning her. A breeze blew the lace at his throat, and it seemed ever more flouncy and unnecessary an accessory.

"You," she said through gritted teeth, "take your hand away from me. Right now."

He did, but her arm hurt where he'd squeezed. "When you become a Handmaiden, you'll do whatever your patron needs, yes?"

"Yes. That's the purpose."

"So why not take me as your patron, then? Do what I need? What I want? What difference is there between serving some stranger and giving me what I require? You'll balk at my affections yet suck a stranger's cock? What sort of calling is that?"

"There's so much more to it than that!"

"Then why not me?" Jacquin demanded.

"Giving you what you want is not the purpose of a Handmaiden!"

"Oh, yes. Solace. Well, let me tell you, sweetheart, I can assure you that I should achieve solace should you just come back home and wed me as we'd arranged, so that I might continue as we planned."

"As you planned, and my father planned!"

"And as you desired!" Jacquin spit to the side.

"I begin to believe you never cared for me as you say, if you could so turn upon me now. I would imagine if your affection was real, you'd be happy for me should I discover this calling is true. If I should decide to become a Handmaiden, I'd be doing good for the world. It's no small thing, Jacquin. If this is truly my path, I would imagine you might be more willing to honor it."

"You're being selfish," he said.

This took her aback near more than anything else he'd said, and the words rose without effort. "Selfish is the heart that thinks first of itself."

"What is that?"

"One of the five principles."

Jacquin's smile stretched thin. "One you've not yet managed to follow, then."

"You're thinking of yourself as well," Annalise said wearily. A dull throbbing had begun behind her eyes. She wanted him to go. She wanted this all to go.

"I make no claims at a calling. Ask yourself what would be the best course here, sweetheart. That's all I want you to do. Think about it. I plead your mercy," he added, a hand over his heart and sounding sincere. "I've spoken out of turn and with anger, and that was never my intent."

She nodded, unwilling to forget all he'd said but unable to replace the affection of years with contempt, now. "I will think about what you said."

"Then I suppose that's all I can ask." He lifted her hand to his mouth and kissed it formally. "Good-bye, Annalise. I'll write to you. Don't let another month pass without doing the same."

"I won't."

Then, with another look back at her, Jacquin headed toward the stables. Annalise waited a few minutes to gather her composure before making her way toward the Motherhouse. She was in sore need of some quiet to think.

Her feet led her there as though she'd been tied to a ribbon being pulled by an unseen hand. Step by step, through familiar halls and past dark rooms, down some stairs, until she got to his room.

She sought peace, but found Cassian instead.

Chapter 20

He was unsurprised to find her at his door. When she pushed past him and into his room, Cassian shut the door behind her and left it unlocked. It seemed likely Annalise would be leaving as swiftly as she'd entered.

She stalked to his dresser, helped herself to a glass of worm. Quaffed it. Wiped the back of her hand across her mouth. Turned.

"Your betrothed has taken his horse from the stables and gone away. And here you are. Is he sending a carriage for you, later?" Cassian formed the words carefully yet didn't manage to keep his tone as neutral as he'd planned.

Annalise's head snapped up, her gaze stormy and mouth grimly set. "No, he's not, no matter how that might please you."

He bristled at once, she ever the oil to his water. "Don't presume you know my mind well enough to speak it for me."

She drew a sharp, hitching breath and turned her back. "I presume naught, sir, but speak my mind as freely as I ever have. If I presume, it's because you yourself have led me to make such a guess as to your thoughts."

"So you're not leaving, then?"

Her shoulders slumped. "Should I?"

He'd thought for sure she'd be gone already. That she seemed hesitant should've set him a bit more at ease, but for the fact that Cassian had long ago ceased to understand the feeling of ease. It was better that way.

"I wouldn't presume to make your decision for you."

In her cheeks, two bright pink spots burned. "No? You have ever made your opinions clear on all else. Yet this time, when I come to you with a clear request for your thoughts, you . . . you . . ."

"Why is this even a question?" Cassian asked, hoping to fend off her tears.

"Why?" Annalise tossed up her hands and shook her head until her braid swung. "This is my life we're discussing, not some random happenstance. My life!"

"*Your* life," he pointed out. He doubted in that moment she'd have noticed any quaver in his voice, but he did his best to keep it calm anyway. "*Your* choices."

When she buried her face in her hands, he thought for sure she wept. Yet the tears but glinted in her gaze; they hadn't yet escaped her eyes. She blinked and turned her face up to the ceiling. She drew in a breath. When she looked at him again, it was steadily.

"I have choices?"

"One always has choices, Annalise."

She gave a short bark of laughter and lifted her glass, this time to drain it. She settled it carefully on the dresser and ran her fingertip around the rim of, then licked it. She looked at him.

"When I came here, I honestly didn't believe I'd ever finish the training, take the vows. I didn't think I'd ever find whatever the others have inside them that allows them to serve. Absolute solace?" she scoffed. "How on earth could I possibly lead anyone toward what I've never known, myself? What I don't believe exists?"

"You needn't have experienced it to provide it to another."

"Pretty words from a pretty mouth." She licked her lips, gaze bright, hectic color still dotting her cheeks. "But it's a lie, Cassian. Tell me it's not."

"I can't tell you that."

"You *won't* tell me. That doesn't mean it's not true."

She made to pour herself another glass, but he strode across the room and took the bottle from her. He corked it. Then he opened the dresser's top drawer and placed the bottle carefully inside and closed it, locked it with the small key jutting from the lock, and tucked the key into his pocket.

"I thought we were friends," she said, "yet you'd be so stingy with your drink, I cannot believe it."

"You've had enough. Come, Annalise," he said softly. "You should go to your room until this passes."

She shrugged off his grip. "Until what passes?"

"This melancholy."

She gaped, then shook her head and backed away from him. "Melancholy? You think this is something as light as melancholy, Cassian?"

"You're intoxicated on worm."

"I'm not," she protested, "for you've stolen it away before I could possibly have drunk enough."

She stared at him defiantly, then dropped her gaze and squared her shoulders. "Never mind. I thought I could come to you with my worries. I see I was wrong."

"If ever I gave you the impression otherwise, I plead your mercy," he told her, uncertain if she meant to leave or shame him further with her accusations. He rather expected the latter. He wasn't certain he didn't deserve to be so shamed.

"You can't have it."

"Annalise." He sighed. "What would you have me do?"

"Be my friend!" She advanced upon him. "Such as you said you wished to be! Such as I've tried to be to you these past weeks, at no small cost to myself, I might add."

"Nobody asked it of you. I didn't ask it of you!"

"Why is it that every time it seems as though you and I are about to make some manner of progress in this, you make sure to push me away? For every brick I take down between us you add two more, Cassian." She gazed at him from wet, bleak eyes he couldn't bear. "Why?"

He had a handful of answers, all of which refused to leap from his tongue. She took two faltering steps toward him and stopped. He wanted to move closer. He wanted to move away.

He didn't move.

"Should I stay and become a Handmaiden, Cassian, or should I leave and marry Jacquin, as he wishes?"

The sound of the other man's name grated in his ears. "If I told you what to do in this matter, Annalise, and I pushed you toward the wrong path, you would ever blame me for so encouraging you."

"And if it was the right path?"

"You would ever blame me for not allowing you to be the one who made the choice at taking it."

She blinked.

"I know you," he told her. "You may not believe it of me, Annalise, but I do. You would ever resent me for being the one who decided for you. And I . . . I find the idea of you resenting me forever unpalatable."

A smile flickered briefly before vanishing. "You would have me stay here? In the Order? With . . . you?"

With me, he thought, but didn't say. "In the Order, working toward the taking of your vows. After which, as you well know, you'd be required to begin taking patrons."

She blinked again. "I know it."

He turned to study the glass she set upon his dresser. He could see the faint mark of her mouth on the glass. If he drank from it now, from just that spot, it would be almost as though he kissed her.

"I would hear you say it, anyway, if such is your preference," Annalise said quietly.

Cassian said nothing.

"Do you remember the first time we met?"

"I'm fair certain I shall never forget it," Cassian said.

"You pointed me to a certain path. You told me then it would take me to where I needed to go. Can you deny you told me true, then?"

His voice, pushed from a throat hoarse and dry, rasped on his reply. "No."

"And yet you cannot tell me now?"

Cassian shook his head.

"Jacquin says he loves me."

He looked at her and long silence spun between them, fragile as spidersilk. "He has every reason to."

Her eyes fluttered against another spate of tears. The color had faded from her tawny cheeks, even from her normally crimson lips. He'd never seen her look so drawn, knew she'd have squawked did she know the state of her features . . . and yet she'd never looked so lovely to him as she did when she turned and left him behind.

"Annalise. Wait."

She didn't stop, convinced she so wished to hear him stop her that she'd imagined Cassian's burr-rough voice saying her name. When it came again, closer this time, she turned as his hand closed around her wrist.

And then his mouth was on hers, hard and sweet. She was in his arms, the floor beneath her sliding away as he lifted her. Cassian cradled her to his chest without ever moving his mouth from hers, only giving way when he lay her on his bed and she gasped against his mouth.

Words would ruin it as they so often had before, from both of them. And yet they spoke—in soft sighs and the small, unashamed groans. His mouth found hers again. His tongue slipped inside, stroking. She opened for him and held him close.

No frantic grappling, no frenzied coupling this time. She'd known from their interlude in the closet that Cassian knew delightfully well how to please a woman swiftly. Now she discovered he knew how to please her slowly, as well.

The buttons at the front of her gown were of carved bone, smooth and easily slipped from their moorings. She'd done it herself dozens of times. Now Annalise stretched her arms above her head, Cassian's hand pinning her wrists as he used his other hand to slide free the buttons and lay open her gown. The thin shift she wore beneath offered no protection from the chill of the air or the puff of his hot breath as he moved his mouth from hers to her jaw, her throat, the first rising swells of her breasts above the shift's neckline.

He flicked open the ribbon and the neckline drooped. Cassian's mouth moved lower. Wet heat engulfed her flesh. Annalise moved beneath him, no longer held in place by his hand. She arched into his embrace.

Cassian sighed over wet flesh and suckled her nipples gently, first one then the other, before moving up to kiss her mouth again. The worm had blunted her tongue but she could still taste him. She put her hands into his hair's dark thickness, wound her fingers tight to keep him from moving away from her.

His kisses gentled. He kissed her mouth, cheeks, each eye. His lips brushed her forehead and the slope of her brows. The curve of her ears and jaw. Then back to her mouth, where he just barely grazed her lips with his.

When he pulled away, Annalise thought Cassian meant to stop, and she let out a murmur of protest. He laughed, low and throaty and entirely unexpectedly. It was the most sensual noise she'd ever heard. Desire splintered inside her, beginning deep within her core but reaching every limb, every part of her within a heartbeat or two.

"Cassian."

He closed his eyes for half a moment, and again she thought she'd lost him. But when he opened them, he focused first on her mouth, then her eyes. "Yes, Annalise."

She wanted to ask him if she were there with him or if some memory had overtaken him, but she sealed the words up tight before they could be let loose. If it were true, she didn't want to know. She would take this now, here with him, no matter what it was.

No matter what it would be.

"Kiss me?"

"Gladly." He did.

He bent back to the work of undoing her buttons, down past her waist and to the hem. She never unbuttoned her gown the entire way and felt laid out like a package now. A gift unwrapped. She slipped her arms from the sleeves and reveled in the air upon her naked flesh as Cassian took her wrist. He held his mouth to the spot where her pulse beat wildly. His teeth pressed her skin. His tongue swiped against her.

He got off the bed and stood to stare down at her. His jacket had the same buttons, same high collar as her gown, and Cassian stripped out of it as swiftly as he'd opened hers. His red shirt went next and he tossed it to the floor.

"Land Above," Annalise said.

She'd known he was lean and muscled. She hadn't guessed he would be so sculpted. His hair, as dark and thick as that on his head, curled around his nipples and in a narrow line leading from just below his navel and disappearing into his waistband. His arms, too, were muscled, the forearms covered in the same crisp, dark hair. She couldn't see the thatch of it between his legs—but if what he had on his chest and arms was any indication, Cassian was thoroughly, utterly male.

The thought of it sent another wave of desire coursing through her. She'd ever found a fondness for men who groomed themselves—oiled their hair, shaved cleanly, dressed according to fashion, and made personal taste of the most importance. But with Cassian, there was naught about the clothes to turn the head. Not of his hair, or use of cologne, or in any affectations.

"You're real," she said aloud. "Entirely real."

He ran a hand over his chest and belly almost absently, then put it to the buttons at his waist. "Is that a disappointment? That I'm not a dream, some myth?"

She pushed herself onto her elbows to watch him slide the trousers over his lean hips and down strong, muscled thighs. "No."

Watching him, so suddenly comfortable in his nakedness, Annalise felt unaccountably shy. Her nipples had tightened. She felt exposed in her obvious arousal and cupped her breasts, the weight of them familiar, yet strange.

Naked, Cassian moved to the bed and up her body to kiss her again. Her gown shifted and bunched beneath them until he reached under her to pull it away. He rolled her at the same time until she ended atop him, sprawling on his broad chest with the shift tangled between them.

He ran his hands up and down her sleeves. "Take this off."

"If it pleases you." The words rose as naturally to her tongue as any ever had. Spoken as a true Handmaiden might to a patron.

Both of them froze, but Cassian melted first. He pulled her close to kiss her mouth, then breathe against her and speak, each word brushing his lips on hers.

"I would have it please you, as well."

Annalise sat upright, straddling him. She tugged the shift off over her head and tossed it aside. His gaze covered her, eyes gleaming. She was no longer nervous.

Cassian ran his hands over her hips and belly to rest just below her breasts. "You are so beautiful."

Heat had followed the path of his fingers; now it flared higher, up her throat and over her cheeks. She bit her lower lip to hold in a sigh, then let it out, anyway. There should be no shame in this, for either of them. It had taken them long enough to get here.

"I always thought you were beautiful, from the first," he said.

Annalise moved on his thighs to rub herself gently along his lengthening cock and smiled when Cassian swallowed hard. "Really? You hid it well."

He pushed his hips upward a little to stroke himself along the heat between her legs. "It would have been unseemly to do anything else."

She leaned down, her hands flat on the bed to either side of his head. She kissed him, long and fully and thoroughly. "I believe I like you when you're unseemly."

Atop him this way, Annalise had the power to kiss him fiercely or pull away, to shift her body so she stroked his cock with her cunt and urged him to gasp. She reached between them to guide him inside her, but Cassian drew her tight against him, forcing her still. She looked into his eyes.

"It has been overlong for me. I would be . . . slower."

"If it pleases you," she teased and gloried in the way he groaned at her words.

"It would not please me to spend myself like an untried boy, Annalise."

She laughed, but kindly, and took his lower lip between her teeth to gently tug when she kissed him. Under her palm, flat on his chest, Cassian's heart thumped steadily and swift. She bent to kiss his skin there, the tickle of curling dark hair tickling her lips and nose.

She breathed him in. "I have ever found your scent so unbearably pleasant."

"How can somewhat be both unbearable and pleasant?"

"Delicious," she told him with a lick of his nipple that pulled it into sweet tightness. "Pleasant, lovely, and yet unbearable as it reminded me all the more of what I could not have."

He shifted beneath her, hands roaming as she kissed and licked and nipped all over his chest. "Yet here you are, with me naked beneath you."

"Ah, but I do not have you," she whispered around the sudden swell of emotion closing her throat.

Cassian tugged off the ribbon binding the end of her braid and ran his fingers through her hair, unkinking the strands. He put his hands to the sides of her face and drew her to his mouth. He kissed her.

"You have me," he said.

Annalise drew a slow, sobbing breath and buried her face into the side of his neck. Cassian held her close, big hands warm upon her naked flesh. They breathed in. Out. Her heart had taken up the beat of his.

She was unsure how she ended up under him again, only that it happened without effort. Their kisses ebbed and flowed, soft and hard, lingering and swift.

She was already languid and liquid when he moved his mouth along her throat to pause in the hollow at its base. He licked, then suckled along her collarbone. Down to her nipples, giving each one equal and thorough attention until she could no longer hold back a cry.

Her hips moved, her cunt slick and empty, clit a tight, hard knot aching to be touched. Heat centered in her belly, and in moments his mouth found it. Over her navel, along the slope of her hip. Annalise held her breath, watching Cassian's sleek dark head move lower and lower.

He moved between her legs and parted her flesh with gentle

fingers. Desire crackled between them, palpable like flames. She had to breathe and could not, waiting.

She thought he'd use his tongue against her, but he slid a finger inside instead. She gasped at the sensation of being so invaded, and before she had time to take in another breath, his mouth was on her.

Land Above, it was sweet.

Sweet, and hot, and wet. Annalise pushed herself up to meet his lips and tongue. She'd thought the pleasure he'd brought her before had been exquisite, but this . . . this was unmatched. To think she might never have known this—

But she pushed that thought from her head, unwilling to give it even one more moment of her attention. Everything was here and now, the weight and heat of his mouth upon her center. His finger stroking inside her. Soon his cock would be inside her, as well, and that thought sent desire shuddering through her.

"Cassian," she murmured, and then again. His name, like a prayer. He made a noise the second time she spoke, and the pattern of his kisses shifted. Became more desperate, and she responded, wanting only to chase this sensation until she exploded from it.

Ecstasy filled her. She overflowed with it. She shivered from it, body quaking as her fingers wound deep within the dark silk of his hair.

"Please," she heard herself say. "Now."

She'd asked for it, and even so it startled her to lose the heat between her thighs and discover it hovering over her body. Passion had twisted Cassian's features, but knowing she was its source only made him all the lovelier. He licked his mouth. Tasting her?

"Kiss me," she begged and took him by the back of the neck to draw him to her mouth.

Her desire flavored their kisses, and Annalise moaned into his mouth. His hands were still working on her body. One slid between her legs. His cock's blunt head nudged at her, parting her, slipping inside inch by slow, delicious inch. Only when he was fully seated inside her did Cassian pause to catch his breath.

Annalise waited for him to move. This was making love, she thought, breathless and aching. *This was love.*

He moved inside her, slowly, then faster when she dug her nails into his back and whispered into his ear how much she wanted him. His sweat painted her lips with every kiss. They rocked together, and pleasure built inside her again, unexpected and welcomed.

He cried her name at the end, and she clutched him in triumph. Spent, he buried himself inside her and his face against her neck. Sweat glued them. Her arms around him held him tight. Short moments later he rolled them both so she lay cradled in his arms, and she murmured faint protest at the loss of him from inside her, only to think, in the end, it was but a small and bearable one. She would always have him inside her. She had, perhaps from the moment they'd met in the forest.

Beside her, Cassian cracked his jaws with a yawn. His eyes closed. His hand stroked her shoulder, tangling in her hair.

"Cassian."

"Yes, love."

The endearment warmed her. Annalise snuggled close. She kissed his chest, the heat of their passion cooling but the salt of their labors still fresh. "That pleased me very well."

He opened an eye to look at her, then smiled. He had such a lovely smile. "Then I am duly pleased."

Sighing happily, she pushed herself up to get a good view of his face. He shifted to return her gaze. Her mind sought the right words, wary of how often they'd tripped her up in the past.

Before she could say anything, a harsh rap came at the door. Cassian looked, but didn't get up. Annalise looked, too.

"Should you answer it?"

He frowned. "At this late hour, the news cannot be good."

"I've knocked upon your door at a late hour," she murmured, wondering for the first time if she were indeed the only one to ever do so. He'd said not, but . . .

"That's entirely different." Cassian leaned to kiss her as another knock sounded. "Fine, I'll answer it. Draw the sheets about yourself, love."

"Should I bury beneath them?" she asked, only half serious.

He looked at her over his shoulder, one leg already in his trousers. "Only if you're ashamed to be here."

So quickly could the spark of passion edge its way to anger, she thought, but knew this enough to avoid it with him, now. "No, of course not. I was thinking of you."

Another knock came as he crossed to kiss her, holding her close. Cassian looked deep into her eyes. "No, Annalise. There's naught to be shamed of. We've broken no rules."

Pleased, she held his face in her hands for a moment to kiss him again. "Nonetheless, I shall take myself to your privy chamber, if you don't mind. I've no need to flaunt myself in front of any late-hour guest."

Cassian's laugh poured through her, honey off a spoon. "I'll get rid of whoever it is. We're not finished yet."

"I'll hold you to that promise." With that, she let him go and made her way to the bath chamber, where she dipped water from the basin to wash herself and smiled at her reflection in the looking glass.

From the other room, the rise and fall of voices caught her attention. Snagging one of Cassian's shirts from a hook on the back of the door, Annalise pulled it over her head. Her braid could be hastily twisted, though she had naught with which to bind it, so she settled for tucking it into a loose bun at the nape of her neck. The shirt hung to midthigh, the sleeves dangling past her fingertips, so she rolled them up and cracked open the door to peek out.

Serenity. Annalise knew her just barely. The woman didn't notice her in the doorway. Her attention was focused entirely upon Cassian.

The serrated blade of jealousy sawed at Annalise. She'd not even known Cassian and Serenity were well-acquainted, and yet he reached for her with casual familiarity. Not intimacy, at least not any Annalise could see, but this was no mere professional relationship.

"I thought you should know," Serenity said. "I wanted to be the one to tell you."

"Thank you, Serenity." Cassian sounded a little hoarse. "You've ever been a good friend."

The door creaked. Cassian and Serenity both looked. Annalise, caught in her eavesdropping, still believed what he'd told her moments before—they'd done naught to shame them. She pushed the door open wider and stepped through it with a nod at the Sister.

Serenity looked solemnly at Cassian. "Oh."

Annalise lifted her chin, jaw gritting, fingers tightening at her sides. Cassian looked from her to Serenity. Silence, thick with tension, built.

"Right. I'll . . . go." Serenity flashed him a small grin. To Annalise she gave only an assessing look.

Nobody spoke again until she'd closed the door behind her. Then Cassian strode to the dresser, opened the drawer, and poured himself a glass of worm. He drank it back in a single gulp, and poured another.

"Will you tell me what she wanted, or is it not for me to know?"

He shook his head and looked at the bottle. "The bedamned worm's all been drunk."

"Cassian."

He looked at her.

"Shall I go, as well?"

The answer she desired was no, and a kiss, and his arms around her. She got none of them. Cassian sighed and wiped his mouth.

"She came to tell me of the arrival of one of her Sisters, long gone from the Motherhouse in the service of a patron."

Annalise didn't want to ask but couldn't keep herself from it. "Was she your lover?"

"Lover?" Cassian laughed. "No. She's my wife."

Chapter 21

She was already with the boy. Kellen shared a room with Leonder, both lads asleep. Bertricia had lit a single taper and held back the glow further with the shield of her hand so that it might not wake him.

That she should sit so tenderly on the side of Kellen's bed, that she should reach to stroke back his hair from his forehead, Cassian found unbearable. His shadow loomed in the doorway. Bertricia turned.

"Hello, Cassian."

Kellen stirred in his bed, but didn't wake.

"A word with you. Outside."

She nodded and stood with a grace he recognized as the benefit of years of training. Age hadn't stolen her beauty, though the years had given her features an edge they hadn't, in the past.

He stood aside to allow her to pass. In the hall she looked him up and down. Her smile didn't quite reach her eyes.

"It's been overlong since I saw you last," Bertricia said. "You look . . . well."

He looked like he'd crawled up from the depths of the Void. Felt like it, too, his eyes sand-filled and aching from lack of sleep. Once he'd told Annalise of Bertricia's return, she'd wanted to know all the details. Had demanded them, in fact. Cassian had kept his secrets so tight to his heart for so long he'd been unable to tell her more than the tale's barest bones.

It hadn't been enough for her. Had he expected otherwise? Annalise was not a woman accustomed to not being granted her way. It was what he . . .

"Cassian? I know this must be a surprise to you. In sooth, it's a surprise to me as well. I'd not expected . . . well." Bertricia gave a soft laugh and shook her head. "Old stories have familiar endings."

"It would be ridiculous to assume otherwise."

Her gaze hardened for a moment, but only just that long. She'd spent a long time in service. He wondered if it were beyond her to be anything but serene.

"Is this the game we shall play, then?" Bertricia said.

"This is no game."

"Ah, yes. I remember overwell how you ever lacked a sense of play, Cassian. I plead your mercy for expecting anything different from you now."

"As you said," Cassian replied, "old stories."

Bertricia drew herself up to her full height, which seemed taller to him than it had in the past. This, too, was because of Annalise, whose head reached the bottom of his chin at just the height to hold her to his chest so they might fit together just right.

"I didn't come here to reconcile with you. That would be ridiculous and foolish, indeed. So if you've a mind to punish me for what happened all those years ago by refusing me, set aside your desire. It can bring you naught but disgrace." Whatever expression showed upon his face prompted her to frown. "Were you hoping I'd come back to ask you for a second chance, Cassian? So that you might deny me? Or have you hoped to rekindle what we had? Have you been waiting for me all these years?"

"I think you know the answer to that."

In the dark and quiet hall, Bertricia's laugh was so far from humor as to be laughable itself. "Yes. I believe I do. But you can't blame me for hoping, at least a little, that you might have been waiting . . . at least a little. Woman I begin and woman I shall end, you know. No woman likes to remember she was cast aside by a man who once loved her above all else."

"Not above all else," Cassian said.

Bertricia nodded, her smile tightening. "Ah, yes, well. In that we were both fools."

"Why did you come back here, Bertricia?" He had to ask, the question burning like bile upon his tongue. Her answer didn't matter; he wouldn't like it whatever it was. But he had to hear it from her lips.

"I came back because the Motherhouse always welcomes us when we need a place to go."

"You've left your last patron, then?"

She hesitated. "No."

"Most in service don't return to the Motherhouse unless they've finished their assignment. Then again," he said, "most Handmaidens don't take years to bring their patrons to solace."

Bertricia had ever had a ready temper, smoothed though it may have been by her time in service. Now her jaw firmed and her eyes narrowed, but she spoke in the same cool voice. "This is for the Mothers-in-Service to judge, not you. You've chosen to give your life to the Order. Don't blame me for everything you've not done these past years, Cassian. Nobody held you here. Nobody forced you to stay on. You might've had a full, rich life, perhaps even a family by now. You made your choices, and I don't stand here and point out to you all the ways you've failed in them. Don't seek to do so to me."

"It's not my place to judge, as you say, your failures. I just want to know what you intend by returning. That's all."

She laughed and glanced toward the closed door behind which the Blessings slept. "I owe you no explanations, not even in memory of what we once shared."

She moved past him, the hem of her gown swirling. He caught a whiff of her perfume, something heady and full of spice, and entirely unfamiliar. Bertricia had ever smelled of lilies. If anything reminded him he no longer knew her, this was it.

"Just so you know," he said to her back, "I'll not allow you to take him."

She paused in her retreat, her back straight, shoulders stiff, her long braid swinging. She didn't turn to speak, but he had no trouble hearing her. "You had the chance to be the boy's father long years past, Cassian, and you refused it. You've no claim on him, you said so yourself. Do not seek to go against me in this matter. You will lose."

He had ever lost when it came to Bertricia, but as he watched her walk away, Cassian determined he would not lose against her again.

For an entire cycle of seasons, Cassian and Bertricia had been happy. He, at least, had been more than content with their life together. He'd been overjoyed. He had his beautiful wife and his service to the Faith. His days were filled with study and service and his nights with love.

He missed his brother, his blood, but Calvis had gone off at the bequest of a minor king who'd wished to hire Calvis's skills with the Art to protect his princess daughter. He didn't write, and no news came of him, but Cassian knew his brother lived. Would he not know if Calvis died? He'd feel it, he knew it.

So the days passed, and if Bertricia had regrets or complaints, she kept them from her adoring husband. They took the house in which he'd grown up, the one with the garden in which he'd seen her for the first time, and where they'd been married. His father died and his mother gladly gave over the household to Bertricia's keeping, preferring instead to spend her days sewing or reading or gossiping with friends while her daughter-in-law made sure to keep everything running smoothly.

It was, Cassian knew, the only way they might have had the life to which Bertricia had always been accustomed. He'd told her his life with the priesthood would preclude large houses and the hosting of brannigans, that new gowns every season and the best of everything else wouldn't be possible. Yet he knew it chafed at her to have to live in his mother's house, even if the old lady had stepped aside as mistress. Bertricia had been raised a merchant's daughter who lacked for nothing, and though Cassian would have preferred a small cottage with a vegetable patch and goat, his lady wife would never have settled for it. It made him love her all the more, that she'd agreed to wed him knowing he'd be unable to provide her with the life she'd always known.

He never asked himself why.

And then, his brother returned.

Calvis looked war-weary, battle-scarred, and yet unchanged. His dark hair had grown overlong, with streaks of silver at the temples and threaded throughout. He'd grown a full beard. He looked as different from Cassian, shaved head and face, as any man could look from another.

There were other changes, too. Calvis had ever moved with grace and strength, but now he limped from a wound he refused to describe. His ready humor, as irritating as it could be, hadn't vanished entirely but had been pushed so deep it rarely surfaced. The flash of white teeth against the dark of his beard most often signaled a grimace, not a grin.

He didn't say where he'd been, just showed up in the dining room one evening as the family supped, and sat at the table as though he'd never gone. He accepted his mother's tears and hugs, the shake of his brother's hand. To Bertricia he said nothing, and later, when Cassian and his wife lay abed, her fierce whisper had cut through the darkness as a knife slices bread.

"Is he going to stay here?"

"I imagine so. He's my brother. This is as much his house as it is mine." Cassian, who had to rise with the dawn to serve at the temple, yawned and closed his eyes.

Bertricia wasn't interested in sleep. "For how long?"

"Love, I don't know. As long as he wants to. As long as he needs to."

The bed shifted as she did, rolling onto her side to face him. "Where was he? He was gone for a year, now he's back, just like that? And looking that way . . ."

"Looking what way, Bertricia?"

"So hard," she said quietly. "So used."

Cassian put his hand on her shoulder beneath the weight of her hair. Her skin, warm and fragrant, called him to touch and stroke it, but when he moved closer to kiss her, Bertricia turned her face. She buried it against his chest, her shoulders shaking.

"He frightens me," she whispered.

There'd been few times during their acquaintance that Cassian had ever seen Bertricia weep. Now he heard the sound of tears in her voice, but when he lifted her face with a finger to her chin, her eyes were dry and bleak in the faint moonlight shining from the window. He was selfish enough to be grateful. He never knew how to react to the grief of another.

"Would you have me send him away? Would you have me put my brother from this house, which is his as much as mine?" Cassian sat to gather her against him, and Bertricia settled herself into his lap, her head on his shoulder.

"No."

"I know you've never approved of him—"

She laughed. "Oh, it's not I whose approval wasn't won."

Cassian knew his brother had never liked her, but he refused to say so aloud to his wife. "He's said naught of his intentions. It's likely he'll not stay longer than a day, a week. He never has before."

But it was longer than a day, a week. Longer than a fortnight. In fact, Calvis woke every morning long after the rest of the household had risen and stayed awake long after they'd all gone to bed. He attended meals inconsistently and without apology for any absences.

"It's like living with a ghost," Bertricia said at night when again Cassian sought sleep. "He comes and goes without a word to anyone. I came upon him in the garden and he looked right through me as though I didn't exist."

"Again, love, what would you have me do? Demand he converse with us in the parlor of nights, play at snap me? What? Wherever my brother has been, whatever he's seen or done, those are his burdens to bear."

"He's your brother, Cassian. Have you spoken to him?"

"I speak to him every day."

Bertricia scoffed. "About what? Mindless things."

"You don't know that."

"I know you," she said, and for the first time since she'd softened to his courtship, Cassian heard disdain in her tone. "I know you won't ask him what you're afraid to know."

He didn't tell her he already knew much about his brother's life and the crimes he'd committed. For the first time in their marriage, Cassian turned his back on his wife, rolled to face away from her, went to bed with anger seething between them upon his part.

"Mayhap if you're so concerned," he told her, "you should ask him yourself."

He would ever wonder if it had been his fault, what happened later. When everything had fallen down around them, when it all ended, broken, Cassian blamed himself. He still did.

Yet he was the one who was still alive.

Ah, Annalise. I'm pleased to have caught you."

Mayhap Serenity meant her smile to set Annalise at ease, but it only set her back a step.

"Yes?"

"I carry a message from Mother Deliberata as regards your current assignment to the afternoon Faith studies with Master Toquin."

Annalise narrowed her gaze. "Oh, and aye? What does Mother Deliberata say of them?"

"You're to be granted your wish and moved from his class to another more suited to your abilities." Serenity's smile thinned a little, her gaze not so serene.

"I see." Annalise had been on her way to that very class, her stomach already churning with thoughts of what she might say to him. Her teacher. Her lover. "At whose request?"

Serenity's gaze flashed, revealing herself not as puzzled by the question as she next pretended to be. "Your mercy, I'm uncertain as to your meaning."

"Who asked it? At whose request was I removed from Master Toquin's instruction?" Annalise paused. "Yours?"

"No, certainly not. I have no say in the manner of such things. At any rate, even if I did, I'd not have asked it." Serenity wet her lips with the tip of her tongue. "Think otherwise of me, but I've no reason to interfere."

"His lady wife? Was it her?"

Serenity blinked rapidly, her cheeks coloring. "His lady—oh, no. I daresay not hers, either. What exactly did Cassian tell you?"

"Not enough. So it was him, then, yes? He asked for me to

be removed from his class, no longer to be his assistant. He did it. Yes?"

"Yes," Serenity said quietly. "But judge him not overharshly, Annalise, unless you know his reasons."

"I can think of reasons aplenty for him to dismiss me from his class, and yet though I requested multiple times in the past to be so removed, no one listened to me. His claim was the Mothers knew best, and you tell me now he was able to petition them for my removal? How convenient!"

"He must've had good enough reason, else they'd have kept you there the way they'd done before. Somewhat must've changed."

Annalise's mouth twisted. "I wonder what that could've been?"

Serenity sighed. "Sister—"

"I'm no Sister of yours. Not yet."

"Annalise," Serenity said with a bit of bite to her reply, "whatever Cassian's reasons for dismissing you, it might be worth your consideration. I've known him a long time and never found him to be unfair."

"No? Unkind, perhaps? Unwilling, unyielding? But not unfair." Annalise swallowed to keep her gorge from rising further. "Was it fair of him to go to the Mothers and ask for what I'd been denied already, and do so without the small, bare consideration of telling me himself?"

"I believe it was his thought you'd be pleased."

"Then he is also unwise."

Serenity looked 'round the empty hall and sighed. "She is not his lady wife. Not any longer, and hasn't been for all the years he's spent here."

"He called her his lady wife. He said naught of a dissolution."

"I believe Cassian carries a great weight within himself as regards the ending of his marriage. One might imagine someone who cared for him would seek to discover it and ease it rather than burden him further."

Annalise choked back a reply. Selfish is the heart, and yet again she thought first of herself. Serenity moved close enough to put a hand on Annalise's arm, though only briefly.

"I believe you are good for him, Annalise."

Annalise shook her head.

"You have ever been his friend since you arrived here. Even when he refused to allow it. And believe me, I do know how fiercely he refuses friendship, for I've tried to provide it."

The women stared at each other. Serenity smiled, finally. Annalise wasn't sure she could have, even if someone lifted the corners of her lips on her behalf.

"I believe he's gone walking," Serenity said at last. "Into the forest, by the waterfall."

"Thank you." Annalise was already moving.

"Annalise!"

She turned to look back. Serenity had clasped her hands in front of her. She unlinked her fingers now to give a small wave.

"Good mazel to you."

Annalise nodded and continued, not toward the Motherhouse's large double front doors, but to a small side door that led 'round to the back. She'd come through the forest on her journey here and hadn't been through it again since then, but she was certain she could find her way.

By the time she reached the forest path her stomach had eased in its twisting. Something in the air's fresh scent, the pungent odor of the trees and earth, calmed her. Or mayhap it was knowing that no matter what happened, it was beyond her control. She could do naught to make him love her if he did not.

Just as she could do nothing to make herself cease.

She let the rushing sound of water lead her past the rock and fork in the path where she'd first met him. She paused only a moment to stare down the long trail he'd sent her on, then back at the way she'd walked. The difference between a few minutes, walk and a full day's journey.

She laughed, finding humor in it for the first time, and kept on. Her slippers were too thin to make this an easy trek. She slid in soft pine needles and snagged her gown on briars and claw-fingered tree branches. Her hair got loose from its braid and tangled about her face. By the time she pushed into the clearing where a small, bright waterfall fell into a tiny pool, her mouth had gone dry.

He was there, as Serenity had said, but Annalise didn't go to him right away. She went to the pond, hardly larger than a puddle, really, and dipped her fingers in the clear water. She drank. She bathed her cheeks and wrists and the back of her neck. She took the time to tidy her hair, though she'd lost the cord with which to bind it and settled for leaving it loose down her back.

Then she turned to him.

Cassian had never looked more severe than he did in his high neck and long sleeves, jacket black as despair. Not even the buttons flashed or glinted. His hair was the only part of him in disarray, and that only from the occasional gust of breeze that swayed the grass and flowers and shook the trees.

He sat on a boulder surrounded by soft grass, both his feet on the ground, boots planted solid. His hands gripped the rock at his sides. He was watching her now, likely had been the entire time.

Annalise went to him. She got on her knees. She Waited, buttocks resting on her heels, the back of one hand resting inside the palm of the other. She Waited for him.

"Get up, Annalise."

She looked at him. She didn't get up. She leaned just enough to press her forehead to his knee.

With a muttered curse, Cassian jerked away and got off the rock. His hands gripped her shoulders, pulled her to her feet. Annalise went readily enough without fighting him, and when he let her go, she was steady enough to keep her feet.

"Don't put me aside," she warned, submissive perhaps in demeanor but not in tone. "I'll have an explanation from you, Cassian. After."

"After . . . what?" he asked, wariness in his dark eyes.

She kissed him. She had to stand upon her toes to reach his mouth and fist her hands in the spare amount of loose fabric on his sleeves. She nudged a knee between his legs, sliding her tongue inside his mouth, open in surprise and not passion.

At least, not at first.

A noise very much like a growl eased from his throat, vibrating on her lips. His hands gripped her hard, one between her shoulder blades and the other buried into her hair at the base of her neck. Cassian kissed her more fiercely than she had him, and Annalise took what he gave.

He broke it first, breathing hard. She was no longer on her toes, but had softened against him as he bent for her. His gaze searched hers.

"Why?" he asked. "Why this, here? Now?"

"Wherever you are, I will go to find you. Think you I would allow you to send me off without a word? Without telling me yourself?" She leaned against him, mouth seeking his again.

His kiss deepened, his hands guiding her as he sat again on the boulder and took her with him. Her feet still on the ground, Annalise leaned into his embrace. Her hands went to his shoulders to keep herself steady.

They kissed for a long time.

She felt his hardness against her and moved her hand to the hem of his jacket, then his trousers beneath. She made swift work of the buttons and slipped her hand inside to grasp him. Cassian moaned into her mouth and made as though to move, but Annalise shook her head and silenced him with another hard kiss.

"Hush," she said against his mouth when he made to protest again.

She couldn't forget the day in the closet, when he'd used his mouth to please her without any for himself. Now she stroked his erection, freed from his trousers, and kissed him until all his protests fell away. Until he gave up to her. Gave in.

Until he broke.

His cock, sleek and hard under her fingers, throbbed as she stroked him. She would gladly have continued, gone even to her knees again for him to take him in her mouth, but Cassian captured her wrist and stopped her hand from moving.

She opened her eyes. He licked his mouth, also licking hers. He slowed the pace for a moment and she thought he meant only to instruct her on his preferences. In the next moment he'd pushed her away just enough to move off the boulder and turn her so her hands went flat against it.

Behind her, Cassian lifted her skirts and slid his hands along her bare flesh. He found her center, already slick with desire; his fingers slid inside to probe and tease. Annalise made a low cry and bent forward as he entered her with his cock next.

She pushed against him, ready and more than ready. She'd thought to please him only, but gave him what he wanted without argument. His fingers found her clit and pinched in gentle counterpoint to the thrust of his prick inside her.

She never would've said something as frantic as this, in such a place instead of slow, well-made love in a comfortable bed, could ever have satisfied her. Annalise crested in moments, body tightening on his. Orgasm danced just out of reach, teasing for only a breath or two before she tipped over the edge into the depths of pleasure.

Cassian followed her, crying her name in a low voice. His thrusts eased. His finger circled gently on her clitoris to ease a small set of new ripples through her.

Her hands had clutched so tight upon the rock she'd scraped the tips of her fingers. Blinking, Annalise eased her grip on the stone. Cassian withdrew, and before she could move even to let her skirts fall around her ankles, she felt the soft press of material between her legs.

She put her hand over it and turned. "Your handkerchief?"

"I thought you might need it."

She raised a brow at him as he tucked himself away. "Anything else would be . . . unseemly?"

Cassian paused, studying her. Then he cupped her face and kissed her softly. He looked into her eyes. "I would never be the cause of your discomfort, Annalise."

"But you are." She arranged her skirts and handed him the handkerchief, watching with concealed amusement as he considered if he should return it to his pocket. "Give it to me."

She took it from him and rinsed it in the basin of rock at the waterfall's base, then spread it on the rock to dry. She turned to find him watching her, obvious admiration in his gaze. She put her hands on her hips.

"You've changed a great deal since first you came to the Order, Annalise."

"Have I? Have you?"

"Yes . . . I think so. I think you've made me."

She sighed and rested, weary now, against the boulder that had so conveniently supported her during their lovemaking. "At least there's that."

He sighed, too, and sat beside her. The boulder wasn't large enough for them both, but Annalise didn't mind sharing the space. It pressed her close to him, and for now she would take every opportunity to be so forced.

"You sent me from your class because we have become lovers." She didn't make it a question.

"I requested once more you be removed from my class because your level of learning was too far advanced for it. This time, the Mothers saw fit to allow the request. It had nothing to do—"

She twisted to stare at him. "Please don't lie to me, Cassian. Above all else, don't lie."

He drew a fingertip across her forehead to push a few curls away. "Your mercy. I should be better spoken when it comes to you."

"Yes. You should."

He cupped her face again. Kissed her. "You have ever been so blunt with me, Annalise. You've never suffered my whims, have you? Even though so many have."

"Whims? Eccentricities, I'd call them. Arrogances, mayhap. I might go so far as to name them hum-grumblies."

His low rumble of laughter lit a fire in her belly, though he'd already so satisfied her moments before. "You have ever been unafraid to say to me whatever was on your mind. You never let me frighten you."

"I've faced more frightening faces than yours." She paused as though thinking. "Not many, true, as yours is fair fearsome."

Again, he laughed and kissed her. His gaze held many emotions, joy not among them. "It's why I . . . care for you so."

"You care for me?" She leaned into him, her head on his shoulder. "You have a most troublesome way of showing it."

"I plead your mercy, sweetheart. I am not . . . I have never been . . ."

"Hush," she told him with a finger pressed to his mouth.

He kissed it and folded his fingers 'round hers to pull them from his lips. "I would tell you, if you'll listen."

"I will gladly lend my ears to anything you have to say," she told him.

And he began.

Chapter 22

Calvis had been gone and now was back; Cassian had been content in his life and now was not.

His time in the Temple fulfilled him, at least parts of it did. He found great satisfaction in bringing the Word of the Book to those unable to decipher it for themselves. Children, mostly, but also those whose minds were incapable of great understanding. He spent his days teaching the simplest concepts, taking the tasks his Brothers-in-Faith found too dull or not challenging enough.

Home was another matter altogether. He had, as he'd told his lady wife, not found it necessary to put his brother from the house in which they'd grown up. Calvis, after all, had a full half share of the house and lands, no apparent desire to buy out his brother, and no obvious means of procuring the funds even if he had.

Living with Calvis *was* a bit like living with a ghost.

He ate and drank at their table and spoke when spoken to, but of the joyous, raucous brother who'd loved to drink and whore and gamble, Cassian saw no sign. He'd once have said he'd be happy to have his brother lose those vices, but now, watching his brother push his food 'round his plate, eyes shadowed, cheeks hollowed, Cassian found himself thinking he might take his brother to a brothel simply to see if he could liven him again.

As summer turned to the harvest and then winter beyond it, Cassian came home from the Temple with night almost fallen. As he crossed the yard he came to his brother, stripped to the waist, breathing plumes of frost into the chilly air. He moved silently, each step precise and certain and lovely.

Striking Serpent.

Leaping Tiger.

Biting Dog.

Cassian didn't know the names of all the forms, just knew his brother had mastered them all. Even without weapons he was deadly. Graceful. Lethal. Those hands had killed. Even now as Calvis finished, panting, Cassian saw his brother scrub his palms against his trousers.

Some stains are never washed clean.

"Cassian," Calvis cried at the sight of him.

It was the first time in a long while Calvis had been the first to speak upon their meeting. The sound of his name in his brother's voice, so much like and yet so different than his own, warmed Cassian more than a slug of liquor.

"Cal."

"Brother . . . you've caught me at my work, I'm afraid."

Cassian leaned on the fence railing to watch as Calvis slipped on his shirt. The warmth had frozen inside him at his brother's words. "Your work? You plan on leaving us?"

Calvis paused, expression unreadable. "I would never leave you, brother. Not entirely."

Cassian forced a laugh to shadow the hint of tension. "When you said your work—"

"Ah, I should've said my Art, but it's not mine, is it? I use it now and again, but I shouldn't claim ownership of what belongs to everyone."

"Not to everyone. Not to me." Cassian laughed, shaking his head.

"Oh, and aye, even to you, brother. Come here and let me show you." Calvis gestured.

Cassian moved forward, reluctantly. "You've ever been the fitter of us."

"Bollocks. We're the same, as the Allcreator made us. Yes? What I have, you have." Calvis tugged Cassian by the wrist to stand beside him. "Now. Plant your feet like so."

It felt awkward, the stance, the stretch. It had been too long since Cassian had even tried these positions. The first few passes left Cassian unsteady and easily knocked off-balance by Calvis, who even pulled his strikes. By the fifth or sixth time, though, Cassian managed a block.

"Most well, brother! Most well indeed!" Calvis looked happier than Cassian had seen him in years. Since they were boys, perhaps. It was better than anything, to see his brother with such joy in his eyes.

"Again," Cassian said. "This time, I'll knock you on your arse."

They went again, in darkness that deepened. Lights from inside the house provided some bare illumination, enough to make this battle all the more challenging. It still ended up with Cassian on his back and Calvis atop him, fist at his brother's throat.

"Stop that!" Bertricia's voice, acrack with fright, rang throughout the yard. She lifted her lantern to shine the light on the brothers. "Stop that at once!"

"We were only playing," Cassian tried to tell her as his brother helped him to his feet. "Naught more."

She didn't seem to hear him. She strode toward them, a picture of feminine fury. She lifted the lantern, and in its flickering light Cassian could see her features had twisted, making her a woman he didn't know.

She slapped Calvis across the face so fiercely his head rocked back.

For a man so well-versed in the Art to take a blow he could so easily have sidestepped meant much, if only Cassian could determine the meaning. When she slapped him again, blood trickled from Calvis's mouth. It looked black in the lantern light, black but bright.

"Enough!" Cassian stopped his wife's hand from a third blow. "By the Arrow, Bertricia, what are you about? Have you gone mad?"

She was shaking, indeed, as though madness had overtaken her. She even snapped her jaws at both of them. Her eyes rolled, a wild horse at the first touch of a saddle.

"I told you I would never hurt him. I told you that." Calvis spit a mouthful of blood into the dirt at her feet. It left a mark in the frost.

Mayhap Cassian had always known from a place deep inside, even back in those garden days when Calvis had called her she-hound the second. Mayhap later when Calvis had hired a whore for his brother's pleasure. But if he had not known so long ago, Cassian surely knew it now.

He stepped away from both of them and tasted sickness so sour he thought he might spew it. "Calvis?"

Calvis's shoulders slumped, but he never looked away from his brother's face. "I will not plead your mercy, brother, for I deserve it not."

"Plead you nothing," Bertricia said in a low, haunted voice. The lantern shook, making shadows dance among the three of them. She wasn't wearing a cloak against the cold.

Cassian held his place on the surface of the world only because to lose it would mean perhaps losing his mind, as well. And that he refused to do. Not over this. Not for her.

"Go into the house, Bertricia."

"I will not! I will not stand aside and let you—" She choked and wept.

Both brothers looked at her, but her husband was the one who spoke again.

"Inside the house, or by the Void, I will make you wish you'd gone of your own accord."

Bertricia went.

Cassian looked at his brother. "What's yours is mine and mine yours, is that it?"

"No, brother. Not like this. Believe me, a thousand times I've regretted this."

"Yet you didn't end it. What did she think you were going to do? Kill me so that you might wed her in my place?"

"By the Void, never. I told her as such."

"She asked it of you?" Horror tried to sweep him into silence, but Cassian forced it away. "Did she?"

Calvis gave him no insult with lies. "Yes. She was crazed. She loves me overwell, brother. Again, I can plead no mercy for it."

"Did you mean for her to love you overwell, Calvis? Did you seek to make me the cuckold you warned me I'd be even before I married her? Tell me you sought this to hurt me, or to . . . compete with me . . . or to have me," Cassian said unsteadily. "Tell me even that, and I will forgive you."

"I would tell you if it were true, but I swear to you, Cassian, she came after me. Always. The first time she acted as though she thought I were you, and I let her because I wanted you to see what a bad choice she would be."

"And now? Surely she can't pretend she thinks us the same now."

"No. Nor did she so believe then, I'd be willing to wager any amount of coin. But I found myself weak, brother. She is very lovely, your lady wife. And well-skilled. And I thought she would never be able to ask of me what other women might—to give myself more to her beyond my cock. I thought she'd be unable to ask such of me."

"But she has?"

"Yes." Calvis shuddered. "Sinder's Blood, I wish . . . I had never gone with her."

"Still? You've been with her recently?" Cassian shuddered, too, throat closing on bile but needing to know.

"Every day."

Cassian muttered a curse so vile he'd never have thought himself capable of taking the Invisible Mother's name in such a fashion. "Why? By the Blood, Calvis, how could you?"

"She threatened to tell you if I stopped, and brother, I didn't want to hurt you. I could not bear it if you hated me. I simply could not bear it." Calvis's eyes flashed. "I already know there's no place for me in the Land Above, but by the Arrow I swear to you, no crime I've committed has sliced me as much as this I've done against you."

The clearing wasn't silent. The breeze soughed through the trees. The waterfall pattered into the basin. Still, Cassian could hear the sound of Annalise's breathing. He turned to her.

"I was angry, and I turned away. My brother left in the night. I never got to tell him I forgave him, or that I would ever have had him in my life rather than her."

Annalise leaned against him, her small hand warm in his. "He betrayed you as much as she. Mayhap more."

"It didn't matter. I could find another wife. With my father passed into the Land Above, I could never have another brother."

She stroked his hand. "What happened to him?"

"He died in a bar fight a few days after he left. He could've easily won any fight against any man. The one who killed him said, in fact, it was as though Calvis fell upon his blade apurpose. It was an argument of no consequence, a drunken fight over dice. The man who killed him hadn't meant to do more than threaten. Witnesses held out his story. He never was convicted."

"Oh, Invisible Mother, Cassian, I am so sorry. So, so sorry." Annalise kissed his hand.

He wanted to pull away from her kindness, but forced himself to stay still. She would offer him herself and he would be no fool, refusing. He could no longer afford to be a fool.

"Bertricia said she'd gone to my brother because she thought she could help him. She tried to make me believe I'd sent her into his arms."

"But he said—"

"With my brother dead, there was only her word. And though I didn't believe all of it, I did believe she thought she could help him. Ease his burden, somehow, even as she eased her own. That might not have been how she started it, but I believe it was how she meant to end it."

"With you as her husband, what burden could she have?" Annalise sounded sour.

He looked at her. "I long ago ceased to imagine her reasons. They only hurt me too much. She entered the Order a fortnight after Calvis's death. She said it was because she'd failed with him and wanted to atone by bringing solace to some others. She found herself well-suited to it."

"And now she's back because she finished with a patron?"

Cassian drew a deep breath and got up to pace, his boots scuffing dirt. "No. She's back now to claim her son."

"Her . . ." Annalise fell silent.

Cassian faced her. "Bertricia was one of the few I've ever seen who took her vows almost immediately upon entering the Order. She was sent to her first patron within a month of arriving. She came to me a month after that, her belly not yet swelling with a child she wanted me to claim as mine."

He didn't blame Annalise for looking sick. He'd felt sick then, too. She tangled her fingers together, perhaps to keep them from making fists.

"You didn't?"

"I'd scarcely been to my lady wife's bed in months, so consumed was she with fucking my brother," he said bluntly. "The child wasn't likely to be mine."

"It could've been your brother's boy."

"And it could've been her patron's get," Cassian said. "She'd not been with the Order long, remember. It's possible the herbs Handmaidens take had not yet begun their job. And Handmaidens who become pregnant while in the service of a patron give birth to—"

"Blessings." Annalise put a hand over her mouth, her eyes wide. "Oh, Cassian. Oh . . ."

"The boy appears to have my brother's eyes, but all else belongs to his mother."

"He has your eyes, then," Annalise said.

"I don't know the looks of her patron. He could have his eyes, for all I know." He sounded angry. Was angry, though not at her.

Annalise rose, then, and went to him. She knew him so well she didn't touch him. He couldn't have borne it, a gentle, pitying touch.

"All this time, you've stayed here so that you might watch over him?"

"So that I might be able to tell if he belonged to my brother. Or me. Yes. But the longer I waited, the harder it was to convince myself he was indeed my nephew, as much mine as a son would've been. Harder still to convince myself he belonged to some unnamed face. The boy is a Blessing, a true Kedalya's Blessing, and he has a life here in the Order. When he's of age, he'll be provided for as handsomely as any prince and set to make his way in the world. Who am I to hold him back from such a future? Who am I?"

She touched him then, and he suffered it without allowing himself to overthink his reasons.

"Someone who loves him," she said.

He clasped her fingers in his. Pulled her close. Stopped himself from kissing her to look into her eyes, instead.

"She's back to take the boy for reasons she hasn't yielded, and I don't aim to allow her to do it."

"No blame will come from me on that account. She sounds vile. And I say that not only because she was your lady wife," Annalise added with a slow smile. "Woman I begin and all that. Her behavior shames us all."

"You needn't be jealous. My love for her ended a long time ago."

Annalise raised a brow. "Good."

She kissed him, and Cassian found it was nothing to suffer, but to enjoy.

"Am I still banished from your classroom?" she murmured against him.

"Well, yes. This has naught to do with that."

She tipped her frowning face to his. "No?"

"Annalise, you need to be with a true teacher, one who can challenge you. You're already far more educated in the Word and the Book than any I've ever taught. You should never have been placed in my class to begin with."

She opened her mouth to say somewhat, but seemed to change her mind. "I don't want to leave. I doubt there's anyone who can teach me more than I know, anyway. I would find it more useful to continue assisting you. Teaching others. Especially now . . ."

"Now what?" He asked her, falling into the deep pool of her loving gaze.

"Now that I understand what it is to really believe. I spent my whole life with the Faith being forced into me yet never once really believed it. And now . . . I do." Annalise had never sounded shy to him. It didn't suit her.

Cassian studied her face, so earnest and sincere. "Sweetheart, I'm not the man to help you on that path."

"Don't be silly. Former priest and all that? You're perfect, in more ways than one." She gave his arse a squeeze he'd have laughed at if her words hadn't so disturbed him.

"*Former* priest," he told her carefully. "Look at me, Annalise. I am not the man to help you in your newfound faith. I have none."

She blinked and frowned. "I don't like you when you make sport of me, Cassian."

"I'm not making sport. I'm telling you the truth."

She stepped out of his embrace. "You have no faith?"

He held out his hands, fingers spread. "No."

"But . . . but you . . ." She stepped back again, and again, expression twisting. "You're a teacher of the Faith! Your purpose is to instruct novitiates in the Word of the Book, to teach them . . . how can you take on such a task with a clear conscience when everything you tell them feels to you a lie?"

"Teaching the Word is my purpose. It need not be my pleasure." He reached for her, and she recoiled. He withdrew his grasp.

Her mouth thinned. "I don't understand you."

They'd spent some few hours in love compared to the many they'd spent at odds. His own mouth twisted on his reply. "If your lack of understanding surprises you, Annalise, I fear I will find you quite foolish."

He knew just where to poke her, to prick and stab. To his shame, Cassian discovered he wanted to. He wanted to force her away from him.

"Then I am, indeed, a fool." Her voice broke and, Void take her, she began to weep. "And I am not at all surprised."

He could have gone after her. It would've taken two of his steps to reach her, one arm's length to grab. Instead, Cassian watched her go.

He was not surprised, either.

Chapter 23

As a girl, Annalise once stumbled upon a bright-plumed bird that had flown into a window and fallen stunned to the ground. No bigger than the palm of her hand, all big eyes and gaping mouth, it had peeped pitifully in her cradled hands. Tiny feet, hollow bones, feathers of blue and red and green. She'd never seen so lovely a creature from so close a view.

She held it only for a few moments, long enough to feel the rapid patter of its heartbeat and the scratchiness of its brilliant feathers. It had seemed a precious and wondrous thing, that tiny bird. Recovering its wits, it had struggled in her fist. Rather than hold it tight to keep it, as she'd wanted to, Annalise had let it go.

Perhaps her relationship with Cassian was like that bird. Precious and wondrous and fragile, fighting against being held so tight. Yet she found herself unable to open her fists and let it go.

She found him in his classroom alone behind his desk, the scent of ink still in the air. "Cassian."

He looked up from the pages he'd been turning. She'd grown overused to his smile upon the sight of her; it stung worse than she wanted to admit to see the old wary coldness in his gaze. He set aside the book and stood.

"I didn't expect to see you here."

"Yet here I am," she said. "I'd like to speak to you."

He didn't move toward her even a hair's distance. "You've said it all, I think."

"Then you'd be wrong." She moved between the rows of desks and stopped in front of his. She wanted to kiss him.

"I stand corrected."

"Why must we ever be at odds? Why must everything between us be a battle?"

His dark eyes showed no glimmer of emotion. He shrugged. "Perhaps it ought to be a lesson to us."

"No. I don't accept that. I won't."

"Annalise," Cassian said, "you have no choice."

"Is that your answer to me, then? I have no choice? You've decided for both of us that we shall remain at a distance from each other? Is that what you . . . want?" She'd aimed to sound strident and managed until the very last, when her voice cracked and broke.

"It was foolish for me to respond to your advances. I know that now, and plead your mercy for it. I ought to have known better. There were other men here who might've taken the place of me—"

"I wanted no other man, and you know it. I made that clear from the first. You might've refused me, but you didn't. Because you wanted me!" She forced the words from a raw throat.

He bent his head a little, eyes closing so that he didn't have to look at her. "Wanting something is not always the best reason to take it."

"I came here believing in little, and much has changed. Because of you, Cassian. Don't tell me you haven't changed as well, for I'll call you a liar."

"You've already called me a liar."

Ashamed, Annalise swallowed against the pain. "I misspoke in anger. I beg your mercy. I was wrong to say such a thing."

"No. You weren't. It's true. I've been a liar for the past ten years. I've lied to the Mothers and Sisters-in-Service who were kind enough to grant me a place. I've lied to the novitiates entrusted to me. And most of all, I lied to myself." He looked at her, eyes bright and hard and cold enough to burn her. "I tried to lie to you, too."

"But you didn't."

"Only because you would not allow it."

She reached but dropped her hand when she saw he wouldn't take it. "Are you familiar with the commentary written by Benvolo Deleon?"

His gaze grew wary. "Yes. I've read it, years long past now, but of course I did during my training."

"Deleon interpreted the story of Sinder and Kedalya by saying that when Sinder came upon her in the woods, she asked him his name. Fearing he would frighten her should he reveal his true nature, Sinder first lied and gave her a false name."

"Deleon's commentary has wildly been denounced as whimsy. What name would Sinder give? What part would he play? As the Allcreator, he'd made the world. Who would ever mistake him for somewhat he was not? Certainly not Kedalya, unless she were an idiot."

Annalise continued. "Deleon's commentary was extrapolated by Garwin Alsider in a pamphlet he distributed himself along with several others."

"I'm not familiar with Alsider."

"You wouldn't be. He was never a priest, just a man who found value in study. He dined out on those pamphlets for many years and was quite popular among certain groups whose common interests featured the Faith. He was a guest of my parents many times."

Cassian raised a brow. "Your point is to make me aware there are commentaries about which I'm unaware? I assure you, Annalise, I know this. But Alsider's pamphlets weren't accepted as canon, therefore they're of no more value than anything anyone could've written."

"Alsider claimed," Annalise continued, determined to make her point, "that Kedalya knew Sinder wasn't telling her the truth. She knew who he was. She allowed the lie because it served them both for him to woo her as another, first. One who was not a god, but a man."

He stared. "Make your point."

"Sinder lied to Kedalya to save her from himself and yet she loved him anyway. It didn't matter what he called himself, or what face he gave her. She loved him anyway."

Annalise wasn't on her knees, but she was Waiting. One hand inside the palm of the other, cupping air. She remembered the beat and brush of wings, a rapid heartbeat, the rush of air as the bird flew away.

"You don't need to save me from you," she told him quietly. "Because I love you."

In her dreams, in the fae stories, such a declaration was always met with a kiss and an embrace, with mingled laughter and tears and followed by a wedding.

This was not a fae story.

Cassian said naught. She waited for him to speak, or even to blink, at least to look at her, but his gaze had gone blank and far away. When her ears began to ring, Annalise realized she'd been holding her breath and let it out. Dizzy, she put a hand on the desk. Surely now, she thought, he will reach for me.

"You should go," Cassian told her.

Annalise managed another sip of air. "No."

Cassian slammed the text closed, the sound like thunder. "Did you not hear what I told you yesterday?"

"I heard everything you said! Every word!"

Now he moved closer, though not in the way she wanted. He

menaced, standing tall above her without touching. His gaze, still cold fire, blazed.

"I do not believe in Sinder and Kedalya. I don't believe in the Word of the Book, I don't believe in commentaries. All of it is pretty fiction, made up by men to satisfy their need for explanation. None of it is true. There is this world and the Void and naught else. I do not," Cassian bit out, "have faith. A priest without faith is naught but a man. And a man without faith, Annalise, is no man at all."

"Don't say that."

"I've said it."

She stepped closer, this time to snag his sleeve. Her fingertips ran down the fine cloth to find his flesh at the end of it. "It's not true."

He didn't allow her to take his hand. Cassian stepped away and made her a detestably formal half bow. "Good day, Mistress Marony."

"Do not dismiss me, Cassian. Please." Once she'd have demanded. She pleaded now.

He'd moved away, but she drew close again, this time to slide her hands up the front of his jacket and then to his shoulders, the back of his neck. His hair, still so unfashionably short, brushed her knuckles. He turned his face and put his hands upon her wrists as she said, "Talk to me. Let me help you. What can I do for you, just tell me. I love you."

She didn't hope for bells to chime this time. She didn't even expect him to reply in kind. All she wanted was him to look at her, but before he did, the door opened.

"Annalise! You've a letter!" Tansy stopped inside the doorway. "Oh, your pardon."

Cassian gently put Annalise's hands from him and stepped away. "Take your letter, Annalise."

"This is not finished between us," she murmured.

Cassian didn't reply. She turned, trying not to slay Tansy with a glare, and took the letter. Jacquin's familiar hand slashed across the envelope, sealed with his family crest. She held it to her chest, eyes closed for a moment. It even smelled of him, the pungent spice of his cologne.

"Thank you, Tansy. Come, walk with me."

Tansy looked over her shoulder as they left the room. "I interrupted. Your mercy. I didn't know."

"It's all right." Annalise forced a smile. "It was naught of consequence. Come . . . I fancy seeing if we can woo Cook out of a sugar bun. I'm fair famished and could use a strong pot of cacao as well. Will you go with me?"

Tansy grinned, then looked crestfallen. "I can't. I was to deliver the letter and then meet Helena and Wandalette for a game of snap me in the library. They claim to have a method of losing I must learn."

"Losing? I might imagine you could do that without being taught."

"Oh, no, it's a subtle way of losing so that your patron need never know you're throwing the game."

"Ah." Annalise said with a lifted brow, unable to take much pleasure in the humor of Tansy's description. "Some can take pleasure only in winning fairly, yes?"

"I suppose so. Are you well? I'll stay with you, should you need me."

"No. You go. I've my letter to read." Annalise waved her friend away. "Make most merry with your friends."

Annalise, when Tansy left, didn't go to the kitchen. She had no appetite and was fair grateful for Tansy's previous commitment, so that she needn't keep on a brave face for the other woman. Annalise took her letter to their room and closed the door. She took a long embroidery needle from her sewing box and slit the seal.

She began to read.

My dearest Annalise,

It's with great sorrow and also the greatest joy I write to share with you our mutual good news. Sorrow, for I had long hoped the pair of us would make a wedded couple; joy to share with you somewhat I know you'll find as amazing and delightful as I.

I've fallen in love and agreed to marry a woman of such worth, such beauty, such intelligence I can scarce describe her adequately with the poor tools of pen and ink. Moreover, my love for her is such that even the physical—dare I say it, especially the physical—aspects of a marriage have ceased to be so daunting. I tell you, my dear one, I'm no longer unable to be a true and good husband.

By the time this letter reaches you, we'll have already said our vows. I trust you'll not despair at missing the ceremony of our binding—I know how important your time in the Order is to you and would never, as your dear and longtime friend and companion, expect you to leave somewhat you find so necessary in order to witness the wedding. Trust you we'll be thinking of you as with us in spirit, for I tell you truly, without your influence the marriage would never even take place.

I wed your cousin, Caterina. As the daughter of your father's only brother and his only heir, your father has considered his niece to be as a daughter to him, albeit one without need of a dowry from his own pockets. My place within the family business is still secure, as are your father's coffers.

As are you.

I pray you'll find peace and joy no matter the path you choose and hold me ever dear in your heart as I will ever hold you.

Your dear and faithful,
Jacquin

The bitterest bile surged into her throat, and Annalise swallowed fire. Jacquin, marrying Caterina? She couldn't even find it within herself to be jealous. Nor disappointed. As far as she was concerned, Jacquin had handed her a gift as pretty and valuable as a diamond on a pillow of velvet.

Why, then, did she feel so betrayed?

Once not long ago, Annalise had told Cassian the Invisible Mother would find her wherever she was. Now, more than ever, Annalise needed Her comfort.

The Faith didn't require its followers to kneel, but Annalise got to her knees anyway. Waiting, Readiness became Waiting, Remorse, and finally, because it was the only way to gain some measure of relief, she slid her hands along the cold stone floor and pressed her forehead to it in the one position she'd sworn she would never make.

Waiting, Abasement.

If this was what it took to gain guidance, she would do it.

The morn would've come too early no matter the hour she was woken, but as the sun had not yet even risen, Annalise was fair irritated to be roused. Blinking, scrubbing at her face, wishing she could convince herself she'd been in the grip of a nightmare, she swatted at the hand on her shoulder.

Tansy didn't seem to take offense. "They want you, Annalise."

"Who wants me?" She spun in her sheets, fighting the tangle.

"The Mothers-in-Service." Tansy sounded awed. "They want you to come right away."

"Is this common?" Annalise asked, annoyed but now also a little anxious at being so summoned.

"They're going to ask your intent, I think."

Some slow-turning tension twisted in her gut. Annalise swung her feet over the edge of the bed and stood. "Do they always do it this way?"

"I don't know," Tansy said more sharply than Annalise had ever heard her speak. "I've never been called."

"Oh, Tansy."

Annalise had never been the sort to seek out casual embrace, but now she put an arm around the other girl's shoulders and gently squeezed. Tansy sighed and rested her head upon Annnalise's shoulder for a moment only before pulling away. She went to the armoire and pulled out one of Annalise's gowns.

"Here. You'll need to dress. Fix your hair. Don't keep them overlong, it won't look good. It's bad enough you didn't wake when Patience came to the door for you. You don't want them to think you're not interested in taking your vows at last."

"Maybe I'm not."

Tansy turned with a frown, dress hanging over her arm. "Of course you are. No matter what happened last night. Maybe especially because of it."

"What do you know of what happened last night?" Once again grateful to be sharing a room with one so responsible, Annalise went to the basin and pitcher and poured out warmish water. She splashed her face and rinsed her mouth. She washed away the final lingering taste of Cassian and refused to regret it.

Tansy shrugged and held out the gown for Annalise to put on. "I'll brush your hair for you, if you like."

"Tansy, you do know I thank the Invisible Mother for giving me you as a roommate, do you not?"

Tansy bit her lower lip. "I wish I could be of more help to you, Annalise. More a friend."

"You've ever been a friend to me."

Tansy cut her off. "No. You've allowed me to be your acquaintance, but not your friend. And I understand, I do. I'm not as skilled, not as proficient. Not as bright."

"Oh, Tansy." The tight knot of coiled tension grew spikes that jabbed. "Is that what you really think?"

Tansy nodded as Annalise took the dress. "It's what I know. It's all right, Annalise. I'm used to it."

"It's not true." Annalise pulled the dress over her head and began with the buttons, undone to her waist, slipping them swiftly into their holes.

It was not the gown Cassian had taken off her. These buttons were a little bigger, of carved wood. More difficult to push through the slots. Her fingers fumbled and slipped, and she muttered under her breath.

"Let me." Tansy finished doing up the buttons with swift efficiency, then reached for Annalise's brush and gestured for her to turn around. "Now, your hair. Sit, it'll be easier."

It was. Annalise closed her eyes at the steady stroke of the brush. Tansy knew how not to snag or pull, though Annalise had gone to bed without tying back her hair—the love tangles had snarled more thoroughly the few hours she'd managed to sleep.

When she'd finished, Tansy pushed at Annalise's shoulder. "There. Lovely. Now go."

Annalise stood but took Tansy's hands. "I plead your mercy for not making you feel as though we're friends. I admire you, Tansy, truly."

Tansy blinked rapidly, her eyes aglint with tears. She bit her lower lip again. Shrugged. A small, pleased smiled tugged one corner of her mouth. "Thank you."

"You should be the one being called. Not me." Annalise studied her appearance one last time in the looking glass. Circles beneath her eyes told of her lack of sleep, but her hair and gown were neat and tidy, thanks to Tansy. "Just look at what you've done."

"Did I choose wrong? I thought the gown was one of your most flattering, though it's one you wear the least—"

"No, it's perfect. Entirely appropriate. But don't you see, Tansy? This is what you're born to do. You're well-accomplished, no matter what you think. I'd never have risen to the occasion for you the way you have for me. I've no doubts you're ready for a patron. Many patrons."

"Sadly for me, you're not a Mother-in-Service."

It was the only time Annalise had heard Tansy speak with anything akin to bitterness. She squeezed Tansy's hands. She hugged her once more.

"I'll speak to them on your behalf."

Tansy sighed. "It will do no good, Annalise, the Mothers decide when we're ready. No amount of pleading can urge them toward it."

"I shall speak to them anyway," Annalise said firmly. "There's no reason for me to be called now and you not. It's preposterous, as a matter of fact."

At this, Tansy laughed. "If you don't hurry yourself toward Mother Deliberata's office, I think your pleading upon my behalf will do even less good than it will now. Go!"

Annalise went through dark, silent halls to Deliberata's office. She knocked. The door opened. She crossed the threshold, her head held high and breath tight in her throat.

"Come in, Annalise. Please, sit." Deliberata indicated a chair set in front of a semicircle formed by a love seat and several armchairs in front of the fire.

Annalise took the single chair facing the others—Mothers Deliberata, Compassionata, and Prudence, along with a Temple priest she didn't know. No Cassian. She didn't look for him overlong, her heart too sore not from what he'd told her hours ago but from what he'd refused to share.

Deliberata took her place in the elegant, high-backed armchair directly across from Annalise. "I'm fair certain you're wondering why the early summons."

"Actually, no." Annalise smiled at the older woman. "It makes sense to make such decisions sooner rather than later."

Deliberata smiled. "Of course it does. But you might be wondering why we called you here this morn, too early or no."

"Tansy said you were calling me to judge my intent. To see if I might take my vows. Take a patron."

"Tansy doesn't speak for the Mothers-in-Service," Prudence said bluntly, yet with sharp words.

"Prudence," Deliberata said with gentle reproof, "I don't believe Annalise was suggesting she did."

"Is she wrong?" Annalise fixed Prudence with a bold stare. Of all the Mothers-in-Service, Prudence was the one she liked the least. The woman had a mouth like a coin-purse drawn tight, but without treasure inside.

"No." This came from Compassionata, who sat to Deliberata's left. "Not entirely."

"We did call you here to discuss your intentions, child." Deliberata gestured at the others. "Perhaps prematurely, but it has been found necessary."

Unable to stop herself, Annalise looked at the priest. "Who finds it so?"

"Sister Serenity raised the concern." Deliberata's smile didn't fade and her gaze continued to be as kind as Annalise had ever known it. "She felt, based upon some personal observances, that it was time to judge if you were ready for your vows. If it was time."

Annalise kept her voice as steady as she could, but it still wobbled faintly. "What personal observances?"

"We didn't ask her." Prudence seemed to find this disappointing or disgusting, mayhap both. "She wasn't required to share them, either, unless the novitiate about whom she raised the concerns desires to know them. Do you?"

"As much as it would seem to please you to hear them," Annalise told the older woman coolly, "no."

"This is why she isn't ready, Deliberata. I told you this and yet you refused to listen." Prudence snapped her fingers in definite disgust and fixed Annalise with a steady glare.

Annalise kept her gaze upon Deliberata. "Prudence is correct, Mother. I'm not ready."

"I disagree. Serenity certainly did, and she's ever had the best of eyes when it comes to matters such as this," Deliberata said.

Compassionata cleared her throat. "You oughtn't feel as though we're forcing you to decide now, Annalise."

"Yet I feel forced." Annalise cleared her throat to keep her voice as steady as it would stay.

"Mother birds sometimes push their babies from the nest before they seem ready to fly," Deliberata said.

Annalise frowned. "And the babies fall to the ground and are eaten by cats."

"Do you think we'd allow you to fall to the ground?" Deliberata tilted her head to match her smile.

Annalise didn't. Not really. "I'm not sure what to choose. I've been uncertain since coming here. I've never felt ready to take a patron, ready to give myself up utterly to service."

"You've excelled in your studies. What may seem minor can be very great. Solace can be found in a simple cup of tea." Compassionata gestured toward the Temple priest, still silent. "It's said when the Allcreator found his bride in the forest, what won him was not her face or body, but the comfort she gave his weary body with a simple cup of tea."

Prudence made a low noise in her throat. "Listen to Annalise. She says she's not ready, she's ever been uncertain of her ability to serve. I say she's not uncertain at all. She knows it's not in her nature to serve. She might've done well enough with mixing herbs and embroidering cuffs, but put a cleaning rag in her fist and see how straight the line of her spine. And of service on her back, well, we all know if skill in that arena was all it took, there'd be no need for the Order at all. Any brothel would suffice, instead."

"Are you calling me a whore?" Annalise looked Prudence square in the face.

Prudence looked slightly taken aback, as though surprised Annalise had dared respond. "No. I'm saying that just because you've managed to acquire a goodly number of bedroom skills, you're no more prepared to take your vows than someone who just walked in from the yard."

"Someone who walked in from the yard might be entirely ready to serve without even a minute's training," Annalise said. "Some are born to it, isn't that so?"

"And some," Prudence said, "are not."

Deliberata had watched this exchange in silence, but now she tutted. "Prudence speaks on your behalf, though it would seem she opposes you. You call yourself unable to serve, and she agrees."

Annalise frowned. "So I should go against her out of spite?"

"No." Deliberata shook her head while Prudence shifted, sighing. "You should make this choice from within your heart. Not because you've nothing to which to return . . . or nothing for which to stay."

Annalise's throat closed and she couldn't speak no matter how hard she swallowed. The Mothers-in-Service knew of her shame, and she couldn't be surprised. She pressed her fingertips to her eyelids, willing back the tears not because she was too ashamed to weep in front of them, but because she feared once begun they would not cease.

"Only days ago your faith was strong. Your decision made. You were as ready as any novitiate I've ever known, Annalise. You'd found your purpose and had taken pleasure in it. Is this not so?" Deliberata asked.

"The fact that much has changed in those few days should be reason enough for me to doubt, should it not?"

Compassionata shook her head. "Oh no, my dear. Any Handmaiden who never wonders if she's chosen the right path is too full of arrogance to be able to truly serve. The fact that you've doubted is a sign to me, above all else, you're ready."

"Should I not know this, someplace in my heart? Someplace deep inside me?" She asked them all. "I thought you might *tell* me when it was time, not ask. I thought . . . many things. Most of which were wrong. And now I'm uncertain of the path I should choose."

"Most paths are uncertain. I say it's those that lead to uncertain destinations that teach us the most," Deliberata said.

"I'm not sure I can bring anyone to solace." There. She'd said it. "I believe myself an utter failure at such a task."

Deliberata shook her head gently. "A flower is made more beautiful by its thorns. Your doubt is your thorn, Annalise."

"Selfish is the heart that thinks first of itself," Annalise replied. "I have ever been selfish, Mothers. I have ever thought first of myself."

"Not in everything," Deliberata said, but went no further than that. Instead she clapped her hands together softly and leaned forward in her chair. "Let me ask you this. If you were granted a lifetime to serve and bring solace to a hundred patrons but knew even those hundred arrows would not be enough to finally fill the Holy Quiver, or if you were granted one patron who needed that lifetime of service before reaching solace, yet his was the arrow that filled the Quiver and brought about the return of the Holy Family, which would you choose?"

"A hundred brought to solace, or only one but his would bring back the Return?" Annalise shook her head, thinking. "Mother, I can't decide that. To be the one responsible for bringing back the Invisible Mother—"

"And the Allcreator, and the First Son," put in Prudence.

Annalise gave her a steady glare. "To be the one responsible for that would be the greatest honor I could ever imagine."

She meant it. Knew her sincerity from deep within her soul. Doubts had batted at her like buzzing flies, mindless and annoying and unswattable . . . but now some of them, at least, began to fall away.

"But to serve a hundred patrons," she continued, thoughts like silken festival banners unfurling in her mind, "to know I'd been able to help a hundred people . . . that too, would be an honor."

She looked at the three Mothers-in-Service and at the priest, too. "I cannot decide. I'm sorry. More proof I'm not fit for the vows."

Deliberata stood and held out her hands. "On the contrary, my dear, you've answered with perfection. Mine was a question without an answer."

Confused, Annalise took the offered hands. Deliberata's fingers were warm and soft, and she squeezed to pull Annalise a little closer. "You are ready to take your vows, child, even if you don't feel it. And it's my pleasure to grant your new name and welcome you as my own dear Sister, Certainty."

The new name settled on Annalise's shoulders, the finest and warmest of cloaks, yet she couldn't wrap herself within it. Not yet. "I fear you've confused me, Mother. Certainty?"

"Oh, yes. For you've ever been certain of yourself, no matter your course."

"Respecta would have been an unsuitable choice," Prudence said with a grudging smile. "But Certainty I will also own suits you."

Compassionata laughed. "Welcome, Sister!"

The priest, at last, stood. He reached inside the draping scarf of his tunic and withdrew a small pot he uncorked and dipped a thumb inside. "Come closer, Sister Certainty, and be anointed, that you might begin your new life within the Order of Solace."

Annalise—Certainty as she was now named, and would she ever grow used to being so called?—let go of Deliberata's hands and moved toward him. He smudged some oil on her forehead. He smiled at her.

"Certainty, do you so vow to spend your days in the service of the Order of Solace, beneath the gaze of the Invisible Mother?"

"I do."

"Welcome," said the priest and kissed both her cheeks.

"That's it?" Annalise touched her face where the warmth of his lips had pressed. "Naught more than that?"

"Naught more," Deliberata promised.

Giddiness swept her, and Annalise felt for the back of a chair to keep her knees from buckling. "I thought there would be more."

"There's naught magic about it, I'm afraid." Deliberata laughed. "Though I think you'll find yourself much changed."

"Indeed." Prudence shook the folds of her skirt as she stood. "But first, I suggest a meal. I'm fair famished. Come, Certainty. Join us."

As simply as that, it was done. No longer Annalise Marony but Certainty, Handmaiden in the Order of Solace, as yet unassigned to her first patron but no longer uncertain she would ever be ready.

It should've been a shining moment and was tarnished by but one thing—she had no Cassian to share it with.

Chapter 24

"You know we would miss you greatly, Cassian." Deliberata poured him not a mug of tea but a glass of cordial, bright as cherries. "You've been an asset to the Order, and I fear we'll not find a worthy replacement."

Cassian swirled the ruby liquid in his glass and sipped, expecting sourness. Unexpected sweetness didn't tempt him to drink. He'd have preferred the bitter. "You know as well as I there are Temple priests aplenty who can provide the same service."

"Perhaps, but not for so long or consistently. Your friend Roget has ever been good to us here as well, yet to imagine him as a teacher of basic instruction is laughable."

Cassian didn't laugh. "There are many teachers you could find."

She sighed and nodded, then steepled her fingers together on the desktop. "You're certain you must go?"

He nodded after a moment, then met her gaze. "Yes. I must. I can no longer in good conscience continue teaching what I don't believe. What I haven't believed for a goodly long time."

"I understand. Though I daresay you've done a fine enough job of it. None of the novitiates you've trained have had any trouble with their teaching."

"They deserve a teacher who believes what he's asking them to believe."

Deliberata smiled. "Of course. So. You shall collect your wages and go. As simply as that?"

He hesitated, knowing the other woman too well to believe she would make it that easy. "Such is my intent, yes."

"And the boy?"

"What about the boy?"

Deliberata tilted her head to look him over. "When you came here to serve, it was with the understanding it was because you wanted to watch over him. You claimed at the time it was your duty. Your Calling, if you will. Perhaps you don't recall saying so?"

He remembered all too well. "I haven't forgotten the boy. He has a home here. He will have a life with what the Order provides."

"What? An education? Food and clothes, shelter?"

"Love," Cassian added, seeing where she meant to go with this. "You cannot deny he's also been much loved."

"By many, yes. And also by you. But that love has come with the weight of guilt, has it not?"

"He wasn't mine, was never meant to be mine. And yet . . . he might've been," Cassian said, "if only I'd been able to forgive his father."

Deliberata smiled, and it was easy to see how she'd brought solace to so many. "It's not too late. Not yet, anyway. Not for forgiveness and not for you and the boy."

"His mother has come to claim him."

"I know. She's petitioned the Mothers-in-Service to take him away. It has thus far not been our pleasure to approve her request. It is not my pleasure to ever do so."

"But others might agree?"

"Others might always agree to what I do not," Deliberata said. "Give me a reason to approve another path for the boy."

"You suggest I . . . ?"

"Cassian, Cassian, Cassian. You have been as much a father to him as he's ever known. Kellen is nearly ten years old, in the shortest of years to become a man. We can offer him much here in the Order, it's true, and we do for all our Blessings. But you know he was not meant for that life."

"I can scarcely provide him better."

"You can provide him with a choice, which shall necessarily be enough. Ask the boy if he'd like to go with you. If he says no, we shall know the Invisible Mother has claimed him."

"If he says yes?"

Deliberata laughed. "Then I believe, even if you don't, that She still has Her hand upon you both."

Cassian nodded stiffly, then drained his glass. He stood. "And his mother?"

"She will abide by the Order's rule or she won't." Deliberata shrugged. "She's found a good life, a pleasure and a purpose. No matter your past with her, she's gone on to make a life. You might've done the same, Cassian. Now's your chance, and too long in the making."

He nodded stiffly. Deliberata sighed. She poured herself another glass of cordial and sipped it, eyeing him.

"And of the woman?"

He could scarcely bring himself to say her name. "I've wronged her. Tell me what penance to provide and I'll do my best to make it."

"I suppose the most obvious solution has escaped you."

It had not, but as much as he couldn't bear to speak her name, so he couldn't stand to speak aloud what he knew Deliberata meant. She smiled, shaking her head. She settled back in her chair.

"As a priest you were required to speak for those who couldn't speak for themselves, yes?"

"Yes."

"So. Though it's not often our case here, sometimes we in the Order do so as well. Come here, child, and let me bless you so that you might move on your way."

Cassian went to her, kneeling to allow her to place both hands upon his head. He closed his eyes, thinking of his mother, long passed. She'd blessed him and his brother just this way.

"May the Invisible Mother bless you and keep you, all the days of your waking." Deliberata tapped his head. "Rise you up and get you gone, Cassian Toquin. And may She keep you in the palm of Her hand. Go, now."

Annalise had thought there'd be much changed after taking her vows. She waited to feel different. Like a Handmaiden.

"Women we begin and women we shall end," she said aloud to her reflection.

She understood it better now.

Still uncertain if the purpose she'd come to accept would indeed become her pleasure, Annalise busied herself with minor studies. She spent long hours in meditation. She took over the teaching of Cassian's class.

A fortnight passed before she was called to Deliberata's office and given, without the fanfare she'd expected, a small sheaf of papers tied with red ribbon and a hand-trunk in which to pack her few belongings. She held the papers and the trunk and waited for her heart to thump with anticipation and anxiety, but all she felt was an overwhelming sense of relief. She packed swiftly and was within the carriage within the span of a few chimes.

She thought she'd have to ride for hours, would have time to thoroughly read and study the information she'd been given. Instead the carriage took her through the nearest town and down a long country lane. It stopped in front of a modest but comfortable-looking stone house surrounded by a tidy yard with gardens behind and forest all around.

"You'll be fine, miss," said Steven, the driver, with a tip of his cap. "Good mazel to you."

Annalise had ridden in the carriage, but Certainty went to the front gate. She opened it. Stepped through. The gravel crunched beneath her toes as she walked, and it seemed quite important she recall every sound, each scent, every sight before her for this first time.

They'd all blend together after a while, she thought as she stood in front of the red-painted door. But this first one, she would have to cherish forever.

She knocked.

He answered.

"If you were given the choice of serving a hundred patrons, providing each with absolute solace yet knowing the Holy Quiver would remain unfilled, or you could have but one patron to serve for the rest of your life but know his would be the final Arrow . . . which would you choose?" Cassian's voice hadn't changed, but he had. No longer clad in the high-necked jacket, he wore a loose-fitting white shirt, a dusting of flour on one cheek and his hair in disarray. From inside the house, Certainty heard the laughter of a child. The boy.

"My answer, sir, is that I would be first grateful to have been given a choice at all."

He drew in a slow breath, his smile hesitant and endearing. "And the second answer?

"I would choose the single patron," she said, stepping up to him. "So long as it was you."

He put his arms around her, and he kissed her. She needed no tinkling bells or flutter of wings to feel in his kiss what his words next shared. "I love you, Annalise."

She didn't correct him. There'd be time much later for the rest of all this—the small acts and gestures that would soothe him and bring him solace. Or not. Somehow, the idea of her task taking the rest of her life was not daunting, but delicious.

"I like you when you love me, Cassian."

He kissed her again, kicking the half-open door all the way open and sweeping her into his arms so that he might carry her into the house. "Then you shall be well-pleased with me for a long time, for I don't intend to stop."

She wound her arms around his neck, holding tight. "I have a question for you, first, before you take me inside."

He paused to look into her eyes. "Anything."

"What would you have done had I not been the one assigned to you?"

Cassion smiled. "I didn't send for a Handmaiden, love."

This answer surprised her. "But you . . . the question you asked when you opened the door . . ."

"Sometimes," Cassian said, "just as the priests speak for those unable to speak for themselves, the Invisible Mother answers the prayers of those unable to pray."

"Sometimes, it would seem the Mothers-in-Service do the same," she said wryly.

"Much to my joy."

She looked at him seriously. "Is it your intent to allow me to try and make you happy?"

He kissed her. "Aye, and yes. It is."

"And what of solace, Cassian? Is it your intent I should try to grant you that, as well?"

Another kiss, softer this time. "Yes."

"Even if it takes a lifetime?"

"In truth, sweetheart," he said as he took her through the door and closed it behind them with a thud, "I intend for it to take just that long."

Which was all she could really ask, and everything she could give.